"Rusty Whitener writes with passion, insight, and power. He won our MOVIEGUIDE® Kairos Prize in 2009 with his script *Touched*, which he turned into a novel, *A Season of Miracles*, garnering two Christy Award nominations and winning a Book of the Year Gold Award from *ForeWord Reviews* magazine along the way before being picked up by Elevating Entertainment Motion Pictures, which is bringing this inspiring, family-friendly story to the screen. This sequel, *A Season of Mysteries*, is another worthy milestone that will no doubt bless, entertain, and enlighten."

—**Ted Baehr**, founder and publisher of *Movieguide*, author, critic, educator, and media pundit

"I love this book! Whitener's beautiful novel weaves together the trials and triumphs of teenagers wrestling with the ordinary, comical pressures of adolescence *and* the extraordinary spiritual forces assaulting their young faith. A perfect sequel to his award-winning first novel, *A Season of Mysteries* is both funny and moving. You'll love it too!"

—**Nancy Stafford**, actress, speaker, and author of *The Wonder of His Love* and *Beauty by the Book*

"Rusty Whitener's *A Season of Mysteries* is a fabulous sequel to *A Season of Miracles*, with a formidable mix of sentiment, inspiration, and intrigue. It brought back strong memories of teenage camaraderie and Boy Scout campfires."

—**Dave Moody**, Grammy-nominated and Dove Award–winning artist, producer, filmmaker

"*A Season of Mysteries* is a multifaceted gem of a story—beautiful, intelligent, thoughtful and, at just the right times, laugh-out-loud hilarious. What I love most about it is that Rusty Whitener uses the voice and eyes and heart of a teenaged boy to examine that most important of questions, "What is Truth?" Not an easy task, but one that this author tackles skillfully and convincingly."

—**Ann Tatlock**, Christy award–winning author of *Promises to Keep* and *Sweet Mercy*

"GRAND SLAM! Rusty Whitener is the Babe Ruth of intrigue, action, suspense, and hope in *A Season of Mysteries*. Brilliantly written, and as one character puts it, 'a perilous quest, seeking both peace and truth.' Play ball . . . if you dare!"

—**Jenny L. Cote**, award-winning author of *The Amazing Tales of Max and Liz*, and Epic Order of the Seven series

"At times haunting and often humorous, Rusty Whitener's *A Season of Mysteries* sends us bounding down the teen lane of Troublesome Trail, where curiosity meets danger, faith sprouts among friends, and the girl is more than worth the chase."

—**Ray Blackston**, author of *Flabbergasted*

A Season of
Mysteries

RUSTY WHITENER

Kregel
Publications

A Season of Mysteries: A Novel
© 2013 by Rusty Whitener

Published by Kregel Publications, a division of Kregel, Inc.,
P.O. Box 2607, Grand Rapids, MI 49501.

ISBN 978-0-8254-4322-0

Printed in the United States of America
13 14 15 16 17 / 5 4 3 2 1

*To my brothers, Mike Whitener and Huck Whitener,
and my mom, Mary Keller Boatwright Whitener,
and my dad, James David Whitener Sr.
If God allowed me to choose my brothers and parents
before I came into this world, I would have chosen the
four of you. I am incredibly blessed.*

ACKNOWLEDGMENTS

Without Kregel agreeing to publish my first novel, *A Season of Miracles*, there would be no *A Season of Mysteries*.

Thanks to Steve Barclift, who allowed me, without an appointment, to push into his hands a disc containing the first rough text of *Miracles*. Steve, you have my sincerest gratitude.

Miranda Gardner's effective edits on that first novel, which established many of the characters used in this new work, were immensely helpful, guiding me through the editing process.

I am profoundly grateful to Dawn Anderson for her wonderful edits and suggestions on my initial manuscript for *Mysteries*. Her editing was also instrumental and supportive in the process of moving *Miracles* to published form.

Thanks to publisher Dennis Hillman, who has always been enthusiastic and kind in correspondence with me.

Thanks to Cat Hoort for working hard at Kregel to market and publicize my work.

Thanks to the entire team at Kregel!

Thanks to Les Stobbe for agreeing to be my literary agent and continuing to encourage me with enthusiasm and excellent counsel.

Thanks to Wheaton College for putting up with my juvenile questions in philosophy courses all those years ago. Much of the dialogues and quandaries that appear in *Mysteries* were spawned in courses like Dr. David Fletcher's "Existentialism," and excellent writing courses taught by Dr. Jill Baumgartner.

Thanks to my friend Chad Huff, who always taught me to value the atoning work of Christ higher than the merits of philosophical inquiries. Chad, you are a great servant of the Lord, a warrior.

Thanks to my wife, Rebecca, who loves me even when I'm tapping the laptop's keyboard at one in the morning. Where would I be without your love, Rebecca? I love you forever!

And thanks to my mom and dad, especially my mom, for introducing me and my brothers to the power and grace of C.S. Lewis's and J.R.R. Tolkien's fiction.

PROLOGUE

I stepped out of the warmth and light of Draughon Library into the dark, still night. Winters in Alabama are frequently wet, but not often white. Tonight was different. A half inch or more of snow crunched under the soles of my boots.

Dr. David Woodruff's home was barely off campus, only two blocks from the library. I was glad I didn't need to drive. The snow and the night spoke to me. A peaceful benediction to a day too full, counseling students who lacked motivation and searching in the library for something I could not find. The books, though, ministered to me in ways a computer screen never will.

I have long sought solace in research, in dodging shadows and deceits, and isolating the illuminations that dispel such shadows. I believe in both; in the Dark and the Light. I am out of step with my time. Nowadays, learned folk acknowledge only Light. And its absence. Notions of the Dark are, to them, fine mythical allusions.

Except they're not.

I have looked for alternate explanations. I mean, other than the obvious ones that soar with angels and slouch with demons.

The research world, though, has turned in on itself. So much access and so little value. We forever mine fool's gold.

Maybe it's not just research. Maybe the whole world is self-destructing, drowning in inane surface revelations. Where are the enlightenments that truly enlighten? Authentic revelation is salvation. Surface revelation is dangerous. We once knew the difference.

My field is a discipline wherein spirits roam unmolested by

scientific inquiry. Anything a writer imagines is possible. Of course, the same possibilities reign in the mind of a sovereign Creator. What-ever the Light breathes into being, is. Our notions of plausibility are beside the point.

———

I'd been to Woodruff's place once before, a private affair with six or seven professors, most from the philosophy department, where Woodruff taught when he wasn't writing first-class poetry. We drank coffee and tea and playfully dueled over the either/or proposition.

Tonight, another man greeted me at the front door. "Come in, come in. Dr. Powell, the literature prof, right?"

"Is this still Woodruff's place?" A stupid thing for me to ask, since this gentleman obviously expected me. But I was anxious, preoccupied, and suddenly felt even more so.

"He's pulling Danish croissants from the oven," the man said warmly, shaking my hand. "I'm Dr. Throneberry."

I stepped inside. Woodruff's voice boomed from the recesses of his kitchen. "Welcome, Richard! Meet Jacob Throneberry."

"Yes, we've just met, thank you," I called out.

"Same with Jacob and myself," he answered. "Yesterday."

"I hope you'll call me Jake." Throneberry smiled and led the way from the front foyer toward the sound of Woodruff's voice.

"I smell those Danish things," I said as I stepped into my friend's postage-stamp kitchen.

"Croissants, aren't they?" Throneberry said.

"Their technical name is Danish melted pastries." Woodruff pulled a sheet of the toasted treats from the oven.

The fragrance was marvelous. "*My* technical name for them is good grub," I jested.

"They do smell like heaven," Throneberry concurred.

"Wait'll you taste them."

"Throneberry here is—" Woodruff started.

"Please call me Jake," the man said to both of us.

"Jake is professor of clinical psychology at Marist College, in Canada." Woodruff set the desserts on the stovetop. "Please help yourselves to the coffee. I have flavored creamers," he said, sounding genuinely pleased with himself. He gestured toward a little wooden countertop tree on which hung mugs and cups of various shapes and colors, each emblazoned with college colors and symbols. "Pick your own."

"I don't see any Auburn or Tigers or some such," I chided.

"I love our university," Woodruff said with some seriousness. "I don't need to prove that by raising a War Eagle mug to my lips every morning. I collect other schools. No other SEC schools, mind you. And by the way"—he turned to Throneberry—"how do you know?"

"I beg your pardon?"

"What it smells like?"

"Excuse me?"

"Heaven? How do you know?" he asked, straight-faced.

Throneberry appeared confused, unsure. A little worried.

"You don't have to answer that," I said. I'm always uncomfortable when others are teased and left dangling. "He's toying with you; he thinks it's funny to play with people's minds."

"Oh. I see."

Woodruff didn't appreciate my cutting in. "Now why did you rescue him, Richard? Here's the sugar if you want it," he said. "And the creams, take what you will, both of you. I wanted to see what he would say. And he was going to answer. Isn't that true, Jake?"

"Well, I thought you were serious. You seemed so."

"I was. I am. And never more serious than when I'm joking." Woodruff piled the Danish treats onto a large platter and set them in the center of the little kitchen table. "We'll eat and drink here," he announced, sitting down with a brimming Notre Dame coffee mug. "And we'll laugh and challenge and encourage our professorial spirits here."

I sat, an Oklahoma Sooners mug in front of me. As did Throneberry, coddling a Stanford cup.

"How did you two meet?" I asked. "I think you said yesterday."

"Jake wrote me," Woodruff replied. "Said he liked my article in the *Journal*. You remember, on the prophetic breaking in on the propositional."

"I remember."

"Said he'd be coming through sometime this week. Could he stay at my place?"

"So here I am." Throneberry plucked a treat from the tray. He broke it into three pieces and set them on a napkin.

"So here he is," Woodruff echoed, laughing. "Eating treats in my kitchen!"

I laughed with him. "It's always good, in our vocation, to meet other believers." As soon as I said it, I realized I had made a great assumption. "I mean . . ."

"Oh yes," Throneberry said through a mouth of Danish. "I definitely do believe."

"I just assumed."

"Quite right," Woodruff chuckled. "They must be cool enough." He took a pastry for himself. "You seem to be making quick work of yours, Jake."

"Well, I will take it as my good fortune you're here," I said to Throneberry. "A professor of clinical psychology should have a great deal to say to me. A great deal to see in me. To explain."

"You're trying to be kind, I think." Throneberry looked at me. "But we psych profs are not psychics. Nor are we sorcerers."

"Yes, of course," I said, as much to myself as to him. I always tend to expect too much resolution in the here and now. My good friend Zack always tells me it's a wonderful trait—to be full of hope, of faith.

"Ah!" Woodruff expelled a good chunk of pastry into his hand, and then onto the table.

"Hot?" I asked the obvious.

"Piping!" He coughed, rising swiftly, shaking his head. "Sorry, fellows." He picked up the chewed dough with a paper towel and threw it in the wastebasket under his sink.

"Some of them must be hotter than others," Throneberry muttered.

"Must be," I mused. "You're all right?"

"I will be." Woodruff stuck his head under the spigot and flushed his mouth with cold water.

"You're sure?"

"It's okay." He grabbed another paper towel and wiped his hands

12

and mouth, sitting back down. "Talk to us, Richard. What's on your impressive mind?"

"Words."

"Words?" Throneberry cocked his head slightly.

"Words. Comments. Conversations. Dialogues stay with me," I said, feeling, oddly, as if I were confessing. "I am haunted by words. I can't get away from them."

"What sort of dialogues?" Throneberry asked. "Actual?"

"Yes. Actual words, real people. From my past."

"How far back?" Throneberry again.

"A long time. Nineteen seventy-six."

"Really?" Woodruff was fascinated. "How old are you?"

"Fifty-two."

"Ah yes," said my old friend. "It takes some balance to walk at the half-century mark and not feel out of sorts, out of time. Not young or old. But able to both remember and forecast; to apply. These dialogues are actual exchanges, you say? People you knew?"

"Yes. It was a remarkable time for me and my friends. Really unforgettable . . ." I stopped myself. "I mean . . . I don't mean . . . I just meant to say 'unforgettable' in the sense of remarkable, not actually, literally, unforgettable. Except that it is, for me, in a ridiculous literal way. The words spoken. I can't forget them."

"You've told me before," Woodruff interrupted, "that you have this very singular ability. It's like a tape. In your head."

"Yes, but that's very short-term memory. I do recall, word for word, daily conversations; but after a few days, that recollection leaves me."

"I'm confused," Throneberry broke in. "Do you mean to say that you remember word for word what people say to you? I mean, for several days?"

"Yes."

"I've heard such claims before," he said.

"And?" asked Woodruff.

"They're not true," he said evenly, staring at me. "I don't believe you."

"I'm sorry to hear that," I said.

"Don't you want to convince me of your gift?"

"I don't consider it a gift. And I don't feel like convincing anyone of much of anything tonight."

I was staring back at Throneberry, but I could see Woodruff out the corner of my eye, watching and waiting to see what we'd say next.

"I don't mean to offend you," Throneberry said softly.

"I'm not offended. I wouldn't believe me either."

"Would you, Richard"—Woodruff shuffled slightly in his chair—"mind sharing a few of the things, the *words*," he emphasized, "maybe even the sentences the three of us have thrown out this evening? It's up to you, my friend. Please don't feel any compulsion, one way or the other."

"Yes, please don't." Throneberry's tone was apologetic.

I surprised myself. My practice has always been to hide my strange ability. It's not something I'm proud of, or something I care for people to know. But for whatever reason, I felt both men should know and I should leave no doubt.

"Okay," I began. "At the door, Jake, you said, 'Come in, come in. Dr. Powell, the literature prof, right?' I said, 'Is this still Woodruff's place?'"

"That's right," said Throneberry.

"You said, 'He's pulling Danish croissants from the oven. I'm Dr. Throneberry.'"

"Then, what did you say?" Throneberry asked.

"No," I answered, "David spoke next. He said, 'Welcome, Richard. Meet Jacob Throneberry.'"

"Fascinating." Throneberry smiled.

"Remarkable!" Woodruff's eyes shone.

"I called back to David, 'Yes, we've just met, thank you.' And you said, 'Same with Jacob and myself. Yesterday.' Should I go on?"

"If you don't mind." Throneberry nodded. "Could you just go through our entire exchange of words from the moment we walked into the kitchen?"

"Oh, see here, Jake," said Woodruff, "he doesn't need to—"

"No, I don't mind," I said. "It feels . . . important."

I started reciting and they listened. I'm sure I didn't miss a word, including throwaway language like "I have flavored creamers" and colorful phrases like "we'll laugh and challenge and encourage our professorial spirits here."

The two of them listened and marveled throughout, as I suppose anyone might have if they'd heard me. I finished with "don't feel any compulsion, one way or the other" and "yes, please don't."

After some seconds of registering awe, Throneberry spoke. "I wouldn't have believed it."

"He's mentioned this to me before," Woodruff said, almost as if I weren't in the room, "but I didn't take him seriously. And he didn't press the issue. Didn't want to convince me."

"It's not something I care to make people aware of," I said simply. "But I thought you two should know tonight. Because of what I'm going to share with you."

Woodruff's awe turned to amusement. "You've already shared the most amazing thing I've heard in a long time. Maybe ever!"

"Yes, remarkable," Throneberry concurred.

"You both understand, don't you," I said, "that it doesn't always happen for me. Sometimes I can't remember . . . it's as if the tape in my head is not working. I can't predict when it will work. Tonight it did. I felt it working as soon as you greeted me at the door, Jake."

Thorneberry looked pleased.

"And in a few days, I will have forgotten these words, what we say tonight. Unless of course I write them down, as I am prone to do. I've journaled since I was in my teens."

"You said"—Woodruff seemed to be thinking aloud—"you've been haunted by dialogues, by words that go back to 1976, I believe it was."

"That's right."

"You were journaling then?" he asked.

"Not much."

"But you've been recalling . . . words from that year," Throneberry said. "And these words bother you."

"Yes. Greatly. I can't get away from them."

"Perhaps you should stop trying," said Woodruff.

"Why?" I asked.

"I'm not sure," he said. "Yet. But go on. Tell us what you want."

"I want . . ." I began. "I suppose . . . I am trying, for lack of a better word, to un-recall these words. To undiscover these things."

"Don't you mean *forget?*" Throneberry said.

I shook my head. "I don't know. Maybe. But forgetting is too weak a word for what I want. I want the words to disappear not just from my mind, but from this . . ." I struggled with what I wanted. ". . . from this realm that we know, or suspect, is real."

"These were scary words, dialogues?" Woodruff said. "That you remember from 1976?"

"Some of them. But others are heroic. Beautiful. If I could pick and choose, I'd let the memories go and just revel in the wonder of that year." I felt tears coming. "If I could only undiscover the scary things that I saw and learned then. If I could undiscover the words that uncovered an evil . . . *reality*. Otherwise, I feel as if I'm in . . . a kind of permanent haunting."

"An intriguing goal." Throneberry nodded. "You want to 'undiscover' something."

"Yes," said Woodruff. "You said that word twice."

"Which word?" I asked.

"*Undiscover*," my colleague said. "Your own crafted word, I should think."

"Yes, I suppose." I sighed. "I don't know how else to describe what I think it is that I want."

"To put something back into hiding that came into your realization?" said Woodruff.

"Yes!" I said, louder. "Exactly."

"You are questing backwards."

"I . . . I don't know that I would put it that way, but yes . . . yes, I think that's it."

"And you're hoping Jake and I can tell you how that may be done. What do you think, Jake?"

I looked from Woodruff to the psychologist.

"There is no unlearning, no real undiscovering for human beings," he said.

That was not what I wanted to hear. "What about, then, just forgetting? Can I make myself do that?"

"That is a matter of opinion among psychologists," Throneberry murmured. "But I believe it's impossible to entirely forget. It's as though we put some things away in the attic. We don't see them, and since they're out of sight, we don't consider them. But they are still there."

"If I don't do something about this, I'm afraid I won't be able to keep functioning."

Throneberry leaned across the table, almost uncomfortably close to me. "You need to write."

"Write?"

"Write everything down. Stop trying to forget it and just let the words come to you. Think of it as a literary catharsis."

"It won't be literary. I'm not a good writer."

"I don't believe you," said Woodruff.

"Believe what you wish, I can't write stories. I've tried. But I'm more a literary critic than anything." I suspect I looked to these two men as if my nerves were leaving me.

"I just see words. I hear words," I said again. "And I try to forget them."

"Stop," said Throneberry.

"What?"

"Trying to forget them. Stop. It can't be done. And it's unhealthy, to boot. Write it down."

"But they're just words. Dialogues."

"Sounds like a journal to me. You'll have some opinions on these words you remember, I'm sure. Write those down, as well."

"I feel like I'm losing it. I don't trust myself."

"A healthy, and likely admirable, place to be," Woodruff said with sincerity. "But you can still listen to yourself. Listen to yourself remember. Few people do that, Richard. And memories surprise us so much; our first instinct is often to dismiss them."

"I *want* to dismiss them," I insisted.

"Why?"

"They trouble me."

"Why?"

"I . . . I want to live a simple life," I said, reminding myself of a favorite protagonist. "I sound like Bilbo Baggins. I sound like some-one in a fairy tale."

"Yes," Woodruff said. "And the best fairy tales are true!" He said it loudly, as if my assertion were an affront. "They're truer than most history texts, especially the rot that's published today. They're truer than many scientific journals."

"How . . . why do you say that?" Throneberry asked.

"Scientific journals are limited to observable, recordable data. Or should be. Lately, there's an ungodly imposition of interpretive truth on top of empirical data."

"What do you mean, 'interpretive truth'?"

"Telling us what to believe about what I call core truths. Justice, mercy, the future, grace, beauty. Not the domain of science. The good scientists know this. The best are always running around telling the others to quit announcing truth and get back to recording data." He took a breath and looked me in the eye. "It's *story* that gets at the heart of truth, Richard. Write down what you remember."

"It won't be a story. Not in the classic sense. It's just what happened. I think it will be just words. And so much dialogue."

"Maybe it's a story, maybe it isn't. But the more you write down, the less burdened you'll feel. Just journal what you recall. Just remember."

"All right."

"And don't let me hear you say 'just words' again," Woodruff sniffed. "Words are greatly underrated in the chase to understand and ameliorate the human condition. Words are nearly everything."

"You say that because you're a poet."

"I suppose so," he agreed. "Still, at least one of the earliest Christian texts agrees with me. 'In the beginning was the Word, and . . .'" He waited.

Dr. Throneberry finished the quote. "'And the Word was with God. And the Word was God.'"

Woodruff grinned. "Very big stuff, this Word. You know, questing backwards is not for the faint of heart."

"Of course," said Throneberry. "You must do it."

"I have to," I said, and both of them looked pleased. "It's all one year."

"What year, again?" Woodruff said.

"Nineteen seventy-six."

"Interesting." Woodruff nodded. "I read somewhere that all our years have different, uneven impacts on us. I think the writer said they have different weights."

"Seventy-six hit me like a freight train."

"Do tell." Throneberry smiled oddly. "Write it all down."

Woodruff pressed me. "You said you just want peace. But I suspect, knowing you, you also want the truth. That is a perilous quest, seeking both peace and truth."

"I do want the truth."

"Then be thankful. The truth is visiting you. In your memories of words and of, as you say, dialogues."

I looked to Throneberry. "Do you think I could be . . . going insane?"

He didn't answer right away. I was heartened that he took my question seriously, but I was glad to hear Woodruff say, "I think perhaps you're going *sane*."

We laughed, lightly. "I'm pretty sure that's not a compliment," I said.

"Oh, but it is!" Woodruff chortled. "We are all prone to suppress what is real and cling to what we prefer to be real. The suppression includes our memory of real events, and truth we discovered at some point in our past. Your mind—and I suspect your heart—is telling you to stop suppressing, start recalling, and write it down. That will ensure that you are going sane."

"Maybe you're just wacky, David," I said.

"Oh, good show!" He laughed. "I'm no doubt wacky. I'm also God's word to you right now. Cull your memory. Begin tonight, Richard. Write the words down."

———

So I begin.

I told them that my problem was recollection. But I believe my real problem is . . . that I *believe*.

Maybe *problem* is not the right word.

What I did not share with the word enthusiast Woodruff or the oddly engaging psychologist Throneberry was the paradox of my 1976 memories. Alongside that year's unnerving recollections are wonderful moments of enlightenment that came to us. My close friends saw it all with me, so much so that I came to doubt illumination ever comes to us in isolation from others.

The "Fellowship of the Rock" is the name we adopted, we band of ballplayers who an unforgettable boy had pulled together and enabled to see things beyond ourselves, and beyond the game. My friends bore the revelations with me in 1971, when we triumphed on baseball fields and the larger field of saving faith. My friends again were conduits of God's truth and grace to me in 1976, a year of revelations of both triumphs and vulnerabilities, many of which I'm certain I have yet to fathom.

I once wanted to believe the Nihilists were right about reducing everything to individual perspective. That would allow me to blame the folly of my narrow perceptions. But my friends saw it too. Peachy and Donnie's dad would chastise me for even wanting to forget. Uncle Albert too. But they're gone now.

It was always my friends, and remains so. The point of origin is Rafer, who inaugurated the Fellowship. (Though I suppose it was the Friend of Sinners who actually started our Fellowship. And all true fellowships. And all things.)

When I was fifteen, I hung on to the broad end of a pendulum, swinging from innocence to danger, from laughter to tears and back again, only to discover that those two conditions are not wholly disparate, but subsets of the ultimate farce of both dancing and warring on a fallen planet.

I don't know what I mean, entirely. I do know there is a real war, a conflict that makes joy and innocence not ways of escape, but necessary weapons in the warfare.

I suspect the worst, and the best, about my 1976. That is, it was a microcosm, a small type, of planet Earth's real history.

CHAPTER 1

The campfire was the centerpiece—not just of the camp but of our camaraderie. It was the epicenter. After days spent exploring woods and trails and lakes and streams, at night we explored out loud our confessions and aspirations, our hopes-against-hope that the world might accommodate our visions. The teenage heart is melancholy; we were beginning to recognize the hard realities imposed by a fallen world, a world that had not changed for our parents before us, and did not seem likely to change for us.

But a Scout campfire is a good place to hope for the unlikely.

We always made our fire bigger than necessary. It is a rare teenage boy who does not approve of excess in all things.

I liked the big fire. My imagination burned red, yellow, white, blue, and black with the coals and flames. There was something both exhilarating and unsettling about chucking sticks and logs into a wood hell.

Boy Scout Troop 44 loved campouts and making much ado about fire and wood. *Campout* is an odd compound word. Who camps *in*? Ours was a tiny troop of nine Scouts, ranging in age from eleven to seventeen. Five of us had a long history together. Zack, Donnie, Duffey, Batman, and I had played together on the Robins, a Little League team that won the 1971 Silas city championship against great odds over the heavily favored Hawks. That year, and that baseball season, was forever imprinted on our souls, not just because of the title, but more so for the impression made on our souls by a remarkable boy named Rafer. Maybe it's hard for others to believe that Little

Leaguers can carry a season with them for the rest of their lives. But that was the case with us.

One of the guys in our troop, Red, had played for the Hawks in 1971. Though my fellow Robins and I still held that season's miracle in our hearts, we wanted to consider Red our troopmate now. But he had to go along with our intentions, and up to now I felt he considered us more like accomplices than comrades. Maybe he didn't know the difference. Or maybe he did. Maybe he preferred being just one of several Boy Scouts on a roster to being in close camaraderie. He was suspicious of communities that accepted rather than excepted. I believe we're all like that, unless a miracle liberates us from our self-absorption.

Our Scoutmaster, in name, was Donnie's dad, Pastor White. But he was a busy man, and much of the time our adult leadership rotated among three other men. My dad and Zack's dad were assistant Scoutmasters. The third man was Mr. Forrester, who was never made an official assistant Scoutmaster, but seemed to be the man most likely to come out with us on any given campout. Forrester was Rafer's dad, and the changes for good that came over him in 1971, and stayed with him even after his boy died, were a big part of the whole package of miracles that came to many of us that year.

It made sense that he would end up hanging out with us Scouts. We all liked him and he was in church whenever the doors opened. He jumped all over the opportunity when Pastor White asked him if he could help out with the troop.

"You don't mind camping out some, then?" the pastor had asked.

"That's about what most folks would say I do all the time. I just camp out in my trailer."

Pastor White and Zack had reached out to Mr. Forrester and Rafer during that miracle year five summers before, and they were the human instruments God used to usher Mr. Forrester into a new birth, a new life. He still lived alone in the same old trailer he'd shared with Rafer. Some people, even those in our church who should have known better, said he was crazy. He wasn't. And as much time as we Scouts spent with him, we would have known. He *was* different. But if different means crazy, we're all certifiable.

On this particular campout, Mr. Forrester had turned in an hour or so before us boys, leaving us to chart our own course through the evening.

Tonight, Batman was telling a ghost story. The rest of us, including Zack's dog, Sawdust, were clustered around the fire. Sawdust slept. We listened to the legend of a Confederate soldier who'd lost his arm in a battle "right about in these here parts."

Batman was the shortstop on the Robins. In 1976, he couldn't catch up to a high school fastball, but he could tell a story like nobody's business. He loved dramatic tales and had found a comfortable niche in the high school drama club. Now he was regaling us with a sinister tale of lamentation for a lost limb.

"He disappeared. The guys in his platoon kinda gave him up for . . . dead." He let the word *dead* hang in the Alabama evening.

"The sergeant was a short guy with a burnt-out face." Batman understood the value of details in a campfire ghost story. "He had wiry hair that kinda grew in every kinda direction."

Batman liked the slang compound word *kinda*; he kinda used it in nearly every sentence, sometimes kinda twice. He used it mostly when he was worried or excited—or when he wanted to make others worried or excited. Like here, recounting a fearsome legend.

"He figured the poor fellow run off, and found some place to just kinda die."

Willie Rowe, an eleven-year-old new to our troop, interrupted. "One of our goats did that. Couple years back. Went off and found a place to die and that was all she wrote." Willie was not yet a Tenderfoot, which placed him squarely in our hierarchy as consummate wood gatherer.

"Thank you for sharing that with us," seventeen-year-old Red said. Sarcasm runs like a wild steed on the adolescent range. And Red never found, nor looked for, reins. Especially with Willie, whose presence in the troop Red found unsettling. Willie was black.

"But this is a man"—Batman recovered the stage—"just like you and me's, men." Which of course we weren't, but the moniker fit us out here by the fire with our fellow "man wannabes." "And this guy hadn't gone off to die. No, he'd gone off to kinda look for something. Whaddya think that was, ya'll?"

"Food," Donnie suggested.

Duffey agreed. "Yeah, I heard them Rebels was always having to scrounge for something to eat."

"Absapositively!" Donnie used a word he fashioned. "Food!"

"Not food, ya'll," said Batman. "Think of what he'd kinda want."

"Food," Duffey said. Duffey was big for seventeen; he'd been big for all his years. He was a wrestling champ at Silas High and the catcher on our baseball team, just as he had been our catcher that charmed Little League season.

Stevie spit a stream of water he'd sipped from his canteen. "He's not thinking about food, you guys. He's thinking about living and dying and junk." Stevie was fourteen, a year younger than me. He was black too, a fact that hadn't seemed to concern Red until Willie arrived. Red was a scorekeeper, and he was wrongly, sadly, threatened by growing numbers.

"So am I." Duffey nodded. "Food."

Zack smiled at me. "Richard's not saying anything."

"I'm listening. That's what I do."

"Yeah right," Duffey scoffed. "You talk up a storm when it comes on you to talk, buddy."

"No, no. I try to listen a lot." God knows why it mattered to me at age fifteen that seventeen-year-old Francis Duffey considered me deliberative. Teens are so sure that no one but their closest friends really understand them. When even they mischaracterize us, we start to think maybe we're better off fashioning ourselves into someone else. A ridiculous quest.

"People talk too much," I said and immediately regretted it.

"Listen to him!" Christopher chastised, chucking another log onto our hellish inferno. Christopher was Batman's best audience because he scared easy, and Batman liked scary, dramatic tales. Funny how people who scare easy like being scared. Or they think they do, anyway.

"Oh, everybody talks too much but you, right?" Duffey joshed. "Zack's the one that keeps his mouth shut lots." Duffey gave me his serious look, which to me was always quite the comic look. "But you know we're pals, Richie."

24

"I know you need my notes in Tylasky's class."

A chorus of laughs and "gotchas" descended on Duffey, who didn't mind in the least, grinning with all of us. He gestured an imaginary stake into his heart and said, "Crush it to da max," his pet phrase for recognizing his notion of an excellent jibe or act.

"Okay, okay, okay, guys, listen up," Batman pleaded.

Three okays did the trick, pulling our train of kid banter back onto his track.

Batman seemed to lean into his next words, and we probably leaned a little back toward him, listening. "He's walkin' around on these grounds right here, draggin' his soul around, up and down Troublesome Trail."

He actually said "draggin' his soul around, up and down Troublesome Trail," which struck me as a powerful image, even poetic. Some people remember images or events. I've learned that some tend to remember emotions and sentiments. Zack Ross is that way. That's a mixed blessing, or a mixed curse, however you're inclined to consider it. I remember words. Spoken or read, or even those I've written. Batman said, "draggin' his soul around, up and down Troublesome Trail." I catalogued it verbatim.

He mentioned the trail again, but reversed the words, for effect. "The Trail Troublesome . . ."

Everybody but Zack and me interrupted at that point, sounding off with some remark about that storied trail, an actual worn path here at Camp Sequoyah. Red, Christopher, and Duffey agreed it was surely haunted, and Donnie challenged their theology.

"Well, maybe it ain't *haunted*," Duffey said. "But it's strange stuff happening there, for some time. Mysterious."

"And he's looking for"—Batman paused for ghost story effect— "his arm, ya'll."

We all sounded off, agreeing and insisting we knew he was looking for that, when of course we didn't. A guy losing his limb is not so horrific if the guy's not real. Stories can scare us. Reality can undo us. Or save us.

Batman's voice was a plaintive tone now, a song in search of melody. "Where's my right arm?" Then a higher pitch. "Where's my right arm?" He made the question sound pregnant with premonition. The man was reaching for . . . what? Not just an arm.

Batman's eyes looked like they grew, right in front of us. "I have to . . . I got to find it."

He had us.

Even Zack, who was senior patrol leader, an incredible, genuine guy who commanded respect without saying a word, was frozen with interest, looking at Batman.

The moment and the night held. At that age, you're readier to believe, or at least pretend to believe. Good things and bad.

Then Batman said, "I know I kinda got to find my arm."

It was the "kinda" that punctured the moment. Stevie said softly, "I guess you *kinda* do," and we all roared.

The first seconds after his spell broke, Batman was ticked. "Ya'll are just . . . can't take it, can you?"

"Is that the end?" Zack asked.

"Yeah, is it over?" Christopher said.

"It is for you guys." Batman snorted, miffed.

"That was a great story!" Willie said with genuine appreciation.

"Naw, it wasn't." Batman kicked at the ground.

"Yeah it was," Willie insisted. "Man alive so dy-no-mite cool."

"I wish I had somebody's arm to gnaw on right now," Duffey said.

"Gross!" Stevie and Donnie chided him.

"I'm hungry, ya'll."

"I got an apple if you want it," said Zack.

"I ain't *that* hungry," Duffey said.

Donnie guffawed. "You just said something about eating somebody's arm!"

"That's one of them speech figurin's," Duffey said.

"Figure of speech," I said.

"Yeah, one of them," he said.

"He got the concept right." I smiled at Zack.

"I got some Jiffy Pop," Willie offered.

"Well, break it out, fella," Duffey said, "and I'll see you get promoted."

"Will you walk with me to my tent?"

Red started to say something snide to Willie, but Duffey stopped him with a look. To Willie he said, "I never leave a campfire unattended—"

"But there's all sorts of fellows here . . ." said Willie.

". . . because a campfire unattended is a calamity waiting to happen."

"I don't want to cause no calamities," Willie said, standing up and taking a few steps before stopping. "I can't see my tent. A guy's gotta be able to see, ya'll."

"Take my flashlight," Zack offered.

"Really?" Willie looked like Zack had just given him the keys to the kingdom.

"It's just a flashlight, son," Red said. "It's not a treasure map."

"But it's Zack's!" said Willie. "He's the senior patrol leader."

"We'll salute him while we eat your Jiffy Pop," Duffey rumbled. "Hop to it."

Willie disappeared, flashlight in hand, mumbling, "Jiffy Pop hop to it . . . Jiffy Hop pop to it." In about fifteen seconds, he stepped back into the glow of the fire.

"That was quick work," Duffey said. "But where's the popcorn?"

"It's kinda dark," Willie said.

"You got a flashlight, ain'tcha?" Red said.

"Still kinda . . . my tent's a far piece over there."

"Get outta here," Red snapped. "Maybe you should transfer to the Special Troop."

Zack stepped up close to Red, getting in his face really, but speaking low. I couldn't hear it, but I'm sure it had to do with Red's Special Troop reference.

The Special Troop was a group of mentally challenged kids in the county next to ours. We saw them often at camp, and they had their own supervised schedule of activities. Sometimes at camp they would join in the events of the larger Scout population.

"I'll go with you," Batman encouraged Willie. "I told the story."

"Good idea," Duffey said. "I'll see you both get promoted."

Batman looked around. "Where's Tall King?"

Tall King was a long, hefty walking stick I had dubbed "Tolkien" only to have the guys pare my fine literary allusion down to a gaunt adjective and hackneyed noun. (Though I suspect the author himself would have chuckled at my friends' characterizing him as tall and Aragorn-like.) We brought Tolkien on every campout, and never hiked without one of us wielding it.

"Holler if you're swinging at anything, and we'll come running," Duffey said as Zack placed Tolkien into Batman's hands. With that, the two boys disappeared into the dark.

I heard Willie ask Batman if Duffey was in charge of promoting Scouts, and Batman answer that Duffey was in charge of eating Scouts.

When Willie reappeared with the Jiffy Pop pan in hand, he was excited, talking a mile a minute. "Did ya'll know Batman's dad talks to airplanes?" He thrust his arms straight out to his sides, palms open and facing downward, like the wings of a sleek jet. The flashlight clattered to the earth and the Jiffy Pop package skittered across the ground toward the edge of the campfire, where Duffey quickly rescued it and placed it gingerly onto a hot log in the fire.

"Easy there, youngster," Duffey cautioned, but Willie was caught up in the moment and didn't seem to notice.

"When I do this," Willie said, raising his left hand straight overhead, "I'm telling the plane . . ."

"The pilot," Batman interjected.

"I'm telling the pilot, 'I *see* you.' When I do this"—he raised his right hand straight overhead—"I'm telling the pilot, 'I *hear* you.'"

"And when I do this"—Duffey put an imaginary cup to his lips—"I'm telling my little friend we're gonna need some cocoa to go with this popcorn."

"Duffey!" Donnie chastised. "It's his!"

"We're sharing, ain't we?" Duffey smiled big at Willie.

"I'll go get it," Willie said happily.

He took a few steps in the general direction of his tent, but stopped. Batman said, "I'm coming," and they trudged off together toward Willie's tent full of goodies.

Duffey used a short thick stick to maneuver the Jiffy Pop pan on the hot log.

"All right now, a lot of that's Willie's, right?" Donnie pressed Duffey.

"Oh sure, sure." Duffey called into the night behind him. "We're splitting it, ain't we, Willie?"

"Sure," his sweet voice called back. "I can't eat all that anyway."

"So, I'm really helping you out."

"Sure." Willie's next words made him sound slightly confused. "But we don't have to eat it all."

"Can't save Jiffy Pop," Duffey gave expert culinary advice. "It goes stale as Halloween candy the day after."

Christopher was impressed. "You don't save Halloween candy? You eat it all that night?"

"I always did. But it's been a while." Duffey looked forlorn, like he was recalling battle campaigns of yore. "I got gypped out of my last two years. I was so big, people thought I was older and they wouldn't give me much."

"My heart bleeds for you," Zack said drily.

"Our senior patrol leader is a hard man," said Duffey.

Donnie said, "Just make sure Willie gets a good bit of his popcorn."

Duffey poked the popcorn pan a couple of times. "What are you, his agent? You talk like I got no self-control."

"We are talking about food here," Christopher teased.

"Ya'll don't reckon this fire's too hot for this stuff, do ya?" Duffey ignored Christopher. "Hard to tell how to cook this thing here on an open fire."

"Have you asked anyone to the banquet yet?" Zack asked me. The banquet was our school baseball team's year-end celebration. Zack and Duffey were starters, Donnie and I warmed the bench. On rare occasions, I would pitch, but my repertoire included a fastball that was not fast and a curve without much break.

"You mean a girl?"

"No, he means a hound dog," Christopher said.

"You told me you liked that one girl," Zack prompted.

"Can I take Sawdust?" Duffey said. "Me and him's getting very close, ain't we, buddy?" He rubbed the sleeping dog's head. Sawdust lazed awake and then dozed back off when Duffey took his hand away.

"You need to get a date too." Zack broke a small stick in half and tossed it at Duffey. It bounced off him and into the fire. "So do you." He threw the other half at Donnie, who batted it away with his hand. "It can't just be me and Rebecca and all ya'll."

"I thought Rebecca liked us," Donnie said.

"She does; that's not it and you know it," said Zack. "But think how much fun it'll be if ya'll bring someone. Might even lead to other dates and stuff. Imagine that."

"Lemme just focus on getting one date," Duffey said, "before we imagine me getting two or three or six. I ain't had one, ya'll."

I tried to encourage Duffey. "I haven't dated yet either."

"You're fifteen! I'm a lot older. And I got no special friend."

After pretending to agree that his two additional years certainly changed everything, I wondered aloud, "Special friend?"

"That's what my mom calls it," Duffey said. "She keeps asking me why I don't have a special friend. She means a girlfriend."

"My mom says that too." Zack smiled. "She adds 'little.' She introduces Rebecca to people as my 'special little friend.' I thought it sounded funny, but Rebecca likes it. You said you liked that one girl," he said to me.

"Julie Prevette." I liked saying it aloud.

"Oh man!" Red sneered. "She's way out of your league."

Duffey, Zack, and Donnie vehemently disagreed, but I thought Red had a point.

"She is pretty and talented and nice and a year older than me," I sighed. "I don't think I have a snowball's chance in that fire to get her to go out with me."

"I guess you don't," Zack agreed, "if you think like that."

I was suddenly worried. "Ya'll promise me you won't tell anybody I like her."

"I promise," Zack said, and Red mumbled "what it is" which is as close to a promise as I'd likely get from him.

"She's that actress girl, right?" Donnie said. "Man, she's good at it, too. I bet Batman could talk to her for you. He does that drama stuff with her and all those theater people."

"Promise?" I stared at Donnie.

"I won't tell anybody," he promised.

"Uh," Zack jumped in. "I wouldn't let Batman approach her. He's a good guy, but it always works better if you talk to her directly. Girls like that, when you talk to them. I know it's weird, but they like it when people talk to them."

He said it so straight, I couldn't tell if he was being funny or if he was acknowledging a very real difference between guys and girls. Some of us guys really do like it when people *don't* talk to us. Or at least we think we like that.

"Duffey," I said. "Promise?"

"Promise what?"

"You won't tell anybody I like her."

"You like who?" He was serious.

Sharing who likes whom was so far off his radar I needn't have asked. "So, who are you going to ask to the banquet?"

"Somebody'll show up," he said. "Just in time." Things did seem to happen for him that way. He poked the Jiffy Pop pan slightly, pushing it into a different spot on the fire. "Can't rightly shake this thing like I'm supposed to even if—"

Boom!

The Jiffy Pop popped in one grand explosion, sending most of us to the ground, reflexively seeking shelter from the blast. Duffey and Zack fell backward off their log seats. A very small hail of unpopped kernels descended on us like tiny nuts falling from trees.

"Ya'll reckon I should have shaken it up?" Duffey drawled.

We erupted in comments, glad to be alive.

"That was *so* loud!"

"It's the magic treat . . ."

"Got another one we can put on there?"

"You and Zack both went over at the same time!"

"Where're they at, boys?"

We had nearly stopped laughing—our safety valve from the shock of the sudden Jiffy Explosion—when the sight of Mr. Forrester with a sizable camping hatchet in one hand and his other hand holding up the trousers he'd thrown on as he stumbled out of his tent kicked off a new round of guffaws.

31

"Duffey's popcorn exploded," Christopher said, making things clear as mud for the man.

"I'm right sorry to hear 'bout that." Mr. Forrester sounded entirely sympathetic. "Yeow!" He hopped then, in his bare feet. "Stepped on a coal or something that popped outta the fire, I did."

That touched off a round of wordplays from the guys on the multiple uses of the word *pop*.

Satisfied that we were all no closer to bodily injury than we'd been when he'd called it a day an hour before, Mr. Forrester hobbled back to his tent.

"Don't stay up all night," he called back. "Less'n a course ya want to."

Enforcing rules was not Mr. Forrester's primary gift. Nor secondary.

Willie and Batman reappeared from the direction of all our tents.

"Where's the hot chocolate?" Duffey said.

"Did ya'll see that?" Batman asked, his face ashen.

"See it?" Stevie said. "We were in it!"

"No."

Something about the way Batman said "no" made us all shut up and listen. "I mean . . . over where we were at. By Willie's tent." He stopped talking. And he looked legitimately scared.

"That old man that's kinda looking for his arm?" Duffey cracked.

The guys laughed, but the look on Batman's face sobered us in a hurry.

"What is it?" Zack asked.

"Two of 'em," he said. "Little flying things. In the air."

"Where?" said Zack. "When?"

"Just now," Batman said. "I mean, just then. They're gone now. It was just that second. When whatever exploded over here . . . what was that?"

"Duffey's Jiffy Pop went airborne!" Christopher squealed.

"Sorry about that," Duffey said to Willie.

"Flying things?" said Zack.

"I guess so." Batman looked lost for a description. "Ya'll didn't see them?"

"Does this mean I don't get no hot chocolate?" Duffey said.

"You talkin' about stuff in the air?" Red asked. "You saw something flying in the air?"

"Not really flying," Batman answered carefully. "Just sittin' there. Hoverin' there."

"Don't you ever give up?" Christopher said. "He's pulling our leg again, ya'll. And he's pretty good at it."

"This is no joke," Batman said, stone-faced. "I know you guys saw it."

"What about you?" Stevie said to Willie. "You must've seen what he saw."

"I was in my tent looking for the hot—" Willie put his hands in his pockets. "I'm sorry, Duffey. I forgot it when he called me out of there."

"No problem." Duffey wasn't worried. About anything. "Go on back and get it."

Willie turned, but Batman stopped him. "Don't go back over there!"

"Come on, Batman." Red scowled. "Drop it. It's a nice act, but it's not flying. Let it go."

It was obvious that most everyone thought Batman was fashioning another campfire story and adopting an actor's scared demeanor to pull off the tale.

Batman said, uneasily, "Okay . . . okay, yeah. This isn't flying. It's not flying." He just sat down on the log next to Zack, looking at the fire. Willie walked back toward his tent, apparently not afraid to go alone now.

Donnie and Christopher put more wood on the fire, and Zack said to Batman, "They were in the air? You said hovering."

"Red is right," Batman mumbled. "We can drop it. It was nothing."

Only he didn't look like he believed it was nothing. He looked like he *wanted* to believe it was nothing.

CHAPTER 2

Donnie's dad, Pastor Nathan White of Silas Baptist Church, was a big part of Zack's coming to faith in Christ. And Zack was a big part of Duffey's and my embracing faith. So I suppose Pastor White was a hero of sorts for all of us, though he would reject that title. Donnie's mom had died in 1974 from a fast-moving cancer that shocked and grieved the church and much of the town, who had come to love her and her husband. Some speculated the tragedy might knock at least some of the faith out of the pastor. But after genuinely grieving, he and Donnie both carried on as if God was then, now, and always giving his children abundant life. Forever.

Pastor White liked to say that Christians are beggars who invite other beggars to come to the feast of God's love, a metaphor I believe he got from the writings of C. S. Lewis.

The Fellowship of the Rock filled almost an entire pew every Sunday. Donnie, Zack, Rebecca, Timmy, Cathy, Duffey, and I sat together. Fortunately for Timmy, and unfortunately for the rest of us who appreciated the nickname, he had outgrown "Tigger" from our Little League days. Cathy was his "special friend." Timmy wasn't in the Boy Scouts, but we still ran into him off and on at school and regularly at church.

A lot of our parents sat in pews several rows behind us, including mine, Duffey's, Rebecca's, and Zack's mom. I suppose it can be a big step in some families when parents let their children sit apart from them in church. For us teens, it just felt natural to sit together; we were closely tied, not only as friends, but as spiritual comrades who'd come to Christ almost simultaneously during the summer of 1971.

Some people marveled at the faith of youths like Timmy, whose parents never attended church. But none of us were going to church just because our parents did. I know that is the case with many, but it wasn't that way for us. We found something true, or it found us, and so we came together to worship that which we had found. It was like drinking water in a desert. Why would you stay away from the water hole?

I asked Timmy once what his parents did on Sunday mornings. He said, "They sleep and then they eat. I told them they could do that anytime and they said, 'Yeah, that's what we're doing.'"

This Sunday, the third Sunday in April, I asked Zack if he thought his dad would ever come to church.

"Sure. I mean, I expect so. He and Sawdust are fishing this morning. He's turning my dog into a . . . what do they call it?"

"A lazy bum?" Duffey suggested.

"No, no. That would be what Sawdust wants to make my dad into," Zack said. "But dad's turning Sawdust into a . . . *pagan*! That's it. Pagan."

"I don't think dogs can be pagans," Rebecca said. "Only humans have the idiot bone in them that says there's no God."

"Very well said," I told her.

"Thank you," she preened. "Sometimes I'm almost . . . whaddya call it—*literary*."

The service had just ended and we all went up to the front to look at Mr. Rodriguez's new guitar.

"That song was great!" Cathy told him, and the rest of us murmured assent.

"Yeah, I like that one too," Mr. Rodriguez nodded. "'Pass It On' was a big part of me coming to faith. And it's good in a worship service. Easy to sing."

"I can't sing that song." Duffey shook his head.

"You can't sing any song," Timmy snickered.

Duffey glared. "Shut up. Dad says I sing like the main man."

"The main man?" Cathy asked for all of us.

"J.C."

Rebecca was intrigued. "Your dad says you sing like Jesus?"

"Johnny Cash, girl!" Duffey looked like it hurt him to think other people didn't know all the words to "Folsom Prison Blues." "What country are you from?"

"Oops! Sorry." Rebecca tried not to laugh outright.

Donnie didn't try. "She's from the country where people think 'A Boy Named Sue' is a song about some fellow in San Francisco."

"Now listen, ya'll," Rebecca clarified. "I know the Sue guy song."

"Sing a line," Zack challenged.

"I don't know how it goes. But I know some words."

"Sing some words," he challenged again.

We all looked at her, even Mr. Rodriguez, and waited for her to regale us with some genuine country-fried Cash.

"He bit like a mule," she sang in a gently lilting soprano. *"And he kicked like a crocodile."*

We doubled over, roaring loud laughs over the din of the congregation milling around talking.

Halfway back in the sanctuary, my dad smiled big and called out, "Carlos! Get those kids under control!"

"It's Rebecca Carson's fault, Rich!" Mr. Rodriguez hollered back.

Rebecca protested. "I'm just singing is all, Major Powell!"

We pulled ourselves together, still buzzing with delight over Rebecca's version of the noted line from Country Music's 1968 Song of the Year.

Rebecca turned to Zack. "Why was that so funny?"

"The mule kicks," he grinned.

"The crocodile bites," Donnie beamed.

"Oh please," she said, but she laughed at herself with us. Rebecca was as cool and warm as Zack. "Richard, tell these geniuses mules will bite."

Before I could respond, Duffey guffawed. "Maybe so, but I don't think you're gonna see Mr. Crocodile standing up on his little hind legs and kickin' nobody."

"How do you know?" Cathy came to her friend's defense. "I saw a gator in Florida eat a golf ball."

"What's that got to do—" Timmy shook his head, but thought better of it. "Never mind."

"Daddy hit the ball off the tee," she said. "And the thing came out of the water and grabbed the ball with its teeth." We were listening pretty close now. "The other fellow told Daddy he had to play the ball where it lay." She stopped talking.

"And?" Mr. Rodriguez looked at her.

"And what?" she said.

"What'd he do?" Rodriguez pressed.

"What'd who do?" said Cathy.

"Your Dad!" most all of us said at once.

"Did he hit it where it lay?" I asked. "The ball in the gator's mouth."

"Well, he went to," she said real serious, lowering her voice to draw us even closer, "but the gator reared up on its hind legs" —she raised her voice— "and started kicking him!"

She and Rebecca thought that was pretty funny, and the rest of us enjoyed pummeling them with church bulletins.

A woman's voice behind us interrupted our after-church banter. "I hate to break up all this fun."

We turned around and saw a familiar face in an unfamiliar place. Nurse Barbara had never been to our church.

"Nurse Barbara," Duffey said.

"You remember!" She was very pleased.

We all concurred with "Oh yeah" and "Course we do" and the like.

"Why don't ya'll call me Miss Barbara? Better yet, Barbara."

"You were real good to us, ma'am," Zack said.

"And real good to Rafer," said Rebecca.

"What kind of nurse would I be if I wasn't good to that boy?" Her eyes shone. "I'm just surprised you remember me."

We're always closer to grief than we know. But grief is not an affliction. Mourning means there are things worth loving, people worth remembering, forever. I noticed Duffey's eyes moisten. Duffey had a big heart. We all missed and loved Rafer.

"What do you think of Dad's church?" Donnie asked.

"I knew your dad was the real deal. Genuine. I saw that when Rafer was . . . when he came to visit Rafer. So I'm not surprised to hear him preaching like, well, honest. A humble man."

Donnie liked that. "Cool."

"What made you come here this morning?" Rebecca asked for all of us.

"Not what," she answered. "Who." She turned and pointed. "See that old guy talking to Donnie's dad? That's *my* dad. He just moved here a couple weeks ago from Ohio. Moving in with me. Wanted to go to a church this morning." She turned back to us. "So here we are."

"Why didn't you take him to your home church?" Cathy asked.

"Cathy," Timmy said softly.

Cathy didn't mean anything by it. "I mean, we're thrilled to have you here, but I was just wondering . . ." She saw it then. "Oh . . . sorry."

"Forget it, honey!" Miss Barbara was genuine. "That's right, I don't go to church."

Duffey thought he'd come to the rescue. "Some of my best friends don't go anywhere. I used to not go anywhere."

Cathy, slightly embarrassed, turned to the big guy. "Duffey . . ."

"Lots of people don't go anywhere." He meant well, and we all chuckled, including Miss Barbara.

"Fact is," she said, "I'm not . . . I don't believe what ya'll do. Mom and Dad didn't go to church, and made it clear there was no God. Mom died when I was ten and Dad convinced me I'd never see her again. It hurt, but he was just being honest with me. That's what we believe, anyway."

"You mean you ain't saved?" Duffey seemed genuinely shocked.

"I'm sorry."

I've always found it interesting that some people feel they should apologize.

"We're just glad you're here!" Rebecca said truthfully.

Zack agreed. "And glad you thought the message was genuine."

"You're very kind," Miss Barbara thanked them. "I've never known Dad to go to church before in his life. Before today. And look at him."

We looked back at the spry old man again, still bending Pastor White's ear.

"Maybe he's gettin' saved," Duffey said.

"More likely he's trying to convert your dad to atheism," she said to Donnie.

"I'd like to buy tickets to see that miracle," Donnie said. "It ain't happening."

"I guess that'd be kind of a backwards miracle, wouldn't it?" said Timmy.

Zack changed the subject. "I saw you at our last game," he said to Miss Barbara. "And your dad."

"Yeah, dad loves baseball. Maybe 'loves' is not the right word. He thinks there's something magical or mystical about it. Anyway, he asked if there was a high school game nearby. I said 'How 'bout we drive over to Georgia and see the Braves,' and he said something like, 'The pros are losing the essence of the game.' He said it'll take a few more years, but the pro game is dying a slow death."

"Sounds like he's brainy." Duffey was impressed.

"He's a ridiculous brain. I should say he *has* a ridiculous brain. He has a Ph.D. in literature and molecular biology."

"You had it right the first time," Rebecca said. "He *is* a brain."

Now we were all impressed. And I was confounded. What sort of person learns two such disparate disciplines? I did not trust science. I liked words; words travel.

I said as much, and my friends looked confounded. Miss Barbara looked interested.

"What about *scientific* words?" She grinned. "Don't they travel?"

"No," I said, seriously. "They never leave their sterile apartments." Everybody got a kick out of that.

Donnie shook his head. "Words live in apartments."

"Not all words," Rebecca corrected. "Scientific words!"

"Molecular biology," I mused aloud.

"I don't know what sort of biology that is," Duffey said. "But any kind is past my head."

"Over your head," Donnie said.

"That too." Duffey nodded.

"Anyway," Miss Barbara said, "we went to the high school ball game and I recognized ya'll from when Rafer . . . well, I remembered some of ya'll."

"Zack saw you in the bleachers," Rebecca said. "He said, 'I think that's Rafer's nurse.' I should have come over and said hey."

"Oh no, you were busy," said Miss Barbara.

I left the group, walking up the center aisle toward the church foyer. Something made me want to listen in on Pastor White and Miss Barbara's dad talking. Duffey and Donnie caught me halfway there, to ask me something.

"What?"

Duffey grinned. "Did you ask that Julie girl yet?"

"I will."

"You didn't ask her?"

"I will!"

"You gotta do it, Richard," Donnie said with an odd expression. A serious rascal.

"I will. How many times I gotta say it?"

"I don't believe you," Duffey said.

"Oh, that's real nice . . ." I broke off, since he started laughing. "Hey, wait a minute. Do *you* have a date yet?"

"No."

"So when are you gonna get one?"

"Chicken on a stick," Duffey said. That meant he wasn't worried.

"Things just happen for Duffey," Donnie said. "Guys like you and me, we have to take action."

"So you got a date?" I asked him.

"You know Mom and Dad don't let me. Till I'm eighteen."

"So don't you think they'd be a little miffed if they knew you were pressing me right now to get a date?"

"That's true," Donnie said. "C'mon, Duffey."

They let me be. Shaking off the weird nerves that harassed me whenever I thought of calling Julie Prevette on the phone, I sauntered close enough to hear the old man talking to the pastor.

"Well, yes," Pastor White said, "I thought it was very interesting when your daughter . . . it's Barbara, isn't it?"

"It is."

"When she said you wanted to talk to me because you thought I was a . . . God-fearer, right?"

"Most people aren't," the old man said. "I'm not sure most Christians are."

"Really?" Pastor White said. "Christians aren't God-fearers?"

"'Christian,' the word, means nothing these days. It means you pat dogs on the head, and let ladies in front of you in the checkout line."

"It still means that a person believes, doesn't it?"

"Does it?" the old guy scowled. "Even the demons believe."

"And they shudder," said the pastor. "James, chapter two."

"Yes." He looked pleased. "You seem like the real thing to me. Assuming I can sense that anymore." He paused, a little fearful it seemed. "Do you know who the Nephilim are? I mean, were?"

"Genesis six."

"Yes. An obscure passage to many, I suppose."

"But not to you?" Pastor White said.

"No."

The pastor opened the Bible in his hands and thumbed quickly to the book of Genesis. "Actually, the verses are not obscure. They're troublesome, maybe, but not obscure. We know what the literal Hebrew words are." He read: "The Nephilim were on the Earth in those days, and also afterward, when the sons of God came in to the daughters of men, and they bore children to them. Those were the mighty men who were of old, men of renown." He closed his Bible.

"What do you think it means?" the older man asked.

Pastor White didn't answer right away; he just looked at him, like he was weighing something about him.

"I mean, do you know anything about the verse? Do you know anything about the Nephilim?"

"Have we met before?" Pastor White said.

The man laughed softly. "I doubt it. Most people remember me after they meet me. I don't mean that in some prideful way. They just do."

"Yeah, I can see that. And I think you're right; we haven't met before." The pastor smiled. "I wrote my master's thesis on these verses from Genesis 6. In seminary. In fact, I kind of got caught up in the research."

"Really," the old man said softly.

"I was looking, academically, at what experts believe about the verses. The comparative and contrasting views, historically. There's a lot of controversy. Rabbinical scholars debate to this day who the Nephilim were. And if their existence means anything for our day."

"What did you decide? Who do you think they were?"

The pastor paused. "The Nephilim were . . . the Nephilim were not people."

"Not people."

"No, definitely not. There's no other way to read the original Hebrew. That's why they're called the sons of God, in contrast to the daughters of men. It's in the same phrase . . . 'sons of God, daughters of men.' They are . . . demons."

"Why would demons be called sons of God?"

"It's a descriptive phrase in the Hebrew, hard to translate into English. The more literal translation is 'servants of God,' or 'attendants of God.'"

"Angels," said the old man.

"You got it. Only what kind of angels are walking, stepping around on the Earth, making their home on the Earth? We're talking about the time right before the flood that God sent to purge the Earth."

"Fallen angels."

"Yeah," said Pastor White, looking around, I think to be sure he wasn't frightening anyone. I was careful he wouldn't notice me, way off to the side. "And these guys," he said, "these guys are so foul, they're actually impregnating the daughters of men, and the women are bearing children to them."

"That . . . is . . . foul."

"It's foul across the board. Think about what these offspring were like, running around on planet Earth."

"I don't have to."

"I don't blame you, I don't want to think about it either." Pastor White sighed. "Anyway, I believe, and a lot of Bible scholars believe, that's why God sent the flood."

"I think they may be back. At least one of them. Maybe a second one."

The two men looked at each other, and nobody said a word for several heavy seconds.

"Barbara says I may have some dementia." He didn't say it to be funny, or like he was admitting anything. He just said it.

"It doesn't seem so to me," Pastor White said softly.

"You're being kind."

"I'm being honest. In fact, you seem like one of the smartest, most honest people I've met in some time."

"I was hoping it was dementia."

Behind me, Duffey said, "Hey, buddy."

I let out a "Whaaa!" and must've jumped, because Duffey jumped and let out a "Heeyyy!" People looked at us, pointed and laughed, and Duffey pointed at me and said, "He's a scary guy sometimes!" That made people laugh more. I'm a lot of things, but I'm not scary.

"The Fellowship of the Rock is going to McDonald's, buddy," Duffey said. "The day's getting better all the time."

"I'd like to talk to Nurse Barbara a little."

"You're in luck. She's going too. With the old guy. Her dad."

CHAPTER 3

McDonald's was always worth the trip, just to watch Duffey order. We recognized our classmate Caroline, the friendly girl ringing up his order.

"Two Big Macs," he said, slow and clear. It was important to him. "Two large fries. Two apple dessert things."

Donnie was next in line. "Why don't you just say two of everything and get on with it?"

"Back off, little man," Duffey scowled. Then, smiling at Caroline, "Two of the regular little cheeseburgers . . ."

"This is just for you?" Caroline was curious, not teasing.

"Just for me and my lonesome," he drawled. "Two fish fillet sandwiches."

"So you really do want two of everything?" She smiled, now teasing, but in a fetching way.

"Sure, I want that, but I ain't gettin' that. Ain't got but so much money here."

A mass exodus began of those behind Duffey in line, moving to the adjacent one, which was actually moving. It included Zack and Rebecca, Donnie and me, and three other customers. My mom and Miss Barbara were already seated with Barbara's dad—Dr. McLeod—who was picking at his burger with a plastic spoon and knife.

"Ya'll got them little chocolate sundae things?" Duffey asked in a tone bordering on the reverential.

"Yes sir."

"I don't think I'm a sir yet," Duffey smiled. "'Specially not to you, Caroline."

She blushed, and then played with him. "How many would you like, sir?"

"I reckon I'll get two of those. Ya'll got the butterscotch ones?"

I heard an older man behind me. "Good grief!" He moved over to the line in motion and said in a loud voice, "Jesus is coming back before that guy finishes ordering!"

A good number of people laughed, and Duffey swung with it. "I'll take three of the butterscotch ones. Jesus likes butterscotch, and I wanna have something to give him."

More laughs.

"You're serious?" Caroline wasn't sure. "You want three?"

"I'm always serious about dessert." I think he winked at her. "I think that about does it."

A smattering of applause went up from people in the line.

Donnie and I carried our trays to where Zack and Rebecca had joined the two women and the man who held two doctorates in seemingly unrelated fields. We sat in the remaining open seats. I was beside the savant.

They were all already eating, except for Duffey and Dr. McLeod. Duffey was arranging his couples carefully in front of him. Priming the targets for assault. Once he started, it would be a brief skirmish. Dr. McLeod fiddled with his Big Mac, separating it into tiny pieces, using what I now saw was not a knife and fork but two plastic spoons.

"Everybody said their own blessing, I guess?" Duffey looked at everyone from the other end of the table.

Mom ended an awkward four or five seconds with "That's right, we said our own."

I bowed my head, a slight move, closed my eyes, and gave silent thanks. When I looked up I saw Duffey was still going at it, thanking God with low fervent passion. I heard "You're so good to me, God." That he was. Duffey indeed had pretty much two of everything on the menu—and of course the three butterscotch sundaes, though one was somewhat promised to the Son of Man.

"Why do you do that?" Dr. McLeod was looking at me.

"You mean . . . pray?"

He just looked at me. Not mean, but intimidating. "Yes. Why do you do that?"

"Because . . . I'm not God. He is." It's what came to me in the moment.

"That's a very prudent answer," he said. "I mean that as a profound compliment. Prudence doesn't seem to count for much in this world. But without prudence, the world would spin down to cinders." He went back to picking at his food.

Mom smiled at Dr. McLeod. "You're not hungry?"

"He was never much into food," Miss Barbara said. She spoke almost as if her dad wasn't even there. "Even growing up, I didn't see him eat a lot. Just enough to stay alive, I guess. That's my dad."

"What do you suppose is in these?" the old man asked no one in particular.

"That's a Big Mac," said Donnie.

He answered himself, low but audible. "Enough saturates and chemicals and rat feces to keep a host of researchers busy categorizing the consumption effects for the better part of a year."

Another spate of awkward seconds passed, until Duffey rescued us. "It eats pretty good, though, don't it?"

"I wouldn't know," Dr. McLeod said.

"We'll be praying for you," Duffey said through a mouthful of saturates.

"Do that." The rest of us laughed, happy to consider that Duffey's culinary expertise might trump the old man's suspicions.

"I'm going to go ahead and change the subject," Rebecca said to a chorus of assent. "Miss Barbara said you were a professor of literature, Dr. McLeod."

"One of my noble pursuits," he said.

"Meaning?" Mom asked.

"Meaning, there were ignoble ones. I wish I had never left literature."

"Richard here is a genius," Zack said. "With literature and everything else."

"So my daughter tells me." The old man looked at me. I looked at Miss Barbara.

She shrugged. "Some of my friends teach there. At Silas High. They all talk about the boy genius, Richard Powell. They mention the Fellowship of the Rock too."

Duffey and Donnie high-fived across the table.

"What sort of Fellowship is that?" Dr. McLeod asked me.

"We had a good friend," I said, "a boy named Rafer, who some of us played Little League ball with four—or now it's been five—years ago." I decided to be very open. "He meant a lot to us. He changed us, really." I started to choke up just a little.

Rebecca helped. "And he gave all of us these rocks. We were just kids then."

"So, we kept the rocks," Zack said. "Mine's still on my dresser."

Duffey reached into his pocket, took out a small rock, and set it on the table in front of him.

"That's so cool, Duffey," Rebecca's voice was tender.

"But that's not your original rock," Donnie said almost under his breath.

"Oh, are we gonna go through all that again?" Duffey boomed.

"We all still got our originals." Donnie had his fun. "That's Tigger's. You lost yours."

"It still counts!" Duffey insisted.

"Yes, it does. Don't listen to him, Duffey," Rebecca said.

"What happened to Rafer?" Dr. McLeod asked.

"He went to Glory," Zack said evenly.

"You mean he died."

"He was a very sick boy," Miss Barbara said. "And it was my privilege to nurse him in the hospital. That's when I met these wonderful young people." She smiled at all of us.

"Why *fellowship*?" Dr. McLeod looked at me. "Why use that word?"

"Richard came up with that," Donnie offered. "Pretty cool."

"It has a couple of meanings for us," I said. "Rafer got us all into Jesus." I didn't plan to say it that straight. But the old man didn't seem to mind. "So we are in fellowship together now."

"You mean going to church," Dr. McLeod said.

"No sir." I didn't. "I mean the bond we have. The new life, the forever life we have together." I thought I might sound preachy, but I decided it didn't matter.

"You've found something that makes your life easier," Dr. McLeod said, surely trying to be gracious.

But I wasn't going to let that lame sentiment get out of our conversation alive. "If we have hoped in Christ in this life only, we are of all men most to be pitied."

"Is that so?" Dr. McLeod seemed mysteriously pleased. "Of all men most to be pitied," he echoed.

"First Corinthians 15:19," I said. "The fellowship is the bond we have because we are new creatures in Christ."

"Crush it to da max," said Duffey through his fries.

Miss Barbara got a kick out of that. "What's that supposed to mean?"

Duffey swallowed and explained. Sort of. "It means, you know, I'm impressed because somebody just went all the way with something they were doing."

"You're congratulating him?"

"Yeah. It's how the guys and me sometimes say 'Wow.'"

I expounded somewhat. "We also use it as an exhortation. It can mean, 'Go ahead and go all the way with the task at hand. Give it your best shot. Crush it to da max.'"

Dr. McLeod caught my gaze and got his grip back on our conversation. "You were saying . . ."

"Going to church," I said, "is going to a building. Fellowship is something deeper."

"Greek word?" He stared at me. A little game. Or test.

"*Koinonia*," I said.

"Impressive," he nodded. "You can't have learned that in school."

"Richard learns tons of stuff beyond school," Zack bragged on me. "I went over to his house last year and he was in his room with like five or six books open on the floor. I asked him what he was doing and he said he was synthesizing."

"Sounds painful," Duffey murmured.

Zack smiled. "I'm sure it is, for you and me. I asked him what he meant and he said—" He turned to me. "How did you put it?"

"Well," I paused, "that's just . . ."

"No, how did you put it?" Zack pressed.

"I like to cross disciplines."

"That's it!" Zack beamed. "Crossing disciplines! He was reading some English textbook and a novel and the Bible."

"Sounds *very* painful," Duffey chimed in again. "All that reading."

"Why do you do that?" Dr. McLeod asked me.

"I'm . . . I'm not sure," I said honestly. "But I guess I'm thinking everything is kind of related."

Dr. McLeod asked several questions quickly. "How old are you?"

"Fifteen."

"Why the Bible?"

"I believe the Bible."

"What novel?"

"*Great Expectations.*"

"You said there was a second reason you called your bond with your friends here a fellowship."

"I did?"

"You did," he said. "Your exact words were, 'It has a couple of meanings for us.'"

"Oh," I remembered. "*Fellowship of the Ring.* One of my favorite books."

Duffey interrupted softly. "Batman comics are mine."

Dr. McLeod kept his eyes on me. "What else have you read?"

"Titles?"

"Authors."

With any other people around, I would have been embarrassed, and even tempted to lie by not truthfully revealing who I read. But these were my friends.

"Fitzgerald, Hemingway, more Dickens . . ."

"Not what your school assigned."

"These are not assigned," I said.

Dr. McLeod actually prayed. "God save us. What else?"

"Steinbeck, Shakespeare, O'Connor . . ."

"Which O'Connor?"

"Flannery." I hadn't heard of another.

"I mean which stories."

"All of them," I confessed.

"How many is all?" he said, seriously.

"Thirty-one."

"Name one of her two novels."

I named both. "*Wise Blood* and *The Violent Bear It Away*."

"Did you like her story, 'Southern Customs Stay with All'?"

"I never heard of that," I said.

"Oh, but any serious O'Connor reader has read that!"

"I'm sorry, sir. I never heard of such a story."

"That's because it doesn't exist." He turned to Miss Barbara. "He's so honest I want to puke."

Miss Barbara asked me if I had a pet.

"Yes. A hamster. I call him Gandalf."

"That's good!" she beamed. "Dad doesn't trust scholars who don't have a pet. He says they're too caught up in their own head."

Donnie was about to come out of his seat. "Ask him something else!"

He looked back to me, and recited slowly, "'Folk must grow weary there, even in their gardens, as do all things under the sun of this world.'"

"Faramir," I said quietly. "*The Two Towers.* Though I guess maybe I could have said the writer of Ecclesiastes. It sounds like Tolkien swiped it."

"Ah." Dr. McLeod seemed pleased. "As do all of us, swipe all things. There is nothing new under the sun. Hemingway too, used—"

Rebecca leaped to her feet and shouted, "The sun also rises!"

Donnie yelped, we all jumped a little, and Duffey, choking on a little bit of burger, coughed and pleaded, "Don't . . . now take it easy . . . you scared the air outta me, girl!"

"Yes, you're right." Dr. McLeod nodded to her. "That's what I was thinking."

"I'm literary! I'm literary!" Rebecca bounced a little, pumping the air with her fists. "Who's the scholar now!"

50

"And you read that on your own?" Dr. McLeod said to her.

"Well, no, it was assigned at school." Her crest fell slightly.

"Glad to hear it," he sighed. "Perhaps there is a God. And you read it. Good for you."

"Well, I didn't read it." Her crest fell completely. She sat down. "But I'm gonna. Sometime."

"What's that called again?" Duffey mumbled.

"*The Sun Also Rises,*" Miss Barbara answered.

"Do they have that in Classic Comics?" said Duffey.

"Probably not." Miss Barbara and the rest of us laughed.

Dr. McLeod prayed again. "Please no, dear God."

"How they expect the rest of us to read it then?" Duffey expounded. "Us that ain't Richard."

Dr. McLeod addressed me again. "So you liked *The Lord of the Rings?*"

"Very much."

"What do you like about it?"

"It's different. The arc, the journey. It's different."

"Explain."

"Well," I took a breath, "most every story has a journey or a path, a mission. Someone or some group is trying to get something or get someplace. But *Rings* is really . . . an anti-quest. Frodo is not trying to *get* something, he's trying to get *rid* of something. And all the good guys are hoping desperately that he succeeds in ridding the world of something. Not gaining something but losing something."

"An anti-quest," Dr. McLeod said, his eyes alive, looking brighter, deeper. "Yes, that's excellent."

A hush settled on the group, quiet now, but for the peaceable sound of Duffey sucking down his third butterscotch sundae. Jesus tarries.

"Miss Barbara says you like baseball," I said.

"Baseball," said Dr. McLeod, "has been my escape. My redemption."

Zack was intrigued. "How is that? What do you mean?"

"I don't expect others to agree," he said. "The stop and start, the rhythms of the strategy and the game's pace itself, mirror the struggle of . . . life. The combination of speed, power, finesse, and mental acuity is, for me, hypnotic."

"Football has all of that in it," Zack suggested. "Other sports, too."

"I'm sure it may, for other people." Dr. McLeod shook his head. "Not for me. I'm also drawn to the individual battles. Pitcher/catcher. Catcher/base stealer."

"Football has similar battles," Zack said. "Receiver, defensive back. A guy blocking another guy trying to tackle."

My mom teased Zack. "Who are you kidding?" She looked at Dr. McLeod. "He loves baseball. He eats it and sleeps it."

"That's true," said Rebecca.

"So I don't know why he's pushing football on you," said Mom.

"That's true. Absolutely." Zack concurred. "I was hoping Dr. McLeod could explain to me why the game holds me in a vice, like it maybe holds him. Sounds like it does."

"Call me Peachy." Dr. McLeod smiled at Zack. "All my friends do. It seems you and I share the same fixation, young man. We have caught the same disease."

"I'm there, too," I said.

"I don't know why you two have it," said Peachy. "I suspect it may have something to do with this boy Rafer and his impact in your lives dovetailing with your playing Little League with him."

Rebecca nodded. "Rafer's a big part of it."

Zack spoke. "I feel funny saying this, but, I feel closer to God when I'm playing. Like he's playing too, with me."

Peachy shrugged. "In my case, I don't know why the game holds a core power over me. I can guess at peripheral reasons. The unique symmetry, the diamond-shaped infield. The more pastoral outfield."

"It's not so pastoral," I said, "for guys having to run down Zack's line drives."

"Zack hits in the gaps a lot," Rebecca grinned.

"On purpose?" Peachy asked.

"I wish," said Zack. "I just try to meet the ball and hope it goes where nobody can catch it."

"It does!" Miss Barbara said. "A lot. He's hitting .380."

"But I can't hit the gaps on purpose. The ball finds the gaps."

"Perhaps God really is involved when you play," Peachy jested.

"But you don't believe in God," Donnie said in friendly tones.

"No, I don't. But I believe in the power of people believing in God. Please do so." He gestured to all of us.

"You believe . . ." I ventured with caution. I liked the man a lot. "You believe religion is the opiate of the masses."

"You *are* well read," he answered. "I do. But a much needed narcotic. The world is much better because people live as if there is a good God."

"I guess . . ." I thought out loud, slowly formulating my next point, "the world may get significant benefit from people living out that belief, even if it is a faulty belief."

"Undoubtedly."

"Unless . . . evil is real."

Everyone, including Peachy, said nothing. He just looked at me.

"If evil is real," I said, "what you call our false belief, our kind of hoping for the best, believing that God's real and that he's good, is not a good thing, or even, I think, a neutral thing. It is a bad thing, this false hope we have, and it enables evil to have its way with us. And with the world."

Amid the usual din of people eating and talking and laughing, our table seemed captured by an odd silence.

"I have never wanted to believe in evil," said Peachy.

"I don't want to either," I said. I thought of Frodo Baggins.

"I have never wanted to believe," Peachy continued. "But I am keen enough to know that reality is not prey to my preferences."

I felt a kinship. "Behold . . . the storm comes, and now all friends should gather together, lest each singly be destroyed."

"Is that from the Bible? Where?"

"Not Scripture. Tolkien," I said. "Gandalf to King Théoden."

He liked that. We shared the moment.

Duffey inaugurated a different moment. "I'm going back up there. Anybody want anything?"

"I don't think I could eat another bite," said Miss Barbara.

"Duffey says that all the time," Donnie offered.

"Shut up." Duffey frowned. "Just for your information, chump

Donnie, I didn't say I was getting anything else to eat. I said I was going back up there."

"Okay, okay, you're going back up there," said Donnie. "Peachy, sir, you should come to our last game. Richard's pitching."

"He's got three pitches," Duffey announced, standing. "Slow, slower, and slowest."

"When is it?" Peachy asked.

"You don't have to come," I said.

"Yes you do!" said Rebecca, apparently energized at the prospect. "It's Tuesday, after school. At the school."

"Can we make that?" Peachy asked his daughter.

"Sure."

Peachy smiled. "I want to see you pitch."

"I'm terrible." I had long ago grasped the benefits of lowering expectations. And by many measures, I *was* terrible. I had no fastball. My curve moved a little. In other words, I was a baseball train waiting to wreck.

"If you're so terrible," Rebecca chided, "why do they let you pitch?"

"Pepper can't pitch every game," said Donnie.

"That's kinda mean," Rebecca said, half serious.

"I been telling ya'll for years I'm no angel," Donnie pleaded. "It's God's honest truth anyway. Pepper pitches hard. And Richard pitches slow and curves it, and the hitters have to adjust. Sometimes they do and Richard gets shelled. Sometimes they don't and Richard is able to crawl from the wreckage."

Everybody laughed at that, even sweet Rebecca. I did too. It was a funny way to describe my pitching. Made funnier because it was the truth. Sometimes the truth is hilarious. Not always.

"If we had a ball and glove," Peachy said suddenly to me, "I could show you something that would help."

"Zack has a ball," said Rebecca. "And two gloves in his trunk. He makes me play catch with him lots."

"I thought you liked that." Zack was concerned.

"I like to go fishing too," she said. "But I wouldn't want to do it every day."

We laughed.

Zack pressed, "What else aren't you telling me?"

"Only that I'm head-over-heels crazy about you, Zack Ross, and probably will be till the day I die."

We roared and Zack blushed and Miss Barbara commented, "Kinda makes you feel like almost nothing else matters, doesn't it, Zack?"

"Almost."

Peachy stood. "Let's go get those gloves and ball. I'll show you something."

I looked at my watch. "I gotta get home. In just a few minutes."

"This won't take more than a minute or two," he said, "in the parking lot right here."

"Might want to get out of the parking lot," Miss Barbara said.

"No, no, parking lot will work," Peachy insisted.

"I'm just saying," she said under her breath. "Accidents happen."

"I'll show you something you can use when you pitch Tuesday."

We threw our napkins and burger wraps in the trash on our way out the door, and walked to the silver 1973 Chevy Vega that Zack's dad was still paying for. Zack popped the trunk and pulled out two gloves, one of which held a dirty gray baseball.

Peachy took a glove and the ball. "We need a catcher. To pitch to."

"Zack can catch," Rebecca offered.

"I'd rather be here on the pitcher's mound," said Zack. "I want to learn whatever Richard's learning."

"Where's Duffey?" Donnie looked around.

He popped out of McDonald's then, smiling like the cat that had brutally ended the canary's angst.

"Get over here," Zack called.

Duffey jogged over. He was very happy, humming some song, and Zack told him he was catching.

Duffey took the second glove from Zack and started walking. "What would ya'll do for a catcher if you didn't have a fat guy around?"

"You're not fat." Mom was kind. "You just carry more healthy stuff in your body than most of the other boys do."

"Thank you, Mrs. Powell."

What Zack had called the "pitcher's mound" was a grassy spot just off the parking lot, beside a McDonald's trash container.

Duffey knelt into a casual catcher's stance at a reasonable distance from Peachy, Zack, and me. Reasonable to Duffey. Peachy paced in measured steps toward Duffey, obviously counting in his head.

He stopped. "Here." He set his right foot at a precise spot on the ground a couple of feet in front of Duffey.

Duffey looked from Peachy's foot to me and Zack, and back to the foot.

"It matters," the man said.

"I'll take your word for it." Duffey shuffled forward to the spot.

"You're a wise young man." Peachy walked back toward Zack and me.

"Naw, I ain't," I heard, in Duffey's soft twang. "I'm kinda slow. But I like me." He was still humming something.

"How do you grip it?" Peachy asked me. "A fastball."

I showed him my standard, two fingers across the seams. "But like we were saying," I gave a shrug, "my fastball is everybody else's changeup."

"Doesn't matter. Let's see it. Wind up and pitch."

"Keep it off the parking lot, you guys," Miss Barbara advised.

"I'm slow, but I'm not wild."

"I'm just saying," she said.

"Fire it in here, old buddy, big man," my catcher called.

Duffey had impressive powers of friendly pretense. I could never "fire it in," I was not old, and I would never be a big man. I *was* his buddy.

I wound up and let fly. The ball didn't zip in the air and pop in the catcher's glove like Zack's would, but my control was excellent. Duffey threw it back to me. "That's the way to bring it."

"Do that again for me," Peachy said without emotion.

I did, and Duffey kept encouraging, tossing it back. "Now you're hummin' it."

"Your windup is perfectly fine. Good, really." Peachy took the ball from me. "And it's long enough, deliberate enough, that you can work on a way to alter it in mid delivery," he mimicked the start of my windup, "so that the ball comes out quicker." He shortened my routine, getting to the pitch delivery much quicker. But he held onto

56

the ball. "That will be very effective when the hitter is expecting you to use the same windup you've consistently demonstrated. He won't expect the shorter delivery; the ball will surprise him."

"I like that." I did.

"Hitting is timing," said Peachy. "If you upset their timing, even just a little, you get a pop-up or a groundout. Even a strike." He looked at me with kind eyes. A little sad too. "We're very much alike, Richard. And for you and me, it will never be about overpowering them."

He gestured toward Duffey, letting him know he was going to pitch to him.

"All right, Mr. Peachy, sir." Duffey pounded his glove. "Bring it in to me. Bring it home to daddy."

Zack chuckled, and I heard Mom and Miss Barbara laughing at Duffey's word choice too.

Peachy counseled Duffey. "This one's going to move on you . . ."

"I got it," Duffey said.

". . . in a rather chaotic fashion."

"Whatever you wanna say, Mr. Peachy, sir." Duffey grinned. "The Duff-man was born to play catcher."

Peachy coiled, tighter, more contained than my loopy, drawn out windup, and let it go.

It was not a slow pitch, but it was not too fast for Duffey to catch. Zack threw harder. But what made Duffey miss it was the rise, an actual hop in the ball just before it got to the mitt. The ball skipped in midair. It was not the rise of a good fastball with movement. It was a real jump. It was not a wild pitch; it would have been a strike. But with that dramatic vertical movement, it sailed inches over Duffey's slightly raised glove, narrowly missing his forehead.

"Whoooaaaa!" Duffey cried out.

The ball knocked hard into the side of a McDonald's trash container and caromed sideways into the parking lot, bouncing off the windshield of a VW bug.

"Ohhhh!" Mom winced.

We walked toward the VW. Only Donnie hustled. The rest of us were in no hurry to see bad news.

Donnie leaned over the windshield. "It's just a little tiny crack."

"Uh-huh," Miss Barbara sighed. She wasn't happy.

"Looks like a little star." Mom tried to sound positive.

Duffey felt bad. "I swear that ball jumped. Right there in the air. Like it had something inside that exploded or something."

Zack picked the ball up off the lot, a few yards from the VW. "How'd you throw that?" he said to Peachy.

Miss Barbara walked back toward McDonald's.

"I'll go with you." Mom came alongside her.

Miss Barbara murmured, a resigned tone. "If he were seventeen instead of seventy, I'd make him come in here and hunt down the owner and apologize and . . ."

"You've got your hands full with him, Barbara," said Mom. They stepped inside.

"What *was* that?" Zack put the ball in Peachy's hands.

"Mr. Paige called it a winged knuckle," Peachy was pleased, oblivious to the windshield mishap. "He was very tickled when he showed me the grip and release and I picked it up so fast."

He held the ball out, turning his hand back and forth so we saw the way his four knuckles spread, two of them pinching it and two of them knuckled under, pressing flat.

"When you release," he said, "the trick is to snap your wrist over the top. Like an overhand curve."

"I got an overhand curve," Zack said. He was keyed up.

"Not me," I said. "But I can try it. I'm left-handed." I didn't know if that made any difference.

"Left or right, it doesn't matter." He showed me again and I took a mental snapshot of his grip. When I took the ball I was able to replicate it.

"That's it," said Peachy. "Now try to snap it off overhand."

Duffey trotted off some ways away, so I was throwing directly away from the McDonald's parking lot.

He crouched. "I know what's coming this time." He looked ready.

"It won't be like that," I said, loud enough for him to hear. "I'm just trying to do what he told me, but, anyway . . ."

I didn't expect my ball to do anything remotely like Peachy's. My curves were never overhand, and now I was trying to snap one off with my knuckles all askew.

I wound up and threw.

It was slower than Peachy's but everybody was amazed when it jump-sailed like his had done and Duffey missed it again. This time the ball grounded harmlessly to a halt in the worn grass behind Duffey. Duffey ran it down and threw it back. Peachy helped Zack place his fingers carefully on the ball.

"That's it," he said. "Now just think like you're throwing your overhand curve."

Zack threw overhand curves in his sleep, so I expected his ball now to do the same as Peachy's and mine. It stayed straight, into Duffey's glove.

"Nothin' there. Sorry," Duffey said, sounding apologetic.

"What's going on?" I said. Zack didn't look disappointed, but he wanted to hear Peachy's explanation too.

"It's odd, I know." Peachy frowned. "Welcome to my world. I've no explanation. Paige showed it to Bob right after he showed it to me. I could throw it and Bob couldn't. Who is sufficient to understand these things?"

"First Corinthians 9:5," I said. "How is it you know that verse, but you didn't know 'We are of all men most to be pitied'?"

"Probably because I am not unlike most men."

"Not according to your daughter, sir," I said.

"Oh I know I'm different. I'm very unusual in many ways," he said rapidly. "I simply meant that people tend to pick and choose which Bible passages they want to remember, don't they?"

"You're not a Christian, right?" I was just making sure.

"Dear Richard," he groaned, like he was disappointed in me, "even unbelievers recognize the worn practice of choosing to recall some words over others because they are more intriguing or attractive and less of a direct challenge. Truth, what's real, is almost never the goal. And preference usually is."

Duffey had walked back to the three of us, and heard most of Peachy's freighted rhetoric. He actually looked interested, so I asked him if he agreed with Peachy's sentiments.

"I don't have the foggiest notion." Duffey looked at the man with a kind of awe. "It sure sounds like something all-fired important. Know what I mean?" He looked at Zack. "Like the world is hangin' on what he's talking about."

"Maybe it is," Zack said.

"And I ain't never seen no ball skip straight up that hard in the air like that." Duffey's eyes shone at me. "You and Mr. Peachy both!"

"Who's Paige?" Donnie asked Peachy.

"Do you know?" Peachy looked at me. He was back in high spirits, suddenly recovered from his diatribe on truth's surrender to preference.

"Maybe. I'm thinking, but . . . when did he show you?" I asked him. "What year did you learn that pitch from him?"

"Nineteen forty-eight."

"Were you in Cleveland?"

"Yes!" He was excited.

"Cleveland!" Rebecca shook her head. "How in the world do you . . ."

Zack said it: "Satchel Paige."

"Yes!" Peachy was giddy. It was hard to believe this was the same man who was lecturing us on the fluidity of truth just moments ago.

For baseball historians like Zack and me, if he had learned a pitch from the famed Satchel Paige, Peachy was immediately a cult figure to us.

"Who?" Duffey and Donnie said at once.

"Man . . . Satchel Paige," I announced with sobriety befitting the legend, "was possibly the greatest pitcher ever."

"I never heard of him," said Rebecca.

"Wait a minute." Duffey looked alert. "I've heard of the great Satchmo."

"Wrong Satch," Zack said. "Satchmo was Louis Armstrong."

"Greatest pitcher ever?" Donnie broke in. "What about Sandy Koufax?"

"Yeah. And Tom Seaver." Duffey wanted to know.

"They're great, sure," I said. "It's hard to compare eras."

"For the historically illiterate, it's nigh impossible," Peachy said.

"I can read and write ya'll," Duffey protested.

"Satchel Paige was black," I said. "They didn't let him play in the bigs until real late in his career. After Jackie Robinson changed things."

"Very late," Peachy concurred. "He said he was in his late forties, but I think the man was in his fifties."

"And you knew him?" Zack beamed. "Did you play with him?"

"Good grief, no, Zack." But Peachy was obviously pleased with the question. "A few of them let me hang around."

"How do you get to hang around a major league baseball team?" Donnie grinned.

"I met Grover Marsh, the man who was a type of medic for the team, in a bar. Grover started letting me hang around him at the ballpark, when I could get off work. He introduced me around. It was different then. You saw ballplayers on the streets, in the stores. Working second jobs. Very different. I guess I was too." He sounded a little sad. Like he'd lost something after those years. Or found something, and wished he hadn't.

"I read once that Satchel Paige had almost a hundred different pitches," I said.

"If you'd met him," Peachy said seriously, "you'd believe it. His variety came from speed changes, delivery changes, and different spins and other things people could only marvel at. Someone asked Willie Mays what his proudest moment as a hitter was and he said it was when he was nineteen and he hit a line drive single off of Satchel Paige in a barnstorming game in the Negro Leagues. Nobody pitched like Satch."

"Who was Bob?" Rebecca asked Peachy. "You said this guy showed the pitch to Bob right after he showed it to you. And Bob couldn't throw it. Who's Bob?"

"Feller," Peachy said simply.

Zack shook his head. "Bob Feller?"

"Now him I heard of," said Duffey. "You knew Rapid Robert?"

"No," said Peachy. "He was just standing there when Satch showed me the pitch and I threw it."

"And Feller couldn't?" Zack marveled. "How do you figure that?"

"Baseball is hard to figure," said Peachy. "It's like life that way. Mysterious. Outcomes no one foresees."

"Other sports can be that way too," Rebecca challenged.

"Maybe so," Peachy said. "I've just seen it up close with baseball. It's the only sport, I believe, where the defense has the ball. It's different."

Miss Barbara and my mom walked out of the McDonald's with a man who was chitchatting and laughing with them, as if he knew them well.

We met up with them at the VW and Miss Barbara showed the man the little crack in the windshield.

"Oh, that," he muttered. "That's nothing. Forget it. My name is Bradley."

"First or last name?" Peachy asked.

The question seemed to flummox the man; he exchanged stares with Peachy.

Miss Barbara rescued the moment. "It's Mr. Bradley, right?"

"Yes," said Mr. Bradley, suddenly smiling. "As I told you when we met inside."

"This fella here," Duffey pointed at Peachy, "played with the great Satchmo."

"You're a musician?" Bradley was impressed.

"He means Satchel Paige," Peachy clarified. "Ballplayer. Taught me a pitch, is all."

"The flying knuckle," Rebecca said.

"Winged knuckle," said Peachy. "It bounced into your windshield."

"You're being awfully nice about it," Mom said.

The man shrugged. "It doesn't pay to make mountains out of little molehills. There are enough real mountains to worry about. Life is too small to fret such things."

"You mean too short," Mom smiled. "Life is too short to fret such things."

"I said that."

"You said life is too small," Mom suggested. "But it doesn't matter."

"Yes." He nodded, awkwardly. "You're right. I meant the other word. I'm old."

"You're not old," Duffey said.

"I'm not?" He looked as if he really didn't know if he was or not. Duffey gestured to Peachy. "*He's* old."

"Duffey!" several of us said at once.

"What?! Am I in trouble again?" He really didn't know.

"Only if I cared," said Peachy.

"I've got to get home," Mom said. "You taking the boys home?"

"Yeah," said Zack. "No problem."

"I guess we're the boys." Donnie put his arm over Duffey's shoulder. "When's your car out of the shop?"

"Whenever my dad lets it come out," Duffey moaned. "It's fixed, I know it is. He just wants me to learn my lesson."

"Barbara said you boys play baseball," Mr. Bradley said. "At the high school."

"Yes sir." The lot of us confirmed.

"I'd like to come watch a game."

"You should come Tuesday afternoon," said Rebecca. "Richard here's pitching."

"Which means," I said, "there won't be anything special to see. Except for Zack's hitting."

"That's not true," Zack said. "You got a new pitch, a devastating rough knuckle."

"Winged knuckle," Peachy corrected.

"A pitch that only Satchel Paige and Peachy could throw before you learned it," Zack said.

Mr. Bradley's countenance brightened. "I would like to watch that, to see that. If I don't forget. And I'm not too busy."

Rebecca had pulled a scrap of paper from her pocket and wrote something on it.

Duffey put his foot in his mouth again. "You don't strike me as someone who stays real busy."

"Duffey." Miss Barbara shook her head.

"What?! Why is that a bad thing to say?"

Rebecca gave Mr. Bradley the paper scrap. "I always remember things better if they're written down," she said kindly.

He took the paper, gestured to Duffey and said, "I don't mind what this one said."

Miss Barbara looked relieved and slightly baffled. "You're kind. I just thought you might take it to mean you looked lazy to him. Or like someone who has nothing much to do."

"I have many things to do."

That sounded a little odd; almost like he really did not have much to do that people would count as worthwhile. But he held up the scrap of paper and said, "And one of them is to watch a baseball game with my new friends—Peachy and the whole gang."

Everyone seemed to decide to go home at the same moment, including Mr. Bradley, who again assured us the windshield was no problem. Driving off, he waved cheerily out the window of his VW.

We all walked toward our separate cars, and I could hear Peachy ask his daughter if she had given his name to Mr. Bradley.

"Sure."

"You're sure."

"I think I did. I must have. He called you Peachy."

"Uh-huh."

On our drive home, I said to Mom, "That guy was a little strange, don't ya'll think?"

"Which guy?"

It took me a second to realize that she might have thought I meant Peachy.

I said, "I mean Mr. Bradley."

"Yeah, I could call him strange," she nodded. "And I could call Peachy strange. And I could call you strange. And pretty much everyone in the world, I could say is strange. Except me. That's the way it works. Everybody's really bizarre, except for you, yourself."

"What if I think I'm strange, too?"

"Then you might be honest, which makes you very compelling." She seemed to be thinking out loud, and enjoying that process. "Because while every person is strange . . . very few are honest."

"Peachy strikes me as honest."

"He strikes me that way too. I guess time will tell. It does that with all of us."

I felt a little lost in her words. "What . . . will do *what* with all of us?"

"Time. Time will tell if we are honest. All of us."

"You're so deep," I said in a teasing tone.

She got a kick out of that. "I'm not deep. I'm observant. My son is deep."

CHAPTER 4

My dreams that night included one that gripped me, one whose images stayed with me into the next day and have remained ever since.

> *I am playing in an important baseball game, a game I recognize as very much like the Little League championship game I played in five years before. But there are differences. And the differences grasp at me, threatening to seize my soul. Or to set my soul free. I can't tell in the dream. In that way, the dream is like conscious life.*
>
> *I'm up to bat. I am ageless. I'm not a kid, nor an adult, nor am I the fifteen-year-old of my conscious 1976 life. Where is time, when we dream?*
>
> *The pitcher is faceless, literally; it has no face. Nothing about its vague form suggests masculine or feminine gender, or even humanity.*
>
> *I bat not against flesh and blood.*
>
> *A baseball is released from the faceless mass. It travels toward me, almost floating, like it's formed from mist compressed into the shape of a baseball. It's coming toward my head, but it's moving so slowly that I sense no need to move, to duck. In fact, I am inclined to watch the mist-ball float toward me. My intrigue turns to horror when, about halfway between the mound and the plate, the mist is transformed into a hard white projectile. The mist is a baseball.*
>
> *Who is sufficient for these things?*
>
> *I duck, dropping to the ground in the batter's box, the projectile narrowly missing my head. The catcher, which has stood to*

catch the high pitch, looms over me. The catcher, like its teammate, is a "which," not a "who."

The catcher says, "That one almost hit you." The catcher's words are a statement, not sympathetic, or even interested commentary. It is simply announcing an indifferent fact.

"That one almost hurt you." Another announcement from this amorphous catcher behind home plate, except the word hurt *stands out in tone.*

The catcher throws the ball back to the pitcher. I am still on my back in the dirt beside home plate. "Who are you?" I ask the catcher.

"I am Fear," it says. "Who are you?"

"I'm Richard."

The catcher shakes its head, and I notice that, like the pitcher, it has no face. I stand up, and look closer, through the catcher's mask. Yes, it is faceless, and I sense the catcher does not notice me staring at it. It has no sense of the most basic communication between humans: eye contact.

"Who is that?" I point to the pitcher.

"He is Fear."

"But you said you *were Fear." I am confused.*

"Did I?" The catcher crouches to catch the next pitch. "I didn't mean it. I never mean anything."

Another misty pitch floats toward the plate, this one coming right down the middle. As I get ready to swing, the mist congeals in what seems a nanosecond and it is past me and into the catcher's mitt with a dull thud.

I am appalled at the speed of the pitch. "I can't hit that." My words are something of a plea for mercy.

"Of course you can't." The catcher flatly agrees, throwing the ball back to the mound.

I notice someone's missing. "Where's the umpire?"

"He's dead," says the catcher.

"Really?" I am more surprised than sad. "So how can we play?"

"Play what?" the catcher asks.

"What's he doing?" I ask the catcher, when the pitcher steps off the mound and rubs the baseball between his hands.

"He's getting the ball ready . . . to hit you with it."

"Oh," I say. I feel sad. And something else . . . resigned. "I get it," I say without emotion.

A new voice breaks over my spirit like water over parched grass. "That's not true, Richard!"

For the first time, I look past the boundaries of the playing field and see faces—of many people. I recognize the one who called my name as Donnie White, my mentor in "spiritual life," a redundant juxtaposition. All of life, including that which is physical, is spiritual.

I look around and see all my friends and my mom and dad standing on the bleachers and crammed in around the fence separating those on the playing field from those watching the game.

"Richard!" Donnie calls again, and I see him standing with some of my teammates behind the fence. "He won't hit you with the ball!" yells Donnie.

"What did you say?" I ask.

Everything goes quiet and still. All the people and images in the dream, including the pitcher and the catcher, are silent and frozen, except Donnie and me.

Donnie sighs, smiling. "All right. Thanks," he says, as if to no one. Then to me he says, "I said, 'He won't hit you with the ball.'"

"How do you know?"

"Because he can't," he says. "But he wants you to think he can, and to believe that he will."

I was scared. "But what if he does hit me? It's gonna hurt like crazy. It might even kill me."

Donnie shakes his head, but seems more amused than frustrated with me. He turns to the boy standing beside him, and I see that it's Zack. If Donnie is my "spiritual mentor," Zack is something like my "mentor by example." Everything Zack does and says smacks of honesty and heroism for me and the other guys on the team.

"Tell him, Zack," Donnie says to his best friend. "He doesn't believe me."

Zack's figure thaws instantly and he talks to me, kindly but firmly. "He won't hit you with the ball. But he can zip it by you. Got it?"

"So then I'll be out."

"Yeah. And the game'll be over," Zack says. "We don't want that."

I had what I thought was a brilliant idea. "Why don't you come in and bat for me?"

"It doesn't work that way." Zack shrugs. "It's your turn to hit. And that's a good thing. You're more dangerous to this pitcher than I am."

"That's not true," I counter. "You know that's not true. Nobody hits as good as you."

Zack starts to answer, but changes his mind and turns to Donnie instead. "Tell him, Donnie. He listens to you."

Donnie fixes his eyes on me. "It's your turn to bat, Richard. Don't you want to see BoDean score?"

For the first time, I notice my teammate BoDean Bonnett standing on first base, frozen, hands on his hips.

"Sure I do," I say, and I mean it. It is absolutely crucial that BoDean score. "More than anything. That's why Zack should be batting." I hold the bat out toward where Zack stands in the dugout. "I can't hit this . . ." I gesture toward the mound, afraid to look at the pitcher named Fear. "This thing out there."

A different voice now comes from the crowd standing in front of the bleachers. It sounds light and fresh, like mountain springwater. I see her then, our friend Rebecca, who is beautiful to everyone because she is kind to everyone.

"You can do it, Richard." Her bright eyes dance in my direction. "You can knock the cover off the ball."

"But this pitcher is . . . fearsome."

"Yes," she nods, and I feel my stomach giving way. Her springwater voice sounds like more than one spring, more than one source. Many waters. "But what is inside you is far greater."

I continue to protest. "I could get seriously hurt. If that ball hits me, the pain will be fierce."

"You say, if that ball hits you . . ." Rebecca tilts her head and smiles at me.

"Yeah, I could get taken out!" I nearly shout. "I mean, taken all the way out!"

"But what if you hit the ball?" Her smile morphs into something else, something like quiet confidence.

"But I can't." I start to cry. "Zack can do it, Rebecca."

She shakes her head. "Zack's not up to bat. It's your turn."

"I'm not good enough," I say through tears. "Look at me. I'm crying. I'm weak."

"What is weak?" she answers. "Who told you that you were weak?"

"Lots of people." That was true.

Her face shines, and in the dream, for an instant, I think she must be the most powerful angel in God's host.

"I believe," the dream-angel says, "the boy Richard Powell will find a power not of himself, an authentic power beyond the cosmetic powers of Fear and Fear's teammates."

I try to process what she is saying. "But what . . . what should I . . ."

"Put the bat . . ." she pauses, and seems to struggle to keep her tone firm. "Put the bat . . ." She laughs now, a beautiful clear sound, swift water on clean rocks. "On the ball. Put the bat on the ball, Richard Powell."

Then everything unfreezes, and it's "Game on!"

The pitcher toes the rubber. I feel more than see all the people watching the game behind me and to either side, beyond the right and left field lines.

I hear Donnie, Zack, Rebecca, and the others calling to me, encouraging me.

The distinct voice of my Little League coach, whom I haven't seen in five years in the conscious world, sounds above all other voices, hollering at BoDean on first. "You better be on your horse, boy!"

It seems to me that BoDean is saying something back to Coach when the pitcher goes into a short, precise windup and throws the ball—hard.

It is coming at me, impossibly fast, almost impossible to see.

But I do see it. I swing . . .

And then I woke up.

CHAPTER 5

So much of life begins to make dangerous sense when you start high school. The school itself is threatening enough. Even more daunting, you start to see that important things are intractable. You can't change your parents, your home, your looks, your intellect. Teachers, the good ones, try to get you to recognize "possibilities." "You can achieve any-thing," they say, "if you're willing to go after your dream." Of course that is not true. I suppose they are trying to get us students to actu-ally pursue our dreams so that the actual consummation at least has something beyond a dreamer's chance. But they phrase the endeavor with much more certitude. I don't know if that's healthy.

In early 1976, I was fifteen years old and "a boy without a class." The tentative plan was for me to graduate the next year, when my peers by age were high school sophomores. I liked that, because I'd be finishing with Zack and the others from the Fellowship of the Rock.

I was the only fifteen-year-old in my English classes that spring. The other students were mostly juniors, two years older. The handful of sixteen-year-olds included Julie Prevette, the girl who terrified me, thrilled me, and mystified me. In other words, I was so crazy about her I couldn't even say hello.

I didn't mind being in class with older kids. The only time I felt out of place was when I felt obliged to talk. That "obligation" never came from my own soul. It came from the teacher asking me some-thing point-blank. Though I suppose *her* soul may have been involved.

This particular morning, Miss Wakefield smiled at me. "Richard Powell. You're being very quiet."

You say that like you're surprised.

"I'm always quiet." I meant to sound humble, but it came out like I was toying with her. "I'm just thinking, is all."

"I'm sure you are." She was kind. "We'd like to get a window into your thoughts."

"So would I," I said.

Everybody laughed and I worried. I thought she might think I was making fun of her. But she laughed too. Miss Wakefield was a gem.

"Tell us, Mr. Powell"—she winked at me—"what makes Dickens such a great writer?"

We were looking at *A Christmas Carol.* Even in the spring months, that novella of haunting fostered remarkable discussion for high schoolers.

"Well . . ." I paused long enough so I wouldn't sound like a know-it-all—which I wasn't, but I was anxious to not sound like one. "I think Dickens's characters are his primary strength."

"Stronger than his story lines?" she said. "His plots?"

"Yes. Those are wonderful too, but the plots seem to me to be born from the characters. Not the other way around. The characters produce the offspring of the plot."

There were some audible murmurs of appreciation from the rest of the class and I felt self-conscious, uncomfortable.

"That's a very interesting observation," said Miss Wakefield. "And well said."

I resolved to keep my mouth shut for a spell. It would be different if I were having a private conversation with her. Or with Dr. McLeod. So much of school is just trying to fit in, without fitting in too noticeably.

"Let's talk about some of the themes," Miss Wakefield began. "I have some other general questions for all of you."

"Your questions always fry my brain," Jason Mann interrupted.

"Good; that's my job," she said. "Why should anyone want Scrooge to change?"

"Because he's a real snot," a boy named Lawrence said. Lawrence always looked angry.

"Agreed." Miss Wakefield nodded. "But what's that to the rest of us? If you don't owe Scrooge any money, and your family doesn't owe him any, why should you care that the guy is so mean? Why does it matter that he's what we might call a 'bad guy'?"

Nobody said anything.

"Let me put it another way," she said. "What business is it of ours that he's not very nice? As long as he doesn't break any laws, why should we care if he's mean? Why should a reader want to read about him changing? Why should a fellow citizen who lives in Scrooge's town care to see Scrooge change?"

A tall girl named Savannah was smart enough to see where Miss Wakefield was leading. "I think you're suggesting that the choices people make, especially personal choices, especially personal choices about what's right and what's wrong, are nobody else's business."

"I'm not saying that's *my* view," Miss Wakefield said. "But yes, many people would say that. Are they right? Is that your view?"

"I don't know." Savannah wasn't dodging the question, just being honest. "I think that's what I'm supposed to believe . . ." she paused. "I mean I think that's how I'm supposed to feel."

"Me too," said a guy in a Led Zeppelin tee shirt. "But it doesn't feel right."

"What doesn't feel right?" said Miss Wakefield.

Savannah shrugged. "Letting people stew. Letting people hurt themselves."

"And listen," Zeppelin said, "he might think his being mean isn't hurting anybody, but c'mon. He's dragging everybody else down. It'd be different if he lived on a desert island, stranded."

Joey, a senior, sang low but loud enough for all to hear, "No phone, no light, no motor car, not a single luxury."

After the others laughed, I said, "I'm not sure Dickens wants us to go around changing people. Or trying to. He's just writing a good short novel that shows how one guy does change, and he's leaving it up to the reader to decide whether the change is a good or a bad thing. And yes, the way the story's written, the reader is moved to see it as a good thing. But the guy doesn't change because people make him. They couldn't do that if they tried. Scrooge's nephew is really the only character that seriously tries to get him to think outside his mean, greedy box. But even he drops it real fast and just says, 'Okay, live the way you want but know that I love you and want you to come to dinner—and even if you don't, I still say, "Merry Christmas."' People don't change him. They don't try. Spirits change him."

You're talking too much. Julie Prevette thinks you're boring.

"Yes," the teacher smiled. "Spirits."

I kept talking too much. "Something beyond the human realm changes him."

"Hmm . . ." she smiled.

"Maybe because that's what it takes."

"Aha!" Miss Wakefield brightened. "Is it? How exactly is a man like Scrooge changed?"

"They scare the snot out of him," someone in the back said.

Julie Prevette leaned forward in her seat.

Please talk! I love it when you talk.

She did! "The story is saying God sent these spirits, not to scare Scrooge, but to rescue him."

"Oh, you don't think Spirit Number Three scares Scrooge?" Phil Bowman challenged her.

"Well, sure, he scares him, but God doesn't send Number Three on that mission," Julie replied.

"Who said anything about God?" Lawrence interjected.

"Well, if nobody else is gonna bring him up, I will," my heart-throb said. "Dickens is asking us to bring him up, right?"

"Maybe the spirits are all in Scrooge's mind," Zeppelin said.

I jumped in. "You mean maybe they're a bit of beef, or underdone potato?"

Everyone, including Zeppelin, got a kick out of that. "Or maybe some special smokes!" he said.

Of course, I only cared that Julie got a kick out of my comment.

"Dickens dramatically wanted to dispel the notion that the visitations were hallucinations," I continued. "The reader must assume the spirits are real. At least in the world Dickens created. And maybe even beyond that."

"What then is the third spirit's mission? Julie?" Miss Wakefield said.

"His mission is to teach Scrooge, to rescue him, to show him he needs to change or his future will be, ya know, scary."

"Why should Scrooge get this . . . rescue, as you call it?" Miss Wakefield asked. "Does he deserve it?"

A chorus of "noes" erupted in the room.

"It seems like an awful lot of trouble," said Zeppelin, "a lot of God's energy you could say, or some power's energy, to spend on such a jerk."

"Maybe God's got a lot of energy he likes spending on us jerks," I said.

"And Scrooge, really, is important," a girl we called Frankie offered. "Scrooge affects a lot of people, has a kind of power over people. Everybody owes him a lot of money."

Lawrence moaned. "So, you mean God picks out the important people to rescue."

"I don't mean that." Frankie laughed at herself. "I don't know what I mean."

"Frankie," Zeppelin said, "I think you've hit on something there." Zeppelin was sweet on Frankie. It's a high school virus. "Scrooge is important in his own head and he's told by the system, you know, everybody owing him and all, he's told he's important. And he needs to be shocked out of that big pride trip he's on. So God spends time on the guy because the guy's a hard case. Not because he's any more important to God than any other person is important to God."

Miss Wakefield seemed to like that a lot. "Excellent, everybody. I have another question."

"My brain's on fire," Jason said, pleading.

"This question may seem easy, but I think, actually, it's quite hard to answer."

When a teacher says that a question is going to be hard to answer, it's a good bet the first answer that rears its head in your head is not the right one.

"Do we really believe it is possible for someone to change?"

Nobody said anything and I feared that would put me in Miss Wakefield's sights again. It did.

"What do you think, Richard?" She looked at me. Her smile was genuine, as always.

"I guess, I think . . . there's at least a couple of things that might be going on when we say a person changes. I mean, they could just be discovering another part of themselves they didn't know was there. If you know what I mean."

"But that's not really change, is it?" Miss Wakefield said, but I could tell she liked my insight. "You said a couple of things. What else?"

"Well, it's . . . supernatural."

Everybody in the class was looking at me, listening.

"I think . . . people can be touched. By a higher power. That changes them."

"You mean God," Miss Wakefield said.

"Yes ma'am, that's one higher power."

"There are others?" she asked.

"I don't know," I said honestly. "I'm just kind of thinking out loud."

"You should do that more," Julie said. "It gets all of us going."

Princess in the tower . . . what was I just saying . . . what was I just thinking . . .

"Richard?" Miss Wakefield gave me a little wave.

She knows. Does everyone? Does the princess? That's good, isn't it?

"Richard," the teacher said again, gently. "Higher powers . . ."

"Yeah, well, I don't know," I said again. "I'd like to think devils aren't real. But it strikes me as just that, what I'd *like* to think. I'm thinking it's dangerous to just believe only what I want to believe is true, is true. If you follow what I'm saying."

"Let me see if I have this straight," Savannah broke in, which was good since I was running out of air. "You believe God is real. And that people can change when God comes into their life. And you believe demons are real. And it sounds like you believe demons can affect our lives."

"I know that sounds kind of strange," I said, thinking how such a discussion would never take place in a public high school science class. God sometimes appears in English class, mostly as an anomaly.

"Why are you so infatuated with the supernatural?" Miss Wakefield said, not unkindly. "You're such a bright boy."

"It's not something I decided to be infatuated with. It's not my preference. Sometimes I wish I could get away from it. But I can't help believing that all of life is supernatural. Maybe I'll find I'm wrong one day. But I don't think that would be good news. If we're all alone here, left to our own resources, we're bound to do ourselves in. Don't you think?"

You are talking way too much. Julie Prevette thinks you're psycho.

"I don't think I want to think too long about that, right now," Miss Wakefield said honestly. "But just to clarify, you don't think anyone can change on their own, apart from some supernatural power ushering in some change?"

"I don't really know," I said and I meant it. "I just feel . . . fated, unable to change on my own. And so I'm grateful for supernatural intervention."

"Such a sad way to feel," she sighed, "at your age."

I said, "I'm not sure I see what age has to do with it. If it's sad to be a certain way when you're young, what makes it less sad when you're older?"

"Now *my* brain is feeling fried," Miss Wakefield said, but she seemed pleased that I'd opened up.

Lawrence turned to glower at me. "Do you honestly think that the world, the universe, is so small, that the loonies who ran the Inquisition had it all figured out? And now you got it down, too, with the tired old simple scheme of God, angels, demons, and hell and heaven to boot?"

I hesitated before answering. But not for the reason he assumed. I wasn't intimidated by the questioner or the question. I was intimidated by the answer I knew I had to give.

"A small universe?" I said. "And a simple scheme? Not to me. I'm really afraid, fearful, that the universe is as big as that tired old simple scheme says it is! Our ideas of angels and demons and heaven and hell, and our ideas of how those real things touch this Earth, are too small. I'm hopeful though, really hopeful, that God is also much bigger than my idea of him."

I chanced a glance at Julie. She was looking at me, smiling very faintly. I couldn't tell, but she looked like she felt something for me or felt sorry for me. One or the other. At least I was on her radar.

"Well," Miss Wakefield broke the silence. "What about the rest of you? We've had four or five people talk up a storm, and the rest of you, I think, are listening. I'm never sure because you're masters at looking like you're listening. What do the rest of you think?"

"I think I'm ready for lunch," said a kid named Morton whose girth rivaled Duffey's. The others groaned, apparently sensing Morton's comment might move the remaining class time in something other than their preferred direction.

Their instincts were probably right. "All right, here's what we'll do," Miss Wakefield said. "I want everybody to take out a piece of paper."

Murmurs of discontent mixed with the sound of people securing paper from their notebooks.

"Don't panic, this is not hard," she said.

"Do we have to write something?" a bushy haired and wafer thin boy in the back asked.

"No, the paper is for you to stare at in the remaining thirty minutes," Miss Wakefield said in a voice too soft to suit the sarcasm. She was gracious; it was hard for her to be as dry and cynical as the teenagers she taught.

"Just two paragraphs, guys," she said. "How hard is that? Just two paragraphs. Write down what Scrooge might say to God, if there is a God, what he might say to God in his own defense. How he might argue his case before God."

Savannah wanted clarification. "So we write it like Scrooge is talking, or can we just describe what he might say, or . . ."

"Whichever you like," Miss Wakefield waved her hands in the air, surrendering to their creativity. Or maybe summoning their creativity. "Surprise me. Richard and . . . Julie, can I see you two up here for a second."

Don't trip over your heart, standing in the same space with her!

I rendezvoused at Miss Wakefield's desk with my secret crush, known only to my fellow Boy Scouts and whoever they might have leaked the secret to under the stress of torture, or in Duffey's case, the stress of large fries. Either the teacher or my dream date smelled like the beautiful wild bushes behind Silas Baptist Church. Honeysuckle.

The teacher addressed Julie first, handing her a piece of paper.

"Take this down to Mrs. Eaton. Her drama class is meeting in the auditorium. She asked for it earlier and I forgot."

"Yes ma'am," my dream answered her. "What about the two paragraphs?"

As if he'd thought of it at the same time, Morton called to the teacher, "Do they have to write these things too?"

"You worry about your writing, and I'll worry about theirs, okay?" Miss Wakefield said.

"I just don't want them to miss out on learning things and stuff," Morton quipped.

"Okay, okay, get to it," she smiled at him. She gestured for my crush and me to lean closer to her. We did so, and I hoped the ecstasy wouldn't fell me. That is, I didn't want to pass out.

Miss Wakefield whispered to us, "You write it when you get back. Don't worry about it. I'm not grading them."

"Yes ma'am." Julie took the paper and stepped out of the class.

"Now, Richard, Mr. Huff wants to see you in the main office."

"Mr. Huff?" He was an assistant principal.

"Yes, he wanted you to come by about ten thirty." I looked at the wall clock. It was ten twenty-five.

"Well, okay. I'd like to write the two paragraphs. I really would."

"I know that. And that is exactly why I'm comfortable with you stepping out to the office for a few minutes." She smiled. "Write them when you get back. Or tonight and bring them tomorrow."

"Yes, ma'am." I stepped away from the desk.

"Richard," she stopped me. "Take your time with Mr. Huff. I think it'll be interesting for you."

"Yes ma'am." Exiting the classroom, I heard Morton mumble my name in the context of bringing him some snacks from the new snack machine by the main office.

I stepped into the hallway and stood there for a few seconds, noting how quiet and still it was when classes were in session. I also considered whether right or left would get me to the office quicker. It seemed it made no difference, given the school was in the shape of a square doughnut and the office was on the other side of the dough-nut. I walked to the right.

Before I got to the first turn in the hall, I smelled honeysuckle. I looked over my shoulder and my dream was shuffling up and walking beside me.

"I thought she might be sending you to the office for something," Julie said, not really looking at me.

My throat went dry so fast I wondered if my vocal cords would work. "I'm supposed to see Mr. Huff about something."

"About what?"

"I dunno. Something." *That was kinda wow. Yeah, you are such a genius with words, Powell.*

"I waited, around the other corner," she laughed out loud, "for y'all to come out of the class!" She announced it like it was great fun, the best part of her morning.

Say something! She likes you!

"You waited," I breathed, "around the corner?"

"Y'all took forever to come out!"

"Sorry."

"Not really forever," she said. "Anyway, I just thought what you said in class was really good. I'm a serious Christian, too. Know what I mean by serious?"

"I do."

"Of course you do, that's what I mean. What y'all said was really cool, really brilliant, and ya know, I just wanted to say that." She stopped walking, so I did too. "I gotta go this other way, to the auditorium. See ya." And she bolted away, back in the direction we had come.

"See ya," I said not loud enough. I was afraid of sounding too charmed by our talking. Foolish are the notions of high schoolers trying to maintain some aura of cool detachment.

She waited for me. She walked up next to me. She walked with me, in the opposite direction from where she needed to go. And she said what I said was cool.

"Was that Julie Prevette?" I looked back up the hallway and Rebecca Carson was walking toward me, smiling.

"Who? That?" I said. "Yeah."

"Did you ask her?"

"Ask her what?"

"To the banquet!"

"The banquet? No . . ."

"You moron!" Rebecca punched my arm, pretty hard. "She likes you."

"Ow." I rubbed my arm. "You think so? How . . . how do you know . . . did Zack say something . . ."

"No."

"Oh yes he did."

"No he didn't," she insisted. "And I'm going to talk to that boy . . ."

"He promised me he wouldn't."

"Well, that's that," she said. "That's why he didn't tell me. Did Batman promise?"

"I tried to get them all . . ." I remembered. "No, Batman didn't promise."

"Well, that's good. 'Cause he told me you liked Julie."

"Batman's a scoundrel. You think she likes me?"

"Absapositively," she said in Donnie-speak.

"I can't tell."

"Of course not. You're a guy."

"How can *you* tell? I mean aside from you being a girl and all."

"The way she was talking with you just now."

"She was just talking," I said.

"Did she sound a little nervous?" Rebecca cocked her head, interrogating.

"She was just talking," I said again.

"Talking kind of fast, jumping around a little with what she was saying?"

"That's just Julie. I can't tell if she was nervous or if she just kinda likes talking that way."

"And the way she was walking."

"She was just walking."

"Oh no, she wasn't. She was walking beside you. In that way."

"What way?"

"It's just a way girls walk when they're interested."

"Guys don't walk that way?"

"No, no, guys walk the same way all the time," she said fast. "And the way she was looking at you."

"She wasn't looking at me."

"You klutz," she punched my arm in the same spot.

"Ow."

"Call her and ask her to the banquet."

"On the phone?"

"No, out your window, Richard. I got to go." She took off down the hall. "Call her!"

I resolved to do so, and told myself what a grand day it is when angels play with our hearts.

CHAPTER 6

I walked into the school office and told the secretary I was supposed to see Mr. Huff. He must have heard, because he came out of a side room and shook my hand.

"I just want to encourage you to consider my alma mater. Vanderbilt is a top-of-the-line school, son."

"Yes sir. I'm only fifteen, sir."

"Well, we know, but we also know you're chugging right along and we know you'll soon be making some of these decisions way before your peers."

"We?" I said softly.

"Miss Wakefield is a Vandy alum too."

"It's a great school, sir."

"You think you might want to go there?"

"I'm not really thinking yet . . ." I wasn't sure how to put it. "I'm just trying to be a kid, Mr. Huff."

"Oh sure." He shuffled his feet like I had said something embarrassing.

"I don't know how this sounds," I ventured, "but the truth is I want to be kind of normal."

"I can understand that"—Mr. Huff nodded—"but who wants to be normal?"

I had just told him that I did. What exactly was it he had just told me he could understand?

"I'm in the Boy Scouts." I'm not sure why I brought that up. "I like it a lot."

"That's . . . excellent." He rendered an official-looking smile, signaling to me that our conversation was ending. "I just want you to be thinking, son, about the future. I know I can get you a ride to Vanderbilt. So we'll be talking. Is that all right?"

"Thanks very much, Mr. Huff."

"I'm happy to do whatever I can for you." He put out his hand.

I shook it. "Thank you."

"You go on back to class, now."

"Yes sir."

He stepped back inside his office and I walked back out into the hallway. I put a quarter and a nickel into the machine and pulled the lever for a Three Musketeers for Morton. Walking the eerily quiet halls again, this time alone, I wondered if Mr. Huff understood what I meant about wanting to be a normal kid with normal high school days. I wondered if I knew what I meant. I sometimes longed to live through *Happy Days* with Richie Cunningham. But that was a chimera.

I ducked into the boys' room. Three guys were in there smoking, one of whom was BoDean, the pitcher on our Little League championship team of five years before. The other two guys, one looking wiry, and one big, and both mean, tensed up when they saw me. I smelled a joint, but I was afraid to see who was smoking it. So I didn't look.

"He's all right," said BoDean.

I took care of my business and tried to ignore them. As I was washing my hands, BoDean sidled up.

"Where's your hall pass?" he joshed me. "Or are you skipping out?"

"I had to go to the office."

"I have to go there lots," the wiry guy laughed.

"Still doing the Boy Scouts?" BoDean said.

"Yeah."

"Duffey too?" he said.

"Yeah. Zack too." I looked him in the eye for the first time. Sad eyes. Not unkind. "You should come back. You'd like it."

The big guy took a step toward me. "Zack. You mean Zack Ross? The big baseball star that thinks he's better than we are?"

"Zack's not like that," I said.

"You calling me a liar?"

BoDean laughed nervously. "He's all right, Shawn. Don't sweat it."

"You can come back," I said to BoDean. "Everybody would like that."

"No, Richie." BoDean used my little kid name. "I can't. Sometimes you just can't go back. Don't you know that?" He wore a smile, devoid of joy.

I wanted to hurry out of there, but my old friend asked me another question. "You go to Donnie's dad's church?"

"Sure. You can go there too."

"No. I can't."

"Sure you can."

"No, I can't," he said again, too soft to be an assertion. I thought maybe he was asking something.

"Everybody goes," I said. "I mean all the guys you know. Batman and Timmy. Course, Donnie and Zack. Rebecca. Duffey too."

"Duffey," BoDean looked off somewhere. "He was such a hoot."

"He still is," I said, suddenly feeling at ease.

"You remember that day," he said, "when you were chasing me on those bases?" I knew exactly what day he was talking about. "And Rafer's old man was hollering and I thought he was hollering to me and all, but he wasn't." BoDean laughed quick and then settled, sad again. "He wasn't hollering to me."

"I remember."

"I miss Rafer," he said. "I still got my rock, Richie."

I smiled. "That's so cool, man." I reached into my left pocket and pulled out the small, rough rock I had carried with me every day for the past five years.

"Oh, I don't believe it!" BoDean said.

"Hey, lemme see that!" Before I saw him coming, the big guy, Shawn, knocked the rock out of my hand. I tried to pick it up, but he got to it first, holding it up and scoffing. "What we got here?"

I felt my body take a step toward him and heard my mind tell my body to stop. But BoDean moved fast, smacking the rock out of the guy's hand and punching him in the chest, hard.

"Ohhh." Shawn clutched his chest, more from surprise than pain.

I grabbed the rock off the floor, and looked up at Shawn holding BoDean against the wall.

"Go ahead," BoDean said in a calm voice. "Knock me around, Shawn."

"You know I can!" the big guy said.

"Go ahead."

I wanted to say something, to do something, but I was terrified. I didn't move.

BoDean said, "Go on, Richie."

Shawn said to BoDean, "Why you always do this to me, man? Why you always gotta make me hit you, man?"

The wiry guy got in front of me. I guess he was trying to look mean. Mostly he just looked high. "You better . . . get out of here," he said. "Less you wanna get hurt."

I got out of there. I thought Wiry Guy would step out and watch me in the hall, but he didn't. I hustled to the office and told them I thought there was a fight in the boys' room.

Mr. Huff asked if I knew who the boys were, and I said a boy named Shawn was roughing up a boy named BoDean.

"What a shock," he smirked, only half hurrying in that direction. "Go on back to your class."

"BoDean didn't do anything."

"*That's* his problem," he said. "He *doesn't* do anything. Except cut class and smoke weed. Back to class, Richard. And remember . . . Vanderbilt!"

Vanderbilt was the furthest thing from my mind.

I saw BoDean later that afternoon in the hall between classes and tried to get by without him seeing me. But he stepped over.

"That was kind of funny, wasn't it?" he said, a big grin on his face.

"You all right?"

"Always, Richie."

"You didn't get hurt?"

"Aw, no. Shawn and me . . . Shawn's okay. We got busted."

"Busted?" I said.

"Three days off," he said. "Start tomorrow."

I felt I had to at least say one brave thing. "I told Mr. Huff where ya'll were. I thought that Shawn guy was gonna hit you."

"He did, but it weren't nothing. You worry too much."

"Sorry I told Mr. Huff." But I wasn't.

"That don't matter. It ain't nothing but a thing," he smiled. "Remember Duffey used to say that?"

"He still does. If you wanna—"

"I gotta go," he cut me off.

"You can come to—"

"You're all right, Richie Brain!" He was suddenly in a hurry to get somewhere, to get lost.

Or maybe to stay lost.

CHAPTER 7

Phones and me are at loggerheads. Warring, really. Phone conversations generally lead where I desire, but the process often feels like traversing hot coals. In bare feet. If I had to cite the war's genesis, I'd guess early evening, April 19, 1976, when I phoned Julie Prevette's residence.

"Hello." A man's gruff voice. Like a bear.

"Uh, yes sir."

"Hello," Gruff said again. "Who's this?"

"Yes, hello, mister."

Good grief, get off the phone before you pass out, Powell.

"You don't know me," I started in, weakly.

"You selling? Not interested."

"No sir. I mean, I'm not selling," I said. "Anything."

"Whaddya want?"

I want to ask your daughter out.

"I was hoping I could, kind of, talk to . . ." I ran out of breath. "Is Julie home?"

"Oh, I get it." Gruff got it. He hollered. "Hey Princess!"

I heard Julie's voice in the background. "Yeah, Dad? What?"

"Some kid wants to talk to you!" Gruff hadn't moved the receiver away from his mouth, so I had to move mine away from my ear. But just for a second, because I wanted to hear anything else "Princess" would say.

"Is it Doug?"

Who's Doug? He is my mortal enemy.

Gruff said, "How do I know?" Then, into the receiver, "Is this Doug?"

"Uh . . ." I hesitated, flustered, my heart shaking.

"Do you know if you're Doug?" said Gruff. His tone sounded serious, and I contemplated the question too long.

Gruff hollered to anyone within earshot who cared to know that an idiot was on the phone, "He doesn't know if he's Doug!"

"Doug?" said a luminous voice on the phone. If I could see her voice, it would be sunlight through the windows. Many times, I have pretended to see the sound of Julie talking.

"No, I'm not . . . my name is . . . you know me from school . . ."

"Hey, Craig."

"No, that's another . . ."

"Oops! Is this Danny?"

"No ma'am—oh, sorry about ma'am . . . this is Richard."

A pause. Probably four or so short seconds, but it felt like forty long seconds and a last meal before execution. "Richard Greenley?"

"No, although he's a good guy. He's in my Spanish class."

"Oh . . . that's nice."

"This is Richard Powell."

"The Brain?"

"Well, yeah," I mumbled. "I guess some say that."

"Sure they do!" Again with that impossibly bright voice. "The Brain!" A shining voice.

"But, um, the rest of me is here too."

She laughed hard at that. And I was able to breathe.

"That was so cool what you said in class today! So what can I do for you, Mister Brain?"

Hold my hand for just one minute. That might do for all time.

I took a breath, quick oxygen, and decided dry humor was my best shot. My throat was dry enough. "It's not *Mister* Brain, it's *The* Brain. The definite article . . ."

She's laughing!

"The definite article . . ." I said again with stronger emphasis, "stresses my unique powers."

She's still laughing! I'm a king!

I tried, to ill effect, to lower my voice. "I am *The* Brain. And there is no other."

"That's hilarious!" she exaggerated, and I loved her for it. "Okay then, what can I do for The Brain? Do you need help with your homework?"

"No, I'm good with that. But thank you."

"I'm kidding! If you need homework help, the rest of us are . . . whatever! Dead, or something!"

"I knew you were kidding." I glanced around our kitchen, looking for more air again. "And I don't mean you're dumb, or not smart or . . . I think you could help me . . . with my . . . homework sometime."

"You are very sweet."

That sounds pretty good.

"You're also about to hyperventilate. Take a breath or two or four. Whatever you need."

"Okay."

"Whatever you need," she cooed.

"Okay." I breathed. "I'm feeling better."

"I knew you would. I get nervous on the phone a lot too."

Probably when you call Doug.

"I don't believe it," I said.

"Hey Brain, are you calling me a liar?"

Who else asked me that today? Oh yeah.

"How can you get nervous on the phone when you do those plays where you're singing and dancing and remembering all those lines in front of tons of people?"

"That's so easy."

"What?!" My voice cracked, high.

Please come back to me, Oh Return to Us, Thou Manifestly Normal Sounding Vocal Range.

"I don't think anything about that is easy," I said in my normal tone.

Thank you, Voice God!

"It's not me," she said. "Up there, out there, on a stage, I'm somebody else. I mean, if I'm doing it right, I'm somebody else. Julie Prevette might feel nervous, but Laurey Williams does not. So I sing and dance and look cute and look sad and have a great old time being somebody else. You know what I mean?"

"I'll take your word for it."

"Never been in a play?"

"No ma'am." I groaned. "Sorry . . ."

"What's this ma'am stuff?"

She's laughing!

"Should I call you sir?" she teased. "Or Sir Brain?"

I laughed with her, a world of pleasure. "I'm just so used to saying ma'am. Especially if I'm on the phone with a woman."

"I'm not a woman! I'm a girl, thank God." Our generation longed for maturity as any other, but we were not fools who thought reaching our teens made us adults. It seems different today, a tremulous, tragic shift, difficult if not impossible to remedy.

Our laughter settled. I said, "I'd rather be drawn and quartered than have to say lines in a play, on a stage and all."

"Drawn and quartered," Julie echoed. "Isn't that like . . . what is that?"

You idiot! What, you think you're knocking around with the guys here?

"It's like . . . it's nothing, really."

Her voice was faint now; she was asking someone close to her, "What's drawn and quartered mean?"

I heard the gruff, low voice of her father. "It's what you do to a pig or a deer, getting 'em ready to roast."

"You mean . . ."

"Ya draw and quarter 'em, ya cut and slice 'em stem to stern . . ."

"Gross! Oh my . . ." Her voice faded.

". . . and hang 'em up in the smokehouse 'til you wanna eat 'em."

"Okay, I'm back," she announced to me.

"Sorry I said that." I sure was.

"You're a funny guy, Brain. You really know how to sweet-talk a girl."

"I'm sorry."

"Oh, lighten up! Take another breath or whatever." I did. "Daddy hunts a lot. Got a couple of rifles. One of them's as big as a bazooka."

"What's he like to hunt?"

"Boys who call me on the phone," she said so straight, I wasn't real sure how to take it. "That's a joke, too, Richard."

She said my name!

"I thought it probably was."

"Why does every boy think my dad would kill them?"

Because he would.

"We're . . . exercising caution."

She liked that too, laughing. All was right with my world.

"I'm sure he loves you very much," I said.

"Oh, you're just a big sweetie, aren't you! You need to call me more often."

I ached to stretch her jest into a serious suggestion.

"Why *did* you call, Richard?"

Oh yeah.

"Um, I understand if you can't and all . . . It's not a lot of notice . . ."

"Are you asking me out?" She sounded shocked. My heart pounded, heavy beats.

"Well, yeah, but I don't . . ."

"Like on a date?" Same shocked tones. I'm sure she heard the pounding.

I talked too fast, and with no control, words crashing. Like a race car spinning off the track. "It's a baseball banquet, except it's just like an ice cream and other desserts . . . like a social get-together now instead of like any banquet like it used to be, so . . ." I paused, hoping she would shoot me quickly so I could hang up, pet my hamster Gandalf, and go to bed.

She was silent. I droned some more. "The guys are like saying I need to bring somebody and I want to bring somebody and I really should bring somebody . . ."

"Somebody?" she interrupted.

I breathed. Again that helped. "I didn't mean to say that somebody stuff." I dropped all pretense. "I don't want to take somebody, I want to take *you*, Julie . . . will you go with me?"

"Richard, that sounds like a wonderful date." Her voice was soft, genuine.

"It does?" My heart rate stabilized.

"When is it? Do we get to dress up?"

"It's this Friday night . . ."

"I can do that!"

" . . . and it's not formal, but we're supposed to wear nice stuff."

She laughed again and my heart rate picked up again. This time it wasn't my nerves.

"I've got some nice stuff," she said.

"But not formal."

"Not formal stuff. Nice stuff," she said. "Are you wearing a suit?"

"They said ties, no suits."

"Okay, I know what they want. Baseball, huh? So is The Brain a big baseball star?"

"I'm a junk pitcher. I barely made the team."

"Pitchers are important," she said.

"You like baseball?"

"I don't know." She was always honest. "I never followed it. I don't know much about it. I'm a dumb actress."

"You're a gifted actress." I suddenly felt like I had all the right words.

"You're a sweet and kind man, Richard Powell." I felt I could hear her smile over the phone. "And a big pitcher on the baseball team!"

"I'm a junk pitcher."

"You said that. Sounds funny. What's a junk pitcher?"

"It's supposed to be someone who can throw a lot of different kinds of pitches."

"Well that's good, then."

"Except for guys like me, it means we have no fastball."

"Oh."

There was a pause, and it occurred to me that she didn't seem in any hurry to hang up. I didn't know the protocol, but I thought perhaps I should thank her.

"Thank you," I said.

"For what?"

"For going to the baseball banquet with me," I said. "I mean the little baseball thing we're doing."

"Little baseball thing we're doing sounds like they'll be little tiny people there and we'll have little tiny plates and cups and . . . like we're all Lilliputians."

"Lilliputians," I laughed. "Do you like *Gulliver's Travels?*"

"Sure. I like little worlds, little people. Isn't that the coolest word? *Lilliputian*. Sounds like some little perfume Barbie puts on to go out with little Ken." Her voice took on a sing-song sound. "Doesn't Barbie smell radiant this evening? She must have dabbed on her new Lilliputian fragrance!"

I chuckled.

"Oh, you like that, Brain, the junk pitcher who's taking me to a little baseball thingy?"

"That was pretty funny."

"Uh oh, gotta go," she said quickly. "Dad's giving me that get-off-the-phone gesture."

"Gesture?"

"A quick swipe of his hand, slicing across his throat."

"Sounds grave."

"Yeah, if I don't get off, he's gonna draw me and make me quartered or whatever that was you said about animals getting cut to ribbons and eaten."

"Sorry about that," I said.

"Don't be ridiculous."

"The Friday night thing is at 7:00. We can pick you up . . ."

"Be a sweetheart and write it down for me," she was talking fast, "and put it in my hand tomorrow at school."

"Okay. Bye. Hope you have a good evening," I said in what I thought was a cool mellow tone.

"Thank you, I will, don't worry." *It was her dad, Gruff, back on the phone!* "This conversation was way too long."

"Uh, yes sir. I'm sorry, sir."

I heard Julie, the Princess, in the background, say, "Oh Dad, lighten up. He's like a genius."

"What do you wanna be?" Gruff barked into the phone at me.

"Excuse me?"

"For a job. Whaddya wanna do?"

"I'd like . . . I think . . . to teach."

"School?"

"Yes, sir. College, sir."

"College? You have my permission to marry Julie." *Click.*

"Hello? Hello?" No response. I hung up.

That night, after I tended to Gandalf, my hamster, and crawled into bed, it was hard for me to sleep. I kept rolling a couple of phrases around in my head and on my tongue. "Eau de Lilliputians" was one. I forget the other one. Okay, I remember. "Doug, drawn and quartered."

CHAPTER 8

If you got an out pitch," our shortstop Pepper Jasper said to me, "this here might be a good time to bring it." When he wasn't playing shortstop, Pepper was our ace pitcher. Of course he knew I didn't have an out pitch.

We were conferenced at the pitcher's mound, Duffey having called time. He and Donnie, who entered the game late to play second, were talking it over with Pepper and me. I'd squeezed two outs from Draper High's batters in this last inning, but now they'd loaded the bases on me. We were up 8–7. I'd managed to barely hold onto the lead, generally frustrating them with my slow junk. But they weren't buying it now.

"They're sitting back," said Duffey, "like they was huntin' in tall blinds."

"Whaddya got to lose?" Donnie said.

"'Cept this game, is all," said Pepper.

"You got an out pitch." Donnie's eyes danced.

"I can't control it."

"Sounds beautiful." Pepper laughed a little. "Those pitches you been controlling all day are gonna kill us. Those guys are controlling 'em real good." He nodded toward the Draper High bench. "Johnny is fixin' to control one over the fence."

Johnny Tuberville was the cleanup hitter, leaning now on his bat just outside the box. Looking at me like I was his lunch.

"You think it's all right with Coach?" I wondered aloud.

"Coach don't give a rip," Duffey said flatly.

That was true. Coach Atkinson wasn't a bad guy, he just didn't care much. He coached because it gave him a little extra money, I guess. He was the polar opposite of Coach Hornbuckle, the terrific coach I'd played for in Little League. Hornbuckle had married and moved to Tennessee. We missed him like crazy; adults don't realize how much youths look up to men and women who are the real deal. Hornbuckle was like a second dad to most of us. He was like the only dad to some of us, like BoDean, who went into his tailspin when Hornbuckle left.

I looked over at our bench where Coach Atkinson was resting his chin atop his folded hands.

Zack entered our circle, having jogged in from his position in center field.

"Hard knuckle time now, boys." He was clearly looking forward to it. It struck me that I should be the one excited and he and Donnie and Duffey should be trying to talk me out of throwing it.

So much of my life moves against the grain, and not of my choice. I have lived by extraordinary unnatural intervention. As if there really is a God. And he enjoys surprising me.

"I can't control it," I said to Zack.

"Sounds beautiful."

"That's what I told him," Pepper nodded.

"And you don't wanna disappoint the old professor." Donnie nodded to the bleachers. Dr. Peachy McLeod was standing up, his right arm raised, flipping his wrist up and down.

The umpire walked toward us. "Let's go, boys. Time's up."

"Can you catch it?" I asked Duffey.

He rolled his eyes. "Like anybody really cares whether I catch the thing. Can he hit it, is what matters."

"Let's find out." Zack tapped me with his glove. "Stand back nonbelievers," he said low key, and jogged back toward the outfield.

Pepper said, "I'm diggin' it," and ambled back toward shortstop, singing low that song about how Watergate didn't bother him and maybe I needed to examine my conscience. And tell the truth.

"Take us home, Big Guy," the real big guy Duffey said over his shoulder, going back to play catcher.

"Play ball," the ump pointed at me, a benevolent command to resume pitching.

Tuberville stepped into the box, and I toed the rubber. I took my time getting the grip right. Normally a pitcher tries to cloak such grips, so the batter doesn't get any clues about pitch selection. This was different; what Tuberville expected would be inconsequential. He wouldn't know the pitch even if I diagrammed it for him. I didn't really know the pitch.

I wound up, a somewhat tighter coil, like Peachy had showed me. I threw.

Right off my fingers it felt good. Like it had the first time. I saw it jump in the air. Johnny swung like thunder and the ball went over his bat and over Duffey's glove. It clanked off his facemask, ascended a few feet and dropped beside Tuberville, whose empty swing had stolen his balance and pulled him to the ground.

"Strike!" The umpire gestured. "You all right?" he asked Duffey who had pushed his mask up and was rubbing the side of his face.

"I'm good." Duffey pulled the mask back down. "Way to bring it, Richard." He crouched back behind the plate.

Tuberville looked at me, said "What was that?" and I shrugged, almost like I was apologizing for getting the pitch by him. It's just the way I was. The way I am.

He got in his stance, warily, and I leaned in again, squirreling my fingers into their odd places on the ball. I wound up again and let it go.

I felt the strange but good release off my hand again and this time had the presence of mind to look for the "jump." I saw it hop over the batter's swing.

This time Duffey got a piece of the ball but not all of it. It ricocheted off his mitt's top and thudded into the umpire's protective gear. The man took a few steps to the side and took a few breaths.

"Strike two," the umpire muttered.

My teammates cheered along with the people sitting in our side of the bleachers. I heard Pepper behind me singing, altering a lyric.

"He's been known to throw a strike or two . . . He picks me up when I'm feeling blue."

Umps trust catchers to stop the ball. The catcher is their shield. Umps don't usually get hurt, but it can happen. They don't like to wonder if a catcher is getting crossed up by the pitch.

"You know what's coming?" I heard him ask Duffey.

"Sort of."

Tuberville joined in. "What's that mean?"

Duffey wasn't going to say anything to the batter, but the umpire's intense look echoed Tuberville's question.

"Neither one of ya'll need to worry," Duffey's tone was earnest, but I knew him well enough to know he was just saying what he thought both of them wanted to hear. "I know what he's pitching and I'm close to figuring out how to catch it."

"Close?" The umpire wasn't amused.

"You might wanna tuck your chin a little lower than normal, is all," Duffey said. He wasn't trying to be funny.

"Is that a knuckleball?" Tuberville called to me.

"Sort of," I answered.

"You don't have to say nuthin' to him," Duffey yelled to me.

"Play ball," the umpire settled back behind Duffey, his head a little lower than his usual stance. "No balls, two strikes."

I threw it a third time and Tuberville swung again, this time a more measured swing, like he was trying to just meet the ball with the bat, like bringing a fly swatter to a close fly. He wasn't close. But Duffey had triumphed.

"I caught it!" he leaped up, the ball in his mitt.

"Strike three!" The umpire looked relieved. "That's the ball game."

I looked over at the stands. Julie was on her feet, clapping and smiling at me. I don't think I would have been any happier if she had been doing cartwheels and singing the "Hallelujah Chorus." Come to think of it, I was already hearing the "Chorus" in my mind.

She waved, a simple gesture. It undid me. I had barely raised my hand to wave back when I was taken to the ground by Donnie jumping on my back. I could barely move as others piled on, and I was happy about it. It was the end of a mediocre season for us as wins and losses measure such things. But it was the last game and we had won a close one and everybody was high on the moment.

When they let me up and I breathed sweet Alabama air again, my teammates started to disperse and gather with their own friends and families.

"Wait till your dad hears"—Mom hugged me—"he's going to brag to everybody on the base. Which is what I'm going to do right here!"

Peachy shook my hand, looking somewhat solemn. "That was an epic endeavor."

They joined Miss Barbara, Rebecca, Zack, Donnie, and Duffey in a little circle around me, joshing me, poking me. Duffey clapped me over the head with his catcher's mitt.

"Unbelievably epic," Peachy said again.

"Thanks for showing me the pitch."

"That was . . . nothing. You did the hard part. You triumphed in the moment."

"We had to talk him into throwing it." Donnie grinned.

"Well, I just didn't know, ya know, what was going to happen and all."

I started swiping clay dirt off my uniform.

"Don't do that," Donnie whispered.

"What?"

"The dirt on your uniform looks cool," he said. He nodded slightly toward the approaching Julie.

"Are you sure?" I said quickly.

"Trust me."

It would have been easier to trust him in these matters if he were Pepper, who couldn't walk the school halls without tripping over girls at his feet. Or if he were Zack, or better still, Rebecca. But even Donnie knew more than I did about these things. Everybody did.

In a suddenness that resembled disappearances the rapture might inaugurate, the circle of folks around me vanished. I saw Miss Barbara smiling and whispering rapidly to the confused Peachy.

"Hi," Julie said.

"Hi."

"I didn't mean to scare everybody off," she said, looking around. But I think maybe she did.

"Oh, they were done talking to me," I babbled, sounding ridiculous.

"I thought you said you weren't very good."

She said it so serious and I was so nervous, I thought she was referring to my sin nature.

"I'm not," I said.

"You just won the game!"

"Oh, that. That was just something . . . I don't even know . . . probably couldn't . . . do it again."

Where did my brain go? Who took my oxygen away?

Mom rescued me. I don't know if she was listening or if she just had a sixth sense her son needed her.

"Hello there," she said in a smooth, kind tone to Julie.

They shook hands. "Hello," Julie brightened.

"Mom, this is my . . ."

My what?

". . . my friend Julie."

"Julie Prevette, ma'am," Julie said. "Pleased to meet you, Mrs. Powell."

"I'm pleased to meet you, Julie. Are you in ninth grade with Richard?"

"Julie's a year ahead of me."

"Classwise," Julie said. "But really I'm behind Richard by about a thousand years in smarts." She laughed. I was encouraged that she sounded a little nervous. Maybe I mattered.

Rebecca and Zack appeared.

"You must be Julie," Zack said. "I think I may have met you at school before."

"I don't think so," Julie said. "But yeah, I'm Julie."

"I'm Zack."

"I know you two." Julie smiled. "I mean I know who ya'll are."

"What do you mean?" asked Zack.

"Oh, ya'll are a couple and everything."

"Oh, is that all," Zack said. Rebecca gave him a look. It worked.

"Yes we are," he rebounded, taking Rebecca's hand in his. Guys don't think sometimes.

Miss Barbara, Peachy, Donnie, and Donnie's dad, Pastor White, flocked around us now.

"All your friends are back," Julie teased me.

"Yeah," I said.

There was an awkward silence. Everybody wore silly smiles. Except for Julie, who looked cool and clean as morning dew.

I felt I needed to say something. "Everybody . . . this is Julie Prevette."

Julie got a kick out of everybody saying hey. "I'm at a disadvantage," she said, playing coy.

It sounded like everybody told her names at once. She bravely, kindly, tried repeating them.

She said what the rest of us had thought, but were afraid to mention. "Peachy's a funny name."

"Is it?" He raised an eyebrow. "Never occurred to me."

"Well, how'd you get it?" she ventured. "Is it your real name?"

"How do you mean real?" Peachy said.

"I just mean . . ." Julie backpedaled. "I was just curious, sir."

Miss Barbara stepped in. "It's a perfectly good question, young lady." She challenged her dad. "Don't be so mysterious. Go ahead and say it."

"I harvested peaches. During the Depression."

"You had an orchard?" Pastor White asked.

"No, I had two hands. I picked them off trees," he said softly. "I stayed alive."

Julie smiled big. "Well, I think it's just about the coolest name I've heard in a long time."

I don't know if she really meant that, or if she just really meant to make Peachy feel good. She said it so big, so warm, and Peachy himself glowed like the world was his field to play in.

"I was always kind of embarrassed about it."

"Peachy!" Julie said. "Peachy is my new friend with the coolest cool name."

It's not *what* she said, it's *how* she said it. Like Peachy was the most important person in her world.

He looked small. "Thanks," he said. He was a boy again.

"Ya know, you're really kinda nice," Duffey said to Julie, like he was amazed to learn this. Everybody concurred. I noticed Zack and Donnie trying to keep each other from laughing.

"Thank you," she said. "It's Duffey, right?"

"That's my name, don't wear it out." It was a silly thing teens used to say.

She eyeballed him. "You sound surprised. That I seem kind of nice."

"Well, you're pretty and everything."

Rebecca and Cathy descended on Duffey like he was the fox in the henhouse. "Oh, pretty girls aren't nice?" "Pretty girls *can't* be nice?" "What, pretty means we think about ourselves all the time?"

"I don't know what I was thinking," Duffey said, a phrase that for him surely carried multiple meanings. "But I surrender."

Zack, Donnie, and I had laughed at the girls setting Duffey straight, and they had laughed at his statement of surrender. So we were all in high spirits, except for Peachy, who was suddenly looking overhead, in the distance.

"I knew it," he said.

I followed his gaze and saw . . . something.

Sunset was still a ways off. The sky was patchy with clouds, except where Peachy focused my gaze. I heard a gasp. Maybe my own.

I saw them for three or four seconds. Two objects. Very small, they looked like tiny helicopters, hovering, only upside down. The body of each object was burnt red in color. Maybe brown. Each had a distinct solitary light at its top. One bright blue, like sapphire. The second object's light was scarlet red.

Though they looked small, I didn't sense they were far off. Not at all.

One of them moved, a short silent sideways maneuver. Then a sort of collapsing in on themselves, and they were gone. A quick evaporation. Like spirits uneasy at being glimpsed. I've always been at some loss describing it.

I looked quickly around. "Did you see that?" I asked Donnie.

"See what?"

"I saw it," Zack said, still looking overhead.

"Did you . . ." I turned around to where the others still talked and laughed. They hadn't.

Our little group were the only people left in the vicinity, everyone else having walked off to their cars.

Peachy said it again. "I knew it."

CHAPTER 9

On the doorstep, I straightened my tie, a massive, lime green thing. Where were aesthetic sensibilities in the mid 1970s? I glanced back at the Buick Estate wagon where I saw Mom laughing and saying something to Dad. Probably something like, "Isn't he cute going up to the door and all dressed up and on his first date!" Or she could have just been saying, "That tie is ridiculous."

It must be nice. Already having someone to love for all time.

That's the way it was with me. I envisioned marriage as a good thing, a marvelous thing. My parents showed me that. But dating terrified me; girls were a mystery to me. For that matter, I was a mystery to me. I still am.

I prepared to knock, but before I could the front door flew open. It was Mrs. Gruff. Known to the world as Mrs. Prevette. Known to me as Julie's mom.

"Well, you must be Richard." She smiled, her expression not unlike the one I'd just seen on my mom's face.

"Yes, ma'am."

"Oh, is that your mother waving?" Mrs. Prevette waved back. "You come on in."

"Thank you, ma'am." I stepped inside and Mrs. Prevette stepped out.

"I'm going to say hello to your parents. I hope that's all right."

Before I could answer, she'd shut the door and left me alone in the front foyer. The place was so quiet. I heard quick steps upstairs, sounding like they were coming my way. My heart was beating fast enough, and loud enough to me that I thought I might be having one of those heart attacks that older people have. Old people and first daters.

She bounded down the stairs and stood in front of me. The little sister. Very little. Maybe eight or so. Face like a little Julie. I had an immediate crush on her. She was holding some albums. The one I could see was John Denver's *Farewell Andromeda*.

"You're not Doug."

"No. I'm not."

"Then who are you?"

"Richard."

"Does Julie know you're not Doug?"

"I think she's figured that out," I said, "when we talked on the phone."

"Do you have a car?"

"No."

"Then how are ya'll gonna go anywhere?"

"My parents have a car . . ."

"That's good."

". . . and they can drive."

"That's good. Do you like the sound . . ." she adjusted gum in her mouth, ". . . of music?"

I hesistated. Did she mean the movie or was her question literal?

"Hey, Richard!" It was the fair Julie, beaming. She was at the top of the stairs. Had she been there long?

"Hey. You look . . ."

She cut me off, her words all spilling out together: "I'll be right down I just gotta get a couple more things you're a little early but that's good this is gonna be fun Lizzie let him sit down for crying out loud." She disappeared. Getting those couple more things.

Lizzie giggled. "You wanna sit down?"

"I guess so."

Lizzie darted into a side room and I started to follow her. I thought better of it, and just stayed put. She reappeared in the foyer, a metal folding chair squeezed under one arm, the albums under the other. In her fruitless attempts to unfold the chair, I saw another album was *Highlights from Handel's "Messiah."*

"Let me help you with that." I took the chair from her and unfolded it.

"Thanks, Richard," she said, a wide smile across her little face.

I looked at the chair.

"Don't you wanna sit down?" she asked.

"Yes." I sat down in the metal folding chair in the front foyer. "Thanks."

"So, do you like it?"

"It's a good chair."

"No, silly. The sound of music."

"I like lots of music."

"No, silly." She laughed all over herself. "I mean the movie. And the record."

I laughed too. It was funny. "Sure I do. Who doesn't like *The Sound of Music*? You like Handel's 'Messiah'?"

"What's that?"

"You're holding it." I tapped her load of albums.

"Oh yeah. I just like number eight. The 'Hallelujah Choir.'"

"Chorus. It's 'Hallelujah Chorus.'"

"I said that."

"You said 'Hallelujah Choir,'" I corrected her.

"What's the diff? Chorus and choir and whatchamacallit. Julie listens to number eight all the time."

"Not just Christmastime?"

"What's Christmas got to do with anything?"

"Handel's . . ." I searched for her thought process. "Number eight is Christmas music."

"Not to Julie it isn't. I just told ya, she listens to it all the time. She said if I learn some of it to sing with her, she'd buy me any album I want."

"What do you want?"

"*Carpenters.*"

Julie cascaded down the stairs, a young goddess in a blue chiffon dress. With two white ribbons in her hair. A silver necklace. I remember more than just words.

"Your sister says you listen to the 'Hallelujah whatchamacallit' year-round," I said to the goddess.

"Whatchamacallit!" Lizzie giggled, rocking sideways, shifting her little weight. I chuckled with her.

"You two are just talking and laughing so much about . . ." Julie looked at the folding chair. "What is that?"

"Lizzie brought it to me."

". . . and why are you sitting in it out here? By the door?"

Lizzie explained. "You said, let him sit down, for crying out loud."

"That is what you said," I nodded with Lizzie.

Julie rolled her eyes. "Please! I meant take him into the living room and . . . never mind."

"You didn't say that." Lizzie shrugged.

"Did Dad come out here?" Julie asked.

"I haven't seen your dad."

"Well, if you did, you need to know he's not as tough as he makes out."

"I haven't seen your dad," I said again.

"He's really a fuzzy bear."

"I haven't seen any fuzzy bears." Both girls laughed at that.

"Lizzie and I've been having a great time," I said. "We both like *The Sound of Music.*"

"Are you a singer?" Julie asked in a somewhat challenging tone.

"I'm terrible."

"Great!"

"Why is that great?" Lizzie wanted to know.

"I'm glad there's something I do better than him, right up front."

"Awww . . ." I didn't know what to say.

"I bet you can curl your hair better than him," said Lizzie.

"You look great," I said. "Just great."

"Look at you! Last time I saw you, you had dirt all over your uniform."

"Oh yeah, guess we better go."

We went out the door; I almost bumped into Mrs. Prevette on the porch. She told us to stand by the birdbath and wait for her to get her camera.

"Why the birdbath?" I asked Julie.

"I dunno," she said. "She likes to take pictures there before I go anywhere."

How many other guys have stood here with Julie? I thought as I smiled for the camera. I guess I was nervous and I said something I probably shouldn't have.

"You go out a lot?"

She looked at me, her voice soft and cool as the May breeze. "I'm excited. I've never been out with Richard Powell before."

I shut up. Mrs. Prevette and my parents agreed it was wonderful to meet each other and Julie told Lizzie yes, she could play her records, but don't touch the eight track stereo player.

Mom and Dad were almost too quiet in the car on the drive to the restaurant. I guess they were trying to give us space to talk. But it was more like giving me rope to hang myself.

"Thanks for doing this with me." *Great. A loser thanking a winner.*

"You mean . . ." She figured out what I meant and was gracious. "Thank you so much for asking me. This is a lot of fun."

I suppressed a chuckle. Sort of.

"Why is that funny?" But she was smiling too.

"This can't really be a lot of fun, I mean, not yet. We're in the car with my parents . . ."

"Oh!" Mom whipped around, looking at me. Also smiling.

"I mean," I stumbled, "we're not even at the banquet yet."

Dad cut in. "All we're gonna do at the banquet is eat. And have them give out awards. The eating part'll be pretty good."

Julie whispered something to me.

"What was that?" Dad said from his driver's seat. "I heard 'Dad' in there somewhere."

"She said you're like her dad," I said.

"Sounds like he's a fine man." Dad had a little wit. A little.

Things were cool at the banquet, it was mellow and festive at the same time. A lot of the team had already arrived when we got there, which gave me a teenager's thrill to walk in with my date beside me and listen to the buzz from my teammates. They were surprised. So was I, still, to be seen in the company of Julie Prevette. I didn't care too much about her esteemed popularity or how she affected my nascent stature with my classmates. But I cared enough to appreciate how pleasant it was to be noticed for something other than my peculiar intellectual distinctives. Of course, to most of my teammates, I was still just a little ninth grader who had learned to throw a weird but effective pitch.

There weren't as many parents as I expected to see, but enough to keep the evening from devolving into an excuse for some restless teens to leave early and party hearty at some locale.

The parents of the Fellowship of the Rock were well represented, a number having shared the same church and the same kid triumphs and trials for a few years. Duffey's dad didn't make it, which disappointed some of the guys since he was a mountainous man whose physique dwarfed even the most muscular twelfth graders on our team. High school guys are really into muscles. The bigger the better. It's the precursor to our adult fixation with money and acquisitions, a wide road to despondency, to grief.

Duffey came in after us, with his date, Caroline, the girl who worked at McDonald's. He made a "Duffey entrance" worthy of his genuine affection for his friends on the team, which was everybody. For all the time he spent with the Fellowship and in the Scouts with the troop guys and me, Duffey still managed to find time to befriend a lot of other kids. He paraded around the banquet room, high-fiving and joshing like he was the Kingfish: "Hey Stan, you're looking like a champ," "What do you say, Fred?" "Hey, Willie, are you and the po' boys playing down on the corner out in the street?" "Who dressed you, Ossie? I know you didn't." "This here's Caroline, and she's mighty fine." "Hey Larry, are you saved yet? You can't buy no stairway to heaven, ya know."

When he'd satisfied himself and the team by making the rounds, he and Caroline circled back to Zack, Donnie, and me and our dates.

Tricia, Donnie's date, was exceedingly serious. "Have ya'll known each other long?"

"Just met Duffey. I'm already tired of him," Caroline said with a straight face.

"Oh." Tricia was stumped.

"Don't listen to her, Trish." Duffey roared and Caroline let go a "Haa!" to let everyone know she was kidding. He deserved a kidder.

"It's Tricia," Donnie's date politely corrected him. "Or Patricia."

"Patricia is my cousin," Donnie said.

"Don't listen to Caroline, Pat," Duffey joshed. "She messes around a lot. With people's heads. 'Specially mine."

Rebecca cut in. "She would have to."

"It's not really Pat," Patricia remarked, way too softly to register with Duffey.

"What's that mean?" Duffey challenged Rebecca. "She would have to."

"You're a card," said Zack, "that needs to be dealt with."

"I swear sometimes I think ya'll are trying to change me." Duffey sounded serious.

"Can I say something?" Caroline asked.

There were a few seconds, a pregnant pause, before Duffey assured us that Caroline would say something whether anybody gave her permission or not.

"I think Duffey is . . ."

"Told ya," Duffey said quickly.

". . . a real hoot and a big fun date and I'm tickled to be here . . ." Duffey beamed.

". . . but if anything, ya'll are probably too nice to him."

Duffey unbeamed. "What kinda . . . whose side are you on?"

"Duff, I know about people." She looked like she did. "And I can see these special friends of yours here are top notch, and sweet as cider and you better keep bein' nice to them right back. That's all."

"That's enough," Duffey deadpanned.

Caroline put up her dukes and hopped around in front of her date like she was ready to box him. We broke up laughing, and Duffey said, "Come here," and she did, putting her arm in his. They matched. Funny how that happens.

Caroline asked Julie how long she'd known me.

"We just met. He called me out of the blue."

"You must be brave," Caroline complimented me.

"No, I don't think so." It's easier to be honest.

Julie's eyes sparkled. "Brave or not, it was very nice."

I smiled back at her. But I considered "nice" a limp adjective.

"Very gallant," she added. That was much firmer.

Duffey asked Caroline if she thought he was gallant.

"I think you're a handful."

Everybody liked that, including Duffey.

Zack and Donnie and I pulled a second long table over to the first where Mom and Dad had parked with other parents. Mom asked Caroline how long she and Duffey had been dating.

"This is our first date."

We kids all said we didn't believe that, but Duffey confirmed it.

"Now I have been over to see her at her work," he confessed. "A few times."

"Oh, now, pretty much every day, Hoss," Caroline nudged him.

"That's true," he grinned. "A fella's gotta eat."

"All you get is coffee!"

"A fella's gotta have money to eat at McDonald's."

I was curious. "But you bought a truckload that day we went after church."

"I was celebrating."

"What were you celebrating?" Pastor White asked.

"We were eating at McDonald's."

"But . . ." the pastor paused. "Never mind."

Duffey decided something. "I was celebrating meeting Caroline," he said with sincerity.

"Awww," all the women cooed.

Caroline didn't say anything, but it was clear she was pleased.

"I had to ask her out that first day," Duffey said. "The Sunday we was all having such a great time eatin' all them things there."

"*You* were eating all them things there," I corrected.

"That's what I'm saying," he nodded. "And she was just as nice as she could be." He caught himself and looked at her. "It's all right I'm talking about you and all, ain't it?"

"Nobody's stopping you," Caroline played with him.

"But she's a pistol, now," he said like that was a problem, but I knew it was a major draw for Duffey's affections. "She'll tell you what she thinks and she'll take on all comers."

"Is that good or bad?" Caroline asked him.

"Sounds like somebody else I know," Zack said.

"Yeah, I hear ya. But ya know, Donnie ain't half as bad as Caroline."

"I was thinking more of . . . never mind."

———

The evening events were straightforward, a good meal and some awards, like Dad had said. All of us, except Zack, agreed that Zack should get the Most Valuable Player award but he wouldn't since he was a junior and they safeguarded such awards for seniors. But then another junior, shortstop Pepper Jasper, won it, and we applauded with polite zeal. Except for Zack. He applauded like a maniac, and everybody knew he meant it. They were both great players. Pepper played with rare skill and pizzazz, with an eye toward how he came across to spectators. Zack just played with rare skill. And there was no question in my mind he was more valuable to the team. Pepper was colorful, gifted. But Zack was clutch. Pepper had more homers, Zack more runs batted in. Their batting averages were within fifteen or so points of each other. I've always believed runs batted in translated to core value.

Our high school coach liked pizzazz.

While our coach stumbled through this and that award, I tried not to look at Julie too much. She was my first date, period. I never went to any junior high dances; I couldn't imagine many events that would terrify me more. But tonight was fine; tonight my high school life took on some shimmering hues. Julie Prevette hues. I was glad my parents were there, and I thanked them more than once for coming. Julie saw that and I sensed she was moved by my thanking them, though it was not my intention. She charmed everybody, including my mom, who introduced her more than once as "Richard's little friend." I guess she and I both, and my friends, were little in many ways in 1976.

My peers, especially the Fellowship, were thoroughly gracious to Julie. They'd seen her at school, but she was a sophomore. They only knew her from her excellent performance as Laurey Williams in Silas High's *Oklahoma!* in the fall.

"You were great!" Rebecca gushed. "I saw it twice. I made Zack go."

"You really were good," Zack nodded. "I'm not into plays really. But you were worth seeing. And hearing. Great singing voice."

"Who was that bozo that played your boyfriend?" Duffey drawled.

"Duffey!" Caroline punched his arm, I thought pretty hard but he didn't seem to mind.

"You mean the guy who played Curly?" Julie laughed.

"Yeah," Duffey said. "Your boyfriend."

"In the play," she emphasized. "My boyfriend in the play."

"Whatever," smiled Duffey.

"There's a difference, you know," Caroline reproached her date. "It's acting. They're just pretending to like each other."

"Gimme a break, I know that," Duffey whined like his feelings were hurt, which we all knew took a lot more than what was happening here.

"That was Ricky Felder," Julie said. "He's gone. Moved to Kansas. Why do you call him a bozo?"

"Yeah, Big Guy," Donnie joshed. "Why'd you call him a bozo?"

"'Cause he was," said Duffey.

"What's a bozo?" Tricia asked, serious. "I mean, what do you mean when you say *bozo*?"

"You know. Bozo," Duffey said, thinking he was clearing up muddy waters.

"Well that explains it," Rebecca grinned.

"I mean somebody that don't know what they're doing. Just flopping around, don't know what they're doing."

"That's like the whole world," I said.

Everybody laughed, including Duffey. He said to Julie, "Am I right or am I right? The Ricky guy didn't know what he was doing."

"It's bad luck to say bad things about another actor," Julie hedged, "but yeah, he was out of his element."

"Out of his element," Duffey repeated. "What's that mean?"

"It means he was flopping around, not really knowing what to do." Caroline took Duffey's arm. "Just like you said."

"Sometimes I get stuff right," Duffey said.

At the end of the evening, one of the parents we did not know, our third baseman Micky Burns's dad, showed some photographs on the wall that he'd made into big slides. Only a few were funny, like Duffey loosening his belt in the middle of a game. While people laughed, Duffey stood up and defended himself. Or flattered himself, however you look at it: "I swear I hadn't eaten anything, I was just *thinking* about eating. And just the thought, ya'll . . ." Caroline pulled him down to his seat and then stood herself and laughed: "Ya'll need to be nice to Duffey, he's probably gonna own the biggest restaurant in town in a few years and he'll remember his friends." Caroline was cool and funny and big as life. Like someone else we knew.

One of the final slides was a photo taken the day I pitched.

"I just got some of these last ones developed and put on slides," Mr. Burns said.

It was right after the game ended, when the team was happily congratulating me around the mound.

"What are those two smudges in the sky?" Duffey blurted out.

"I haven't figured that out yet," Mr. Burns said. "I think those marks were something that happened when they developed the photo."

"Right," Zack said, giving me a look that told me my suspicions were his.

"Look like UFOs to me," Duffey said, sparking animated laughter.

"Maybe they are!" Mr. Burns said innocently.

He went on to the next slides, and the "smudges" didn't reappear.

At the banquet's end, Zack and I approached Mr. Burns and asked if he would put the "smudge" slide back up.

The photo clearly showed, in the sky over our heads, bigger than life—Earth life anyway—two objects. Different colors.

"We saw them," Zack said. "That day, in the sky."

"Get out of here," Pepper Jasper said.

"You ready to believe that Zack's lying?" Duffey challenged him.

"No," Pepper backed off. "But it's just he thinks he saw it. They weren't there."

Donnie said, "So what do you think we're looking at right now?"

"Something we can't figure out," Pepper said. "Could be anything."

"Exactly," Rebecca said. "That's literally what UFO means. Unidentified Flying Object. It might be something the sun does coming through certain clouds at certain times of the day, but it might be something else. It's *unidentified*."

"It is that," Pastor White said. "Can I get a copy of this photo, Mr. Burns?"

"Sonny's the name. Sure. I'll get it to you."

"You think it's a photo lab thing?" Pastor White said.

"Not really. I think Rebecca's on target. I think it was something in the sky that day, something we can't identify. That doesn't make it scary or threatening. It's just something we can't call by its name."

"Yeah," Pastor White said. "Could be anything. Anything at all."

CHAPTER 10

I wasn't sure how to take Pastor White's suggestion when he told Zack, Rebecca, Donnie, and me after church it was time to bring in a "new man" to help us sort through some of the odd phenomena.

"I met this guy in seminary," he said. "A super great guy. You're gonna love him. Brilliant. He knows about all this stuff."

"All what stuff?" Donnie asked his dad.

"Well . . . that's it, right?" he said. "We need somebody who can make sense of what's happening. Albert is the man. Already called him. He's coming down from Cleveland. He's excited."

"Can anything good come from Cleveland?" I said, with enough lilt in my voice to let them know I was parodying Scripture's comment about Nazareth.

"That's funny," the pastor said. "You know, you can be funny when you want to be."

"He's a preacher?" Zack asked.

"No. Not really."

We waited for him to elaborate.

"Although he does preach, sometimes. In churches. And he preaches to . . . whoever, whatever, will listen to him."

"He's an exorcist," said Rebecca.

"Well, I don't know if he uses that term. He's not happy with the movie. You know, the movie and book with that title."

———

Zack, Rebecca, me, Julie, and Duffey were enjoying Shakey's Pizza in Dawson, waiting for the "new man" and the "Old Squad."

The latter is what Duffey called Peachy, Miss Barbara, and Pastor White. Not to their faces, of course.

"What are you going to call this new fellow?" Rebecca asked him.

"Well"—Duffey swallowed most of a sizable bite of pizza and looked quite serious—"I been thinking on that. And I think what I oughta do is add him onto the other three, instead of giving him some separate name."

"So they'll all four be the Old Squad," she said.

"Naw, naw," he swallowed the remnant. "They can't be the Old Squad if they's four of 'em. Can they?"

"I guess not."

"So I'm thinkin' we could just call them Creepy Days."

The rest of us looked at each other, a mutually confused society.

"You're off the wall," Rebecca said, shaking her head.

"Where did you come up with Creepy Days?" Julie asked him for all of us.

"It's a takeoff, in my mind, of *Happy Days*. You know, on TV."

"Go on . . ." said Rebecca.

"A lotta kinda creepy stuff goin' on, and these four'll be like Fonzie, Potsie, Ralph, and Richie. It's almost perfect. Pastor White, see, he's Richie, always trying to do the right thing. And this new guy'll be Fonzie."

"How do you figure that?"

"Fonzie always comes in to explain life and stuff. That's what this fella's doing. At least, that's what you guys said this guy might do . . . explain some stuff to us. Am I wrong?"

"Which one is Miss Barbara?"

"That's why it's not perfect, just almost perfect. She, bein' a woman, messes it up. But she and her dad are like Potsie and Ralph. Always hangin' out together."

"You're so far off the wall." Rebecca laughed. "You're off the reservation."

"You're kinda hard on me."

"I figure you're a big boy," she said. "You can take it."

"I like that." He took another slice of pizza, folded it over, and stuffed half of it into his mouth.

The so-called Creepy Days crew walked in just then—Miss Barbara, Peachy, Pastor White, and the new man, Dr. Albert Crumpler. He was short and thin. *Little.* This sixty-year-old Fonzie wore glasses. Filthy glasses.

Zack and Rebecca stood up. Julie and I started to. Duffey never moved.

"Hey ya'll." Miss Barbara smiled. "Keep your seat, keep your seat. Well, four chairs, just for us."

We had brought the chairs to the table ahead of their arrival.

Peachy was chuckling.

"What?" his daughter asked.

"Hey ya'll," he tried to drawl.

"Oh, excuse me." She chuckled with him. "Hello, all of you."

"This is Dr. Crumpler," Pastor White introduced the newcomer as they sat down.

Zack reached across the table and shook the man's hand. We all followed his example. Dr. Crumpler already knew our names, and he matched them to each of us, without our saying who was who. He repeated our names aloud, as if each name's sound were a crucial, important idea. Maybe they are.

"You guys coached him!" Rebecca said to Miss Barbara and Peachy.

He was odd; I liked odd. Except in myself.

"Let's have all of you call me Uncle Albert," he said. "A little girl, ten or so, told me once that Dr. Crumpler sounded to her like a Dr. Seuss character. I discounted her remark. A few days later, she showed me a poem, a rhyming verse she'd written called Dr. Crumpler's Rumpled Dumplings."

"I like that!" Julie brightened. "Dr. Crumpler's Rumpled Dumplings."

"A gifted girl," Peachy said.

"As is this one"—Uncle Albert gestured to Julie—"the actress."

"How'd you know about that?" Julie said, taken aback.

"Barbara filled me in on all of you," he gestured to encompass the entire table.

"Oh boy." Rebecca glanced at me and Zack.

"Good things. Truths about you fine young people, of whom she is quite fond."

"That's true," Miss Barbara concurred.

"Zack is a gifted ballplayer, and a leader." He smiled at my hero. "And you," he said to Rebecca, "are a strong young woman in the Lord."

Rebecca tried not to blush. Instead, she got serious. "But anything like that is all God's grace."

"As I said, you are a strong young woman in the Lord."

"What am I, Uncle Albert?" Duffey asked, big as life.

"You're a strong brave soul—"

"That's right, ya'll!" Duffey liked it.

"—who is unafraid to share the gospel."

"People need to get saved," Duffey said, "like we all do."

Uncle Albert nodded. "Well spoken."

"What'd she say about Richard?" Zack asked. He knew I wasn't about to.

"Ah, Richard," he said in an affectionate tone. "Boy genius." Audible affirmations from my friends. "Softhearted." More affirmations. "A little mysterious." Denials. They thought I was *very* mysterious. Except for Julie.

"You don't strike me as mysterious," she said with a gentle nudge of her elbow.

"That's good," I said. I liked hearing that from her. But I feared I actually was mysterious, though I did not want to be. I wanted to be normal, like I'd told Assistant Principal Huff. I still want to be.

"All of you should have heard Richie in Mr. K's class!" Rebecca was the only person who still consistently called me Richie. She was like the big sister I never had.

"I didn't really mean to interrupt him," I mumbled.

"Don't apologize!" Rebecca beamed. "You were awesome!"

I played with my fork on the table in front of me. "Mr. Koslowski is an excellent biology teacher. Most of the time."

"I don't understand anything that guy says," Duffey droned. "Everybody like pepperoni?" He was anticipating ordering. Again.

"Most of the time," Peachy echoed my words. "When is he not?"

I hesitated, self-conscious. "I don't know . . ."

"Yes you do," Miss Barbara said with warmth.

"Ya'll don't want to hear about bio class."

"On the contrary," Uncle Albert said. "I very much want to hear what Richard Powell knows, what he thinks about."

"Please, Richie?" Rebecca said, a falsetto, teasing voice.

"Hey, that's my job," Julie told Rebecca. Then to me, "Please, Richard?" with the same comical voice. She batted her eyes. Everybody else was tickled by her performance. My heart was bowled over.

"He misses some things," I said slowly. "He overlooks stuff."

"What sort of stuff?" Uncle Albert's eyes sparkled.

"Well, ya know . . ." I was terrible at announcing what I thought. I wrestled to avoid sounding pedantic. ". . . nonmaterial phenomena."

"Quite." Uncle Albert sighed heavily. "Rather to be expected with American high school biology teachers . . . especially in our times."

"Were you born smart?" Duffey asked me.

"C'mon, Duffey." I frowned.

"No, really," he pressed. "Or did you just kinda grow up that way?"

I patted Zack on the back. "Was Zack born cool, or did he just kinda grow up that way?"

Duffey pressed some more. "If Zack's cool, what am I?"

I thought about it a few seconds, and said, "You like pepperoni pizza."

Duffey raised his voice, good natured, over the laughter. "You're saying I'm fat, is that it?" He gave me a cold stare, but I could tell he was trying not to laugh.

Peachy gave him a little love. "You can knock a baseball a country mile."

Miss Barbara sincerely encouraged him. "And you're quick as a cat behind home plate."

"Okay, okay," he accepted the overtures. "Let's do what we came for."

"Ah yes," Uncle Albert said, "talk of UFOs and demons and such." It sounded pretty odd put in such blunt terms, though I guess it would sound odd in expansive terms as well.

"That and eat pizza." Duffey turned in his chair and raised his hand for a waitress.

"I thought ya'll already ate," Miss Barbara said.

"That was just the first round," Duffey said.

"We did," Rebecca said to Miss Barbara.

"This here's second round," Duffey said mostly to himself.

"I'm a little confused," Rebecca said. "I thought that spaceship stuff, UFOs and all, are . . . like against God . . ."

"Quite true." Uncle Albert nodded.

". . . because they're not real," Rebecca finished.

"On the contrary," Uncle Albert proclaimed.

Julie broke the awkward pause that followed with a simple request. "Do you mind if I clean those?" She pointed, a tiny gesture. "Your glasses."

"Be my guest." He gave her his glasses, and she pulled tissues from a pocket on her sweater.

"These are stove top lids," she said quietly. "A guy's gotta be able to see."

Her words and inflection were surprisingly identical to Willie's on the night of Batman's sighting . . . of something.

Pastor White looked at his friend. "You look a little cross-eyed without the spectacles." He passed his hand not ten inches in front of Uncle Albert's face. "See that?"

"I saw something," said Uncle Albert.

"So you think UFOs are real," said Miss Barbara.

"Quite."

"Dad thinks they are, too. So I'm inclined to believe they must be."

"I appreciate your solidarity," Uncle Albert, still blind, said to the air. "Of course, our perception of reality does not alter it."

"There!" Julie announced, proffering the glasses. He almost saw them. He reached into the air and missed them with his first swipe, grabbed them with the second.

"Good grief," Duffey drawled. "You're blind, Cyclops."

"Duffey!" We all chided in unison.

"He's not blind," Miss Barbara said.

Uncle Albert put his glasses on and smiled at Duffey. "Not yet. Though I suppose it's inevitable. After the Franklin affair in Akron."

"Akron," Duffey muttered. "That's foreign, ain't it?"

"Akron, Ohio."

"Thought so," Duffey nodded. "Outside God's country. Outside Bama."

"However, your allusion is not appropriate. Cyclops, before Ulysses bested him, had one large good eye. I have two small bad ones."

"We're so glad you're here," said Miss Barbara. "I've been trying hard to learn as much as I can, as fast as I can, about the occult."

"Hmmm." Uncle Albert leaned back in his chair. "Should we applaud you or pray over you?"

"Either one is good," she chuckled. "What was the Franklin affair? In Akron?"

"It's rather a long episode; I'm sure you don't want to hear it. Suffice to say I found myself temporarily blinded by the flash of a camera of all silly things. My sight returned in moments. But my eyeglasses called for a much stronger corrective prescription thereafter."

"It was just a camera?" Peachy asked.

"I should say, it was a camera held by a man possessed of a demon." He said it like he was talking about the weather. "Which leads me to suspect there was more to the flash than just a camera. Spiritual warfare wreaks havoc on our ordinary expectations. I read of an incident in the Belgian Congo where a missionary, a very fine, excellent man of God mind you, found himself unable to speak when he was on certain grounds. Grounds he was told belonged to the devil and the devil's servants."

Miss Barbara was skeptical. "I find it hard to believe there are beings who alter the laws of physics. There must have been something else going on that kept him from speaking, something that paralyzed his throat muscles."

Uncle Albert kindly nodded, seeming in no hurry to dispute her contention. It was Peachy who raised a defense.

"Maybe demons are *part* of the laws of physics," he said. "I spent some time in the Congo . . ."

"I know, Dad."

"And I saw some things the physics texts fail to address."

"You've said that, Dad. It just sounds—"

"Too extraordinary." Uncle Albert smiled. "I understand. But there's very little that's ordinary about demons. Or angels. Or God, for that matter."

The waitress approached, a large woman wearing a button that said "Your server today is SERENA."

Duffey worshiped. "Thank God for pizza! Mother of us all!"

Serena pulled a pencil from behind her ear. "Ya'll want the pepperoni special?"

"You mean to eat?" said Julie. I'm sure she didn't realize how it sounded.

"No, to wear on your head," Duffey teased her, and immediately felt bad about it.

"Is she for real?" Serena teased too.

Duffey, suddenly a young gentleman, looked over at Julie. "I'm sorry I said that, I swear. I'm just excited. Eating pizza and all."

"That's all right." Julie laughed it off.

"I like you and everything," he said, sincere. "You're real nice."

"We're still deciding." Rebecca smiled at Serena.

"We know she's for real." I nodded toward Julie. "But we're still deciding about the pizza."

"I'm not," said Duffey. "We need at least three large pepperonis."

"Do you have any pizza without the tomato sauce and cheese?" Peachy asked.

"You mean . . . bread?" Serena said without expression.

"I guess it would be," he sighed.

Pastor White took charge. "Two large pepperonis and Cokes all around."

"Water for me, please," said Peachy.

"And bread?" Serena asked him, gentle-like.

"I'll make do with what my friends are ingesting," he answered.

Serena stepped away from our table, mumbling about how her day, her whole day, was from the underworld. For her it was just an expression.

Pastor White folded his hands in front of him on the table. "Al, do they know how many UFOs are sighted? On an average day."

"The FBI says they average one hundred sightings reported each day."

"A hundred!" Rebecca was incredulous.

"On average," Uncle Albert said evenly. "Lately it's been a lot more."

"More than a hundred a day?" said Julie.

"Those are just the documented, reported sightings. They get 'call-ins' that they don't document."

"You mean, if they don't think the sighting is serious?" Miss Barbara asked.

"Yes, or they think the sighting is too serious, too sensitive, to list it with the other sightings."

Peachy shook his head. "I don't follow."

"Well . . ." Uncle Albert paused. "There is no solution . . . no valid, working hypothesis that the scientific community recognizes as an explanation that accounts for the UFOs."

"But *you* have an explanation." Peachy looked at Uncle Albert.

"Well, it's not just my idea," he said. "In fact, this hypothesis, this explanation has been around for quite some time. Centuries."

Zack said, "We're wide-open." Zack had clicked into that focus he had, that ability to consider things beyond the school day notions where most of his friends lived. I was smarter than Zack, then and always, but I don't think I was ever deeper than his deep thoughts. Only one other person had been. And Rafer Forrester was gone. Gone from us, anyway.

"They are angels," Uncle Albert announced.

Duffey gave a low "What?" and the rest of us just sat there, looking at him.

"Angels," Rebecca repeated.

"UFOs are angels?" Julie was incredulous.

"Fallen angels," he nodded.

"Fallen?" Zack said. "You mean demons?"

"I do."

"You mean," said Zack, "you think they may be aliens who act like demons?"

"I mean *demons*," he said with emphasis. "Angels who rebelled against the Power who made them."

"Dr. Crumpler," Peachy said gently, "can you give them some data? Why they can't be aliens, like Zack suggests?"

"They *can* be. I just think it's implausible."

"There are a lot of people," Rebecca said, "including a lot of churchgoers, who would say the idea of demons is not implausible, it's impossible."

"But Rebecca, *you* wouldn't say that," he countered. "Zack, you wouldn't say that, would you? Because you take the biblical account literally. Duffey, you trust Pastor White's preaching, right?"

"Course."

"Then you believe as he does and as I do," said Uncle Albert, "that the reality of angels and demons is no less a fact than the existence of God. And the atonement in Christ alone."

"The ten of us at this table are intelligent believers." He pointed at each of us, like he was choosing up sides for a ball game.

"Thank you," Duffey said, grinning. "Nobody's ever called me an intelligent anything."

Julie said, "I think you're very sharp, Duffey," and the rest of us murmured our assent.

"Ya'll are just bein' nice, but I'll take it." The big guy looked around. "Should be some pizza here any second now."

"Am I right?" Uncle Albert asked us. "Am I right to say that we all believe the Bible is true?"

We nodded without hesitation.

"And it's not just truth," he continued, "but it is literal truth. It says what it means, and means what it says."

I was intrigued. "What other sort of truth is there?"

He took a deep breath. "For lack of a better phrase, let's call it figurative truth."

"That sounds pretty deep," Julie said through a smile.

"Yeah," Zack spoke for all of us. "Can you take us along for this ride in your brain?"

"Some people think the Bible *contains* truth," he said, "even God's truth, but that it ought not be taken literally. That we should look for the truth it contains, but avoid granting the Scripture literal historicity. So, these persons often particularly do not consider the passages that deal with the rebellion in heaven, and the resulting Satan and his follower demons as historical fact. It is allegory to them."

"Convenient," I said simply.

"Yes." Peachy's eyes widened. "But only convenient until the truth breaks into our world in the form of demonic activity."

"All right," said Rebecca. "We all believe angels and demons exist."

"Agreed," Zack nodded. "And if we take Scripture seriously, and we do, we also believe they not only exist, but they are active. Angels and demons have an agenda they're actively pursuing in our world—"

Uncle Albert interrupted. "How committed are they?"

"How committed are they?" Julie echoed his question, her pretty eyes intense.

"What do ya'll mean?" Duffey asked.

"I mean," said Uncle Albert, "it's one thing to say they're active. But how active? Are they hot and cold, sometimes committed to their agenda, and sometimes indifferent?"

"I'd say," Zack answered, "by definition, by who they are, they *gotta* be committed."

"Assuredly," Uncle Albert nodded darkly. "Employing a local colloquialism, you can bet your backside they are committed. You can bet the farm."

Serena arrived, carrying two pizzas. "Oh, bet your backsides, but don't bet the farm, children. The farm is the family's future, ain't that right?"

Rebecca gave her a warm look. "Yeah, that's right."

"No sir," the waitress said with sobriety. "When the bad guys come, and it's the end of the world, you hole up in that farm. Oh my, I forgot ya'll's drinks. I'll be right back." She bustled away.

Zack looked at Duffey and said, "Do you want to say grace?"

Duffey demurred. "Ya'll are all better at it."

Zack took issue. "There's no good pray-ers and bad pray-ers. There are just people who pray and people who don't. We know what you are, so get to it."

Duffey prayed then, simple straightforward thanks for the pizza, and how God was giving us more food than we needed.

Serena was at our table again, dropping off a trayful of Cokes and Diet Cokes.

"Do you pray, Serena?" Miss Barbara asked.

Peachy stared at his daughter. "Do *you*?"

"I'm just asking the woman a question." Miss Barbara stared back at her dad. "I'm curious, okay?"

Serena, who obviously got a kick out of their exchange, said, "I got nothing happening to me that I got a right to complain about. I would like my arthritis to find a new home. And my old man to remember his old home and come on back."

"I'm sorry," said Rebecca kindly.

"Why?" The waitress eyed her. "It's not your fault, girl."

"What's his name?" Rebecca said. "I want to pray for him."

Serena looked at all of us now. "She must be desperate to update her prayer list." She shook her head and plodded back toward the kitchen, mumbling the fearful outlook that some people don't deserve to be prayed for.

Julie shrugged at Rebecca. "Sorry . . . sorry she didn't take you up on that."

Zack gnawed on a pizza slice. "You were saying they're committed," he said in Uncle Albert's direction. "Demons and angels."

"More than committed," said the exorcist. "They're zealots. Made by God to be his servants in the heavens and earth he created. But they *rebelled*." He emphasized the word. "They were 'cast down,' it says in the Word. Agreed?"

He looked at me. "Agreed," I said.

"So they have an agenda in this world, and they are zealous about it. So why don't we encounter them?" he asked quickly.

"Encounter them?" Julie looked troubled.

"In our daily lives."

"Well," I ventured, "a lot of Christians, most Christians, would say that we do encounter them."

He smiled. "The reasonable ones would say that, yes. I mean of course, the ones who exercise reason and logic in their deliberations."

Peachy thought that was funny.

"You like that?" Pastor White chuckled with him.

"It's a very entertaining premise," Peachy said. "The notion that reasonable, logical Christians would believe we encounter demons in our daily lives."

Miss Barbara stared at him. "But you believe it!"

"Exactly. And I am not a Christian. Furthermore, most people think I'm habitually unreasonable, and I've been told recently I am illogical."

"Nobody's perfect," Julie joshed with a straight face. After a silent second to process her comment, the table erupted in laughs. She laughed with us, blushed, and flicked her hair over her shoulders. The blushing may have been for effect. It worked.

When the air was quiet enough, Uncle Albert proceeded. "The reasonable, logical Christians would add, of course, that we simply do not see them." He tilted his head, to address all of us. "Why not?"

"Because . . ." Miss Barbara smiled and tilted her head back at him. "They're invisible."

"How do you know that?"

"How do I know that?" Miss Barbara repeated. "Because . . . I've . . . never seen them." She saw his point.

"Exactly. It's the most basic fallacy in logic. Claiming something is universally false or nonexistent, only because you haven't observed it or experienced it. Humanists are so quick to say logic trumps everything in the quest for truth. But they become experientialists when it's time to talk about Christ and spiritual truth. If they haven't experienced it, then it can't be true. Especially if there is no evidence that someone else experienced it."

"In our particular case, of course," Pastor White said, "we do have a phenomenon that persons claim to have experienced. Peachy, Zack, and Richard all say they saw the same objects in the sky on that same day, at the same time. And"—he pulled a print photo out of his brief-case—"we have evidence that supports their experience."

He handed Uncle Albert the photograph. The exorcist removed his glasses and held the photo very close to his eyes.

"Are there other photos?" he asked.

"No," said the pastor.

"Who took it?"

"Mr. Burns," said Zack. "His boy Micky is on our team. He takes photos for all of us. At our games."

"And he brought you this?" Uncle Albert asked Pastor White.

"No. He didn't even notice the things in the sky. He was just showing this slide at the boys' baseball banquet. He thought they were smudges, marks that appeared when the photos developed."

"He said that to you?"

"To me," said Duffey. "Well, to all of us really. It's just that I asked him what they were. He said he didn't know, but he thought they were just blurry stuff on the photo. I said they looked like UFOs and he said maybe they are and he just kept going with his slide show."

"Sounds innocent enough," Uncle Albert said. "I mean the man. The way he reacted. Though it takes some faith to honestly believe these are smudges."

"That's what I thought," Zack said. "I mean they're pretty clear."

"Yes." Uncle Albert set the photo on the table and most all of us leaned in and looked it over. Again. We'd all seen it before. Pastor White had made a point of showing it to Peachy and Miss Barbara. Two small objects, appearing to have some little light on top of them. One blue-ish, the other a red shade.

"It's one of the reasons I thought you might want to come here, Al," said the pastor. "To check this out. So what do you think?"

Uncle Albert answered with a question. "Who sees UFOs?"

"Farmers," Miss Barbara said. "Kansans."

"Be serious." Peachy tried to gently admonish his daughter. He knew better.

"I *am* serious." She put down her pizza slice. "If you want to see a UFO, you go to the back hills of Arkansas or some farm in Kansas where only one farmer and his family live. Nobody sees UFOs in metropolitan or suburban America. It's a rule," she snickered. "If you're a UFO, you can't show up in suburban Atlanta or Birmingham."

"That's funny," Rebecca said pleasantly. "You're really kind of funny, Miss Barbara."

"No, I'm not." But she smiled. "I know I'm not funny, because I always wanted to be funny. She's funny." She pointed at Julie.

"I am not!" Julie defended herself, or maybe she was agreeing. Actors are tricky that way.

God help me, she is pretty, and sweet, and fine. There must be something romantic I can say, something alluring, or at least cute.

"I thought we were talking about demons," I said to Uncle Albert.

"Yes." He folded his hands on the table. "I believe UFOs are not aliens. They're demons doing impressions. Pretending to be aliens."

"Why would they do that?" Zack asked.

"Lots of reasons," he said simply. "But principally, their goal would be the same as it's always been. Deception. Demons want to deceive, especially spiritually. They want human beings to be blinded to the truth. Blind to who we are, God's creatures made in God's image for God's purposes. If people get the idea there are multitudes of higher terrestrial beings, then human life isn't such a big deal. The happenings of this grain-and-granite planet don't count for much if we're just one of a vast array of intelligent life forms. And not very high on the food chain, if other species are visiting us like they're going to the zoo."

Pastor White got it. "So UFOs encourage people to view Earth and human beings as substandard, almost irrelevant really, given the expanse of space."

"You are an impressive man of God." Peachy eyed the pastor with respect.

"I'm just a country pastor."

Peachy shook his head but kept his countenance placid. "If God is real, then there is no such thing as 'just a country pastor.' Not the way you mean that."

Uncle Albert soldiered on. "And how do you think this plays in God's throne room, if more and more humans see themselves as a blip on a cosmic screen? He gave his Son. He puts his Son through the dust of this Earth and then up on a cross because he cares that much about saving humans. He loves humans that much."

I looked at Peachy, for any sign that this gospel proclamation might speak to him. His reserved countenance did not change.

"Everything about redemptive history," Uncle Albert continued, "about the cross, is screaming testimony to the value—the immense value—of human beings."

"The sanctity of human life," Rebecca said.

"Yes, thank you," he said. "The sanctity of human life. Ours is a glorious existence. Demons don't want humans to see any of that glory. And extraterrestrial sightings obscure that glory, if they don't hide it altogether." He lowered his voice, slowed his words. "If I were a demon . . ."

Duffey made a cross with his arms in Uncle Albert's direction.

"That's not funny, Duffey," Rebecca scolded.

He dropped his arms. "I bet if Julie did it, ya'll would think it was funny."

Julie and Duffey comically glared at each other.

"If I were a demon," Uncle Albert resumed, "I'd be hyperactive about manufacturing UFO sightings. My point being, we should not be surprised by multiple sightings. I marvel there are not more reported sightings."

"I think maybe," Pastor White said, "*reported* is the operative word. People probably see stuff all the time, they just don't report it."

Uncle Albert nodded. "I think you're right."

"Why?" said Miss Barbara. "Why don't they report it?"

"Because people are not as stirred by paranormal activity as we think they would be. People are captive to the mundane—like food, fishing, money, and who will win the big game this weekend."

"Which game is that?" Duffey said, around the pizza in his mouth.

"I rest my case." Uncle Albert smiled gently. "It makes me think of Christ's citing of Isaiah's words: 'While seeing they may see and not perceive.'"

Julie leaned close to me. "We have to go."

I stood up with her. "Sorry. We have to go. Very good to meet you, Uncle Albert."

"We understand," Uncle Albert said in a kind voice. "I'd be interested to know what you think of everything I've shared."

I didn't know how to respond. "I think . . . I think you're helping us understand some things. See some things, as they are."

"You're very kind," Uncle Albert said.

I thought I should add something. "It scares me."

"And well it should," he said. "But I should emphasize . . . demons are not the towers of strength the movies make them out to be. I've seen demon-possessed souls crack and crumble under the slight weight of a child's rebuke."

"You're kidding," I mumbled.

"I kid you not. It's another aspect of spiritual warfare that's hard to divine. But they—demons, I mean—often seem confounded by children. Still, the main thing to believe, to know, is that Christ has crushed the Serpent's head. We are fighting the end skirmishes in a war that is really already decided."

"Yes sir." I pulled dollar bills from my pocket that Mom had given me to spend on "pizza with all your special friends." But Miss Barbara wouldn't let me put the money on the table.

"We've got it covered," she said.

"Mom gave me this money," I said before I realized it sounded like I was about ten years old.

"Wonderful," she said. "Take Julie out on a date."

"This was"—I shrugged—"kind of a date."

"No," Rebecca and Miss Barbara said together. Julie wasn't saying anything, just looking impossibly sweet.

Peachy spoke up. "This was more like a battle strategy bull session."

"Some dates are kind of like that," Zack said. Rebecca gave him a look, but it was obvious she got a kick out of the remark.

"Go play Putt Putt or whatever," Miss Barbara said.

"It's called miniature golf," Peachy mumbled.

"Not down here, it ain't," his daughter said.

"I like Putt Putt," said Julie.

I put the dollars back in my pocket.

"Goodnight everyone," Julie said, inaugurating a chorus of warm words and expressions from our old and new friends.

We were almost out the door when Peachy put a hand on my shoulder from behind.

"I want you to have this," he said. He put a very old-looking black-and-white photo in my hand.

"Is this you?" I said, intrigued at the images of two men in front of a thatched hut.

"That's me and . . . a guy I knew. Twenty . . . or twenty-five years ago."

Julie looked at it. "Wow."

"You should keep this," I said.

"No. I got other photos. That one's for you. We can talk about it later." Only he didn't look like he was looking forward to talking about it. He retreated to the table and Julie and I stepped out into the dim light of dusk.

She tried to play with the moment. "Kinda makes you look at the sky a little different, doesn't it?"

"Yeah." It was an odd moment, a mix of fear and intrigue and confidence in our Lord, who we knew loved us with an everlasting love. It was really an odd year, recognizing real battles, real mysteries, and the splendor of fellowship with believers like Uncle Albert and Pastor White, who had walked many perilous roads and danced in many grace fields.

In her parents' Pacer, a car that resembled a space bubble, Julie turned the key in the ignition and let it idle a few seconds.

"Is your life always this weird?" she asked with a smile.

"No," I said. I decided to be a little funny. "Not at all. Sometimes I go for weeks, just Gandalf and me humming along peaceably through life, without even thinking about demons and angels and all that stuff. Months even."

"Months even!" She thought that was funny. "Gandalf and you. How is the little fellow?"

"He's a hamster wheel addict," I said. "But he's not obsessed with demons. Nor am I."

"That's good," she said.

"But I'm kind of obsessed with God."

"That's better," she said.

She backed out of the parking space and pulled onto the main road that would take us back to our homes.

"There's so much to it," she said. "To this God thing. So many people think it's just about being good and going to church, and Easter eggs."

I sighed. "Actually, we probably underestimate what it means to be good, and what it means to go to a church and worship. I'm guessing those things have a bigger impact in the cosmos than we ever consider. I don't know about the Easter eggs. They may not matter."

"I loved dyeing the eggs!" she whooped. "I still do! Don't tell me Easter eggs don't matter!" she teased.

"I'm just shooting it straight up," I joked.

"No!"

"But I will say this. I think there is more happening in the cosmos when children delight in the little things like dyeing eggs. There's something powerful in their joy, their smiles, something that threatens to tilt the demonic world into oblivion."

"Wowwwww!" She hung onto her word of exclamation.

"What?"

"You say things that are so incredibly cool, Richard Powell!"

"Thank you."

"Man, I want to write that down." She sounded serious.

"Really?"

"Really?" she mimicked me, a breathtaking, charming tone.

I envisioned myself hanging onto the pendulum, the one that swings between innocence and warfare.

"What a strange year," I said. "Beautiful. Strange."

It was as if strong otherworldly winds blew that year in the lives of my new and old friends and me. The veil between this material world and the spiritual world fluttered in the breeze. We saw things, or sensed things, hidden in other years. Those revelations, coupled with the simple joys and trials of being fifteen, sixteen, and seventeen years old, changed us in odd ways. In 1976, we were sharpened and broken at the same time. As if God's intent was to break us, focus us, and equip us for things beyond the foibles of Earth.

And of course, that was, and is, his intent.

CHAPTER 11

Gandalf died.

Somehow he'd gotten his neck caught between some of the tissue he slept on in his cage and the metallic wheel he ran on, and he'd choked on the tangle. Freakish.

I'm not sure why it struck me so hard, but after I'd buried him under the tree in the backyard, I sat on the edge of my bed and cried. I think it bothered me to consider I was the only other living creature who ever paid him any attention, only I hadn't recently. I hadn't played with him or petted him much or even talked to him. I told myself he was just a hamster, but that only reminded me he had no creature encounters except for with me.

I wished I had not known that God notices when a sparrow falls. Everything matters too much. Except of course those things we spend all our time on.

I almost took solace in the talk about UFOs that had morphed into a talk about demons. It helped me see a larger picture. You'd think the Fellowship and I would have talked about it incessantly. But we rather avoided it. It was as if we tried to shelve the whole matter, at least for the moment.

Come to think of it, that is pretty much what most people do with notions of evil's reality.

I was very grateful we had a big campout that weekend and I could focus on the preliminary requirements for the canoeing merit badge. The Boy Scouts did so much to help me prepare to be a man.

I escaped with fellow Scouts to the outdoors, the solace of strong simple things like campfires, the night's visible stars in between tall treetops, canteen water that slaked like nothing else could, and sleeping and rising with the sun. They were plain things, but laden with hidden and obvious lessons that serve a part in seeing life for what it is, rather than what we prefer.

Mr. Rodriguez, the guitar player from church, joined Mr. Forrester as our adult leaders this campout. He'd brought his guitar, but he didn't pull it out straightaway the first night. But after Mr. Forrester, prodded by Duffey, sang all three verses of "Ole Slew-Foot," accompanied by nothing but his hands slapping his thighs, and threatened to sing it again, I asked Mr. Rodriguez to please get out his guitar. I like "Ole Slew-Foot" as much as anybody, but such musical revelry can be overdone.

"What should I play?" he asked, tuning by the fire.

"J.C.!" Duffey barked. Mr. Rodriguez started up "Folsom Prison Blues" before anybody else might suggest otherwise. It was cool; but when we got to "blow my blues away," I was ready for those Blues to *be* blown away, to be over. I think everybody but Duffey felt the same, including Mr. Rodriguez, who immediately started up "Pass It On."

If you haven't sung, or just heard "Pass It On" around a campfire, I wonder what you've been doing with your life.

It only takes a spark . . .

Some of us sang, some of us didn't. It was a lot like church can be, that way. Some sing, some mouth the words, and some don't even toy with the appearance of singing. We are so self-conscious; it keeps us from surrendering, I think. But none of that mattered here. Some of us sang, some of us didn't. All of us breathed the truth of the song, whether we planned to or not. It was in the air. Church worship services can have that same effect. I am convinced more people are drawn to Christ by exposure to genuine worship than by intellectual presentations of Christianity's validity. Of course, God uses any number of means to draw people to himself.

Red didn't sing. I'd like to have looked into his mind while we did. I think he chalked up our singing to our inherent good natures.

136

What else could he have thought? Christopher did sing, softly. Neither he nor the rest of his family were churchgoers. He had told me so. The rest of us were believers, though, largely through the influence of Rafer, our miraculous friend of five years earlier.

Willie and Mr. Forrester formed a common bond by almost simultaneously requesting "I'll Fly Away," and then finding they were the only two who knew every verse, every word. I can still see them, pointing at each other while they recalled the words and sang at a clip that kept Mr. Rodriguez's guitar hands blurry.

Before I turned in, I sat with Zack, Duffey, and Batman around the fire. We told Batman what Uncle Albert had said about UFOs. I thought it would trouble him, given what he had seen that night he told the ghost story. But he seemed relieved to hear that what he had seen was not simply his hallucination. You never know about people. A lot of us would prefer to hallucinate.

"I thought when we told you this stuff," I said to Batman, "what this man says about UFOs, you'd be, I dunno, terrified."

"Are you?" said Batman.

"Well, I'm trying not to think about it."

"You're not doing a very good job. If you're asking me about it, then . . ."

"Yes," I said. "It terrifies me."

Batman frowned. "You don't look like it."

"I'm trying not to think about it," I said again, as if repetition had some power.

"Oh, give me a break," Duffey scoffed. "You're thinking about it and that's okay. We're all thinking about it."

"Gandalf died," I said.

"Who?" Duffey looked at me.

"My hamster."

"Bummer," said Batman. "Was he old?"

"No." I told them about the tissue bizarrely intertwined with the spokes on the running wheel.

"So he hung himself," Duffey deduced. "Your hamster committed suicide."

He thought it was funny, a pure Duffey-like joke. I thought it was crass, rude. But that was Duffey. Raw.

Batman and Duffey laughed.

"Thanks for understanding." I pitied myself. And Gandalf.

Zack had the grace to change the subject. "I know I don't like thinking about the UFO stuff. But I want Richard thinking about it."

"What?" I said. "Why?"

"Because your brain can take it."

"I'm not that smart." I don't know why I said that, except that I wanted no responsibilities beyond my own psychic survival through this demon mess.

"Oh please," said Batman. "We know you're brilliant and you know you're brilliant."

Duffey joined in. "Everybody knows you're brilliant, so let's just move on from there."

That made me laugh.

"What's so funny?" Batman asked.

"I don't know. No one's ever put it to me like that before."

"We're just cutting to the chase, Powell." Duffey chuckled with me.

I sighed. "I don't want to be me." That was simple enough.

"Get in line," said Zack. "You think you're special? Nobody wants to be who they are." I didn't expect that from Zack.

"I think Doug Gillihan does," Duffey said.

"Okay, but he's the exception that proves the rule," said Zack.

Duffey snorted. "I ain't never understood what that means, but I'll take your word for it."

"But really," Zack backtracked, "even Doug doesn't want to be who he is. He'd rather be Richard because Julie likes Richard. So he's not the exception that proves the rule after all."

"Okay." Duffey nodded. "I'll take your word for it that he's not that thing I don't understand."

We drifted into quiet then, looking at the fire, listening to it spit and pop. Our words were few. Walking to my tent to get some sleep, I heard Zack's voice behind me.

"Sleep is a gift," he said, "from God."

It's amazing how a little truth like that comforts us.

———

"But you don't have the canoeing badge," I said to Donnie in the haze of the early morning light, trying not to sound too much like I was begging.

"I know I don't." He put another log on the huge fire we'd kept raging throughout the night. "But Batman asked me to work the mile swim with him. It's important to him. I said yeah."

"It's all right." I fought against sounding like a martyr. "I can do it by myself. Or maybe . . . where's Zack?"

Stevie's voice escaped one of our pup tents. "Zack's gone, ya'll."

"Our hero's gone?" Batman feigned concern. "How we gonna make it through the morning?"

Now Stevie escaped the tent, rubbing his eyes. "He and Christopher and Red are helping with the rowboats, on the other side of the lake."

"You got canoeing?" I asked Stevie who was hopping around carefully, looking at the ground.

"Where's my other shoe?"

"Is your foot hurt?" Willie asked.

"What did ya'll do with my shoe?"

I frowned. "Like we really are gonna take your shoe."

"I threw it in the fire," Duffey calmly announced.

Stevie looked like a car had hit his dog. "Why would you throw my shoe in the fire?"

"I didn't know it was your shoe."

"Why would you throw anybody's shoe in the fire?" Stevie stared at him.

"You look funny," Willie giggled. Stevie still had one foot on the ground and one airborne. Balancing.

"I thought it was some old throwaway," Duffey said. "You know, somebody just left it here in the woods."

Stevie hopped closer to Duffey and the shoe-consuming fire. "That shoe was brand-new!"

Willie giggled again. "You hop funny."

"Shut up," Stevie chastised Willie. "These socks are brand-new too."

"Who cares about new socks?" Batman wondered aloud.

"You still got one," Duffey said with no expression.

Now I knew Duffey was just taking him for a ride. "Yeah," I said, "you still got one."

Stevie surrendered, beaten, sitting on one of the bigger logs we had dragged up close to the fire.

I took pity. "Tell him where it is."

Duffey lost it then, laughing and clapping his hands on his thighs. "I had you," he chortled. "I had you going and coming."

Stevie looked not amused but not angry. Pathetic.

"Why did you leave one shoe out of your tent?" Duffey wondered. "I mean just the one shoe."

"I had both of them in there. Zack said something smelled. I knew what it was, so I set it outside."

"Just the one shoe?" Donnie asked.

"It's always that way for me," said Stevie. "My right foot leaves a smell in my shoe."

"Left one's okay?" Batman asked.

"I know it's weird. But that's the way it is." He looked at Duffey. "Where is it?"

"On the other side of that log." He nodded toward a sitting log on the opposite side of the one where Stevie had surrendered.

Willie hustled over to it and picked it up.

"Toss it here." Stevie held his hands out.

"Across the fire?" Willie looked anxious. "I'm not good at tossing."

"Just make sure you get it over the fire," Stevie said roughly.

Willie hesitated.

"Toss it!" Stevie commanded.

The little guy was so concerned about throwing it too short and not clearing the fire that he heaved it way over Stevie's head.

"I'll go get it, I'll go get it," Willie said overtop of our laughs and jeers. He ran past Stevie, who shook his head, defeated by the morning's first events.

Stevie sighed. "I shouldn't have come this weekend. I coulda stayed home and watched the Game of the Week and sucked down a Coke and some chips."

"What you doin' this morning?" Donnie asked. "I mean after you get your shoes on?"

"Zack asked me to go down to the rowboats. Help him out."

"You'll be in the water all day," Duffey snarled. "You didn't even need your shoes."

"I gotta walk down there, don't I?" Stevie snarled back. Willie bustled up to him, holding the shoe out on his open palms like it was some kind of peace offering. Stevie took the elusive shoe and shoved his foot into it.

"What in . . ." he took his foot out, looked in the shoe, and held it up, shaking the leaves out.

He looked at me. "I ain't done nothin'," I heard myself say in the slang of those early days. I held up my hands. "You know I ain't." Early on, I noticed my conversational language and tones would sometimes shift to accommodate the setting and my friends. I talked differently around adults and oftentimes around girls. On a campout with the boys, well, I blended.

Duffey raised an index finger, like he was about to make a serious point. "That's to teach you to always look in your shoes when you're camping out, before you put 'em back on again. They could have spiders that bite or snakes or just about anything in them."

"Something's not right with your head," Stevie grumbled.

Duffey nodded, chewing. "That's the honest truth." He was back to pounding down his breakfast, some egg-like substance that had started as a powder.

Willie had taken off his own shoes and was looking inside them, all serious and everything.

"I ain't . . ." Duffey paused to swallow the last of his breakfast gruel. "I ain't got it," he said. "Canoeing."

"I know," I said too fast.

"You know?" he cocked his head. "But you ain't asking me."

"Duffey, we're supposed to partner up with people about our own size."

"Uh-huh." He looked a little hurt. But he might have just been playing with me. I couldn't tell with Duffey. He shook his head a little. "I think you just don't want me in the same boat with you."

"You know that's not true."

"Naw, I don't. It's okay, I understand and all that nice jazzmo."

"Duffey, they made a big deal outta it," I insisted. "We're supposed to be the same size. Or just about. And you're . . . you're . . ."

"Fat," Christopher said.

"He's not fat. You're not fat," I said to Christopher and Duffey at once.

Stevie had slumped down off the log to sit on the ground, staring into the fire. "My mom got mad at me for calling somebody fat once. I asked what should I call them then, and she said 'comfortable.'"

"That's solid." Duffey turned to Stevie. "I'm *comfortable*. Something's not right with my head, but the rest of me is pretty comfortable."

"You're a ways past comfortable," Christopher teased.

"Oh, like I don't know I'm oversized."

Donnie sounded pleasant enough. "That's not so bad. Being oversized."

"Oversized for what?" Willie licked a wad of peanut butter off a plastic spoon.

"For life," Duffey said. He still wasn't really mad. I would've been mad.

"But life's a pretty big deal," Willie said in his preadolescent, mouse-like voice. "I don't see as how a guy could be too big for life and all."

I smiled at him. "That's a very deep thought."

"It is?" He dug in the jar, loading up the spoon again.

"Oh please," Duffey whined in Willie's direction. "We got enough deep thinking stuff and deep talking happening around here with Richard. Just spare us, okay?"

"You don't like the way I talk?" I asked.

"It's okay," he backed off. "It's even a little cool. I just don't think we need another genius around making the rest of us feel stupid."

"I make you feel stupid?" I was concerned more about my likability than his feelings.

"Everything does," Duffey said, laughing a little. "So don't sweat it so much, Richard."

I wanted to remedy something. "You know what?" I said, trying to sound like some thoughts were just now occurring to me. "I don't think it really matters about the size difference. I could use your help. It'd be great if you can come with me."

"Thanks." Duffey stood up. "But I got some junk I need to do around here."

I knew that wasn't true. But I also knew that guys have to give each other room.

———

Down by the edge of Lake Cross where they kept the canoes, I stood with other merit badge "wannahaves" and listened to the counselor, an eighteen-year-old with a stern face and voice.

"You can call me Counselor Randall or Counselor or Sir. Take your pick."

A brave soul raised his hand.

"Yes?"

"Counselor Randall, sir, is this badge hard to get? I need something easy."

He was brave, but his question was fuel on Counselor's fire.

"You're in the wrong place," Counselor rebuked him.

"Ain't this the canoeing merit badge class, Mister Counselor Randall, sir?" Brave But Foolish Soul asked.

"How many names you gonna give me?"

"I thought you said—"

"Either Counselor, Counselor Randall, or Sir. Pick one."

"Sorry, Mister Sir." I heard snickers all around. It would not have been nearly as funny if the fellow had been messing with Counselor's mind. But he was genuinely confused. "I mean Mister Counsel. I mean . . . where's the right place, 'cause I gotta get there?"

"This is the canoeing merit badge class." Counselor tried to sound off like a drill sergeant, but he seemed to me to be playing a role and even trying not to laugh. I sensed some of the older kids next to me saw that in him too. A general sense of calm and budding camaraderie came over us.

"And I don't think any of ya'll have what it takes." Counselor played his role fine, amused by his own overly dramatic countenance.

"This is going to be a tough badge to get. But I'm going to give you a shot. If you listen close, and do exactly what I tell you, you might—I say, you *might*—come close to getting the highly sought after, chick-magnet merit badge called Canoeing."

He paused for effect. "Canoeing is something you need to do mostly with a partner." He started pacing back and forth in front of us like we were in some military formation. "We tried to get that bit of information out to all the troops participating here. That it'd be good to come with a partner." He stopped pacing. "Did y'all come with a partner?"

There was a general buzz of assent, though none of the kids said anything real clear in response. But most all of them seemed to be standing pretty close to some other kid.

"I say again, did all y'all come with a partner?"

I said nothing. I heard "Yes," "Yes sir," "uh-huh," and "What happened to Ernie?"

A small voice said, "He fell into the latrine."

"All the way in?" a bigger voice asked.

"No. But he needed to clean up."

Counselor looked at me. "What about you? You got a partner?"

"I was hoping Ernie would throw in with me."

"It's my understanding," Counselor said, "that Ernie may not be pleasant to be around today."

I shrugged. "I need a partner."

"No you don't!" a voice hollered behind us, and Duffey pushed his way through the guys and stood beside me. "Duffey and Richard are partners," he said to Counselor. "Sir."

"You guys aren't exactly the same size."

I started to say something, but Duffey beat me to it. "We've known each other a long time, and we can look out for each other in the boat, sir."

"You guys aren't exactly the same size," Counselor said again.

"Give us a chance, sir," Duffey said simply.

"Okay. I like your can-do attitude." Counselor nodded sharply. "That's what it's gonna take."

This wasn't my first Scout merit badge class, so I knew a can-do attitude was helpful. But the main thing was to do exactly what we were told when we were told.

"What's that smell?" Counselor frowned. "It's like . . . Aqua Blue."

"Ernie just got here, Mister Randall," a boy behind us said. "We're all paired up now."

"Ernie!" Counselor grinned at the sheepish boy. "You smell real nice. Like my granddaddy. Aqua Blue aftershave, right?"

"Yeah."

"But it's like a hundred granddaddies! Ya think you put enough on, boy?"

Ernie started laughing now. "It's all over my clothes. I tried some on my face but that stuff stings!"

"You don't put it on until you shave. Hence the name."

"I don't shave."

"I figured that."

"I put it on to cut the latrine smell."

"Mission accomplished," Counselor nodded. "All right everybody, over to the docks." He pointed and we all ambled over toward where several tied canoes were floating in the water. A fine Aqua Velva aroma ambled with us.

Duffey whispered to me, "I reckon I need to tell you something."

"Thanks for coming, Duffey." I meant it.

"Sure. We're close, right?" He gave me a serious look. "Fellowship of the Rock and all."

"That's right. What'd you want to tell me?"

He said low, "I can't swim."

"You can't swim," I said with way too much volume.

A few heads turned to us; not Counselor's, thankfully.

"Course I can swim," Duffey announced to the world. "What are ya, crazy?" Then, after a few seconds passed, he muttered low again. "I can't swim. But it don't matter. We're in a boat, right?"

I realized something. "Do you want the canoeing merit badge?"

"What would I want a little badge for?" He was only here because he wanted to help me. That was Duffey. "Who needs a little badge?" he said. "Now, I wouldn't mind having another of those big badges."

"You mean a First Class? Then a Star, and all?"

"Yeah, another one of those big ones."

"You have to get the merit badges, the little badges, to get the big badges."

"Is that how it works?" He looked like that was news. "What a racket."

Counselor had stopped in front of the boats and we had all stopped in front of Counselor.

"If you can't swim," I whispered, "we got a problem."

Counselor heard my whisper's tone of angst, but not what I'd said. "Is there a problem?" he said to Duffey and me.

"No problems here, sir," Duffey said with a big grin.

"Good," Counselor said, satisfied. He then proceeded to tell us how important it was that we all could swim well enough, should we end up outside a canoe after starting inside it.

I whispered again to Duffey, "Can you at least float?"

"You mean on the water?"

I couldn't help myself. "No, in the sky like a hot air balloon."

Counselor heard something. "Don't talk while I'm talking."

Duffey got his conversations mixed up, and told Counselor, "I can float. I mean, on the water. I mean . . . we're through talking."

Counselor was confused. "Ya'll are both . . . y'all both got screws loose."

We laughed and agreed. "Yep," I played along, "that's us." Duffey chuckled, "We don't know what we're doing."

"Stop talking."

We did.

"Stop laughing."

That was a little harder, but we did.

Counselor proceeded to tell the lot of us what a paddle was and what each part of the canoe was called and other terms that accompanied the time-honored practice of canoeing a canoe.

He read a name off his clipboard. A sandy-haired boy that was easily as tiny and young as Willie shuffled forward, tentative.

Counselor played with him a little, calling his name again, after the boy was already up front. Sandy Hair raised his hand to make himself visible. "That's me. Sir."

"Oh, there you are. You're not the one that said I shouldn't discriminate on the basis of age, are you?" He knew he wasn't.

"No sir. You can disintegrate all you want with me."

"I thank you." Counselor laughed. "Good grief, boy, my blisters are bigger than you."

"Yes sir."

"I think Chuckles over there might eat you for breakfast."

Duffey played along. "I've ate biscuits bigger than him, Mister Counselor, and that's God's honest truth."

When I stopped laughing, I whispered to Duffey that he might not want to say God like that. I didn't think he heard me in the chatter and laughs bouncing around the group.

"Okay, Mr. Tolliver," Counselor used Sandy Hair's real name, "what do you think this is?" He held up an orange flotation device.

"I dunno."

"I think you're being modest," Counselor said.

"Naw, I ain't," young Tolliver said.

"Are you sure?"

"Sir . . . when you're as little as me, you're not sure about nothing."

"Take a guess," Counselor said over the rest of us snickering. "What is this?"

"It's a vest. A big orange one."

"Good! That's the right answer. What for?"

"You mean, what for am I giving the right answer?"

"I mean what for . . ." Counselor caught himself. "What is the purpose of this vest?"

"So's a fella don't drown."

"Exactly! This vest is called a PFD. Anybody out there want to say what a PFD is?"

"Police and fire department," a tall boy hollered in a high voice.

"Get some hormones," Counselor teased him. He looked serious for an instant. "Don't anybody say I said that; I'll get in trouble. Okay, PFD? What's it stand for?"

I knew Duffey wanted to say something. I nudged him. He said, "I gotta behave."

"PFD, anybody?" Counselor pressed.

"Pusillanimous Fragmentary Demons." I don't know. I just said it. Loud and clear.

The other Scouts said "oooh" and "aaah," ribbing me, but I could tell they thought the words were cool.

Counselor looked at me with new appreciation. "As opposed to pusillanimous but whole demons. Widespread demons."

"Yes sir."

"Okay, back to Earth," he said. "Mr. Tolliver, could you show us all how to put this on?"

Tolliver took it and asked, "So what's PDF?"

"PFD. Personal flotation device."

"That's what I was gonna say," Tolliver mumbled, "but that smart kid got me mixed up."

"I know the feeling." Counselor faced the group and said again, "Personal flotation device."

Somebody behind us said he knew PFD wasn't about anything like demons, and some people need to get serious. If he only knew.

When Tolliver got the PFD on, it looked like a big orange balloon had sprouted two little legs and arms. And one itty-bitty head.

Tolliver offered, "This here one might just be a hair too big for me."

"Think so," Counselor agreed. "Can you move around with it on?"

"All's I got to do is reach and hold the paddle."

"Can you move around with it on?" Counselor asked again.

Tolliver took a couple tentative steps forward and then walked in a tight circle too small to play marbles in.

"You don't seem to be real sure of your steps," said Counselor.

"I can't rightly see my feet."

The vest swelled out under Tolliver's chin. He really had fastened it on quickly, securely, and properly. Counselor said so.

Duffey said, "That little guy's done this before."

"I got the canoeing booklet," Tolliver said.

"I gotta start reading," said Duffey.

Counselor got that vest off of Tolliver and onto Duffey, and then all of us into PFDs roughly fitting our sizes.

He got in a canoe and demonstrated how to launch from the dock, canoe in a straight line, and how to turn the canoe in a pivot all the way around and back to your starting point without moving the canoe laterally through the water.

Now it was our turn. Instead of launching, most of the boys pushed and pulled away from the dock like turtles scrambling off their sunning logs. There were enough canoes and enough room along the dock for everyone to go at it at the same time, two bodies per boat. That led to a few collisions, some muted curses, and one confused capsizing. The two canoers were confused, not the canoe.

It's not the easiest thing to do, to capsize a canoe, but these two Scouts managed. I didn't see how it started, but I saw enough to know the canoe knew what it was doing, kicking those numbskulls out. I heard, "Let go of my paddle, you chump!" and turned to see two Scouts leaning hard into each other and both apparently claiming right to one particular end of the canoe. They pressed the point sufficiently, and pressed the canoe too, tipping it far enough to one side to take on water and not recover. That takes some doing in a canoe. We all applauded.

Counselor rowed toward their two heads peeking out of the orange vests bobbing in the water. He was saying something about how we were not swamping the canoes until summer camp and would they please turn the canoe over and get back in. He could just as well tell them to orbit Jupiter. They bobbed. And shouted each other down.

Duffey and I did right well. We launched like champions. And where many canoes clustered in odd circles and moved in curving lines that were supposed to be straight, Duffey and I skimmed over the water strong and smooth. Duffey was stronger, I was smoother, but we were both on top of it.

We had escaped the canoe-jammed fracas and were far enough from the group to only faintly hear Counselor calling to us.

"He wants us to come back," I said.

"Is that what he's saying?" Duffey mumbled. "I can't exactly hear him."

"He definitely wants us to head back."

"We will." Duffey gave no indication that would happen anytime soon.

"I'd like to get the canoeing merit badge."

"You'll get it," Duffey assured me. "I'll tell him I made you go this far away. He'll see I'm just mean, and you couldn't do nothin' with me."

"You're not mean."

"He don't know that."

"I think we're pretty good at this," I said.

"You're jolly well right we are. Did you follow all that J-stroke and sweeping and push-away stuff?"

"Pretty much."

"Me too, I reckon," Duffey mused. "That J-stroking stuff is just common sense. Fact is, a lot of what he said was common sense."

"Pretty much," I said again.

"Fact is, a lot of what teachers tell us at school is common sense."

"A good bit of it," I agreed.

"Is it just me, or is a whole lot of life not just common sense?"

"It's not just you. I mean, you're right. But the fact is," I used his own phrasing, "common sense ain't all that common."

"You're jolly well right there too. Shop class this week, we were all nailing two plyboards together. Joey Voris hammered a nail through the two boards and his shirttail and into the desk underneath."

"Oh man," I laughed.

"Mr. Jurgens asked him what he was thinking. Joey said he was thinking about nailing the boards together and he can't be blamed for his shirt and the desk getting in the way."

Duffey stopped paddling, and pointed. "Who do you think that is?"

I looked with him to our left, at someone obviously watching us from the woods just off the lake's bank. Whoever it was didn't want to be seen, and quickly disappeared into the woods' recesses.

"That's kind of weird," said Duffey. "Looked like a big fella. By himself. No Scout uniform."

"A Scoutmaster?"

"Maybe. I don't believe so. Didn't look like no Scoutmaster to me. Lotta them got uniforms too. Who wants to watch us canoe, anyhow? Talk about boring. I'm the one canoeing and I'm boring me. Can't imagine how lame it'd be to have to watch me doing this."

While we were still looking that direction, something whizzed by between us.

"Wooaa!" Duffey looked around. "That was . . . what was that?"

"Hornet?" I guessed.

"Maybe. That'd be a big sucker."

Something small pinged against the side of the boat.

"You don't reckon," Duffey thought out loud, "somebody's got a pellet gun. BBs or something?"

My paddle was out of the water. Something small hit it hard, and dropped into the water.

"Get goin'!" Duffey said.

"What?" I wasn't sure.

"Somebody's shootin' at us, Hoss! Get paddlin'!"

We turned the canoe on a dime and paddled hard, back toward the docks.

"If you want, you can duck," he said. "But I'm thinking ain't nobody, not Davy Crockett himself, can hit us moving this fast."

CHAPTER 12

Duffey convinced me we should not tell anyone about the pellets being shot at us.

"We don't know that it was actually a pellet gun," he said to me.

"Well, *something* was sure pinging off the side of the canoe."

"They'll just shut the camp down and send us home and the party's over."

"I'd rather not party where someone's shooting at me."

"C'mon Richard, I know you don't want to go home."

"Well no, but . . ."

"They'll cancel the War Club Race and everything."

"I know but . . . I don't want that."

It was not the first time Duffey's pleas overwhelmed my assessment of the situation. Nor would it be the last. It's hard to counter a friend you know loves you as much as Duffey did me.

It was called the Indian War Club Relay Race, a moniker that today would dramatically fail all tests for political correctness. *Relay's* okay, given our contemporary affinity for community and joint efforts. *Race* is a little more risky; it implies victors and vanquished. We still laud champions, even idolize them. But we're uneasy acknowledging that champions inevitably leave behind non-champions.

If the words *Indian War Club* echo in forgotten halls, the words *morally straight* from the Boy Scout Oath are threatened with interment in the grounds under the halls. And "On my honor" and "do my duty to God and my country" are next in the burial line. As is the entire Boy Scouts of America organization, which refuses to "evolve" and is duty-bound to its commitment to duty. It's one of the few duty-bound organizations still recognizing *duty* is a virtue.

———

"Did they just make this up?" Duffey wanted to know.

"I don't think so," said Mr. Forrester. Mr. Rodriguez had left to find a spot on the lake to fish, and because he had to get home this afternoon, he wouldn't be here for the relay race. So it was left to Zack and Mr. Forrester to give us the race particulars and challenge us to compete.

"It does sound like something that just came to them." Batman looked a little worried. "And now they're trying it out on us to see if it works."

Mr. Forrester nodded. "Sounds like that, I know. But they've done it a lot before. Just not recent-like."

"Whaddya mean, not recent-like?" asked Willie, sitting a few yards away from the group, trying to whittle on a too green, too thin branch. It was almost as green as he was.

"They had to stop a few years ago," Zack said. "One of the kids got hurt."

"Whaddya mean, got hurt?" Willie stood up.

Mr. Forrester said, "It was something . . . on the trail, I think."

"Whaddya mean, on the trail?" Willie stepped closer to Zack.

"I don't know." The man shrugged. "He bought it on the trail."

"He *died*?" Christopher sounded more anxious than Willie.

"Did I say he died?" Mr. Forrester said to the whole group. "Who said nothin' 'bout died?"

Duffey asked for us all. "You said 'bought it.' Some guy 'bought it.' 'Bought it' means he died."

"C'mon guys, 'bought it' means something bad happened," Mr. Forrester corrected.

"S'what I'm saying," Duffey said. "Something bad did happen. The kid died."

This sort of talk happens all the time with teenage guys. About the age of thirteen, we come to know all there is to know that's worth knowing, including the meaning of all cool expressions and all slang.

What we don't know and so have to learn later, about the age of eighteen, is that all our understandings are nuanced in accord with our distinct perspectives. Later, usually in our mid twenties, we suspect that nobody really knows anything. Except for our grandparents, who really *did* know everything but lacked the cool slang to communicate it to us adolescent Neanderthals.

I don't suspect teenage girls have the same conversational experiences. They seem to recognize abstractions quicker than boys. And they are not so prone to dispense with mystery, but rather welcome it. Teenage girls link or even equate mystery with romance, a tendency almost entirely lost on teenage boys.

Christopher thought he might clarify. "When people say 'he bought it,' they're sayin' he 'bought the farm,' they're just not sayin' all the words. 'Bought the farm' means he croaked."

"'Croaked' means dead, ya'll," Duffey said. "That's the kind of thing, the kind of word, I know." He was downright proud.

"Okay, lookey-here, okay, lookey-here," said Mr. Forrester, sounding like an electronic typewriter. "Maybe I don't know exactly what 'bought it' means."

Tenderfoot Willie was worried. "But you're the Scoutmaster."

"Assistant Scoutmaster. Filling in and happy to do it. But there's boatloads of stuff I don't know."

I leaned toward Willie and patted his narrow shoulders. "He knows all the important stuff."

"Okay."

"That's true." Mr. Forrester beamed. "I can skin a buck. And fish without a pole. Now listen, he didn't die, ya'll, he just broke something. So they stopped doing it for a while."

Batman asked him, "What'd he break?"

"I think they said it was a hand or neck or something." Mr. Forrester gestured toward Tall King, the thick walking stick in Christopher's hand. "Can I have it?"

The rest of us sounded off with loud questions, variations on a theme, accenting different words. "Did you say *neck*?" "You mean he *broke* his neck?" "Break a neck and you *die!*" "Hand ain't so bad." "You can't get a new *neck!*"

Mr. Forrester laughed, looking around at each of us. "I'm glad to hear you say a broken hand ain't so bad, since that's what happened. I just didn't want any of you bailing out." From his back pocket he pulled a rough map he and Zack had drawn up, with different colors crayoned in lines on it. "This thing is going to be a lot of fun. We just need all of you on board, and I mean every single one of you rascals."

We liked that. *Rascals.*

"Even me?" Willie asked, eyes large.

"Especially you, buckaroo."

"There's nine on a team," Zack announced. "So this'll take every last one of us."

Stevie started counting, quietly, pointing at us.

Zack smiled. "You can take my word on that."

"The toughest leg of the relay," said Mr. Forrester, "we're thinkin', is the long-distance swim."

"We got Christopher!" Donnie beamed. Christopher swam for Silas High.

"Just don't put no pressure on me." Pressure was not Christopher's friend.

"We can win this thing!" Duffey was into it. "If you haul it across the lake like the barracuda swimmer you are, we'll have a lead that won't die. All the way to the relay end, Topher."

"You're not helping." Christopher was less than enthusiastic. "I'm not a barracuda. More like a tugboat. And don't nobody call me Topher but my baby sister."

"All you gotta do," said Zack, "is make it across the lake, without losing the war club."

"I can't swim holding onto that."

"Stuff it down your cutoffs," Mr. Forrester countered.

"That works," said Donnie.

"What if it falls out?"

"You'll know if that's happening," Mr. Forrester said. "Stuff it back down in there."

"Wait a minute," Christopher raised his hand like he was in class, then dropped it when we laughed at him. "Afore I go stuffin' anything down *there*, or stuffin' anything *back* down in *there*, I need to know what kind of thing I'm tryin' to stuff."

"He's got a point, ya'll," Duffey sympathized.

"How big is it?"

"You should have plenty of room down there," Red deadpanned.

"Oh hardy har har," Christopher dismissed the slight.

"It's about the size of my hatchet," offered Mr. Forrester.

"I ain't putting no blade down there."

Donnie teased him. "Already circumcised?"

"What's that?" Christopher honestly didn't know.

"It's when they cut off . . ."

Zack cut *him* off. "There's no blade on it, Christopher."

"It's two sticks tied together in a knot," Mr. Forrester said. "Just figure out exactly where to put it before the race starts."

Zack agreed. "Then when Duffey hands it to you, take your time putting it right where you want it. Secure it down there."

Not entirely convinced, Christopher mumbled, "I don't rightly want to secure nothing down there but what God's already secured down there."

"You say Duffey's handing it to Christopher?" Donnie asked.

"That's right," Zack affirmed. "The sprint swimmer hands it to the long-distance swimmer."

"Duffey can't swim," said Christopher.

Duffey agreed. Sort of. "It's not my best thing."

"You can't swim," Christopher repeated.

"But I can hang with it." He was more than confident.

"You can't swim!" Christopher was nigh apoplectic.

"I'll get the hatchet to you, Topher."

"But you can't swim!" Every troop at Camp Sequoyah must have heard Christopher's concern.

"What you mean is, I can't swim the right way."

"What I mean is you can't swim!"

You'd think Duffey'd get mad, even use his fist. I'd seen him lose his temper many times over, when we were younger. But in our teens, Duffey developed some kind of sliding scale about when to throw

down, when to keep persuading, and when to just josh. He was joshing with Christopher, who was right. Duffey couldn't swim.

"I can dog-paddle." He grinned. "I'm tellin' ya, like a big dog, ya'll."

Christopher, exhausted by Duffey's intransigence, took his case
to a higher court. "He can't swim, Mr. Forrester."

Zack shrugged. "We don't have much choice. There's nine on a team.
For us, that's everybody, the whole troop. Duffey's got to take some slot."

"And ya'll know I can't run. Not farther than one base to another."

Christopher started to sound resigned, fatalistic. "You can't swim
neither."

"There ain't no boxing or wrestling in the relay." Duffey was
totally serious. "It's running and swimming, and if I try to run more
than a hundred feet or so, our troop will end up last. Is that what
you want?" he asked Christopher, whose resistance was folding like
a newspaper.

Red spoke. "I don't guess they have a 'chow down' leg in the relay.
Something at the mess hall."

"Yeah, Duffey'd rock and roll with that," Stevie chimed in.

"Ya'll are real funny." Duffey reached across the table to hit Red,
who dodged the blow.

"Why ain't you swinging at Stevie?" Red filed a grievance.

"Stevie and me's buddies." He looked over to Stevie. "You pray
for me when I'm in the water. So's I don't drown."

"Come off it," Christopher whined. "You can't drown, with everybody right there by the pier watching, and you doing a dog paddle."

"I might surprise you."

"Okay, okay." Zack commanded attention. "Duffey leads off. Our
Sprint Swimmer."

"Be buoyant," Donnie whispered to the big guy.

"He hands it to Christopher, the Long-Distance Swimmer,
who will take the war club across the lake. To here, on the bank."
He pointed to a spot just off the water on his map. "That's you, Batman, First Trail Runner. Batman takes the Yellow trail through these
woods." He traced a short distance on his map.

"Good-bye, yellow brick road," Batman sang, "on the south of
society house!"

"Them's not the right words," Red said.

"But those sound like the right words," said Batman. "I mean those words sing pretty good, don't they? It's Elton John."

Red frowned. "Them people from England can't sing plain English."

Zack pressed forward. "Yellow trail stops at Blue trail's top. That's you, Donnie. You're Blue."

Batman sang to the tune of Elvis. "You'll be on bluuuue . . . trail . . . this Christmas!"

"Can it," Duffey drawled.

"Okay."

"Donnie runs the trail here, south, until it breaks off southeast, here, at the top of these other woods."

"Will I see it break off like that?" Donnie wondered aloud.

"Just stay blue," said Zack. "Stay with the blue markers—"

"You'll be on bluuueeee . . ." Batman started off again.

" . . . until you see Richard," Zack finished.

Duffey stopped Batman again, this time with a hard look.

Batman pleaded and teased at the same time. "I got the music in me."

"I got it in me too," Duffey countered, "but it ain't like it's the sum total of my conversation."

Donnie grinned. "Sum total. Listen to Duffey's vocab."

Zack looked at me. "You're the Long-Distance Runner."

"Yeah, baby!" Duffey high-fived Zack and me.

I was good at distance runs, but I didn't compete on the school team. I thought it took too much time. I couldn't read all I wanted to if I had to sacrifice time running.

Red said, "Richard'll run like Marty Licorice, ya'll."

"It's Liquori," I said. "I'll do what I can. It'll be different holding on to the war club."

Donnie couldn't resist. "You could always stuff it down *there* and circumcise yourself."

"What kinda size is circumcise?" Duffey honestly asked.

"Circumcise means to cut," said Donnie.

"To cut," Duffey repeated.

"It's when you cut . . ."

"Listen up, ya'll!" Zack broke off Donnie's explanation. "So then Richard runs with the war club!"

"What color does Richard follow?" said Batman.

"No color," Zack said.

"Shoot." Batman was disappointed.

"Just a diamond shape like this here." He drew a little diamond on the side of his map. "Oh wait, I remember now. The diamond shape is white."

Batman sang softly, "Louie was whiter than white . . ."

Duffey's voice was soft too. "You're gonna get hurt, son." Batman had stopped, but it was clear he only wanted to sing the one line anyway. It was also clear Duffey wasn't going to hurt him. Not on purpose.

Mr. Forrester smiled at me. "If you're able to run like I think you can, we might have a chance."

"I'm not . . ." I paused. "I don't run to compete real well. I run for me. To relax."

"That's fine," Mr. Forrester said. "Just relax."

"It'll be hard to relax with other runners ahead of me and behind me and beside me and . . ."

"Be cool," Donnie said. "You're uptight just talking about it."

"Running is personal for me."

"That's cool," said Zack. "But just this run, kick it in for the team. It's just one little race."

"I'll do my best." If Zack had asked me to run around the world, I would have said "I'll do my best" and meant it.

"I know it," he said. "Cool. Okay, Richard hands off to me, here by the old Arrow Cabin. I'm the Long Sprinter."

"That sounds a little strange," Donnie said. "How far's a long sprint?"

"This one's about like a two-twenty," Zack said. "It's not bad."

"What's two-twenty?" Stevie frowned. "Two-twenty what?"

"Yards. Two hundred twenty yards."

"Calamity Jane!" Stevie's eyes popped out. "How far is Richard running?"

"No more than two miles," Zack said.

"It jolly well better be less than two," I said, probably saying "jolly well" for the first and last time in my life. School buddies have that effect on us.

"It is, it is," Zack insisted. "But a good part of it is through the woods."

"I don't mind that. The less I see of other guys, the better."

Zack pointed to the spot where he would hand off to Stevie. "You're the Short Sprinter."

"How far?" Stevie was suspicious. "How far is short?"

"About fifty yards."

"What color is Stevie?" Batman ventured.

"Stevie is black, ya'll." Duffey declared in a loud voice.

Everything seemed to stop, including the air we breathed. We were all as still as a windless, snowless winter night. Our eyes moved a little. We looked around to see how everyone was processing Duffey's declaration on this fine Alabama evening in the late spring of 1976. The short end of the processing was that Duffey was on point; Stevie was black. He and Willie were two of the few blacks on the entire Camp Sequoyah complex. The white and black issue was a mystery to me. My family wasn't from the South. We'd moved from Colorado in 1969 because Dad, an air force pilot, was stationed down here. Dad was born in California and Mom grew up in Washington state, where, she said cheerily, "nobody has any color whatsoever. Even the Negroes are white there, it's so cold and wet."

I'd sat in Silas Baptist Church with Zack, Donnie, and Duffey when Donnie's dad preached with quiet strength and clarity from Galatians 3:28: "There is neither Jew nor Gentile, neither slave nor free, nor is there male and female; for you are all one in Christ Jesus." I had read *To Kill a Mockingbird*, watched the movie and cried, and understood a person's color was an immense issue for many people. But I was sure my friends and I had escaped that dragnet. If I suspected any racial tension, it came from Red, whose feelings were finely cloaked. Maybe too finely.

The reason Duffey's declaration stopped us in our tracks like train brakes is we'd never mentioned it before. It wasn't an issue for us in Troop 44. Fun was an issue. Camping and hiking and fishing and swimming were issues. Not skin color.

It occurred to me in those seconds that if Duffey were a bigot, he would not have made such an audacious, almost whimsical announcement. He would have been coy. Prejudice, of whatever ilk, is wickedly cautious when it's around the non-prejudiced. Duffey was bold.

Duffey confirmed, in a loud voice. "And black . . . is . . . beautiful, ya'll."

The air moved for us, audible sighs of relief and ordinary breathing.

"Yes it is," Zack concurred. "Okay, ya'll, Stevie has no color, the colors are gone at this point. We don't need them anymore. I mean, we don't need them to know where we are and . . . what we're doing . . ."

His voice trailed off and birthed another pause, easier than the last. His literal meaning was that Stevie had no color to look for on the trail. The subliminal, heavier substance of his words wound around all of us, binding us. Grace is organic. Willie started to giggle and that allowed the rest of us to chuckle and laugh and enjoy the moment.

"It's just you and me's left," Willie smiled up at Red, who stood just beside the table where the other eight of us sat crowded together.

"Uh-huh," said Red.

"Now," Zack started back in, "just before Stevie hits the mud pit . . ."

"Whatcha mean 'hit' the mud pit?" Stevie worried.

"Just before Stevie gets to the mud pit," Zack edited quickly, "he hands the war club off to Willie—"

Willie did Scooby Doo's "Oh no" sound: "Rut row."

". . . and Willie goes down the obstacle course lane, crosses the line and Troop 44 wins the 1976 Camp Sequoyah Indian War Club Relay Race!"

"All right!" Donnie shouted and started a hand drumroll on the table and everybody but Red joined him, including Mr. Forrester, for about ten loud, table-slapping seconds.

"There's just one catch at the end, you guys," Zack said. "No part of Willie's body can touch the ground throughout the time he's carrying the war club and traveling that lane in the obstacle course. All the judges, the camp counselors, will be looking."

Duffey said, "Run that by me just once more."

"And Red here"—Zack stood and put his hand on Red's shoulders—"he'll be making sure that happens. 'Cause Red will be the Scout Bearer, carrying Willie, who is the War Club Wielder carrying the war club. Can you do it, Red?"

"Oh, I can do it," he said. "But I think Duffey oughta carry him. He's bigger and stronger than me. I can be the Sprint Swimmer."

"It's not allowed," Zack said. "The Scout Bearer, the guy who carries the guy who carries the war club, cannot weigh more than a hundred and fifty pounds. I didn't ask Duffey, but I'm guessing he's a mite over that."

"Just a shade," Duffey confirmed. "A mite on the north side of two hundred."

"What about you?" Red asked Zack. "You're stronger than me, and you could haul Willie like nothing."

"You're at least as strong as I am," said Zack, talking fast, pressing Red to take on the task. "It's perfect! You're about as strong as anyone under one fifty. And Willie's about as tiny as a Boy Scout gets."

"I ain't heavy," Willie said.

Batman sang, "He ain't heavy . . ."

Everyone but Red sang, "He's my brother!"

"We need you, Red." Zack's leadership was pivotal.

"Course I can do it." He sounded more resigned than eager.

"One more thing," Zack said. "The Special Troop, you know from the Home, might be participating in certain parts of the relay. Mostly the simple trail running, I think. I'm told they might, or they might not. But they are *not* in the overall camp competition. They're just doing some of the simpler events. I know ya'll will be good to them, be kind."

Mr. Forrester said, "I love those guys. They never do anything but smile."

Zack concurred. "I expect we could learn a lot, just watching them. But don't worry about where they are in the race. They are not in the actual competition."

Zack looked from Willie to Red and back. "You two will have to figure out the best way for you to have Willie hold onto you, so you get through the obstacle lane while Willie keeps the war club from touching the ground. Nothing to it."

"Let's go look at the obstacle lane now," Red suggested. "All of us. I need ya'll to help me see, ya know, how to hold the guy and what all. Ain't easy carrying a guy."

I noticed Red avoided saying "Willie." It's easier to hold onto the narrow corners of prejudice if the other person is nameless.

CHAPTER 13

"All ya'll ready to do this thing?" Zack shouted.

We were in a prerace huddle, a tight closed circle, arms on shoulders, looking at each other. The only one absent was Donnie, who was already in place with the other troops' Trail Runners on the other side of Lake Cross.

Most all of us shouted, in a few quick words, that yes we were ready, we were born ready. Willie's words weren't as quick or few, so we heard him, after the rest of us were silent, squeak, "Man alive, this is really so dy-no-mite."

His voice was so high the other troops heard it and teased us, mimicking Willie's eleven-year-old falsetto.

"So dy-no-mite!"

"Man alive! Dy-no-mite! Man alive!"

"Which troop has Mighty Mouse?"

Duffey asked Zack, "You want I should bust their heads?"

"Uh, no," Zack said in a light manner. "That's not necessary."

Duffey raised his head from our huddle and hollered all around, "Can it! Less you wanna talk out of your belly button."

Duffey's gladiator spirit was legendary. No one wanted to open a new vocal cavity.

"All right." Zack held our gazes. "This *is* gonna be wicked cool and loads of fun and I'm serious, ya'll, I think we can take it. And wouldn't that be the talk of the camp, if Troop 44, with nine guys to pick from to fill relay spots, ends up beating out all these other troops that have fifty guys to pick from to fill their nine spots?"

We all looked around at each other, still in the huddle, and realized for the first time the size of the task in front of us. But we also saw the possibility of upsetting many expectations. The other troops, of course, and also our own unspoken doubts.

Zack eased up then. Real leaders know when to lighten the atmosphere. "Just have some fun," he said. "If you're having fun, everything else will fall into place."

Christopher, often my only real rival for the "serious one" of the troop, said, "You want us to win or do you want us to have fun?"

"Now you've got it," Zack said with a straight face. "Batman?"

Pastor White had given us a troop chant, a variation on poet Robert Service's "Law of the Yukon." While we looked at him, Batman intoned the words in his rich baritone.

> Send not your foolish and feeble.
> Send me your strong and your brave.
> Strong for the red rage of battle.
> Brave for the sinner to save.
> I wait for the men who will win me.
> And I will not be won in a day.
> And I will not be won by weaklings.
> Subtle, and suave, and mild.

We all joined in here:

> But by men with the hearts of Vikings.
> And the simple faith of a child.

And we all shouted: "Be brave!"

It was another time. An era of sentiments long past. Easily forgotten, and forever missed.

Batman left us, jogging easily toward his starting point. He would take the club from Donnie who would get it from Christopher out of the water.

We had all scouted the entire relay route, and I knew I would be able to watch the first two legs—Duffey's start and Christopher's long swim—before I had to get to my spot at the midpoint ready to take the war club on the long-distance run. Once I finished my leg of the race, I would also be able to watch the final stretch, when Red would carry Willie through the mud pit. Though I wouldn't be able to watch the others, I was looking forward to hearing from Batman, Donnie, Zack, and Stevie about their Viking-like efforts.

Zack and I waved across the lake at the little figure of Batman in his Scout shorts and one of the tee shirts Zack's mom had dyed yellow, our troop's color for this event. The tee shirt would help Christopher spot Batman on the bank while he swam toward him. Batman waved back.

The race would start with a whistle blown by Camp Sequoyah's ranger, Mr. Burkett. We were instructed to call him Ranger Burkett or Mr. Burkett or Sir. Among ourselves, we called him Yosemite because, with his overgrown mustache and all, he looked like a real-life Yosemite Sam. His voice also reminded us of what Yosemite Sam sounded like on the Saturday morning cartoons. Furthermore, he seemed to have the character's edgy, self-important, brusque temperament. Like he never considered other people, except to reckon them nuisances or roadblocks to his personal agenda. In a cartoon character, that comes off as funny. In a real person, it comes off as foul.

After Yosemite blew the whistle, Duffey and about a dozen and a half other Sprint Swimmers would dive off the far pier, swim to the near pier and hand the war club to their troop's Long-Distance Swimmer. Well, Duffey would likely jump rather than dive.

"You know my dad's half Cherokee," Duffey said to Zack.

"Oh yeah, I know."

"And he says the real name of this here water is Lake Etowah."

"I like that," Zack said. "Lake Etowah."

Every other Sprint Swimmer tucked the war club down their cutoff jeans or swim trunks. Not Duffey.

"You're good with it like that?" Zack asked.

"Dis'll be da ways zime doin' dis." Duffey snarled around the club's handle in his mouth. He looked like a pale walrus daring the world to take the chew toy out of his mouth.

"Okay," Zack nodded. "Good man."

At first, the other swimmers tried not to laugh at Duffey, though more out of fear of him than respect, but soon enough the sight of him moved everyone to good-natured laughs. I thought he'd take umbrage, but he seemed to revel in the attention. He saw the others swinging their arms and shaking their legs to warm up, and started stretching himself. His arm swing went fine, but his leg shake looked like something was going to pop out of place. So he just stood still and surveyed his competition, all smaller, sleeker animals. Gumption can take you pretty far, and Duffey was always ready to roll. But this was a different sort of rumble. I didn't expect him to keep pace with the pack.

He surpassed my expectations. When Yosemite Sam blew his whistle, the pale walrus cannonballed into Lake Cross, sending a magnificent geyser high into the air and creating a wake for the other swimmers to struggle through. All the onlookers were cheering for their teams so loudly, they didn't hear my buddies and me yelling for Duffey to please surface for air so we wouldn't have to jump in and haul him out of the water.

When he finally reappeared—and to this day I don't know how he did it—he surfaced alongside the guy who was swimming a close second behind the leader! Ol' Duffey was flailing his arms and spouting water high in the air like a mini model of Old Faithful; I worried about how much water he might be sucking in, even while he kept the war club clenched tightly in his teeth. All the while he dog-paddled furiously, like a Saint Bernard trying to reach a drowning victim. A couple of smooth-stroking swimmers passed Duffey, but as the pack neared the end of this very short swim, Duffey was holding on to fifth or sixth place. If he didn't drown.

"Maybe I should jump in," Christopher hollered over the cheering to Zack and me. "He's drowning!"

"Think so?" Zack considered it.

"I can't tell." I shook my head.

"Could be," Zack said loudly. "But, even dog-paddling, he's hanging in like crazy. If he's not drowning and we jump in to get him, he'll kill us for stopping him. Let it go."

It struck me as bizarre that Zack would say "let it go" about whether our friend was drowning. But he had a point. Duffey would kill us if he wasn't drowning and we jumped in to get him.

"I think he's all right," I said.

The first and second swimmers reached the dock and climbed up, fumbling with the war clubs in their trunks. The third and fourth swimmers followed close on, as the lead troop's Long-Distance Swimmer dove off toward the far shoreline. Duffey reached the pier and dropped the war club out of his mouth onto the pier like an obedient, faithful retriever. Christopher picked it up, shoved it down the side of his cutoffs, and dove in. The swift transition from Duffey's mouth to Christopher's cutoffs outpaced the fourth-place team's awkward transition, and we watched Christopher gliding over the lake's surface not far behind the third-place team.

"We're in third, guys!" Zack pumped his fist in the air, and we shouted our heads off.

With considerable effort, we were able to haul Duffey onto the pier. He just lay there, looking up at the sky, gulping chunks of air like miniature doughnuts and saying something hard to make out.

It sounded to me like, "Ice wall . . . lard kneel and bout . . . Moses . . . duh hole Edna."

We took our eyes off Christopher's masterful swimming long enough to make sure that Duffey was going to be all right.

Zack looked at me. "Can you make out what he's saying?"

"Ice wall . . . lard birth . . . near Moses . . . duh hole Edna," Duffey repeated.

I made a go of it. "Something . . . about Moses and Edna."

As Zack leaned over to listen a little closer, the walrus grabbed Zack's tee shirt and pulled him down hard, close to his mouth.

"Ice wall . . . lard kneel and bout . . . near Moses . . . duh hole Edna."

"I can't make out what you're saying, big guy." Zack smiled at Duffey. "But you did great! Christopher's in third place!"

"Second place, now!" Red said.

"Second place now, Duffey!" Zack told him.

Duffey let Zack's tee shirt go, and put his head down, breathing a little easier now.

I had a spark of inspiration. "Hey, Stevie, get over here." He and Duffey were kind of close. Stevie hustled beside me. "What's he saying?" I gestured. He got down close to Duffey, listening.

"Ice wall . . ." Duffey moaned. "Lard . . ."

Stevie translated, processing Duffey's accent exaggerated by the ordeal and his uneven breathing.

"I swallered . . ." said Stevie.

". . . pert near . . . ," Duffey continued.

"Swallowed pert near . . ." Stevie paused. "Swallowed pretty near . . ."

". . . duh hole lay Edna."

". . . the whole Lake Etowah." Stevie smiled the smile of success. "I swallowed pretty near the whole Lake Etowah."

"Coulda drown, ya'll," the walrus muttered. That part we all understood.

Batman yelled again, "Christopher's in second, pressing toward the shore!"

"We're in second, Duffey!" said Zack.

Duffey pulled himself up to rest on one elbow, looking far out over the lake. "Khrushchev ketchup," he mumbled.

I looked at Stevie, who said, "Chris should catch up."

Zack told me I probably should start moving toward my starting point, so I wouldn't be winded when Batman reached me. I trotted easily in that direction, pumped and primed with many visions of what was happening. Christopher gliding smoothly across the lake, while other competitors halted and started and halted again in the long stretch over the water. Duffey churning through the water like an overloaded tug, but dropping the war club easy for Christopher.

I couldn't see Batman running, but I knew he was a trooper who would navigate the trail smart and fast, preserving whatever advantage Christopher's long-distance swim had gained. Donnie . . . was not a runner, but he was a gamer—a much leaner version of Duffey. Donnie would give it his all, and it wasn't like he had a long way to go to get the war club to . . . me.

I was ready; just an edge of nerves. That would benefit me, as long as I kept my heart peaceable while I ran. A two-mile run, or anywhere close to that, is a sizable haul through woodlands and paths with up and down slopes. And that's what I'd be running; I'd walked it with Batman the day before while the others were checking out the rest of the course.

"Ever think about going out for a play?" Batman had asked me.

"You mean like, trying to act? In a drama?" I didn't see myself doing that—ever.

"Ever think about it?"

"I'd rather be boiled in Crisco."

"Is that a no?" he said with a straight face, for laughs.

"I got enough drama in my life without stepping into all of it on a stage." I made small motions with my hands.

"What're you doing?"

"I'm tracking the turns through the woods. My hand moving, it helps me remember."

"You're nuts," he said quite kindly.

"*You* are nuts. Getting people to watch you on a stage. On purpose."

"Julie does it."

"I know," I said. "That's one reason I like her. She's not like me."

"As good as she is, at drama, in real life she's just like a little kid. I mean, she's not big on herself. She's swell. You're lucky."

"I know. Thanks."

"We need to let her in. Let her into the Fellowship of the Rock. Rafer'd want that. Rafer would like her."

"I think so too," I said. Batman was all right.

Reaching my start line, I recognized only one of the other runners who stood around, some stretching, some joshing. Pepper Jasper gave me his superior look that said he knew, definitively, that his troop would annihilate any and all others today. Of course, he especially found our troop unworthy. He'd joined another troop, one that was much larger and not sponsored by Silas Baptist Church.

I thought about what Batman had said. He was right, I was lucky—or like Pastor White would say, blessed—to have met Julie, and gotten to know her in a sweet special way. Thinking of her now helped me both to relax and get ready to do my best at the same time.

She had that effect on me. I wanted to be peaceable and strong at the same time. Thinking of her made me feel I could be.

Looking strong but not peaceable, Pepper made an announcement. "We're ahead, you guys. Way up." He sang the little ditty that Dandy Don Meredith drawled on *Monday Night Football*: "Turn out the lights, the party's over."

"Shut up, Jasper," said a little kid with a crew cut. Despite the other kid's slight size, Pepper must have known he was tough, because he shut up right quick.

Far down the starting line from me, one of the other runners waiting was a little guy from the Special Troop. He looked just like the rest of us, except his smile was massive. I gave Smiley a little wave. He waved back, a huge, demonstrative gesture.

"What'd you see last?" Frazier, a boy I barely knew, asked me.

"You mean . . ." I stopped. I didn't know what he meant.

"At the lake," said Frazier. "You just come from there, right?"

"Oh yeah. Well, it looked pretty close, I guess." I sensed lots of eyes on me. "Close, the top four or five."

"Really?"

I shrugged. "But I don't know what's happened after the long swim."

"I see him!" Pepper was excited. "That's Tony! My guy!"

We peered a good ways out in the distance. The runners were not easy to make out.

A guy who looked old enough to be in college, with a big white band on his arm that told us he was an official judge, warned us to stay behind the line, a long and very shallow mark made by lime chalk across the dirt in front of us.

"You can cheer your guy. But if you're across that line when you get the war club, your team is disqualified." I recognized him as the archery and rowing merit badge counselor. Most everyone clustered close to the line. I stayed well back.

"Somebody's right behind him," said Crew Cut.

I looked hard. It wasn't Donnie.

"That's Chili Bowl!" Frazier lit up. "And somebody's on *his* tail, too."

I looked hard again. I saw him then.

C'mon, Donnie, rock and roll! Don't let a guy named Chili Bowl ace you.

Donnie was puffing hard, giving his all.

The lead guy, Pepper's man, kicked hard, stretching his lead.

"All right, Tony!" Pepper jumped up and down, waving like a madman. It occurred to me that he was already burning precious fuel, given the distance we had to run. Tony crossed the line and Pepper just about ripped Tony's shorts off trying to get the club out.

"Ow, man!" Tony complained. When Pepper was not deterred, Tony, who was about Pepper's height, slapped Pepper upside the head. That worked.

Pepper stood quite still, and Tony clinically pulled the club out and gave it to him. Pepper said "thanks" and took off while the rest of us stifled laughs.

"You're doing great, Donnie!" I called to my friend.

"Bring it home, C.B.!" Frazier encouraged his guy.

Another runner, in a green tee shirt, came in view not far behind Chili and Donnie. I looked again at the runners around me and noticed for the first time a lean kid to the side, wearing a green tee, quietly stretching in a manner that implied he was a practiced distance runner. Slender but strong, he looked to be all legs and lungs, and dark curly hair.

"That's Gillihan," a kid with a gentle smile said to me.

I recognized the smile. "Aren't you the Aqua Velva guy?"

He didn't answer. "You know"—I thought I had to remind him—"the canoeing merit badge guy who—"

"Yeah, yeah," his smile threatened to leave, but he was a good soul. "I'm trying to live that down, ya know?"

"Sure," I spoke softer. "You stink."

"Thanks."

"Who's Gillihan?"

"Big cross-country runner for Dothan High."

A suspicion crossed my consciousness on a jet stream. "What's his first name?"

"Here comes your guy," said Stinky.

"What's Gillihan's first name?" I readied myself for the war club exchange.

"I dunno. He's Troop 21. Ask him."

Chili Bowl and Donnie crossed the line and collapsed. Donnie had carried the club in his hand so I was able to grab it and go.

"You did great, Donnie!" I said to my friend panting on the ground.

"Men with"—he took a breath—"the heart of Vikings."

"And the simple faith of a child." I started running. I had to know. "Gillihan!" I called back over my shoulder. "What's your first name?"

"Doug," Gillihan answered. "Go get 'em." He waved to me, gave me a genuine smile, and winked at me! One of those incredible winks that only the coolest of the cool can actually bring off. The rest of us look like we have something in our eye. What kind of rival is that? At least be a jerk. I waved back. I didn't wink.

I ran a little faster, trying to distance myself from the notion that I was not the only guy Julie Prevette had hung around with and laughed with and winked with.

A foul pox on Troop 21 . . . c'mon Powell . . . get your head in the game!

I glanced back and saw Frazier pacing very slowly, and far enough behind me that I couldn't imagine him overtaking me. Unless he was some kind of a closet champion cross-country runner who just happens to show up and run us amblers into the ground; there are such types on the prowl.

Get a grip, Powell! Focus. This race is enough of a dragon. Don't worry about slaying any more while you're already straining to see through this one's fiery breath.

Pepper, of course, was nowhere in sight. But I suspected he was the type that would run too fast, too Peppery. If I paced well, and if he burned out like I imagined, I could catch him. Or at least close the gap for Zack when I handed off to him. I knew Zack would burn up his 220 yards like a man on fire. It could be very interesting down the stretch, with Stevie, who was not going to lose sprint yards to anybody, handing to the Willie/Red Mud Pit Mobile. I smiled. Even if the contest wasn't in doubt, that mobile would be entertaining to watch in motion.

I tried to relax mentally, and that seemed to help my muscles and lungs. Pete Schumann, one of the track distance guys at Silas High, once told me that a runner's endurance is best served by contemplating things that calm, or things that delight. Most people don't realize this, and mistakenly believe they can stir up more endurance by thinking of things that excite them or challenge them.

"It's better to sing Simon and Garfunkel or Jim Croce in your head than Grand Funk Railroad," said Pete. "Unless of course you hate Jim Croce. For sprinters, it's different. They want to explode like a blown gasket. We distance guys want to coast like a canoe on still waters."

When I told him he should be a writer, he'd said with a straight face, "I write poetry. But if you tell anybody, I'll set your hair on fire."

I'm pretty sure he was kidding, but it's hard to tell with distance runners. A different sort altogether.

Following the white diamond markers on trees and posts stuck in the ground, I turned onto a trail and into the woods. I took solace in the trail's labyrinthine winding, an up and down, back and forth maze I knew would be a bear for bigger kids who would have destroyed me in a shorter run on a level track. The path was over-diamonded, but I guess they wanted to be sure nobody got off course. I went through "The Sound of Silence" in my head and "The Boxer," a song I thought should have been a bigger hit than it was. The boxer was recalling the gloves that brought him down when I heard someone coming up behind me. I glanced back, seeing no one but hearing the certain sounds of a runner gaining on me.

I quickened my pace and realized my brain was surging through the words and music of "I Am a Rock." I was telling myself it was good to be chased; the will not to be overtaken would fuel me. And it did, until I miscalculated a sharp break to the left in the path. My right foot slipped on a sizable patch of moss that a dying elm had spawned. I fell forward, so fast I couldn't get my arms in front of me to break the fall. My forehead met a sizable rock. A rock feels no pain. I didn't either. My last conscious thought was of the rock's gray shades in front of my eyes.

CHAPTER 14

The blackness receded, the gray color returned.

A man's voice said, "Wouldn't you like to join your friends?"

I raised my face up off gray, concrete flooring, and came to a kneeling position.

I was just inside the front door of a one-room cabin. The walls were stacked lumber. The cabin was entirely empty except for six silver metal folding chairs in the center of the room, facing one wooden chair occupied by the man who'd spoken. His back was to me; he faced the silver chairs, in which sat Rebecca, Julie, Duffey, Caroline, and Donnie. My friends looked concerned, sober.

The man spoke again. "Wouldn't you like to sit in a chair with your friends?"

I stood and stepped toward the chairs, stopping beside the seated man. For the first time, he looked up at me. The revolver in his hand was pointed at Duffey, though it was clear he was also watching everyone else very closely.

"You recognize me, I'm sure," said the man.

"No," I said honestly.

"Yes, you do."

"No," I said again. "I'm sorry, I—"

Then I did. He was the man in the old photograph. The one Peachy had given me.

He saw in my eyes that I did recognize him. "I don't normally like being recognized." He smiled. "It can make things much harder for me. But in your case, I consider it an honor to make your acquaintance."

He still had the revolver aimed squarely at Duffey. As it began to dawn on me that I was close enough to the man that I might could grab his arm and count on my friends to help me wrest the gun from him, he said softly but firmly, "I would feel much more comfortable if you took your seat. I suspect we all would."

I sat in the one empty chair.

Julie gave me a sympathetic look, and put her hand on my arm. "Are you okay?"

"I kind of ran into a rock. I mean my head ran into it." But I smiled at her; I wanted her to know I was all right.

Duffey wanted to know how my head could run into a rock. I started to agree with him that it wasn't easy, but Caroline's brave words to the man cut me off.

"Holding a gun on kids make you feel like a man?"

He replied in an even tone, "The weapon is for your benefit. It would not do for me to use my other means. Yet." But he lowered the gun to his lap, his right hand still gripping it. He was seated far enough from us to preclude any notions of rushing him.

He slowly repeated some of Caroline's words. "Feel like a man. A horrid suggestion."

"You're a demon, then?" Donnie asked.

He must have thought the question funny, because he tried to laugh. When the odd gurgling in his throat stopped, he made an assertion. "I am the real power." He didn't raise or alter his voice in any way. He simply said it.

A few seconds passed, his assertion hanging in the air like a snake from a cypress.

I said, "I've been told, many times, that demons do not exist." I didn't add that I'd recently been told they do.

"I'm sure you have. I'll go so far as to say I'm glad that is what you are told. I don't want anyone to believe. I don't want any believers."

"What about us?" asked Caroline. "Are you afraid that we believe?"

"I am afraid of nothing," he said. "No one. Certainly not six teenagers."

"He's a demon." Donnie pointed at the man. "Only a demon is stupid enough to count our side as six teenagers. There's sure enough somebody else in here with us. Right now."

I was not ready to concede Donnie's assertion. I thought it more likely he was a very intelligent but sick man, perhaps oppressed by an evil force, an evil personality. The idea of outright possession by a real evil spirit, an actual evil personality, seemed beyond reasonable conjecture. And even if possessions were real, what had Uncle Albert said? "Demonic power is ultimately so much smoke hungering for fire it cannot command."

The man's words now were mystifying, smoky with a perverse charm.

"I think, maybe, it's important we get to know each other." His voice was temperate, passive. "I always enjoy talking with your kind."

"Our kind?" I said.

"Human."

"I thought you meant Christian," said Caroline.

He smiled without joy, a manufactured facsimile of human expression.

"My kind do not distinguish Christian from non-Christian; the distinction is vapor. Of course in our ongoing . . . mission, we do differentiate those who claim to embrace the un-god and those who make no such claim."

"Un-god?" Duffey frowned.

"You call it God," he said. "Your allegiance is asymmetrical. I'm sorry about that. Really, I am. And I'd like to help you, all of you, find the truth. What do you say to that?"

Caroline said, "I reckon we might say . . . why would you care?"

"A very fair question," he nodded. "You're a very fair young woman, aren't you? The answer is, this is what I do," he continued. "Help people find the truth."

"I've been taught that the one you follow is the father of lies," I said without rancor.

"John 8:44."

"You know the passage."

He smiled. "Your un-hero sharing his un-wisdom. He is, of course, speaking about his un-self." He recited, a melodious incantation: "Ye are of your father the devil, and the lusts of your father ye will do. He was a murderer from the beginning, and abode not in the truth, because there is no truth in him. When he speaketh a lie, he speaketh of his own: for he is a liar, and the father of it."

"Word for word from the King James," Donnie whispered low to Caroline.

That entertained him, a dry chuckle. "Where's the point in not memorizing precisely?"

"I take it you don't accept the verse's premise," I said.

"Oh, but I do." He leaned toward me, not threatening but as if taking me into his counsel. "The premise is faultless, only the subject is, I say again, asymmetrical. Your un-god is the father of lies, and my Lord is he who stands in truth."

"You'll forgive me, or," I paused, "maybe you won't, but that sounds exactly like what someone would say who has been schooled by the actual father of lies."

"We can't help what the truth sounds like, can we? And don't your hero's own words presage the notions of falsehoods masquerading as truth and truth as falsehood? It appears to me—and I'm never wrong about facts, my friend—that the issue is narrow. One says the other is a liar."

"He said, she said," I muttered.

"Yes. Only for our purposes, the question carries the weight of all things, doesn't it? If your un-god is God, then I am undone. And if my Lord is found to be the true Lord, then you are . . . wasting your wonderful intellect and insight on what is not true."

"I thought you were going to say . . . then I would be undone," I said.

"My Lord is not wrathful." He appeared to believe that. "Hell is your un-god's creation."

I was silent, long enough for him to think I might be unsure.

"Why do you think your un-god made such a place?" he asked.

Caroline waded back in. "God doesn't need us to defend him."

I glanced at Julie. She hadn't said anything after asking me if I was okay. But she didn't look scared. She looked exceptionally sure . . . about something.

"We're just talking," he tried to sound friendly; that made him appear creepier, if that were possible. "I enjoy this, really."

I don't think he enjoyed anything.

"Richard, what exactly is this thing we keep referencing, this thing we call truth?"

"Pilate's question."

"Pilate was a fool," he said.

"I'd think that guy was a hero of yours," said Donnie.

"Then you don't understand me. He stupidly let your hero become a victim. But tell me, what is truth?"

"Truth is a person," I asserted. "I am the Way, and the Truth and the Life."

He frowned. "That's no answer. I could myself say truth is a person. And the person is that of my Lord Satan."

"That's part of Truth's confirmation. Satan did not say he was the Truth, and Christ did. Such things don't occur to your puppet Lord. He is forever piggybacking on the true Lord Jesus' words. And on God the Father's creation."

The man didn't like that. We all saw it.

Duffey said, low but clear, "Crush it to da max, Richard."

Our captor shifted in his seat and looked away. He appeared, abnormally, to be swallowing something. He looked back.

"You can't mean," he said to me, "that the one who speaks first, who makes the claim first, is the Truth."

"I do. In this context, I mean that very thing," I said. "There's something to be said for being the first to create, the first to move into void and"—I hunted for what I meant—"generate non-void."

"Non-void is not a word." He tried to laugh. It came out more like a sick man clearing his throat.

I felt strong. "After your *un-god* and other *un-things*, I didn't think you'd mind my playing with a word to get my meaning across."

Duffey shrugged and said flatly, "It ain't nothin' but a thing, ya'll."

That struck me as very funny, but before I could laugh, the man said, "Speaking, as we are, of the Truth concept, you must know . . . it's dying."

I said, "Tell us what you mean." I thought that would be fascinating. A personality that thinks it is a demon, discoursing on the death of Truth.

"You are drowning in your subjective view of objective truth," the man said evenly, "which is swiftly on its way out."

"What is?" Donnie asked.

"The airy pretense your Western civilization has enthroned and called objective truth is entirely perception and perspective. The very reason you, Richard, an extremely brilliant young man, and me, a fairly competent demon"—he tried, but failed, to smile—"hold a starkly different view of reality is that we view the same objects with differing perspective. Your un-god is my devil. My Lord is your devil."

Caroline jumped back in. "What would you say if I said that one of you, either Richard or you, is right, and one of you is wrong?"

"That is another way of saying we have differing views on the same subject. We see different angles on the same object."

"So you're both right?" she asked.

The man grimaced, as if in pain. "Why is everything reduced to who is right and who is wrong? If you hold to that extreme position, you strike me as lacking that amazing grace your faith loves to sing about."

Duffey couldn't take that. Shaking his head, he said, "Now the demon's telling us about amazing grace."

The man ignored him, addressing Caroline. "You make it sound as if a choice is possible. That we can decide what is right and what is wrong. I grant that making such choices would amount to power mongering, demagoguery. We would label our friends right and our enemies wrong."

Duffey drew out his first sentence. "Which is nearly 'bout . . . what you do . . . ain't it? Your demon friends, them you call 'right,' and God and God's people, you call 'wrong.' Try and tell me I'm missin' something here?"

I looked at Julie again, and she looked like she was swimming in peace like a river. That fed me.

"Since you brought up friends and enemies," I said, "I feel led to mention that we Christ-followers are given some outrageous commands by our leader. We are told to pray for our enemies. And bless those who persecute us."

"Which, of course, you have consistently refused to do throughout history," the man said, as if he were telling us something we didn't know.

I readied a comeback that would have attacked this present enemy but exposed my proud, malicious spirit.

Thank God, Caroline spoke ahead of me. "Yeah. We haven't done that well." Her admission unsettled him far more than my snide rebuttal would have.

"You have in fact failed him," he announced. "All of you. All your lives. And he cannot countenance what he regards as your constant, consistent sin. You do consistently sin, do you not? Tell me I am wrong about that," he challenged.

I felt sickened. The prospect that he was saying something true folded over me like a blanket of death.

It was Caroline who sidestepped his challenge and pulled the blanket back by addressing a separate but related issue. "The thing is . . . we can't really tell. You might not be a demon. You might just be a human being who needs Jesus. Which makes you no worse a sinner than me or Richard or Julie or Duffey or Donnie or Rebecca." It was like listing forgiven sinners—naming them—had power. "Or Zack or Rafer or Rafer's dad or—"

"I am greater in every way than any one of you," the man said with some heat, though his voice was not raised.

"See," Caroline answered, "when you say something like that, I'm pretty sure you are not an actual demon."

She said nothing more for several seconds.

It was not easy to tell, but I thought he was intrigued. "Why do you say that?"

"I could be wrong," said Caroline. "But I'm just thinking, . . . a real demon, it's like, they wouldn't have to say they were greater or more powerful than some human being. It would be obvious. Know what I mean? A real demon wouldn't have to tell everybody that it was bigger and badder than some human beings."

I spoke. "Unless of course demons in our earth realm really do struggle against humans. I mean, maybe the powers of fallen angels don't translate well to our earth elements. Peachy's always reminding me you guys just don't mix well with others."

I wondered if we might really be touching something in the man's or demon's psyche. It was impossible to tell. He simply said, "Un-god does not care for you. He cannot. You have all disappointed him. You and all your kind. All his church, throughout history, has collapsed, and is even now collapsing further. By your failure, and by your words, and often by your very silence, you deny him."

"You're halfway right," I said, "which is a perilous place to be theologically." I recited, "If we deny him, he also will deny us."

"Yes!" the man almost cheered.

"If we are faithless, he remains faithful; for he cannot deny himself."

His voice deepened. "Do you think we haven't already processed and dismissed ancient creeds that you deem have power?" He spit the words. "Do you think we fear such trivialities? Do you think we fear anything?"

He cocked his head in Julie's direction. "You've not spoken one word this entire time."

"That's not true," she said softly. "I said, 'Are you okay?'"

"I know what you've said aloud. What have you said in silence?"

"Nothing," she said softer. "Just praying."

"That's not nothing."

"Leave her alone!" The authority in my voice surprised me.

"You don't tell me." He was threatened. "You don't command me."

"Christ commands you," I said with surprising force. "If you were really in command, even of your own self, you wouldn't have to protest my assertion of command, would you?"

After five or so long seconds, the man/demon seemed to deliberately settle down. "I'm finding myself pleased," he lied, "that we're all getting to know each other better."

I thought his words bizarre and would never have guessed what he said next.

"You like drama?" he asked Julie.

"Love it," she answered, downright breezy, given the company we were keeping. "Nothing is real. All pretend. It's like a backwards world. All backwards."

"All backwards," Duffey echoed. "That's like your world," he challenged the man.

"I think not . . ." he said, appearing to stumble over his words. "I know not . . ."

I realized Julie was humming a tune.

He glared at her. "Stop that."

Julie didn't, or couldn't. "It's just a song." She hummed louder. I recognized the music.

"Hear me!" he commanded her.

"Leave her alone!" I said.

"You will . . . stop it," he insisted.

"I can't and I don't want to, so I won't," she said, looking very composed. I felt someone tell me to let them talk.

"What is that?" said Duffey.

"I know that!" Caroline beamed in Julie's direction.

"Sure you do," Julie nodded.

"Handel's 'Messiah,'" Rebecca announced.

"Everybody knows it," said Donnie.

"Everyone in the universe," Julie said to the man. "You know it, too." She was not challenging him. At least, that was not her intention.

"Stop," he ordered.

"I don't think I can," Julie said truthfully. She sang then, softly. "He shall reign forever and ever. And he shall reign forever and ever . . ."

"King of kings," I said, also quietly.

Julie sang, louder. "Forever, and ever. Hallelujah. Hallelujah."

I raised my voice too. "And Lord of lords."

Julie let her lyrical, bright soprano loose. "Forever, and ever! Hallelujah! Hallelujah!"

In a swift move, the man stood and pointed the gun at Julie, and I sprang to my feet. I'd taken a step toward him, but froze. His gun was now pointing at me.

Julie had stopped singing.

"What happens now?" Duffey said low. I peeked behind me, and saw all my friends were standing, still.

The man took another step back, the weapon still raised.

Julie said, "You don't sing, do you." It was not a question. "But you used to. Didn't you?"

No one spoke or moved. I felt the scene dissolving, and my eyes opening.

CHAPTER 15

Smiley. Smiling.

The face of the boy from the Special Troop was inches from mine, grinning. His countenance was so big and bright; it was like he was pouring life energy into me.

"That's my favorite word," he said.

I got on my feet. Too fast. My head felt like it was expanding. "Ow," I said.

"I'm glad you're not dead," said Smiley.

My head receded to its normal mass, and I was pleased to realize I felt okay. Just a slight throb in my forehead.

"Is it over, then?" I asked. "Must be by now."

"Is what over?"

"The race. The relay."

"No. It's not over. We're in it. We're right in the middle of it. Uh . . . I think you're number two and I'm number three."

He stepped to the other side of me, standing in front of me. "Now, I'm number two and you're number three."

I rubbed the crown of my forehead. No blood, but a bump rising. "But I feel . . . I know I've been laid out here for a while." I didn't recall all the unconscious dream, but enough to guess I had slept on the path by the big rock for a long time. Had to have been.

"I don't know what 'a while' is. I saw you fall and I ran up to you and looked in your face, and you said, 'Hallelujah,' and I said, 'That's my favorite word' and you stood up and—"

"How long did that take?"

"How long?"

"How long was I sleeping?"

"If you were sleeping, you were sleeping . . ." He thought about it. ". . . The time it takes me to count to ten."

Was that possible? Maybe. "How many passed us? Running."

"Nobody."

Was it possible? Had I only been unconscious for a matter of seconds? The dream seemed to last so much longer. But maybe dreams are that way. Maybe, at least sometimes, our unconscious time actually only amounts to a few seconds of conscious time.

"*Nobody* passed us?" I asked again.

"Nah. Nobody passed us. Hasn't been enough time for that, I guess. But that nice Gillihan guy is right behind us."

"Well, c'mon then!" I said, bolting onto the trail, with Smiley right behind me, both of us back in the race.

My head was okay, for now. I could run, though my breathing and pace were labored.

Smiley paced and breathed so quietly, I looked over my shoulder to see if he was running with me. Seeing him encouraged me. The trail narrowed to next to nothing in some places and twice I thought I'd lost him. But there he was, so quiet, nearly close enough to touch.

"You're running great," I said.

"Thank you." A very soft voice. "It's good that you didn't die. I thought you might die. When you fell."

"Oh no, no, I'm okay." I felt bad that he'd been that concerned. "My name's Richard."

"My name's Lewis."

"Do you run a lot?"

"I'm running a lot now."

"Watch out," I said, ducking a low thin branch. I heard it brush hard against what was surely Lewis's face and I felt terrible. "Man. Sorry about that."

"It was the branch." I heard him spit something. "It wasn't you."

His steady pace was impressive; I was sure he was a better distance runner than I was. I wasn't wondering whether he could pass me, but why he didn't.

"You can pass me," I said between breaths, impressing myself with my gracious spirit. "If you like."

"No. I don't like running alone."

So then, something else that makes us different. Except right now, I *do* want to run with this guy.

"Me neither," I said. It wasn't a lie, not for this race. "I'm so glad we're running together."

"Me too."

We were at a clearing, big enough for him to shuffle up beside me, on my right. He smiled so big I thought it must hurt his face. I smiled back. Just that quick I saw a couple of tears on his still smiling face.

"Something in your eyes?" I said.

"No. I'm crying." His smile faded. "My dog died."

"Oh no."

Our pace actually picked up slightly. I don't know why.

"He died today?" I asked.

"No."

"When?"

"A lot of days ago."

I didn't know how many that was. It didn't matter.

"I'm sure sorry about that."

"Thank you, Richard." He smiled again.

I hunted for the right words. "You miss him?"

"Yes. A lot."

I started to cry. Not sobs, but obvious tears.

"Are you sad?" said Lewis.

"Yeah."

"He wasn't your dog," he asked.

"I know."

"Can I hold your hand?" he said simply. "We do that a lot in my troop."

My troop had seen them do that, and we had made fun of them. "Sure," I said, taking his hand. "That's a good idea."

"Is it all right with you if I pray?" he said.

"Fire away."

"Does that mean it's all right with you if I pray?"

"Yes. Please pray, Lewis."

"I'm gonna keep my eyes open on account of I can't see where I'm going when I close them."

"That's a good idea." It occurred to me that more of us should pray with our eyes open, for precisely the reason Lewis gave.

I felt my runner's second wind kick in.

Lewis, breathing easy, didn't seem to need a second wind. "I still miss Boo-Boo, God. Is he okay? Oh, good. That's so good. Thank you for my new friend Richard. Thank you for the kind things he says."

I noticed we weren't running smaller trails now. We could stay side by side, holding hands while we ran.

"Everything's okay, Richard." His smile was bigger than life. "See?" He held his free hand, his right, straight out to his right side, his little fist closed. His hand held nothing but air.

I glanced, for his sake. "See what?"

"This is little Jesus." Lewis introduced me to the empty air beside him, just as if I had said that yes, I did see someone. I can't help your unbelief, as Lewis could not help mine in that moment.

"I don't see—" I caught myself. "Yes, I see. Everything's going to be all right then, isn't it?"

"Yeah." Lewis nodded, looking ahead. "Let's just keep going the way that we're going."

"I agree," I said, Lewis still gripping my right hand.

"Little Jesus says this is the way," said Lewis. "We should run in it."

I couldn't see anything or anyone beside him. But it was enough that he did. It was more than enough.

Those two kept up a running dialogue. Felling dark armies.

"If you gotta go, that's okay," Lewis told him. "Cool . . . I like all these trees . . . Do you play out here by yourself? . . . Oh yeah, I forgot . . . Well, what do you want to sing? . . . Sure I do."

Lewis sang, still running and breathing easy like a racehorse trotting through warm-ups.

I got a home in glory land that outshines the sun . . . way beyond the blue . . .

I took Jesus as my Savior, you take him too . . . I took Jesus as my—

Lewis stopped singing and started talking. "Hey, this song is about you . . . You can't sing about you . . . Yeah, I guess so."

He sang a slightly altered version.

They took Jesus as their Savior, you take him too . . . way beyond the blue.

"He wants me and him to run up ahead," Lewis told me.

"Sure, ya'll go ahead."

I was a little disappointed. He must've seen it. "I'm gonna see ya again, Richard."

"Sure, that'll be great."

He smiled and took off. And I thought I was a strong runner.

I coasted like a champ now, pacing like a thoroughbred. I thought of Julie, and I started to remember what she'd said and sung in my dream after I collided with the rock. Seeing it again in my mind's eye calmed and delighted me at the same time. It also challenged me, excited me. According to Pete the Poet, that would drain my endurance rather than expand it. I wondered if this was normal. That a girl would calm you, delight you, challenge and excite you. I noticed the inherent rhyme and said it aloud.

"Calm you, delight you, challenge and excite you."

It sounded like a song, so I sang it: "That girl will calm you, delight you, challenge and excite you. Yeah she will calm ya, delight ya, challenge and excite ya!"

"Did you make that up?" A voice right behind me scared the peace out of me.

CHAPTER 16

Whaaaa!" I glanced back. It was my rival.

"Sorry," Doug Gillihan said. "Didn't mean to sneak up on you."

I don't believe you. You're a mean and gutless guy and how did you catch up to me?

"S'all right," I said. All of a sudden, my breathing was labored. Doug drew breaths like Lewis had, like he was lying in a hammock. Off and on, he sang pieces of Jim Croce's "Time in a Bottle."

"Man, you've had a pretty good clip goin' here," he said. "I thought I'd never catch up."

Humble. Bummer. I wanted to hold you in low esteem.

"You run for Silas?" he said.

"How'd you know . . . I go to . . . Silas?" I said between breaths.

"Just guessing. I haven't seen you at Dothan. You run?"

"Naw."

"I do," he said.

"I figured."

"But it's a little different carrying this battle axe around." He shifted the war club from one hand to the next. It suddenly felt heavy in my own left hand. I put it in my right.

We rounded a bend in the woods and there was our old buddy Pepper, still moving but looking like he was going to keel over at any minute.

"Reckon we should club him in the head when we pass him?" Doug joked.

"Naw."

189

"You're right. Let's be nice," Doug whispered to me. "He's feeling the strain."

We coasted by Pepper, whose face was so red I worried for him.

"You okay?" I tried to say it without suggesting he looked like he was not.

He grunted, enough of a snarl for me to know yes, he was okay, and no, he didn't want any concern coming from the likes of Doug and me. He grimaced and wheezed as we passed him.

My labored breathing told me I had something in common with Pepper. "I know . . . you're going to . . . run ahead of me," I said to Doug.

"Yeah."

"What's keeping you?"

"You don't like my company?"

No I don't. Please feel free to confirm my suspicion that you're a jerk.

"Sorry," I huffed and puffed. "I don't mean . . . nothing by it."

"You're like, ya know, one of the nice guys," Doug said.

I tried to sound cool. "Don't tell anybody."

"I have a strong suspicion . . ." he paused.

At last he's taking a breath in the middle of a sentence!

". . . that you being nice isn't a secret to anybody." He started to leave me. "See ya in the winner's circle. Second place is pretty good."

Aha! A phrase from his lips I can consider prideful!

"See ya, Doug."

"Say," he called back, "what's your name?"

"Prefontaine."

He smiled big and started his own Prefontaine stride.

Deciding I never liked Jim Croce, I ran harder, trying to keep my rival in my sights. If I could hang fairly close to him, within some reasonable distance, Stevie and the Red/Willie duo might have a shot. The mud pit might be an equalizer. The relay's designers, Scoutmasters and Badge Counselors, obviously saw it that way.

I picked up my pace, hoping there wasn't too much ground left for me to cover. Doug took a left and disappeared ahead of me.

That has to be the back straightaway! Start striding a little longer, and get ready to kick.

I cut then to the left, where Doug had cut. It wasn't the straight-away, not yet.

Duffey was there, along with a huge contingent of other Scouts and some adult leaders. He jumped up and down, beside another break in the running path, this one to the right.

"Cut this way! Cut this way!" Duffey hollered, fearful I wouldn't see the break in the path. Honestly, he hollered at me, like the world would end if everyone for miles didn't hear him.

"Circumcise this way! Circumcise, Richard!"

To this day, I can't hear the word in church or read it in my Bible without recalling Duffey's entirely innocent and thunderous pro-nouncement. I suppose the humor of the incident could have worked against my efforts, draining my energy. It didn't.

I forgot about Doug as a courter of Julie and dwelled on my bud-dies in the troop. Duffey's antics gave me an adrenaline rush; the guys buzzed in my head, a mythic corps of brothers. In my mind's eye, I saw Duffey virtually drowning but pulling out a game short swim for us. And Christopher skidding over the lake to give us a real shot at this. I hadn't been able to watch Batman, but I imagined him now running along the crest of the hill on the opposite side of the lake. Donnie, a very mediocre runner, probably lost us a little ground, but not for lack of effort. He collapsed getting me the war club, mouth-ing our troop chant about having a bold heart and a simple faith. If such sentiments, particularly the pursuit of goals larger than our self-interest, take root in our teen years, our adult ones are graced.

I took the cut to the right. Down the straightaway now, kicking early, I hoped I had enough wind to not give out before crossing the line. I was heartened to see Doug not far ahead.

"All right, Richard!" I heard Batman hollering a little ahead and to my left. I saw him and Christopher jumping up and down, the lat-ter yelling too now. "Way to go you brainiac! Kick it in. Go, go, go!"

I saw Zack now, waiting for me to get him the war club, and I felt my runner's kick quicken rather than wilt. The first line of the Scout Oath invaded me, fueling me.

On my honor, I will do my best . . .

Just as Duffey had, and Christopher had, and Batman and Donnie. And all the Scouts, from all the troops.

To do my duty . . .

In my mind I heard Donnie singing by the fire when a Scout day was done: . . . *Silently each Scout should ask, "Have I done my daily task?"*

To my right, kept off the runner's straightaway by a boundary rope, Donnie clapped his hands, said, "Crush it to the max!" and almost fell over cheering me.

It occurred to me, though the outcome was yet to be determined, the race was already won by the standard of embedding camaraderie and deep effort in the hearts of boys soon to be men.

Doug crossed the line and surrendered the club to his troopmate.

I could not move my legs any faster than the rubberlike sprint that had captured them. I counted seconds. One Mississippi two Mississippi three Mississippi four Mississippi . . . not stopping until I crossed the line and said the fourteenth Mississippi. I felt my legs give way, played out, sending me sprawling on my face in the rocky dirt. I turned over onto my back and held the war club straight up in the air. Zack seized the talisman and disappeared. But not before I heard him say, "You're my hero, Richard."

I tried to stand up, but it didn't happen. Duffey and Donnie were over top of me then, picking me up, one under each arm. We stood motionless for a few seconds watching Zack's backside whipping away from us like he was running down a long line drive he had no business catching. Zack had what they call "game speed." He was not a track star, but put him in a game situation and he seemed to find speed that didn't belong to him. His heart was bigger than his ability, and that made the difference when it counted.

My friends turned me to the right and started walking me. I felt some juice coming back into my legs.

I looked around. "Is that troop of mentally . . . you know, mentally handicapped guys around here?"

"Haven't seen 'em," said Donnie. "Reckon they're not participating."

"They did the run," I said.

Duffey said, "I don't think so. Zack told us they decided not to."

"But they did," I insisted. "I ran with Lewis."

"Who's Lewis?" the two said at precisely the same time. Duffey parroted, "Bread and butter, dad and mother," which was supposed to banish the curse incurred by randomly saying the same words at the same time.

"Superstition is not—" Donnie stopped, seeing that Duffey was chuckling and obviously not harboring genuine superstitions. "Anyway, the Special Troop's not doing the mud pit finish. You know that."

"I know," I said.

"Step lively, boys." Duffey grinned. "'Bout twenty yards or so through these trees, big guy. Can you make it?"

"You're bleeding," Donnie said.

"It's nothing," I said. And it wasn't. I was so pumped up. Just like every Scout that day.

Duffey was tickled, trying not to laugh. "You didn't cross that line. You fell over it. Is it okay if I . . ."

"Go ahead and laugh. I know I looked funny."

The three of us laughed together.

I felt my legs getting solid. "Let's pick it up. I want to see the finish."

They helped me hop and skip and hustle through the sparse line of trees to the edge of the mud pit. Scouts and Scoutmasters were lined up on either side and we elbowed and "Duffeyed" our way in so we could see.

Red and Willie looked ready, side by side, watching the spot ahead where Stevie and the others would emerge from over the top of three long horizontal trees felled by a storm a couple of years back. They had carved footsteps up the front side of the trees, hidden from our view, so everyone could get over them. The goal was to get over them fast, and slide or step down on our side of the trees and not drop the war club. Then get the club to your mud pit guys.

Zack was wise to give this task to Stevie. He was nimble, surefooted and sure-handed. He'd get over the trees and get to the pit fast with the club in his hand.

The crowd—all of us by the mud—was quiet, listening for clues to the race hidden in the distance behind the felled trees. Exciting things were happening, we heard yells, sounding, by turns, triumphant and concerned. We waited, hushed, to see someone slip over the top of the three trees.

A long green tee shirt slithered over the top and Doug and his troop cheered. But while their tall boy was shimmying down the tree wall, Stevie and his little yellow tee shirt appeared at the wall's top.

We shouted variations of "There he is!" and "Stevie," our cries mingling with those of Doug's troop for their boy.

Donnie said, "Zack must've burned up his . . . whooaaa!"

All of us watched in a mix of horror and amazement as Stevie jumped from the top of the high tree wall. We measured it later as a fifteen-foot drop, and it looked every bit of that distance now, seeing Stevie's legs folding into his chest when he landed on the ground. For a second, I thought he was stuck there, or something like an ankle or worse might have broken. But he rose and ran, about two strides behind Long Green who was more tall than fast.

No other Scout would come over the tree wall for many minutes. It was a two troop race.

They reached their last handoffs simultaneously, Long Green handing off his war club, and Stevie handing ours to Willie. Red, our Scout Bearer, bore Willie on his shoulders, mirroring Troop 21's two-headed anchor team. With Willie's little arms draped close around Red's head, it looked like Red was sporting a Willie helmet.

The two two-headed bipeds ran into the knee-deep mud that hazarded the forty-yard obstacle lanes in the last leg of the Indian War Club Relay Race.

Everybody was shouting so loud, I couldn't make out what anyone was saying. Maybe they weren't words. Even the Scouts from other troops were captivated by the neck and neck finish, particularly since their troops were far behind. I tried to gauge who these third parties were yelling for to win and decided there was no clear favorite. Except of course that a sizable number were hoping one of the teams or both would drop their Club Wielder and themselves into the mud. I don't think they cared about disqualifying them so much as they cared to see the mud triumph.

But both Scout Bearers were strong and careful, and both teams were locked dead even. They reached the first obstacle two-by-four at the same time, dangerously close to bumping into each other. The Green Bearer was a tad taller and thinner than Red, but their strength was about the same. They were both crossing the first two-by-four with relative ease, given the top heavy weight of the little Scouts on their shoulders. But both Willie and the other Club Wielder flipped around in the process. That is, they started with face and knees facing forward, and they both swung around in the process of their Bearers getting over the two-by-four.

Now Red was pressing forward and Willie was facing backward, looking over the top of Red's head but trying to turn back around, without dropping the sizable War Club.

Troop 21's contingent was suffering precisely the same calamity, making both teams' Bearers struggle mightily to see ahead.

It's amazing what you can hear over the roar of the crowd when you focus on single voices. I heard Red's admonitions and Willie's squeaky rejoinders.

"Don't drop it!"

"I swear I won't!" Willie promised.

"Stop squirming!"

"I swear I can't!" Willie explained. "Can you see?"

"It don't matter!"

"God help us!" Willie petitioned.

I thought one of the Troop 21 guys must be named Bartholomew, because it sounded like that's what the troop was shouting. I found out later that their Bearer's nickname was Mule and their Club Wielder, a kid every bit as little as Willie, was named Bart. Come to think of it, "Bart-on-a-mule" was not a bad descriptive for the confused creature that struggled mightily through the mud that day.

The contestants actually collided fairly violently at one point. Both war clubs waved innocently in the air, staying out of the fracas. But Red's and the other Scout Bearer's heads smacked together like balls in a bowling alley ready tray. This was their first great collision.

Somewhat miraculously they righted themselves before any war club or any War Club Wielder was dropped. And both Bearers managed to see enough around their human choke collars to get to the second two-by-four obstacle and start climbing over.

They were neck and neck, so close they were unintentionally bumping shoulders.

The little fellow Bart wore glasses. Why he hadn't set them aside at the start of this day is an excellent question. Maybe he was blind without them; the lenses were quite large. As both teams flopped over the final two-by-four, Bart's glasses came off.

The sound of someone crying out in fearful despair is a different cry from the masses' cries of excitement. Bart's cry, inimitable, transcended all others.

The glasses plunged into the deep, watery mud.

"Stop!" Willie and Bart shouted, intense, at almost the same instant. And Red and Mule both stopped, right beside each other. And all of us watching were stopped, still and silent. It was as if someone had turned off the hurly burly world just at that second.

There were still no other competitors in sight. Troops 44 and 21 had far outdistanced the other competition.

In a quick move, Willie leaned down and dove his free arm, the one not brandishing the club, under the muddy water, a move that resembled a kingfisher breaking the water's surface. He kept his hand under for three or four seconds, and then pulled the mud soaked glasses out, holding them high like Arthur's sword from the stone.

Everybody cheered and laughed at the same time. Willie wiped the glasses off quickly on his tee shirt, a futile act. He handed them to Bart, a gesture noble and childlike. There lies the honor.

Bart said, "Hey, thanks man."

Willie said, "A guy's gotta be able to see, ya'll."

Mule said, "Are you ready, Bart?"

Bart put his muddy frames on. "I'm ready."

Mule asked Red if he was ready and Red said he was born ready, so Mule said "Go!"

And just like that, the world was turned back on.

We exploded into cheers as Mule/Bart and Red/Willie rampaged exactly alongside each other, shoulder to shoulder through the last forty feet or so of the mud that went from waist deep to thighs to knees to shins and naught and then . . . their second great collision.

CHAPTER 17

There must be some universal law about the shifts and accompanying weight displacements that affect little guys on bigger guys' shoulders when two competing Bearers are so evenly matched. The law is one of magnetism. The Bearers are drawn together.

Inches from the clear chalk finish line, Red and Mule crashed, as if collapsing into each other. The impact separated Mule from Bart, knocking Mule to the ground short of the finish line, but sending Bart on a short effective flight crossing the line in the air, still holding the war club aloft as he landed on, of all things, his feet. I don't believe he could actually see the ground through the mud on his glasses, but he landed standing upright. I applauded, dumbfounded by the sight.

In bizarre confluence, Red and Willie stayed intact at impact, the crash jettisoning them across the finish line seconds after the airborne, bespectacled Bart.

Troops 44 and 21 descended on the four muddy racers with delirious shouts of praise for whichever tandem we thought had won. It was obvious to us that Red and Willie had won, because they had stayed together and crossed the finish line as one while the other team had come undone. It was just as obvious to Troop 21 that they had won since their War Club Wielder had crossed the line ahead of our guys and no part of his body had touched the ground before he crossed the line.

"Everybody clear off of the finish line," Ranger Burkett motioned to all of us. "The rest of the teams are coming through here any minute."

"Who won?" Duffey asked.

"We'll decide that when everybody's finished here," he said.

We cleared the course. It was very entertaining to see the others navigate the mud pit, with varying degrees of comical success and hilarious failure. When you know you're not a contender for the title, you have more liberty to laugh at your efforts and even tease yourself. They did. I noticed too that Willie and Bart were hanging out, joshing around like they were best buddies while they watched the finishers.

When all the teams had finished, Mr. Forrester gathered us around and he and Zack said how proud they were of us for the incredible race we'd run.

Our little Troop 44 and the enormous Troop 21 gathered around Ranger Burkett to learn the final, official results.

"Give me that sheet," the ranger said to another man. "The rules." The other man handed him the sheet that would determine our fate. The sheet was folded many times, and stained. It looked like something these men may have written up over breakfast this morning. But at least they'd written something down.

"Good grief, Fred," Ranger Burkett said, still unfolding. "What is this? Bacon grease?"

"Those are the official rules," Fred announced somberly, as if his official tone could sanctify the document.

"Okay, here's the mud pit." Ranger Burkett waved a hand to cut off our mumblings and rumblings. We listened. "On the final leg of the relay, no part of the War Club Wielder's body may touch the ground while he carries the club and travels the obstacle lane . . . and then in parentheses . . . the mud pit." He looked at Fred. "That's it?"

"That's what we have," Fred said. "What's written there."

Doug Gillihan, obviously one of his troop's Scout leaders, said "Ranger Burkett, in these circumstances, Troop 21 is honored to accept the official result is a tie."

There were groans from some of his troopmates, but when Doug looked over his shoulder and said quietly, "Guys," the dissenters shut up quick.

Zack looked briefly at Mr. Forrester, who pretended not to see him. It was Zack's call.

"That's all right with Troop 44," Zack said.

"Let me see the four," said Ranger Burkett. We all knew which four he meant.

Red and Mule stepped to the front, both looking serious.

"Where's the two little guys?" Ranger Burkett looked around.

Willie and Bart emerged, joined at the hip.

"Your glasses are looking a lot better," the ranger said.

"Yes sir." Bart giggled. "I cleaned 'em off. Licked 'em."

"Uh-huh. Ties . . . I don't like them. A tie is like . . . hugging your mom."

Someone deep in the Scout crowd said, "Your sister."

"What was that?" Ranger Burkett asked, his tone gruff.

Someone said, "Kissing," and someone else said, "It doesn't matter."

"If you've got something to say," the ranger growled, "speak up! I'll not abide all that mumbo-jumbo."

Duffey whispered to me, "Yosemite Sam."

Willie raised his hand, like he was in school. I gave him a quick look, trying to spare him. But he kept it raised.

"Whaddya want?" Yosemite barked.

"I was just thinking, sir, that if we called it a tie, it wouldn't be like nobody won. It would be like both teams won. Wouldn't it?"

"Not to me it wouldn't," Yosemite snorted. "Maybe to you." He said "you" like Willie was a lower life form.

Duffey chimed in. "Troop 44 would be real proud of a tie."

Yosemite glared at him. Some people don't need a reason to be angry. They live there. "Who are you?"

"Second Class Scout Frances Duffey. Apple of my mama's eye."

"Are you speaking for the whole tribe, Mr. Duffey?" Yosemite knew Duffey was part Cherokee.

"Every last Injun," Duffey said with a big smile, sparking lots of Scout laughs and a sharp eye from Yosemite, who told us all to pipe down. I feared for Duffey, but Doug Gillihan spoke up before Yosemite could take a bite out of the big guy.

"Sir, Troop 21 agrees with Troop 44," said Doug, sounding like he was running for office. Some guys just can't help that. "And we want to thank you for this awesome and fun race."

"You're welcome," Yosemite said with an odd nod. "Are you the senior patrol leader?"

"Emeritus, sir." Doug put his hand out. "Doug Gillihan, sir."

Yosemite shook his hand. "Gillihan?"

"That's right, sir."

"You feel a tie is the right thing to do here?"

"In this instance, yes sir, I do." Doug sounded like he was chairing a board meeting. In his adult years, he would chair many.

"All right, then." Yosemite raised his voice so every Scout heard. "The 1976 Camp Sequoyah Indian War Club Relay Race is hereby declared a tie. Troops 21 and 44 will share the title."

"What about the banner?" someone shouted from the cluster that obviously represented Troop 21.

Yosemite shrugged. "That's up to you two troops. Work it out."

"We don't care about no banner," Duffey said, raising protests from Batman and Christopher.

"It'd be nice to see on our troop flag," said Stevie.

"We ain't got no troop flag," said Duffey.

The two winning troops' power brokers, a group that included Doug, Zack, Mr. Forrester, and a man who was apparently serving as Troop 21's Scoutmaster but had stayed entirely mute throughout the discussion over race results, gathered with the four boys that had collided at the finish line. Red's right forearm leaned on Willie's left shoulder. Red said something to the little guy and Willie laughed, a monumental breakthrough for Red.

Yosemite climbed into his Jeep. Willie's courage was not entirely spent; he ran over to the ranger.

"Is it all right if I bring you some tomatoes from our garden, sir?"

The man was confounded by the request. "Why in thunder would you do that?"

"Because they're homegrown. Them's the best kind. Ma and me live just down the road a ways from your ranger cabin."

The ranger started to repeat the same question, since Willie had, intentionally or otherwise, avoided answering. But he dropped it, said, "Suit yourself," and peeled off down the narrow camp road that led to his cabin.

Christopher made an observation that, for a Boy Scout, was borderline philosophical. "It's funny how having a Jeep makes you look so powerful, when everybody else is moving everywhere on foot."

"I'd like to hit these trails on my bicycle," Stevie mused.

I asked Stevie if his legs felt all right.

"Yeah, that's right, oh man," Batman jumbled his words. "What's the idea of scaring us all like that? Jumping off the top of them trees like it was a house on fire!"

"The other guy was ahead," Stevie said matter-of-factly. "I told myself before the race that if I had to, I could probably jump from the top and hit the ground and close the gap with a fellow. You know, if he was ahead of me."

"Probably?" I asked.

"Well, I coulda got hurt," he said without emotion. "And that woulda been kind of a drag."

"You coulda broke a leg," Donnie agreed. "We should be taking you to a hospital right now."

Stevie recited folk wisdom in a sing-song voice. "If coulds and shoulds were candy and nuts, then we'd all have a Merry Christmas."

While the rest of us looked at each other, laboring over the translation, Duffey asked him where he'd picked up the saying.

"BoDean," he said.

"That pothead!" Duffey gawked at him.

"I don't think he was high when he said it to me," Stevie said, serious. "He was smoking in the boys' room—"

"His home away from home," Christopher smirked.

". . . but it wasn't nothing but a Marlboro. I told him he could come back to church. And he should join our Scout troop and all. He said if coulds and shoulds were candy and nuts, we'd all have a Merry Christmas. I thought he was trying to be funny, so I laughed. But he didn't laugh."

Nobody said anything. We all missed BoDean.

Stevie felt obliged to elaborate. "So I could have or should have broken something, but see I didn't—"

"We get it," Donnie cut him off.

I looked at Duffey. "You kind of annoyed the ranger."

"I don't know how that happens," he said. "I don't aim to get under the skin, but it's like I just do with some people."

"Like me," Christopher said. "I hate you."

"Shut up, maggot. I'm glad that Gilligan fellow started talking."

"Gillihan," I said.

"He seems like he kind of fancies himself," Duffey continued, "and he sounds like, I dunno, like he's about to invite us all over to his fancy restaurant, but in a nice way, ya know?"

"I know," I said.

"His dad donated the bulk of the money to build this camp," said Donnie.

"How do you know that?" I hoped it was hearsay.

"He told me. In a very nice, subtle way."

I'm competing with the heir to Rockefeller's estate. Only he's a nice heir. Great.

"That explains why Yosemite gave in all of a sudden," said Batman, and then in his Yosemite voice, "Gotta be nice to the rich critter! He ain't just another varmint!"

"What's Americus mean?" Duffey asked me.

"What?"

"Yosemite asked Moneybags if he was the senior patrol leader and he said he was Americus."

"Emeritus," I clarified.

"That's what I'm saying. What's it mean?"

"It's like . . . being retired. I guess he used to be their senior patrol leader."

"Sounds important," Stevie said.

"That guy could tell us he was going to the latrine," said Duffey, "and make it sound important."

"It is important for him," Christopher said.

The power brokers broke up their powwow. Mr. Forrester walked off talking to the other guys' Scoutmaster and our guys and Doug Gillihan walked over to us.

"They can have the banner," Duffey said.

"No, no," Doug said.

"There will be two identical banners," said Zack. "A second one will be made in the next couple of weeks and both troops will have one. In the meantime, the original banner will stay here at Camp Sequoyah, in the main office."

"An equitable solution for all." That was Doug. "I told Zack you should be running for Silas. On the track team."

"Oh well, that's, I don't know," I fumbled.

"I'd like to shake your hand again, Mr. Willie." Doug took Willie's hand and pumped it enthusiastically. "Come by our campsite tonight and we'll share a round of mocha."

"Moke uh?"

"A mix of coffee and cocoa."

"Cocoa sounds good, sir."

Duffey clapped Willie fondly over the head. "He ain't a sir."

Doug addressed Stevie. "I see you survived your jump off the top of Timbuktu. You're a brave soul."

"Seemed like the thing to do at the time."

"You're a brave soul."

"Cherokee, right?" Doug said to Duffey. "And a bit of Choctaw."

"How'd you know that?" Duffey was pleased.

"I'd like to say I just knew, but I asked Zack here."

"Dad was born Choctaw," Duffey said real serious. "But he's kind of Americus now."

"Beg your pardon?"

Troop 21's Scoutmaster called out that the troop was leaving together.

"See you guys later. Been a pleasure." He gave a wave and trotted off.

Red put a headlock on Willie. "Forget that cocoa junk. Stay in our campsite tonight and we'll drink Dr. Pepper till we puke. Okay? Okay?"

"Okay! Okay! I will!"

Red released him, and Duffey said, "That Doug guy's got my vote."

"For what?" Zack said.

"Me too," said Stevie.

"For what!" Zack said again.

"I dunno," Duffey shrugged. "But he's obviously runnin' for something, don'tcha think? It's weird, he's real nice and all. And I think he's serious about being nice. He just sounds like he's running for Congress."

"Maybe he was just born that way," Donnie said. "Born to run for office. Dad says you got to kiss a lot of babies to be a Congressman."

"Gross," Red frowned.

"Congress . . ." Christopher sounded sad. "Well . . . can't nothing be done for him."

"You guys are Loony Tunes." Zack shook his head. "There are worse fates, ya know."

"Than kissing babies?" Red's face contorted.

We started walking back to camp, basking in the glow of having spent ourselves in the grand task of carrying a wood mallet across Lake Etowah and over hills and down trails and to the top of Timbuktu and down again into Amazonian mud.

We spontaneously split into pairs, talking. Red and Willie buzzed and chattered, reliving their mud adventure like it was the last leg of an Olympic contest. I heard Duffey tell Donnie that yes, he sucked in more lake than he did air on his first and last foray into competitive swimming.

Zack and I walked and talked. I told him Doug and Julie had dated a lot.

"No kidding?" He got a big kick out of it.

"You think that's funny?"

"Oh no." He did. "Um . . . does he know you've been seeing her?"

"I don't think so. First I thought he did. That she must have told him and that's why he was being so nice to me. But then I see him being nice to everybody."

"Yeah," he laughed. "Kissing all of us babies."

I tried to laugh with him. But he could tell.

"What's the matter?" he said.

"I really like her. I'm maybe crazy about her."

"Maybe crazy?"

"I'm definitely bonkers about her."

"That's good," he said. "'Cause she's definitely crazy about you."

"You're just saying that. This Doug guy—" I went through the bleak list—"his dad's a millionaire, and Doug's tall and talented and popular and on the track team and senior emeritus patrol leader, and on top of it he's a really nice guy."

Zack didn't say anything.

"Well?" I said too loud.

"Well what?"

"Aren't you going to tell me he's not all those things?"

I guess he didn't want to lie. Even for a buddy. "I don't know if he's talented," he said finally.

"Oh that's—that's great."

"And he's not really that tall."

"He's taller than *you!*" I said. "And you're a high school god!"

"I'm sure that means a lot to him." It wasn't like Zack to be sarcastic, but I think he was still enjoying my angst.

"I want you to worry with me," I blurted out. "Why won't you worry with me?"

"Because it's silly. She likes *you*, not him."

I liked the way he said that so plain. But I still needed something more. "How do you know that?"

"I don't know that."

What kind of high school god are you? But I didn't say it.

"Look"—he found mercy—"I can't know that, and you can't know it, on account of we're guys. We have no antennae to pick up who likes who and who's crazy about who. But girls, they have like an entire sub-space station crammed with antennas for who likes who and how much. So, ask Rebecca who Julie likes. She'll tell you. Ask her privately, so she can really open up. She says Julie thinks you're dreamy."

I was greatly encouraged. "Dreamy's pretty good, isn't it?"

"Oh yeah. Right up there. Way better than cute."

We walked for a time without talking. Satisfied to listen to the other guys chatter and tease and promise and break confidences.

"His dad's a millionaire," I said.

"Some girls don't care about money."

"I liked it better when you weren't lying to me."

"Some girls don't care," he said again, confident.

"Fitzgerald didn't think so."

"Who?"

"F. Scott."

"Oh," he said. "The Gatsby guy. Writers don't know everything."

For whatever reason, Donnie, Batman, and Christopher took off running, leaving the group. Probably a contest of sorts.

Red, Duffey, Stevie, and Willie apparently decided on their own contest. They knelt in the dirt road and Stevie climbed on Duffey's shoulders and Willie on Red's. The two carriers stood up, and all four of them were laughing so hard the game was almost impossible. They gave it a go, racing to what Duffey called "that lonesome pine there." Red and Willie had just about won a close race when Duffey leaned over and basically dropped Stevie into Red, so the four of them crashed short of the tree.

"You weigh too much," Duffey scolded Stevie.

They were a sight, the four of them lying on the side of the road. And Red laughing so hard with little Willie.

"See you back at camp," Zack said, as we passed them.

"Oh, we'll catch up, ya'll," said Duffey.

We walked on.

"I guess you know," I said, "that if Red had run in your place, and you'd been the one carrying Willie on his shoulders, we'd have won the race outright."

"I don't know that. And you don't either."

"Red's faster than you. And you're stronger in the shoulders and all around. To carry Willie."

"To carry the Scout," Zack said, "you can't weigh more than one hundred fifty."

"I remember the weigh-ins for the baseball team."

"Red's not on the baseball team."

"You're barely one forty-five."

"I know that," he said. "And you know that. But Red doesn't."

The four of them passed us, running the same competition, Duffey toting Stevie, and Willie slipping around on the back of the complaining but amused Red.

I asked Zack if the Special Troop had participated in the relay race at all.

"No. I guess it just didn't fit their schedule."

"What about the kid that finished the Long-Distance first? Ahead of Doug Gillihan."

"Nobody finished ahead of Gillihan."

Don't sweat it, Powell. There are a number of possible explanations. Maybe Lewis just veered the course near the end and traipsed off to rejoin his troop. Did you think of that? Or maybe . . .

I said, "You ever think maybe we need an instruction manual to help us know . . . just basic stuff?"

"Basic stuff like?"

"What's real and what's not."

"We got one," he said. "The Word. And not just written. The Word became flesh and dwelt among us."

"Dwelt among us," I echoed those words. "Do I ever say stuff that you find hard to believe?"

"Richard, you could tell me the earth was made of diamonds and dust and I'd believe you."

"It *is* made of diamonds and dust. Spiritually. Things eternally significant, and things that are worthless and so much dust. Everything falls into one of those two categories."

"Like I said. I always believe you."

"I think maybe my problem is that sometimes my imagination kinda takes off."

"That's a problem? I'm thinking . . . our imaginations are part of the new creation we are in Christ. They're sanctified. Or at least becoming more and more sanctified, along with the rest of us."

"You sound like Pastor White."

"Thank you." Zack grinned. "Anyway, I trust your imagination more than other people's observations."

We stopped talking. We walked side by side, surrounded by distinct summer breezes blowing through the tops of the trees at Camp Sequoyah.

CHAPTER 18

According to the ads on TV when I was a kid, girls were invited to "sing around the campfire, join the Campfire Girls." Their name could just as easily have been Campfire *Singing* Girls.

We Boy Scouts were not singers, save one song Donnie sometimes sang in the late evening, by our fire, no more than a couple of times. He tried to get us into it; said it was a Scout song from way back.

"Cousin Ernest taught it to me," Donnie said. "He's a Life Scout," as if that would move us from skeptics to enthusiasts.

As usual, it was Zack who meted out grace. "I want to hear it."

"Yeah," Christopher said. "We want to hear it."

"Who's we?" Duffey glared comically at Christopher, who was but an arm's length away. Then Duffey jerked a fist as if he was going to pound on Christopher, and Christopher jerked away from him. Such things meant that he was accepted in Duffey's world.

"Okay," Duffey said to Donnie. "Let's hear it."

As possessed as I am with the spirit of word recollection, I cannot recall the song's precise words. My cursed gift seems to dwell with spoken and written words, not those sung. I do remember themes, questions, in what Donnie sang. It was a short song, with questions a Boy Scout ought to ask at night, before he goes to sleep. Have I kept my honor bright? Can I guilt my sleep tonight? Have I done what I ought to be prepared? Have I dared to be prepared? The latter question struck me as unusual. In what manner is being prepared answering a dare? Is being prepared courageous? I suppose it depends on what one prepares for.

This campout was different; Peachy wanted to camp with us, one night only, and Pastor White made it too. He was pleased to have another man "spend some time with the boys." I think he felt bad that he leaned on Rafer's dad so much to camp with us, since he was often pressed for time. He needn't have felt any guilt. Mr. Forrester was solid and sincere; we boys all knew that he genuinely cared about our well-being, including our spiritual formation, which he referred to as "ya'll getting deeper into Jesus and Jesus getting deeper into ya'll." It's not often as complex as we make it.

Peachy talked Uncle Albert into coming this weekend, and the pastor liked that even more. Batman kicked off a round of laughs when Uncle Albert asked him what he and the guys found to do all day out in the woods.

In his best shot at a Liverpool accent, Batman said, "We're so sorry . . . Uncle Albert. But we haven't done a blessed thing all day."

Uncle Albert said, "That's the Monkees, right?"

"I been waiting so long to have a shot at saying that . . ." Batman stopped. "Monkees?! My British accent was good, wasn't it?"

"Oh yes," Uncle Albert encouraged him.

Duffey straightened out Batman. Sort of. "Maybe he don't know which bands is American, and which bands is foreigners. Ever think of that?"

"I meant to say the Beatles," Uncle Albert clarified. Sort of. "Your British accent was very fine. Excellent."

"You know," Zack told Duffey, "in another country, we Americans are the foreigners."

"You're kidding me." Duffey was unsure how to process that.

———

Later in the evening, I sat by the fire with an odd mix of men: a brilliant agnostic professor, an exorcist, a pastor, and a sometimes-employed housepainter. I stepped in and around many obscure notions in my mind while my teen friends stepped in the darkness toward their tents. I heard Willie say, "A guy's gotta be able to see."

"Hey Willie," I called.

"Yeah."

"Have you met Julie?"

"That's your girlfriend, right?"

"You ever met? Ever talk to her?"

"No. But she must be real nice."

"How do you know that?" I asked.

"Because you are you."

"Night, Willie."

"G'night, Richard. Ow. Can't see over here."

Peachy, Pastor White, Uncle Albert, and I were left around the fire. We could tell the others were not all sleeping. Duffey's tent housed a poker game, the dim flashlight beam shuffling intermittently with the cards.

"You're sure they're not betting money?" Pastor White asked me.

"They use M&M's," I told him honestly. "It's not so much an integrity issue for them. They don't *have* money. And Duffey likes to eat his winnings."

"Savage instinct," Uncle Albert mused.

He and Peachy sat in cloth folding chairs they'd brought for the purpose. Pastor White sat on a thick, long log, and I sat on the ground.

"Doesn't that feel a little cold?" Pastor White asked very politely. "I mean, the ground, on your backside."

"I like it," I said. "It keeps me from overheating this close to the fire."

"That's . . . interesting." I'm sure it was more humorous to him than intriguing. Pastor White was a kind man.

He looked at Peachy, who was looking into the fire. "You want to go through with this?"

"I do. You all need to know."

"Richard too? What about the others?"

I didn't know what they were talking about.

"No," said Peachy. "I'm glad the others are nestled all snug in their tents."

Christmas surfaced in my mind. "The children were nestled all snug in their tents," I said. "While visions of . . . something . . ." I considered what danced in my head at night. "Baseballs danced in their heads."

"Why is it Christmas seems always with us?" Pastor White said with breezy cheer. "Even here. In late spring."

"Because it's the epicenter," Peachy said, staring down the fire. "It's the primal invasion."

Donnie's dad, Uncle Albert, and I exchanged looks.

"I used to think," Peachy said slowly, "of Christmas as a harmless season. One wherein people reminded themselves to look after each other. Care for those less fortunate. The season wherein Scrooge learns to care for those less fortunate. Now I wish for bigger things. I wish for Scrooge to go beyond learning. To be changed. Made a new creature, as the apostle claims is possible."

"What do *you* claim is possible?" the pastor asked.

"Many things," Peachy said. "Too many things."

"Your salvation?" Pastor White asked.

"Not all things," he said. "Tell the boy."

The pastor took a long breath in, before saying, "Richard, Dr. McLeod . . ."

"Peachy," he said in a quiet voice.

"Peachy wants to tell us something. Things that are happening to him. He thinks I might be able to help him." Pastor White paused, looking at Peachy. "You tell me if I say anything that's not right."

"You're good," Peachy said. I think he meant what the pastor was saying was accurate. But Peachy's tone also had a declarative sound. Like he considered the pastor a good man. Unusually good.

"Well, as I say, he wanted to tell you, Richard, Uncle Albert, and me. The three of us."

"Sure," I said. I had no idea what was coming. "If it's easier for just ya'll three to talk, I can go to my tent."

"No," Peachy said. "I need your insight."

That totally threw me. I figured if you had Pastor White, a remarkably wise and humble man, for insight, and Uncle Albert too, you were set. I started saying so, making reference also to what I thought was the salient fact of my being "just a kid."

He didn't buy it. "Stop drawing 'I'm just a kid' like it's a white flag when you want out of a fight." He didn't say it mean. But it wasn't a suggestion either.

"Okay."

I thought Uncle Albert might say something, but he seemed content to listen and watch the fire. More than content; he seemed to enjoy Peachy's one-sided banter with me.

"When you heard me say the words 'primal invasion' a few minutes ago, what was the first thought that came into your mind?"

"Are you talking to me?" I said, sure that he was.

Peachy looked like something occurred to him. "I was. But first you, Nathan. I say primal invasion. In reference to Christmas. Your first thought."

Pastor White didn't hesitate. "I do a simple little jump in my head and I think of Jesus invading this world. God's Son comes to Earth. He will make salvation possible."

"Excellent!" Peachy said. "Directly on point, and precisely what I guessed a man of your background and sincere spirit would focus on."

"Thanks." Pastor White smiled the calm smile of people who know how to humbly receive kind words that they really do not need for self-affirmation.

"Now you," Peachy said swiftly to me. "Primal invasion." He threw the words at me. "Your first thought."

"First thought?"

"The very first. Don't think. Just go!"

I didn't think. I just went. "Primal suggests there are other, secondary invasions. Incursions in the wake of the primal, perhaps in response to the first."

"Whew," Pastor White breathed low.

"Anything else?" Peachy asked.

"Primal also, in my mind, conjures images of disruption. A primal invasion is not benign. It's not easily remedied. Its effects are long-standing."

"Whew," the pastor said again.

Uncle Albert smiled. A sad smile, I thought.

"Does that fit Christmas in your mind?" Peachy asked.

I liked his question. "If you mean does it fit Christmas as traditionally celebrated by popular American culture, it does not. If you mean Christmas as the prophets foretold and the Christ fulfilled, then yes, Christmas can dovetail with primal invasion in my mind."

Pastor White asked if it was all right for him to change his answer.

Peachy chuckled. "That may be the prudent course."

"What *he* said." The pastor laughed.

I remembered Peachy's words from the first day we'd met. "Without prudence," I smiled, "the world would spin down to cinders."

"Richard is gifted," Peachy said as if I weren't there. "I don't just mean he's sharp. A genius I'm sure. He also has insights into . . . spiritual realities. Most people, almost everyone, collapse reality into human initiatives. Man causes everything, including his own demise. Wars, internal and external, are conceived and carried to term by humans. Fix humans and all is well. The real war eludes them. Richard not only sees past the human footprint, but he has an instinct for considering the war up front. One of his first instincts is to frame what he hears and sees and feels in terms of the war."

"By war, you mean . . ." Pastor White waited for Peachy to finish the sentence.

"What do I mean, Richard?" Peachy said.

"God and Lucifer."

Long seconds passed with no one speaking. Time around a campfire is drawn out, isn't it?

"It's not something I consciously . . . manufacture," I said. "I'd rather have visions of baseballs dancing in my head."

"So would I," Peachy said soberly. "Truth doesn't ask our preference. Or our permission. It just is."

"Yes," Pastor White sighed. "But I'm afraid the day is coming when people will, I don't know"—he sought the right words—"push Truth off the map, and set up their preferences as the boundaries in which they'll live."

"That's a very poetic image, Nathan," Peachy said.

"Don't look so surprised," he jested. "I'm no Richard Powell, but I can come up with a colorful metaphor once in a blue moon."

"Truth off the map," Peachy mused.

Pastor White recounted a passage from memory. "For the time will come when they will not endure sound doctrine; but after their own lusts shall they heap to themselves teachers, having itching ears . . ."

Peachy said, "And they shall turn away their ears from the truth, and shall be turned unto fables."

"That's it!" Pastor White was impressed.

I felt the liberty to add, "and will turn away their ears from truth and will turn aside to myths."

Pastor White eyed me with some wonder, or maybe he was just being kind. He was that way. "How is it you know that verse?"

"You just preached it," I said.

"I know, but . . ."

"Second Timothy 4. Around verse 3 or so."

"I don't expect my congregation to remember passages word for word."

"They don't," Peachy said. "Richard does."

"Not always," I clarified. "But those verses just struck me. They sounded important. Scary important."

"So they are," Uncle Albert remarked, reminding us he was there.

"How is it," the pastor asked Peachy, "you know Scripture as well as you do, and still you don't . . ." he paused.

"Believe?" Peachy said.

"I was going to say that, but the word doesn't quite fit your situation. You do believe a lot."

"He does," Uncle Albert agreed.

"But you don't believe you can be saved. Still, you seem to believe others can be."

"Yeah," said Peachy. "That's it."

"If I believed as you do," the pastor said, "I would go insane. I couldn't stop screaming."

"I'm screaming now," Peachy said. He tapped his head with his fingers. "In here."

"I'm sorry," Pastor White spoke from his heart.

"You think it's okay that I tell Richard?"

Donnie's dad nodded. "Richard's strong. The Word has made him that way."

I liked how he put that. I couldn't guess what I was about to hear. But, for different reasons, I trusted both the pastor and Peachy entirely.

The wood popped, sparks living short lives overtop shiftless, shifting flames. I had long before discovered more colors in fire than we can name.

"At night," Peachy began, "in the apartment, when I'm trying to sleep, and I can't, which happens quite a bit lately, I lie there for some time. Then . . . the wall in front of me moves."

Out of the corner of my eye, I saw him give me a quick glance. I kept my gaze on the fire. I wasn't sure I wanted to hear this. But it was obvious he felt he needed me to hear it.

"I'm just going to start telling all of you," he said, sounding like one of my teenage friends, "and you can think what you want to."

All four of us looked into the fire.

"The wall opposite my bed turns in on itself. It's like the wall has a pulse. And the pulse generates a kind of spiral. Counterclockwise. It looks to me like the wall expands and shrinks. Different colors come and go. Always in the same order. Starts out yellow. Lemon yellow. Then gray. Different shades of orange. Then red. Very deep red. Covers the entire wall. Just that wall, opposite me. Then the red gets darker. So dark a pitch, it's really almost black. My eyes tell me it's black, but I know in my head it's still a deep, deep red. I know that sounds ridiculous. I recognize the color. The walls beside me and behind me are unchanged. The ceiling is unchanged. Off white. I always hope it's a dream. Maybe it is. But I've had other dreams, where I tell myself to wake up and I always do. This one just . . . doesn't listen to me."

I looked at him. He kept his eyes on the fire. As if to look away would silence him, and he wanted to tell all. I looked back at the fire.

"Then . . . it starts talking. The wall. Same voice. Same tone."

"Do you recognize the voice?" Uncle Albert asked. "From your acquaintances when you're awake?"

"No."

"How about from your past?"

"Do you mean my past life awake?" Peachy looked at the man. "Or my past . . . dreams?"

"Either one."

"I recognize the voice." He looked back at the fire. "Past dreams. Long ago dreams. At least, I was sure at the time they were dreams."

"Go on," Uncle Albert encouraged. "What does the voice say?"

"He talks about the past. My past."

"He?"

"It's very personal," Peachy said. "I have supposed it is a he. It's certainly not a she. When I heard the voice years ago, I always answered it as if it were a . . . man."

"How many years ago? What year or years? Precisely."

"Nineteen fifty-two and fifty-three."

"You're sure?" Uncle Albert said. "That's a long time ago."

"Not to me. Twenty some years feels like yesterday. Especially now. With it happening again."

"Do go on. What does it . . . what does *he* say? You mentioned your past."

"Well . . ." Peachy paused and I felt he might be deciding, as perhaps he had done many times, how much to share and how much to conceal. Then he opened up entirely, with a rush of some of the most unforgettable words I have ever heard.

"He says it's nice to remember. And he wants me to remember things with him. And I try to keep my mouth shut because . . . it never helps to talk to him. But the pull . . . I don't know how else to say it . . . the force from him, from the wall, is fierce. I tell him I don't want to talk. And he says I don't have to anymore, because we're such old friends and he can talk for both of us. He says he wants the formula, but he asks for it like it's no big deal, like it's nothing. I tell him every time I'm not going to give it to him, and I always expect him to get angry and, I don't know, maybe come after me, but he just keeps asking, in a kind of sick, polite way. But the threat . . . is always there. And he knows that I know the threat is there. So far, I think that's what has saved me."

"Saved you?" Uncle Albert asked.

"I don't know what he'll do if he thinks he doesn't need me anymore."

We took a short break then. Peachy from talking, and us from listening. Pastor White stood and plucked a big chunk of dry wood from the stack and set it carefully down on a good spot of coals. It ignited. He smiled at me and sat back down.

"I used to think," Peachy started in again, "all problems, yours, mine, and the world's, were philosophical. What makes one thing bad and another good? Why do people do bad things? Things that hurt people. Why do some people consistently do helpful things? Not haphazard, or accidentally, but consistently. I thought the answers were all epistemological. All captive to our perceptions."

When he took a long pause, Uncle Albert said, "But you don't think that way now."

"No, I don't," Peachy murmured, as if he were apologizing to himself. "I've become a supernaturalist."

"Congratulations," Uncle Albert said in a low voice.

"I hear of people believing in God and angels and such at a young age, and then coming to a time of doubt when they're older. I'm backward. In so many ways. I never believed in a higher power, from my youth through middle age. It's only now, in my seventies, that I doubt my agnostic materialism. I've become a believer."

"In . . . ?" Pastor White waited. As did I. Peachy didn't answer right away.

"You mentioned God and angels," Uncle Albert said.

"I believe God exists. I don't know about angels."

"What don't you know about angels?"

"If I accept the premise of angels, I may be haunted by the prospect of . . . fallen angels."

"It is clear you are already haunted by such a prospect," Uncle Albert said. "What we're considering is whether you are haunted by something more than the prospect."

"Yes," Pastor White said, with virtually no emotion. He did not appear threatened in the least by what Peachy had shared. He actually looked like he was at peace with all things. Later he told me he was praying without ceasing while Peachy shared.

Uncle Albert asked, "How many other people did you tell about these . . . times when the wall spoke to you?"

"I told one doctor, in 1953."

"Psychiatrist?"

"No. I don't trust psychiatrists."

"I understand."

"This was a pig doctor," Peachy said.

"It sounded like you said *pig* doctor."

"Yes. He was a vet. People in the village lived off their pigs. He was a good friend of mine."

Uncle Albert didn't raise an eyebrow. "Did he give you good counsel?"

"He gave me some pills, which I threw away. I don't trust pills. Especially from a pig doctor."

I couldn't help it; I laughed. I was so glad Pastor White laughed with me.

And Peachy smiled. "He said I should eat more fruit."

We laughed again.

"It gets funnier," Peachy said. "Only I don't know if you're going to think this is ha-ha funny or this is funny-strange. I started eating more fruit and the wall went away."

We didn't laugh. Hearing him say "the wall" struck our sober nerve again.

"Well," Uncle Albert tried, unsuccessfully, to raise himself a little from his chair's deep cloth seat. "I feel like this chair is swallowing me." He stopped trying, and smiled. "I suppose there are worse fates. Let me see if I've heard you right, and if we're all tracking on the same line."

"Please," Peachy nodded.

"You're having trouble sleeping nights. Sometimes, while you're lying there, the wall opposite your bed turns different colors and starts to talk to you. You recognize the voice and the wall display from visitations you had some twenty-three years ago. You had not heard the voice or seen the wall since 1953."

"That's right."

"Let's call him Wall Man. He wants something from you. I believe you called it a *formula*. You're reluctant to give it to him. And the recurring visitations by Wall Man . . ."

"I don't know that I'd call them visitations," Peachy interrupted.

"Well someone or something is visiting someone or something

else," Uncle Albert said kindly. "It is perhaps your own mind visiting itself."

"You mean I'm crazy."

"I mean we are *all* crazy," Uncle Albert said, "to the extent that we are all prey to dreams and even hallucinations. Some of us more than others."

"So I'm crazier than others?"

"On the contrary. You are saner."

"That's a scary thought," said Peachy. "I was hoping I was more insane than not. But you know, if I were, I wouldn't know it, would I?" He looked like he was trying hard not to laugh. At himself, I supposed.

Uncle Albert saw it too. "Go ahead. It's all right to laugh about these things."

But he didn't. Given permission, he didn't see the humor any longer.

"It doesn't feel like a dream," he said. "I always want it to feel like one. It never does."

"What do you do when Wall Man leaves?"

"I go to sleep," Peachy said. "Very soon thereafter."

"And your dreams?"

"I don't have any that I can recall."

"That makes sense," said Uncle Albert. "If your mind is tricking you, your subconscious is quickly, suddenly, at rest when the mind stops the trick. And you are released to sleep. So you do. It's quite natural. Just as people doze off quicker when they feel at peace about their lives and their circumstances."

"So what do you think?"

"I think I need more information."

"What do you need to know?"

"Before I answer that," Uncle Albert paused, "I need to feel that you will be honest in your responses to my questions."

"I will."

"How can I know that?"

"You can't," said Peachy. "I'm just telling you I will be honest. You can believe me or not. I wish you would. I think you can help me."

"What I ask you, you must answer straightaway."

"I will."

"Why?" asked Uncle Albert.

"Why . . ." Peachy was confused.

"Why will you answer straightaway? Why will you do as I ask you?"

"Because . . . because I want Wall Man to go away."

"Is that all?"

"Because . . ." Peachy hesitated. "Because I want to be free."

"I don't know." Now Uncle Albert hesitated. "I can't give you what you want, if I don't know what it is. And I can't know what it is, if *you* don't know what it is."

"Listen, man!" Peachy was suddenly angry. "I am visited by a demon! Can you get him out of my life, or can't you?"

"So you *do* believe." Uncle Albert almost smiled. "All right. Answer. Without pausing."

"Yes!"

"Where did you live in 1952 and 1953?"

"Belgian Congo."

"What did you do there?"

"For a living?"

"Yes."

"Biological research."

"Specifically."

"I tested pigs and other small animals."

"For?"

"Resistance to germs."

"Who hired you?"

"It was a directive grant. From MIT."

"The research went well."

"That's not a question."

"Did it or didn't it?"

"Yes, very well. They were very happy."

"Who is *they*?"

"My benefactors, I suppose."

"Their names?"

"There were no names. I saw only one person."

"His name?"

"Throckmorton."

"First name?"

"Jan. At least that was the name he was going by."

"What do you mean?"

"I'm sure Jan Throckmorton was not the man's real name."

"I thought that's what you meant," Uncle Albert said. "When a demon takes over its host, it likes to assert its own identity, not that of the host. So the demon-man calls itself something other than the man's real name."

Nobody said anything for a few long seconds, before Mr. Forrester said, "God Almighty," and Pastor White gave him a gentle reproving look.

"Oops," Mr. Forrester said. "I don't wanna take it in vain. God's name."

"Good man," the pastor nodded. "Then say it, brother, like you're telling the world God's name."

Mr. Forrester did so, raising his arms and declaring in a loud voice, "God Almighty is God Almighty . . . Almighty God!" He obviously meant every word.

From the recesses of a tent behind me, Stevie called to us. "Everything all right out there?"

"Perfectly fine," Pastor White hollered back.

Duffey's voice confirmed that my friends were glad to know all was right with the world. "Glad to hear it. Keep the faith." And in a lower voice, "The pot's shy, fellas. Ante up."

Uncle Albert said, "Yes. Demons have a strong interest in asserting their own names." To Peachy, he said, "What is the formula?"

"It's something I got far along with, but it never crystallized. I never came to the final formula."

Uncle Albert sighed. "I would very much like to believe you . . ."

"But?"

"I like you, and I think, now, you want to do what's right."

"But?"

"You've wanted to live right ever since you went back to teaching . . ."

"That's right!"

"But . . . I don't believe you." Uncle Albert didn't say it with any animosity. He could just as well have announced, "I don't eat cabbage." "I don't believe you did not come up with something very close to a workable formula. And apparently Wall Man doesn't believe you either."

"I didn't!" Peachy was intense. "Yes, I came close. Another couple of weeks and I would've had it. That's why I left. I didn't want it."

"Of course you wanted it. You were working toward it. You were isolating the variables."

"I can't make you believe me."

"I wish you could." Uncle Albert tossed a small stick into the blaze. "More to the point, I wish you could make Wall Man believe you."

"I don't expect him to," Peachy sighed. "He's a demon."

"Don't underestimate their capacity to know some truths. They do believe, you know, and have through the ages. Which is more than we can say for so much of humanity through those ages."

Peachy stood up. "I'm not looking to save my hide."

Uncle Albert agreed. "I believe that. And that is exactly why you are sitting in the salvation window, but still wavering, looking out and in."

I couldn't tell if Peachy had resolved something in his mind or if he was afraid to concede that he had not.

"I'm going to sleep," he said. "I'm tired."

I suddenly felt very close to him. I stood up. "Me too."

"Me three." Pastor White stood and stretched.

None of us moved, though. I thought Peachy would say one more thing. He did.

"I'd like to wake up dead tomorrow." I don't know if he intended that to be funny, but it sounded so to me. I laughed. I was alone, and very quickly stopped.

"I'm sorry," I stammered awkwardly, tumbling over my apology. "It's just, you can't wake up if you're dead. And then, for somebody to say they'd *like* to wake up dead . . . I'm sorry."

"Waking up dead *would* be problematic," Uncle Albert concurred, and that set me off again. But I caught myself, and cut my laughs off.

"Especially if someone is . . . lost," said Pastor White in a quiet, kind voice.

Peachy looked hard at Uncle Albert. "I want you to believe me," he said to the exorcist, "when I say I don't have the formula."

Uncle Albert returned his stare. "I think very highly of you."

Peachy took a few steps into the night. Pastor White stopped him, calling his name.

"Yes?" Peachy answered.

"Jesus said, 'In the world, you will have tribulation. But be of good cheer, I have overcome the world.'"

"Nathan . . . how did you know? John 16:33 is my favorite verse."

"Then you can, you must, have the peace Christ offers." The pastor asked what I'm sure all of us wondered. "Why is that your favorite?"

"I guess I'm still foolish enough to hope. To hope there is one who has overcome." He walked toward his tent.

"Will you be warm enough?" I called after him.

"I will be burning up," he said, disappearing in the shadows.

"He has a good heart," Pastor White said.

"He does," Uncle Albert agreed. "A big heart. Big enough to keep something hidden."

"You think he's protecting people," I said.

"Yes."

"What people?" the pastor asked.

"I'm not sure," the exorcist said, looking into our fire. "Maybe . . . I suppose . . . the people of this planet."

CHAPTER 19

It was very early. I'm one of those tortured souls who rises early and stays up late. Ask me when I sleep and I'll tell you I don't know. It's more acute if I'm away from home.

Usually my Scout tent buddy was Willie. If he got up in the middle of the night, and he consistently did, I heard his arms and legs sliding along his lime-green nylon sleeping bag. I also heard his reason for getting up, announced in whispers to himself that cascaded over my head.

"I'm awake," I would say.

"Oh," he would say, "then I don't have to be quiet."

His moving so as to "be quiet" sounded identical to his movements when he felt emancipated from concerns about quiet. But I wasn't going to tell him that. Willie was a gracious soul.

That early morning, I crawled out of my sleeping bag quietly so as not to awaken Willie; though if I fired off a twelve gauge in the tent, Willie would have mumbled, "Okay," turned over, and stayed rooted in Dreamland.

I stepped out of the tent and into my tennis shoes and ambled toward the dormant fire. That was odd. We always kept the fire strong through the night. We split the evening into hour segments of "fire watch" for that very reason. I thought I remembered Batman's name at the bottom of the roster we had Stevie write out when we set up the night's schedule. It wasn't like Batman to just drop the ball. Maybe the guy before him didn't wake him up.

I walked softly to Batman and Christopher's tent and pulled one flap to the side.

"Get away!" Stevie yapped at me in his preadolescent high pitch, peeking with one open eye out of the top of his sleeping bag. "Oh, sorry, Richard. Man, you scared me."

"Where's Batman?" I said.

"Who? How should I know?"

"You're in his tent."

"He's not in my tent," Stevie said, the other eye finally opening.

"I didn't say . . . this is where Batman and Christopher are. Isn't it?"

"They can't fit in here! What's wrong with their tent?"

"Who's that?" I nodded toward the sleeping bag opposite Stevie. Whoever's head was entirely inside the bag that housed a snoring symphony.

Stevie grinned. "Can't you tell? That's Duffey's early mornin' snore." He poked the body through the bag with a finger and the snoring stopped. For a couple seconds. The cloaked body murmured something like "sorry witches" or "sausage biscuits" and picked up the symphony again.

"Go back to sleep," I told Stevie. "You got another hour before the sun's up."

"Okay." He put his head down and looked to be sleeping within seconds. What a gift.

I dropped the tent flap and stood up, looking around. My eyes were used to the dark now. I went back over to the smoldering firepit and put some small wood on it, blowing low on the coals, evenly, and it started to look like a fire again. I put a bigger log on where I thought it'd catch.

"Who moved the fire?"

I turned to see Red hopping up behind me in his sock feet.

"Where's your shoes?" I said.

"I don't know." He didn't sound too worried. "I figure Duffey did something with them. When he gets up, I'll get my shoes."

"Where'd you leave 'em, after your watch?"

"Just outside the tent," said Red.

I walked in that direction.

"Where you goin'?" he said.

"To look around the tent," I said.

"I left 'em by *my* tent."

"That's where I'm . . ." I stopped. "Are you sleepwalking?"

"What's that?"

"It's when people walk around but they're still asleep."

"People do that?" he asked.

"Some people."

"On purpose?"

I stepped up to his tent and looked around on the ground. No shoes. I found Pastor White's boots. Caked with mud.

I walked back to the fire. Red was sitting close, warming one foot's sole and then the other.

"What did you mean when you said, 'Who moved the fire'?"

"I just wondered," he said. "Cause it was yonder," he pointed, "and now it's here," he said casually.

"Nobody moved no fire." I had retreated into bad English. Early mornings on Scout campouts could do that to me. My grammar pendulum swung. "Fires don't move hither and yon."

He shrugged, expressionless, as if to say I could think what I wanted, but the facts as he saw them were different.

"Who moved the fire?" Zack stepped up alongside me, scratching some beard stubble. Very light and very sparse, but it was there.

"You got a beard," said Red.

"Naw, I don't." Zack kicked at the edge of the fire.

"What do you mean who moved the fire?" I said.

"You gotta shave, right?" said Red.

"It's no big deal," said Zack.

"Why do you say somebody moved the fire?" I pressed.

"I guess," Zack hesitated, still waking, "because fires don't walk around on two legs."

"I told him," Red rubbed a bare foot. "He didn't pay me no mind. He said it was yonder and now it's . . . hither."

"Why on God's green earth," I said to both boys, "would any of us put out one fire in one place and start another in another place in the middle of the night? Does that make sense to ya'll?"

Red drawled, "I don't rightly know what God and the green earth gots to do with it."

"Zack?" I looked at him.

Red drawled again, "But I don't ever try to make a lotta this camping-out stuff make sense. We come out here and we're in another world or something."

"Maybe it's a Duffey prank," Zack said.

"Lotta them goin' around," said Red, like it was a virus.

"Did ya'll move your tent?" I asked Zack.

"Yes."

"Thank God," I said. I wasn't certifiable.

"We moved it to Nebraska," Zack deadpanned. "I'm going to put some water on. Coffee. Where's the big pot?" He looked at me. "The pot. We heat the water in it."

"I'm telling you, Zack, somebody has moved nearly everything here," I said, straining to sound earnest but not so fretful.

"Did you switch with Batman?" Zack said. "This last watch was his."

"That's what I thought," I said. "And no, I didn't switch with him."

Zack walked toward the tent where I'd found Stevie and Duffey the Snore Master earlier.

"If you're looking for Batman, he's not in that tent."

"Sure he is," Zack said without turning around.

"Them's my shoes right there." Red hobbled a few yards to a tree where he plucked his shoes off a low hanging branch. He looked them over carefully, and smacked them against the tree's trunk to make sure there would be nothing in them but his feet when he put them on.

Zack passed by me and the fire and said, "Batman's not in that tent," and walked fast toward the other tents.

"Oh, really?" I said, sarcastic.

Stevie and Duffey both exited their tent clothed, Stevie first and then Duffey rolling out and into Stevie like a bowling ball taking out a nine pin. Stevie laughed and took a hold of Duffey's leg while Duffey dragged him in our direction, a thick human sock around his ankle.

"Hey ya'll," Duffey said over Stevie's giggles. "I can't find my other sock. I can't walk around with just one sock on."

I was still unsettled by the morning's mystery, the shifting fire and tents, but Duffey and Stevie's antics were sweet medicine. I laughed with Red as the strange creature with the oversized right ankle stood next to me.

"Zack's looking for Batman," said Duffey.

"I know," I said.

"He ain't in my tent."

"I know."

"You gonna hang around there all morning," Duffey said to his new sock, "or what?"

"I guess not." Stevie let go and stayed on the ground like a dog on his back warming up by the fire.

"Well, that's kinda funny . . ." Duffey looked behind him, back to the fire, and all around.

"Don't tell me," I said.

"I coulda sworn the fire was . . . say what's up with Donnie?"

I followed Duffey's gaze and saw Donnie stomping the ground by his tent.

"Donnie!" Zack hollered from the far tent.

"Fire," Donnie hollered back.

We all ran to him, including Pastor White and Peachy who'd hustled out of that same tent. The tiny fire outside Donnie's tent was out even before we had all clamored around to extinguish it.

"No problem," Donnie said. "Sorry I yelled. Just kinda surprised me."

His dad looked at the little remains. "Dried leaves," he said. "And some sticks big enough to act like kindling." He glanced at his son. "Did you start it?"

"Why would I do that?"

"Kids do crazy things sometimes, son," said Pastor White. "I was a kid."

"I'm not crazy, Dad!"

"Maybe by accident?"

"Not that crazy, Dad," Donnie insisted.

"I don't think this was an accident," Zack said, looking over the scant charred remains. "All the leaves around here are wet, and somebody had to bring some dry sticks or paper or something here and light it. Least that's how it looks to me."

"It's not an accident," Peachy said. He looked at me. "Was anything else unusual this morning?"

"Unusual?" I guessed what he might mean, but I wanted him to say more first.

"About the grounds here, the camp. Anything out of the norm?"

"Well, yeah." For whatever reason I was reluctant to say.

"Everything's all backward," Red gushed.

"How do you mean that?" said Peachy. Before Red responded, Peachy pressed me. "How does he mean that?"

I shrugged. "Well, it's like the camp is reversed, sort of. Only it wasn't. It's like somebody moved some things. I thought everybody's tent was moved, but then I realized that was impossible . . ."

"Not many things are impossible," Peachy interjected.

"Yeah, anyway, I think what did happen is somebody put out our fire and started another one, and that made me think they had moved our tents, which would be impossible with us in them," I insisted.

Zack's voice reached us from a distance. "Here it is." He had wandered off while we were talking. "The first fire," he said. "Our first campfire."

We all sidled up to him as he brushed aside blackened, cured leaves and faint indiscriminate black spots and other signs of the first fire. It had not been at the center of where we pitched our tents, otherwise I wouldn't have confused the tent occupants. It was to the side, our tents set in disparate, uneven relation to the fire. That's normal. Scouts pitch tents where the ground is amenable, not in regard to the campfire.

What is not normal is the day dawning with the campfire having been relocated under darkness of night.

All Peachy said was, "He was here," but that was enough. Pastor White decided we should break camp early and head for home. That sounded like a plan to the rest of us. When I had my stuff tied off in my backpack, I sat down next to Peachy who was poking the new fire in the minutes remaining before we would have to put it out entirely.

"Why do you think he would do something like this?" I asked. "It seems kind of silly."

"It is."

"It's silly?"

"No," he said quietly, as if uncomfortable with others hearing. "I mean *it* is silly. The creature itself. If by silly we mean confused about reality, disconsonant with reality. The Rebellion is silly, isn't it? Telling God he is not God and you are."

"But you don't believe," I said.

"I *do* believe. In God. I don't believe in my personal redemption. Which is to say, I don't believe in the power of positive thinking." Fearing he had offended me, he added, "I'm not correcting you, Richard. I am trying hard to make myself clear. Even to myself."

"I get it." A moment later, I started smiling and even laughing a little. I had to ask again. "Why did he move our fire?"

"It is active. They are active. They love being noticed. Crumpler tells me angels are active too, but they are reluctant to be recognized."

Donnie, who had stepped up behind us, said, "Maybe that's why certain angels fell. I mean, rebelled. They wanted to be recognized. Instead of putting the focus on God."

"An astute observation," Peachy said.

"More of a theory than an observation," said Donnie. "I haven't observed anything."

"Yes, you have," Peachy mumbled. "This morning."

"What do they want?" Donnie asked.

Peachy heard him. But his considerations were elsewhere. "Life's not the bargain it looked like when I was a young scholar, full of promise, full of myself really."

"It's no bargain at all," I agreed. "It's Robert Frost's forest with no trail, no path. 'Birches.' You know it?"

"I do!" We had found another nexus. "Remember the cobwebs, near the end?" He was excited.

I recited. "Life is too much like a pathless wood where your face burns and tickles with the cobwebs broken across it." I paused. I knew the next line. Strange how in that moment I ached to hear someone else say the words.

"And one eye is weeping," Peachy said softly.

"Yes," I said.

He finished the line. "From a twig's having lashed across it open."

He took a deep breath, like the recollection or the recital had taken something out of him. Or put it in him.

"Nothing good comes," he said, "from a pathless wood."

"What do they want, sir?" Donnie asked again.

"Nothing good."

CHAPTER 20

When I recall Peachy's disclosure of Wall Man's visitation and the startling circumstances of the campfire's nocturnal migration, I should have been very much afraid for some time thereafter. But when you're fifteen, you move from zeal to fear and back again with ridiculous frequency.

Less than a week after that mysterious campout, I agreed to join my friends on a mission fraught with jeopardy. What high schooler wouldn't?

Donnie was convinced someone was breaking into the church at night. "Nothing's missing," he said. "Yet. But it's not right, and, well, I think we can catch the guy."

That was enough for our adolescent mind-sets to make plans to apprehend the intruder. We figured it would be fun, the sort of thing teenagers do on a Friday night if there's nothing to see at the theater.

"What if this intruder guy is not a guy?" Caroline asked.

"Then we'll apprehend a female," Duffey said.

"I mean, what if it's . . . you know, a demon," she asked, her eyes bright, alert to that redoubtable possibility.

"Then we'll apprehend a demon." Duffey's eyes met hers in what I'm sure he considered a romantic moment.

Julie and I walked silently, bent over, from tree to tree so as not to be seen by . . . whoever, making our way to where the tree line ended behind Silas Baptist Church.

"This is so, so creepy," she whispered. In the fading light, I couldn't tell if she was bothered by our odd venture this early evening, or fascinated.

"Welcome to Richard Powell's world," I said, trying to sound a little tough, a little cool. I felt cool. Julie Prevette was hanging out with me. I was beginning to believe she really liked me. At that age, you're so anxious about acceptance and camaraderie and, yes, puppy love that barks like a basket of bassett hound pups in your heart, you're tempted to not mind even the incidental appearance of demons.

I whispered back. "I'm sorry. I know this is kind of off the wall."

"It's not off the wall, it's on the other side of the wall, Powell." Her playful use of my surname encouraged me.

"You're okay with it?"

"I think it's splendiferous." In her good moods, her wordsmithing rivaled anyone's. "This is like the coolest. Breaking into your church at night."

"We're not breaking in," I said, buffering her enthusiasm. "We're seeing if somebody else does."

"That's splendiferous too," she laughed, a melodious schoolgirl giggle.

"Besides, Donnie's here."

"You see him?"

"Yeah," I said. "I told you he would be. So we're all right. Rebecca's here too."

We crept up beside them so the four of us were behind bushes on the backside of the little church where Donnie's dad preached.

"Why don't you make some more noise?" Donnie whispered.

"Could you hear us?" I tried not to laugh. The evening felt funny.

"Only every word," he said.

"No way," I disputed.

"Splendiferous," Rebecca said. Her whisper made the word sound magical.

"It's my fault," said Julie. "I'm not used to all this cloak-and-dagger."

"It's kind of cool, isn't it?" Rebecca leaned her head close to Julie, who looked very cute wearing a Cubs cap her uncle had sent her and Lizzie that year from the Windy City.

"Well," Donnie sighed low, his eyes on the church, "you better get used to it if you're gonna keep hanging around with us. It's like we can't get away from it."

I heard something right behind me, and whipped around, ready to run or maybe hit something. It was Duffey.

"Hey guys," he kneeled beside us.

"Can we possibly be any louder?" Donnie grumbled. "What are you doing here?" He wasn't upset. He just wondered how Duffey knew.

"Zack called me," said Duffey proudly.

"He's got to finish a report for Mrs. Quitko," Rebecca said.

"Said he thought you were coming," Duffey looked at Rebecca, "and wanted me to look out for you."

Rebecca wasn't buying it. "That sounds nice, but really . . . I can't see Zack telling you that."

"Don't you want me to take care of you?" Duffey played a lame masculine sympathy card.

"Who takes care of whom?" Rebecca challenged him. You can speak your mind in the Fellowship of the Rock.

"Maybe we could hold up a big sign," Donnie moaned. "Hello . . . demons and aliens and crooks."

"Oh my!" Julie and Rebecca chimed in with the Oz gang's fearful mantra.

"*I'm* glad you're here, Duffey," Julie patted his massive shoulder.

I fished for her affection. "What about me?"

"I'm more glad you're here, Mr. Powell." She locked arms with me and pulled in tight. I still revisit that moment.

Rebecca was suddenly very still. Because Donnie was. "What is it, Donnie?"

"The far window." He pointed quickly, covertly.

I looked. Nothing.

"It passed by," he murmured. "Head down."

"It?" Rebecca asked under her breath.

"Well, I couldn't see clear enough," Donnie whispered.

"There . . ." Julie's voice caught. ". . . it is."

We all saw then. Something had passed by a different window, close to Donnie's. A light traveled with it. We kept looking. But it was gone. For now.

"It's so big," I said, marveling.

"Can we just stop with the 'it' word?" said Rebecca.

"I'm here for you, sister," Duffey said, obviously delighted that we'd seen someone. Or something.

"Call the police," Rebecca said.

"By the time they get here," Donnie said, shaking his head, "it's over. It's gone."

"Donnie," Rebecca insisted, "someone's broken into the church. Call the police."

"Why would it break into the church?" said Julie. "I mean, there's nothing inside but God."

"Uncle Albert said they do," Donnie answered. "Kind of a lot. People who are into demons and stuff like to, I guess, make an offering to the devil in a church."

Rebecca said, "Let 'em go build their own church."

"They do that too," Donnie said.

"That's so wacky." Julie winced.

"What do you think?" Donnie glanced at me, still keeping his gaze mostly on the windows in the back of the church.

I confess I was high on adolescent pride, my reason hazy in the glow of Julie's attentions. "Let's see what it . . . I mean, who he, is. Let's get closer."

"Richard!" Rebecca gave me a look, like I was loony several times over. "What if he . . . has a gun? Or what if it . . . has demon fire coming out of its mouth!"

The gun slowed me. The demon fire was laughable. Back then.

"He could have a gun or something, Donnie," I said.

He acted like he didn't hear me, moving out in a kind of quick creep toward the back of the church.

"Come on," I said to Julie, who moved with me. The sky overhead was rapidly losing the last vestiges of daylight. I welcomed the shadows; I was every bit as comforted by Julie's company as she was by mine, though I preferred she not be able to see that.

Rebecca had hustled up close to Donnie almost as soon as he

went forward. The Fellowship sticks together, debates over strategy and protocol notwithstanding.

We got to the building and kneeled behind and beside a big air-conditioning unit, which did not entirely conceal us.

"Follow me," Donnie whispered. We wouldn't have done otherwise. "Door on the far side . . . opens to a supply room . . . I got the little key." He held it up.

"Where's Duffey?" Rebecca looked around. We all did.

"Maybe he stayed back there," Julie whispered.

Rebecca shook her head. "That'll be the day."

"He must've gone to some other door or something," I said.

"Still glad he came?" Donnie whispered to Julie, frustrated.

"He's got a big heart," she said, gracious. "Know what I mean?"

"He's got a fat head," Donnie answered.

It was loud. Something crashed, more than once, in the church. We heard someone yelling. It was not Duffey.

"C'mon!" Donnie stood up running and we ran after him.

"You guys are crazy!" Julie yelled, excited, not afraid. I was afraid.

At the far side door, Donnie jammed the key into the lock and opened the door in one motion, moving inside fast. We followed him in, just as fast and stopped where he had. The crashing and yelling had stopped, as suddenly as it had started, and the resulting silence was far more threatening than the previous bedlam. Silence is never empty.

The supply room was dark, but as our eyes adjusted, Julie gasped. I turned sharply and saw her pointing to a monster: a life-size poster of a clown with the letters VBS on his head and TONIGHT on his torso.

Donnie cracked a door open, just barely. There was still no light in the building's interior. He put his head close to mine, whispering, "I'll go in first. Wait two—no, three—minutes. If you don't hear anything from me, ya'll need to just get out of here. Call the police, I guess."

Yes, we were idiots about this. Teens can be that way.

"Okay," I breathed. "Three minutes."

Donnie crept out, and I told Rebecca and Julie the plan.

Rebecca was practical. "Look around. See if there's anything we can use as a weapon if Donnie hollers." We were fools. But we weren't stupid fools. If Donnie hollered, we were hitting the beach armed. Okay, we weren't thoroughly stupid fools.

I found a long pole, light enough to swing, but thick enough to break a demon's bones. Or so I hoped. Rebecca found a hammer. Julie found a sizable two-handed yard clipper. I started to say something to her, but she looked so seriously intent on wielding great powers of persuasion with those clippers that I just let it go.

"Is that three minutes?" Rebecca asked, ready to drop the hammer and run to a phone to get the police.

"I think so," I agreed.

Donnie's loud voice jumped us out of our tennis shoes. "Come on in!"

I started to go in and Rebecca grabbed me, talking fast. "He didn't say everything's okay. What if someone's got him? You know, holding him."

"Come on out!" He hollered again.

Julie's eyes were as big as Alabama. "He still didn't say it's all clear!"

"Bring what you've got," I said, solemnly. "Your clippers."

I stepped out, still holding the pole, ready to club the powers against us. A light came on in a room on the other side of the church.

"Over here," Donnie called to us. "Everything's good, ya'll."

We breathed easier and walked into the lit room, the Sunday school classroom for us high schoolers at Silas Baptist.

Duffey and Donnie were sitting on the floor, facing us as we stepped inside the room. A thin line of blood traced down one side of Duffey's head. The intruder, his back to us, sat deep in a bright orange bean bag chair, head down.

He was big, big as Duffey, and that was sizable.

"You're bleeding," Rebecca moved to Duffey. Julie stayed by me, by the door. I could feel her sticking close, her arm against mine.

"Sorry 'bout dat," said the intruder.

I've heard that voice before.

"I got a big old hard head," Duffey said, gently. Rebecca set her hammer down on the floor and knelt, looking at Duffey's wound. Duffey kept his eyes on the fellow in the big bean bag.

"I didn't mean . . ." the intruder's voice trailed off.

But the voice was deeper now . . . Where have I heard this man? When?

Rebecca glanced at the intruder, stood up, and froze. She recognized him. She looked at me.

The intruder's shoulders rose and fell, small spasms. Quiet sobs.

I stepped deeper into the room, Julie following. We circled around the crying intruder to where Rebecca stood. Duffey and Donnie were still seated on the floor. Looking at him.

His face was in his hands. In between tears he said, "I can't do it . . . just gettin' up another day . . . and just . . . gettin' up . . . can't do it." He took his hands down and lifted his head to look at us.

Booger!

Booger Clark was the Hawks' catcher who'd taunted me— haunted me, even—when I was ten, in Little League five years before. Pitiless, he'd told me my dad was likely dead when he was MIA in Vietnam. When Dad was rescued, Booger had pretty well told me my dad *should* be dead for "dropping bombs over there." He had disappeared after that season five years ago. I'd heard one kid at school say Booger's family—what family there was—had left Silas, Alabama, for Delacroix, Louisiana. Good riddance. I would have excised him from my memory if I had any power to do that. I had managed to forget his real name.

And here he was, in a Sunday school room in Silas Baptist Church. Crying. Sitting in a bean bag chair on the floor.

"What makes ya'll," he said, his breathing labored, "get up . . . in the morning?"

Rebecca, mercy minded, suggested that she and Julie "might could step outside and let ya'll boys talk."

"No, please." Booger's voice was so little coming out of such a big guy. "You're part of these guys, Rebecca."

"I can let all ya'll talk." Julie took one step back toward the door.

"Are you friends with Richard?" Booger asked.

"Yes," she smiled. "We're friends."

"Richard is . . ." He swallowed hard. "Richard is . . ." He smiled a little. "A really cool guy."

"I think so too," she said.

"If you're friends with him," Booger said, "then you must be tight with all these guys. Please stay here." His crying faded; it looked like he fought to stop it. So he could talk to us. It was crucial for him to talk to us. Life was at stake.

"Ya'll are all so . . . happy. You're like . . . some kind of family inside the other family you got." He looked like he was thinking hard, trying to imagine our lives, lives that to him seemed unreal with purpose and joy and many good things that were lifelong strangers to him.

"I been watching you guys. Spying, I guess. The Boy Scout camp and all."

"So that's it." Duffey looked relieved. "You messed around with our campfire. That was you."

"Campfire? No. I don't know nothing about no fire."

Duffey and I exchanged looks. "What about the BBs?" I said. "Duffey and me canoeing?"

"What BBs?" Donnie asked.

"I'm real sorry about that. Real sorry." Booger meant it. "It's just . . . I was mad. Both ways mad. Mad in the head like crazy. And mad that ya'll are like . . . so close . . ." His voice kept breaking. "I just don't . . . don't think I could have anything . . . like that."

"BBs?" Donnie said again.

"I'll tell you later," I said, my eyes assuring him that was a pledge. Right now we needed to hang out in Booger's soul. Booger was inviting us in.

This was something Donnie was great at, bringing God into the mix of confusion and self-doubt and world-doubt, leading fellow beggars to the feast. But it was Duffey who led this time.

"We're just like you, Freddy."

Freddy! Duffey had remembered. Duffey cared.

"That ain't true," Booger shook his head. "I'm bad . . . down to my heart . . . just bad."

"You don't look so bad," Julie said quietly.

"I am." His voice held steady now, but tears rolled down. "Ask Richard. He'll tell ya. I was bad back then, and I'm worse now. I've done just about everything to get myself in hell. Nothing left for me but to die. Feels like it's happening."

"You *are* dying," said Donnie.

We waited. Donnie knows what to say and how to say it. That is, the Spirit knows these things.

Donnie sat down on the floor by the bean bag. "This is your day to die," he said without drama or pity or any other affectation.

Duffey sat down on the other side of Booger, and said to him, "You're so close, man."

If their words confused him, Booger didn't show it. He kept the same look of grave remorse.

"All I ever wanted," Booger said, "was to be normal."

"I can't help you with that," Duffey said. "Ain't never seen normal. But if you wanna be changed, we got something to show you."

Rebecca, still standing, leaned against the wall, her eyes closed.

"Ya'll can't change me." Booger said it with resignation. A fact.

Donnie nodded. "You got that right. But if you're ready to die, and you said you were, you can be born again."

If the words sound tawdry or showy, it is we who have colored them with pretense. To Booger, they sounded like life.

"I want that," he said. "More than anything I've ever wanted."

"Do you know what it means," Donnie said, "to be born again?"

"I'm settin' here asking God in my head if he would tell you to tell me," Booger said. "I heard it before. Born again," he said with reverence.

I tried to back out of the room, Julie with me.

"You're born again, too, aren't you?" Booger said to me.

"Yes."

"Yes," said Julie.

"Okay," he said, almost giddy with anticipation. Things were already leaving and entering him. "Stay in here, then. Please."

We did.

They walked him through it, Donnie and Duffey showing a fellow desert vagabond the water. It didn't take long. Not in those moments. Booger's wandering and wounds, his own and those he'd inflicted, had been a long, circuitous thirst for water he was sure did not exist.

We watched him drink.

When he picked his head back up, he was newborn, like a baby.

Duffey hugged him, a great bearlike embrace. I'd seen the two wrestling and punching five years before in a brutal fight.

All of us hugged him.

"You won't be normal," Duffey said, chuckling. "You said you wanted to be normal. Normal is dead. Going the way of the world," he said, impressing me with his insight. "If you follow Jesus, you ain't gonna fit down here."

"I feel so clean," Booger said.

"You are!" Rebecca blurted out.

"Ain't never been clean before."

"You're still gonna sin," Duffey said.

"I don't want to."

"That's good!" Rebecca said.

"But when you do," Duffey said, "your sins are forgiven. By his blood. Forever. Your sins are covered. And you'll get stronger in the Lord."

We say such things to newborns as if they are actually fitted with some novel kind of "God radar" that will demythologize complex truth for them with every beat of their new heart of flesh. And they are.

We stood there, the six of us, in the high school room at Silas Baptist Church, and just let the baby's breath hang in the air around us for a few silent seconds.

Then Duffey spoke, in the chummy manner of brother to brother. "So that was your sorry backside shootin' BBs at Richard and me in the canoe on the lake?"

"It was a pellet gun," Booger said. "I'm right sorry about that."

"Ain't nothin' but a thing." Duffey smiled easy.

"I did make real careful sure, ya know, I wouldn't hit either one of ya'll."

Donnie's eyes were massive. "You shot a pellet gun at them!"

"But careful not to hit 'em," he said.

"How?" said Rebecca.

"I aimed right at 'em," he said, "so's I wouldn't hit 'em. I got a right awful aim."

I thought it was funny; Julie not so much. "You aimed a rifle at Richard?"

"A gun, Julie," I said. "Pellet gun's not a rifle."

"You aimed it at Richard? And Duffey? And fired it?"

"I'm right sorry about it," he emphasized again.

"And we forgive you," I said. "And better, God forgives you."

Duffey put an arm on Booger's substantial shoulders. "Say, do you wrestle? You could transfer back into our district and one of us could wrestle heavyweight and the other get down to one eighty-one and we could go to the state finals!"

"Do you forgive me?" Booger looked at Julie, pleading. He was twice her size.

Never answer for someone else in such moments. We waited for Julie. She cocked her head slightly, like she heard something we didn't.

"I have myself . . . shot off at people. With what I've said . . . that I shouldn't have said." She smiled then at Booger. "I'm sure I've shot at people more times than you have."

"You a hunter?" he asked, appearing impressed.

"I'm a sinner," she said. "And God keeps forgiving me. And I'm learning to shoot less and less."

He got it then.

And I fell even deeper into love with Julie and with our Father.

We went out for ice cream, all of us. Duffey and Booger were intrigued with the prospect of both wrestling for Silas High the next year, and Booger vowed he would work to get his weight down to one hundred eighty-one pounds to wrestle in that weight class. Just as soon as he finished his chocolate peppermint sundae.

Julie reaffirmed her love affair with the jukebox, playing Chicago's "I've Been Searching So Long."

"That's me, ya'll," Booger said. "Everything's new and strange."

"And good," Julie said.

"Yeah," he said. "Good."

He was himself. Booger Clark. His mask off.

CHAPTER 21

The Fellowship of the Rock decided to approach BoDean and see if he wanted to canoe one afternoon with a group of us on Lake Cross. Duffey and Batman went with me to ask him.

I stumbled through too many words and sentiments, trying to tell BoDean we cared about him without him thinking we were trying to rescue him. Which of course we were. But people who need help are often the last to want it or take it.

"It's just we thought you might"—I stumbled through pauses—"could use some time, ya know, to talk about some things and—"

"Look," Duffey cut me off, mercifully saving me from drowning in my own words. "We're gonna eat by the lake until we're ready to explode. Then we're gonna jump in canoes and see if we can knock around on the water without killing ourselves. Are you in?"

BoDean said, in a voice strangely mellow and edgy, that he didn't need lectures from any of us.

"That's good because we don't give lectures," Batman said.

"I don't need any preaching either."

Duffey said, "It's a picnic. With canoes. No hymnals. No offering plates. No pews."

BoDean smiled. "Who all's going?"

"Probably eight or ten of us," I said, rattling off names of guys he'd known since he was in grade school. And a couple girls he didn't know.

"Who's Julie?"

"She's somebody I been seeing a little," I said. "Off and on."

"You got a girl?"

"Ya know . . . off and on."

"They're going steady," Batman said.

"We're not going steady." I thought I should clarify. "I don't know what we're going, but we're not going steady."

"Maybe this is news to you," Batman said, "but Julie turned down the lead in *The Curious Savage* because she wants to get to know you better instead of rehearsing all her spare time. And that girl's a drama addict. She's gotta be super serious about you."

"She told me she didn't want to wear all that old woman makeup," I said. "For Mrs. Savage."

"You think a drama nut like her cares about wearing that makeup?" Batman scoffed. "Actresses like her live for roles like that. They'll put on a plaster of paris body cast if they can be the lead in *Mrs. Mummy Goes to Town*. You're going steady."

"Have you kissed her yet?" BoDean weighed in.

"No!"

"Man, she's nuts about you," BoDean said seriously.

"What!" I was confused.

"You haven't even kissed her, and she's still hanging out with you. Batman's right. Ya'll are steady. Anybody else going?"

"Duffey's girl," said Batman. "Caroline."

"Now *they* are going steady," I said.

BoDean stared at Duffey. "She that girl I saw reading you the riot act in the cafeteria?"

"That's her," he said, laughing with all of us. "I said something I shouldn't have and she let me have it."

Batman beamed. "Man, that was funny! You just stood there, nodding to whatever she was saying, your eyes on the floor. You looked guilty . . ."

"I was."

"And repentant . . ."

"I was."

Batman nearly doubled over laughing. "Like somebody's Saint Bernard caught barking when he shouldn't and hearing a mouthful from the little girl of the house."

"I saw that," BoDean said. "Yeah man, that was seriously wild."

"What was that about?" Batman asked.

"I don't remember," Duffey said without guile.

We thought that was even funnier, mostly because that was pure Duffey, straight up.

BoDean made a decision. "Okay, I'll go. I got nothing to lose these days."

I wasn't exactly sure what he meant by that. I took it as a hopeful sign that he was at least making some attempts at being honest with himself.

———

That weekend found the Fellowship and BoDean, the Fellowship's prodigal, at a Lake Cross picnic site. We invited Booger, but he had to "bust up a barn." I thought it was another way of saying "raise a barn" but he said, no, he was helping his cousins tear one down that was "fixin' to keel over on its own, and that ain't nothing but bad news. Generally keels over on top of somebody or somebody's goats and such."

I was sorry he couldn't come to the lake with us, but Donnie said it was likely just as well since "rescuing BoDean's a big enough project for us this day. God'll give us another day to pull Booger deeper in. God plans these things."

The nine of us that God planned to get together this day were crammed around one picnic table, wolfing down burgers, hot dogs, chips, slaw, potato salad, and sodas.

"Save room for my cookies," Caroline said.

I was afraid it'd be awkward; people would be too quiet. And maybe BoDean would feel a little on the spot. I should have known better. There was so much amused chatter and vocal buzz around the table, I forgot all about watching BoDean to see if he was having a good time. When I did remember, he looked like just one more in this little gang of carefree American teens.

Donnie said we could probably pull a second picnic table over and put it up against the one we had and be more comfortable.

"No," Rebecca said. "This is the best. We're all of us together, just like family."

She was the sort that could say that, even in a group of teens, and nobody thought it was silly. In fact, the general response was amicable agreement.

"I kinda like sitting here," Duffey beamed from his seat at the head of the table. "It's like I'm looking over my kids. All ya'll!"

"You must be Papa Bear," Batman laughed, the rest of us agreeing.

"I have a question," Julie announced. The table quieted down. "Everybody else here seems like . . . really close. Like really tight."

"'Cept you don't mean me," BoDean said.

"Sure I do." Julie dismissed his comment, which made BoDean and the rest of us feel real good. "You fit in with these guys like you were born with them. All ya'll fit together like a dream. And the weird thing is, I feel like I fit in here that close to ya'll, too. And Caroline and me are the two newcomers to this group, but am I wrong, Caroline? Don't you feel like there's something like a family here, and now you're in it, and you don't want to be anywhere else?"

"Sure that's what I feel," Caroline said. "Who wouldn't feel that? You guys are like a big love machine."

That was a little uncomfortable for the guys, but Duffey broke us up with, "I always wanted to be part of a big love machine."

"Well, you are!" Julie said. "And it's beautiful."

Batman, beside me, whispered, "Drama people say this stuff."

Julie heard him. "That's right, I'm a drama person. So are you Batman, and who cares? I'm just saying what I see. More people should do that, don't you think, whether they're drama people or whatever."

"You had a question," I said.

"Yes, thanks, honey," she said without thinking. "Oops!"

It seemed like everybody blushed except for me and Julie, and Duffey who had managed to secure a cookie even though Caroline hadn't opened the tin yet.

"What?" Duffey mumbled through peanut butter cookie dust. "Oh man, I miss everything. What did somebody say?"

"Julie just called Richard *honey*," Rebecca said, and everybody felt they had permission to laugh.

"How did you get that cookie?" Caroline asked Duffey.

"They're in your tin."

"I know that. I haven't opened it yet. How'd you get it without me seeing you?"

There was no good answer, so Duffey ventured a little humor. "I got special powers." Caroline didn't look entirely pacified, so he said, "It's a picnic! Can't a guy sneak a cookie on a picnic?"

She liked that. "Okay, I buy that. Picnics change the rules a little."

"You'll make a great mom," Duffey said.

She liked that too.

"You had a question," I said again.

"Yes!" Julie almost shouted. "Why are ya'll so close? I mean, you're all so different in so many ways."

"She means Richard's smart and I'm clueless," Duffey said, joking.

"No I don't! I mean Batman's into drama and Duffey's into wrestling and Richard, okay, he's a brain and into writing, and Donnie's a preacher's kid and okay, Zack and Rebecca I can see hanging out together, but the rest of you . . . and BoDean . . ." She looked at him. "I don't know what you are yet, but you seem different from the others, but like them too in a way I can't put my finger on."

"I'm a pothead." He said it like it meant nothing. Like your grandmother would say, "Looks like it might rain." But he was revealing something about what he thought. Or what he believed.

"You might smoke pot," Rebecca said firmly. "But you're not a pothead. You're BoDean."

He gave a little smile.

"Anyway," Julie charged on. "What is it that makes ya'll so close? Caroline and I want to know."

Caroline confirmed. "That's right. We were talking about it."

"We did play on the same Little League team a few years back," Zack said.

"So what?" Julie said. "I played on a girls basketball team when I was eleven or so. But I don't hang out with those girls anymore."

"It's a God thing," Donnie said.

"I believe you," Caroline said. "Now tell us more."

Donnie did; he went the whole length of the true story and more. He told them of an unforgettable season of miracles from the year

1971. He told them about God and Rafer coming into our lives, and God's Spirit and Rafer's spirit refusing to ever leave us.

———

There were three big canoes. That split the nine of us evenly, three to a canoe. After some discussion, it was resolved that each canoe would hold two guys and one girl. Zack, Rebecca, and Donnie were together, as were Duffey, Caroline, and Batman. Julie and I were paired with BoDean.

I think we had more fun launching and bumping into each other near the shore than we did out on the lake. With two oars to a canoe, one occupant just enjoyed the ride while the other two paddled. All three girls insisted on starting with oars in their hands, and we guys were wise enough not to object. The girls were all in the rear of the canoe, where most all the steering takes place. Rebecca and Caroline knew what they were doing. Julie, well, steering was lost on her, but she was having a good time. Which, of course, meant I was having a *great* time, even if I complained.

"You have to steer back there," I said over my shoulder.

"I don't have to do anything," Julie laughed. "You can't watch me back here!"

The pivotal question was whether the three canoes should stay together and travel the same direction, or split up. The Zack-Donnie-Rebecca vessel wanted to stick together, but the Duffey-Batman-Caroline canoe lobbied for all of us going different directions.

"What do ya'll say?" Zack asked us.

"I don't rightly know how we can go three separate ways," BoDean answered. "There's left and there's right."

"Port and starboard, Captain!" Batman dramatized.

"Yeah, whatever," BoDean said. "I guess we might could go straight up in the air."

"Which we may actually do," I said, "if Julie keeps steering like a crazy woman back there."

She slapped her paddle at the water's surface, a deft move that hit my face with a thin slice of lake.

"Hey! What's that for?"

"Gee, I don't know, *honey!*" she emphasized my new moniker. "Something just came over me."

"What kind of a reason is that?" I swiped my face with the back of my hand.

"That's the best reason to do anything."

Duffey called gleefully, "Ya'll might could go straight up in the air, if BoDean shows you how to get high!"

I thought that comment was a grave mistake, but BoDean loved it.

Zack gave directions. "We'll go right here. Ya'll go left there," he said to Duffey. "And ya'll go where you want to," he told us.

Julie was all for being bold. "We'll go straight out, away from the shore."

"How far?" BoDean said.

"When we almost can't see the shore, then it's time to turn back!" said the adventuress.

We broke then, in the three directions. We resolved our steering woes by my switching places with Julie, which placed me in the back and her in the middle. The simple act of changing seats was interesting, even a little exciting given the canoe's narrow confines and our uneasy balance on the water. She grabbed my shoulders and gave a faint shriek like she might have gone over the side had I not been there to catch her. I couldn't tell if she was just toying with my affections.

We made good time, traveling a fair piece over the water without talking. After a while, BoDean decided to open up.

"When I was a kid, I thought life would be cool," he said. "But life's not cool."

"You're sure about that?" I asked.

"I ain't sure about nothing. Except I'm messed up."

"That's the first step," said Julie. "To being all right."

"All right," he echoed. "All . . . right. Not possible. I can't be all right."

"Of course you can," Julie answered.

"I'm not like the rest of ya'll. I don't fit no more. Some people get that way, ya know. We just don't fit."

"Fit what?" Julie said.

"In. Fit in."

"Who wants to fit in?" Julie said.

"The rest of us do," he said to her. "People like you, girl, you're talented and pretty and kind and fun . . ."

"Are you getting all this, Richard *honey*?"

"I am," I knew what to say. "And I entirely agree."

"And Richard's so smart," BoDean said. "He can write a lot of his own ticket . . . wherever he wants to go. Whatever he wants to be. I'm not mad about that. I'm happy for him. I'm just saying that most of us got to find someplace to be. Someplace to belong."

I noticed Julie's slightly bowed head, her closed eyes.

BoDean kept paddling, and opening up. "I feel like I gotta make who I am. And I don't have enough stuff to make anything with. And what good stuff I got in me, I've probably smoked away."

We sat still in the water for some moments, more giving our minds a break than our arms. The canoe twisted a little, but mostly just sat there. As did we.

"We make ourselves," BoDean philosophized. "We have to. All the teachers say that, over and over to us at school. I wonder if they know how depressing that is."

Julie's head was still down, and she was slightly frowning. I figured that was okay. Sometimes prayer is not easy.

"You feel like you can't make yourself"—I was telling him, not asking—"into who you want to be."

"I don't want to make myself. I don't trust me."

"God doesn't always ask what we want," I said, my tone a little sterner than I anticipated. "He probably never asks. We just think he does."

I saw Julie's frown was sharper, deeper. "Are you okay?" I asked her.

"I don't . . . feel so good," she said, her voice a kind of monotone.

"What's wrong?" I leaned to her, my hand on her small shoulder.

"I gotta lay my head down . . . can I lay down a little here?"

I helped Julie lie down in the canoe's belly, an awkward shuffling of wet legs and arms.

"I got you," I said, removing my flotation vest and putting it under her head. Her eyes were still closed, but she wasn't frowning quite so hard.

"I thought you were praying," I whispered to her.

"I started to," she said. "And then my head just . . . hurt so bad."

BoDean was already turning the canoe, pointing it back to the shore, which suddenly appeared a long way off.

"Came out farther than I thought," I said, paddling strong in concert with BoDean.

"Naw, we're good," said BoDean, sounding confident and glaring at me to climb aboard the confidence train. "Ranger station's right there. They'll take care of you, Julie." He used a Duffey slogan. "It ain't nothing but a thing, ya'll."

The lake had seemed placid paddling out. Now it seemed to have a force, not a current but something like a strong lapping of little waves. The lapping worked against us.

I J-stroked hard, on one side, opposite BoDean, but we seemed to creep over the water's surface. I despised my weary arms and whatever spirits were plaguing our hearts and, now it seemed, our bodies.

"We are moving," I said. "Aren't we?"

"We're moving and we're gonna make it, and every little thing is going to be all right." BoDean fairly hurled the words into the air over the lake.

I noted that BoDean was the courageous one and I was feeling distraught; my faith should have been strong enough to buoy him and me and Julie as well. But I determined to feed off BoDean's sanguine spirit and not curse my own deficiencies.

"Alternate sides," he barked back to me. "When I switch, you switch."

"Right," I said. "That'll pace our arms." It made scant grammatical sense, but we understood each other. "We're going to make it back in no time now," I said in a strong voice, hoping Julie was conscious enough to hear.

It was like the water resisted our strokes; like pushing a stalled car on an incline, no matter how slight. You look to see, not how far you can go, but when you can stop.

"Change," BoDean said. I stroked on the other side.

"How're your arms doing?" I asked.

"My arms feel . . . they're just dead weight." He whispered it, but Julie heard.

"I'm the dead weight here," she said. I marveled at her attempt to be funny when I knew she was in pain.

BoDean grunted. "You don't weigh nothin', girl."

"I weigh ninety-five pounds," she murmured.

"My uncle's cat weighs more than that," BoDean lied.

"Big kitty," Julie said.

"He don't move off the sofa," said BoDean. "'Cept to roll to the food and the kitty litter. And then roll back up on the couch."

Julie breathed heavily. "A cat can't . . . roll up onto a couch."

"This one does," he said.

"Maybe you shouldn't talk, Julie." I thought she should save her strength.

"No, that's all right," BoDean said. "All of us should be talking. Julie needs to stay awake."

I didn't know how he would know that. But he sounded sure about it.

"I won't . . . can't . . . sleep here," Julie said softly. "Wet. Filthy. But it is kind of nice."

"Stay awake, girl!" BoDean said it with a vocal force I didn't know he possessed.

Julie's eyes caught mine, and I saw for the first time that she was scared. I couldn't have known that from what she said or the tone of her voice. But her eyes were wide with unspoken fear. Was she crying? I couldn't tell; her face wet with lake water or sweat or tears or some mixture.

"Change," BoDean instructed.

I felt a sudden strange and strong peace, in mind and body. "We got you, Julie," I said. "We got you."

Our minds are amazing. In the midst of great trauma, you'd think mental processes would fold in the heat, collapse under the weight of the trial. That can and does happen. But it's not automatic. Our heads and our hearts are just as likely to crystallize with purpose, in the heat of the danger. We focus.

I was not afraid. My mind targeted what had to be done. My heart, too, was busy. Silently telling myself I could do it. Audibly telling Julie all would be well.

"It's going to be all right," I said.

She smiled, her eyes closed.

The biggest question is a short one: Is God able? It's enough, it's sufficient, if we believe God knows what he's doing. If we know that, we know everything. And the deepest pits level out for us.

"Julie!" BoDean called out.

"Yes, Lord," she answered. That scared me. Her eyes were still closed.

"You're in a canoe," he said over his shoulder.

"I like canoes," she mumbled.

"Julie, you're with me," I said. "Richard."

"I like Richard," she declared.

"And BoDean," I said. "In a canoe."

"Bo who?"

"Dean," I said.

"Dean who?"

"BoDean!" My friend trumpeted his name.

"Oh yeah, mister that, far-out BoDean," she rambled. "That boy, that pot guy who is . . . changing."

BoDean appeared to get a kick out of her rambling, but wasn't sure how to take her claim that he was changing.

"We're in a canoe!" he said bizarrely.

"You already said that," she chided softly. "That canoe thing."

I thought maybe she should open her eyes. I said so.

"That's so . . . hard." Her voice floated. "Go away."

"What's your favorite song, Julie?" BoDean demanded.

"I like . . ." Her voice faded.

"What'd she say?" he called to me.

"She didn't." I answered. "She didn't say."

"Sing something!" BoDean said to me.

"I'm not really . . ."

"Anything!" he roared.

I got a little mad. It's silly, but people get silly in such moments. "Why don't *you* sing!" I blurted.

BoDean turned his head swiftly, his big eyes pleading.

I sang: "You are the dancing queen . . . young and sweet . . . only seventeen."

"Wow," Julie said in a small voice. "That song . . ."

"Do you like that song?" BoDean said, still attacking the water.

"I hate that song," she said, loud enough for both of us to hear.

He looked at me, between his fierce J-strokes. "Sing something else."

"It's hard to think of—"

"Sing!" he hollered.

I sang: "Everybody was Kung Fu fighting . . . those cats were fast as lightning."

"Change!"

I paddled the other side, and sang: "In fact it was a little bit frightening . . ."

"You're terrible." Julie giggled.

"She kind of laughed a little," I said to BoDean.

I sang more: "But they fought with . . ." I stopped. "I can't remember the words." I announced it like it was news to them.

Julie cooed, a little girl's sigh. "A show tune."

"I remember!" I said, and sang: "They fought with expert timing . . ."

"A show tune!" BoDean called. "Sing what she wants!"

I pleaded ignorance. "I don't know those . . ."

"Sing!" BoDean roared.

"Feed the birds . . . that's how it starts . . . something, something, something in the bag."

Julie interrupted. "That's not . . . a show tune."

I defended my choice. "It's Mary Poppins."

"Are you paddling back there?" BoDean wanted to know.

"I'm paddling, yes, paddling." Then to my wounded special friend, "That old lady makes the birds come down."

Her words were still slow, but her voice was clearer now. "Show tunes make . . . bring the house come down . . . sing something faster."

I did: "Ohhhhhh . . . klahoma where the wind comes sweeping down the plain."

"Oklahoma!" BoDean piped in.

"And the waving wheat can sure smell sweet when . . . I don't know but something makes it sweet!"

She smiled again. I paddled like an Olympian.

BoDean shouted, "Somebody's jumping up and down and waving."

I thought he meant one of our friends in the other canoes, but I didn't see either one of them on our left or right. I looked hard at the shore ahead and saw Willie Rowe grinning, waving his arms at us.

"Willie!" I hollered, my voice strong. "Julie's sick!" In a lower volume, my voice shaking, I asked BoDean if he thought Willie could hear me.

"I dunno," BoDean said. "He's lookin' this way, but . . ."

Julie looked unconscious.

Willie suddenly put both arms straight out to his sides, palms facing me. He raised his left arm over his head, and then his right.

"Thank you, God," I croaked, and hollered to the boy, "Run to the ranger and call an ambulance!"

He waved his right arm quick overhead and then took off up the hill toward the ranger's house.

"Thank you, God," I said again.

"Switch sides!" BoDean commanded. "Who's Willie?"

"He's in the Boy Scouts with me and the guys."

"He's black."

"He's terrific!"

"What's he doing out here?"

"I don't know. But thank God."

We steamed fast to the shore, just as Willie and a ranger I didn't recognize scrambled down the hill. The ranger carried a large first aid kit in his right hand and some long thing in his left.

"Ambulance is on the way," he said, touching Julie's forehead.

"Where's Ranger Burkett?" I asked him.

"He's been transferred. I'm the new sheriff in town. Ranger Franks."

"Man, that is so good." I said precisely what I felt.

Julie was conscious, but she was in pain and her head felt better if she lay still and quiet.

"Can you stand up?" Ranger Franks asked her.

"I don't know."

"Don't try," he said immediately.

"Grab her ankles," the ranger told me. I did, and he put his arms under her shoulders. "Pull that thing open," he said to BoDean, nodding to the canvas stretcher his left hand had dropped on the ground.

BoDean stared at it, trying to figure it out, but Willie pulled it open and tied it off neatly, quickly.

"Good job," BoDean said.

"Thanks."

The ranger and I pulled Julie out of the canoe and set her carefully on the stretcher.

"I'm so sorry," she muttered. "It's my head . . . hurts."

"No, no," Ranger Franks comforted her. "You're going to be fine. You're just lucky you had these fine young Scouts to get you in to shore so fast."

"And the other one," she said, not lifting her head or opening her eyes, but putting her right hand out, open. "Thank you."

"Willie," I pulled him over.

"Me?"

I put his hand in hers. She squeezed it tight. "Oh, you're a little boy," she cooed and smiled tiny.

"Yes ma'am," Willie said.

I saw she thought the "ma'am" was funny, but her pain kept her from laughing.

"Thank you for . . . running for help."

"I—I wish I could do more," he stammered.

"You've done plenty," Ranger Franks said.

Because I knew Julie would like hearing it, I said, "Willie's got the heart of a Viking . . ."

"And the simple faith . . . of a child." She'd memorized our troop chant the first day I told it to her.

Ranger Franks and I carried her stretcher up the hill, BoDean and Willie hustling beside us.

"I'm not a Boy Scout," BoDean said to Willie.

"You're kidding." Willie sounded amazed. "Whatcha been doin'?"

We reached the top of the hill just as the ambulance arrived, blowing the top layer of dust off the dirt road like a chopper's descent.

Julie said again, "I'm so sorry."

The medics moved swiftly, purposely, transporting her effortlessly from the ranger's cloth stretcher to their gurney and into the back of the ambulance.

I told Ranger Franks I should call Julie's parents and he pointed at his cabin, not forty yards away.

Running off, I heard BoDean tell the ranger he was not a Boy Scout.

"Nobody's perfect," Ranger Franks answered him.

I thought I'd be nervous on the phone with either parent. For whatever reason, I was glad it was Julie's gruff dad who answered. I told him what had happened.

"She'll be all right," Gruff said. "See ya at the hospital."

I hung up, thinking how it should've been me telling Gruff that his Princess was going to be all right, instead of him assuring me.

I stepped out of the cabin and saw Rebecca and Caroline talking up a storm with BoDean, who was filling them in. Zack and the guys were scrambling up the hill.

"Tying off . . . canoes," Duffey stammered, breathless.

"Something's wrong with Julie . . ." I started in telling the guys, but Rebecca and Caroline were already filling them in.

"Let's go," Zack said, waving all of us to the two big cars we had come in. I started to run with them, but stopped when I saw Willie standing to the side. I ran over to him. I didn't have to ask. He knew what I was wondering.

Willie said, "Sorry about that. I was spying on you big kids. My house ain't but a mile that way, over yonder."

"How'd you know we'd be here?" I asked.

"Ya'll talked about it at the last meeting. Troop meeting."

"Oh yeah," I said.

Duffey hollered at me from the cars, telling me to get my backside in gear.

"C'mon," I said to Willie. "Let's go."

"Oh no. I can't."

"Why not? We can call your parents. Drive you home."

"Because I'm . . . because I can't."

"Richard!" Duffey yelled.

"Go on, Richard." Willie looked embarrassed. "It's okay."

For all my smarts, it just then occurred to me why he didn't feel comfortable coming with us white kids to the hospital.

"I'll pray for her," he said. "My whole family will. My church too."

"I'm sure glad you were here." I shook his hand. It wasn't enough, so I gave him a quick hug. For the first time that day, I started to cry. "You did good, Willie."

I took off for the car, hearing his small voice behind me.

"We won't stop praying."

CHAPTER 22

As soon as I walked into the hospital, a nurse intercepted me at the emergency entrance.

"Julie Prevette is absolutely fine," she said.

I was confused. "But . . . how did you know—"

"She told me her friends would get here immediately, and here you are. That you'd be worried, and you look it. But she's fine, really."

"Can I see her?"

"Maybe. But you'll have to wait."

I heard a familiar voice behind me say, "Hurry up and wait."

"Hey." I was glad to see Peachy. "How'd you . . . who told you about this?"

"Barbara."

"Is she working here today?"

"She is now. Your mom called her and told her."

"My mom! Who told her?" I immediately felt guilty for fearing Mom was upset with me. I should've been entirely preoccupied with Julie's welfare. I was, primarily. But seeking shelter from the specter of parental discipline is a reflex in teenagers.

"Julie's mom," said Peachy. "Mrs. Prevette, right? She called your mom."

He looked like my angst tickled him. It occurred to me that he wouldn't appear this amused unless he had encouraging news of Julie's condition.

"She's going to be fine, Richard." He put a hand on my shoulder.

"They told you that?"

"Barbara's on top of it. And she's already said it's going to be fine."

"Thank God." Now I could worry about myself a little more. "She was doing great. I don't know what—" I stopped talking, because Peachy had suddenly shifted his gaze from me to something down the hall. He looked gravely concerned.

"Something wrong?" I ventured.

His daughter stepped out of a door I took to be the entrance to the emergency ward.

"Richard!" Miss Barbara smiled big. "Julie said to tell you that you are a really fun date!"

"She's all right, then?"

"She's fine. She'll be . . ." She looked at Peachy. "Dad, you look like you've—"

Peachy took off, a semi-jog, hustling down the hall at quite a clip for his seventy-three years.

Miss Barbara and I went after him, concerned, jogging ourselves. Peachy approached a man in the hallway and said something to him. The man dropped his mop and faced Peachy squarely.

From my vantage point, I could see the man's face, vaguely familiar, prompting an indefinite recollection in me. Did I know him?

Peachy did. Their faces had to be inches apart. The man said something; something that didn't sound like English. Then he raised his right hand; I thought he might strike Peachy. But he just smiled, gave a little wave, and took off running, a sprint, in the opposite direction.

We reached Peachy. He was out of breath, pale, and sweating.

Nurse Barbara swore under her breath. "Are you trying to give us all a heart attack?" She took him by the shoulders, turned him, and started walking him back up the hall.

"You don't understand," said Peachy.

"I understand you need to sit down. Maybe lie down."

"That man," Peachy said. "You don't understand—"

"Sit down," she commanded in her head nurse's tone. They had stopped by a room from which Barbara quickly dragged a chair.

He sat down. He was already physically more in control. As if he had accepted something and begun to deal with it.

"Who was that?" Peachy asked, gesturing back down the hall.

260

"That was Jack. And you must have said something to scare him like that, because he's a very mellow guy."

"He's not mellow."

"He's very quiet."

Peachy shook his head. "Do you know him? Do you talk to him?" His breathing was almost back to normal. "What's his last name?"

"You're scaring me, Dad."

"*I'm* scaring *you*," he said. He gave an odd little smile. More release than amusement.

A nurse walked around the corner. "Are you on tonight, Barbara?"

"Hi, Lisa. No, no. We're checking on a girl that just came in. A friend. And we're chasing my dad down the hall here."

"You're chasing . . . well I declare." Lisa shook Peachy's hand. "You raised a wonderful daughter, Dr. McLeod. Barbara's the best."

"Yes," Peachy said. "You know the man who mops the floor?"

"He saw Jack," Miss Barbara sighed. "He saw Jack and ran up to him and—"

"The janitor down the hall," said Peachy.

"Custodian, Dad."

Nurse Lisa looked. The hall was barren now, except for the mop bucket he'd left. "We see Jack pretty much every day. But nobody knows him. Very quiet."

"What's his last name?" said Peachy.

"Thornton," she answered. "Jack Thornton."

"Have you talked to him?"

Lisa shrugged. "We say hello to each other. But that's all. I should do more, I know, but I'm not good about talking to everybody. Not like Barbara is."

Peachy said to his daughter, "Don't talk to him. Ever."

She ignored him. "Do you know Richard?" Miss Barbara introduced me to Nurse Lisa.

"Richard Powell, ma'am." I shook her hand. That tickled her.

"You're the perfect gentleman, aren't you? Are you related?"

"No ma'am," I said. "And I'm not the perfect gentleman, but thank you."

While Miss Lisa insisted I was, and I insisted again I was not,

Peachy exchanged confrontational words with his daughter: "You said you didn't know him well."

"I didn't say that." Miss Barbara shook her head. "I didn't say anything remotely like that."

"So you do know him?"

"I don't. Not well at all. We've exchanged pleasantries and—"

"Stay far away from him."

"That's gonna be difficult," Miss Barbara said. "We both work here."

"Don't talk to him. Don't listen to him."

Nurse Lisa diplomatically took a few steps away from us. "I'll catch you later, Barbara. Nice to finally meet you, Dr. McLeod."

"And you also," Peachy managed to reply.

His daughter gave him a look that said she loved him, was embarrassed by him a little, and concerned about him a lot.

"Are you going to tell me what's going on in your head right now, Dad?"

I took a cue from Nurse Lisa and made a demonstrative step to walk back down the hall. "I can see ya'll back at Julie's." I said it like "Julie's" was a restaurant or tavern down the hall.

"No!" Peachy said too loud. "Richard, you have to know . . ."

"C'mon, take it easy, Dad."

"Jack Thornton is . . ." He lowered his voice. "He's not . . ."

We waited, both of us, for him to finish either sentence.

He looked down the hall, but the man had still not returned to finish mopping. He looked back to us, and decided something.

"You need to know," he said, "that unless I am seriously mistaken, and that's unlikely . . ." He paused, and started another new sentence. "If Uncle Albert and Nathan White are right, and if demons do in fact exist . . ." For the life of him, he couldn't finish a sentence.

"Dad. You know I love you."

"I know that."

"But I'm never sure why you say such . . . what is the purpose of saying such things in front of Richard?"

"It doesn't bother me," I said, wanting to bring some peace to both of them. And it honestly did not bother me. It was not yet a real entity. It was just something that haunted an old man.

"You're kind, Richard," Miss Barbara said. "Always kind, but—"

Peachy interrupted her with words that seemed to freeze our senses. How does anyone respond to such words?

"The purpose is to save the boy's life. And to prepare him. To equip him. You think I want to say these things? He has to know."

"Who is Jack Thornton, Dad?"

He whispered. He was sharing secrets, lecturing discretely. "It's not human. The man, that custodian, is human, but it has long taken up residence in him."

"You can't believe that," she said.

"I can't *not* believe it. I've tried. You think I want to believe it? I worked with that man twenty-three or twenty-four years ago in the African bush—"

"That's it," I said. "The guy in the photograph."

"—and, yes, that man. He went by Throckmorton then, but it's the same man, only twenty some years older, mid to late fifties now or—"

Miss Barbara said, "How could you possibly recognize him, know it was him, spot him down the hall like that?"

"I didn't know. So I ran to see. Because I've been looking for him to show up. The wall told me. He told me he'd show up."

"Why would he tell you that?"

"I don't know." He shook his head. "Demons are prideful, Albert says, and I think he's right. And they feed off the fear they engender if you're anticipating their arrival."

"Since when are you an expert on the psyche of demons?"

"Since the demon Jackalthorn took over Jan's body in Africa." He spoke fast now; it was difficult for me to isolate all the fears spawned by his words. "It was my fault. Jan wanted to stop. And I wouldn't let him. I pressed on. But I didn't know. I couldn't know. Could I?"

Miss Barbara's tone softened. "Maybe you should talk to someone who can help you, Dad."

"I've been doing that. Pastor White, and Albert as well, have both—"

"I mean someone who can tell you . . ." Her voice trailed off.

"What? The truth? I think the pastor and Crumpler are onto truth." Now Peachy's tone softened. "I know they are *being truthful*. That's what terrifies me. The possibility that they are right."

In what felt like a simultaneous silent decision by father and daughter, the two of them stopped talking. While we walked back toward the end of the hall where my friends were gathered, I considered mentioning to Peachy my dream, my concussion vision, of the man holding my friends and me hostage. Again I decided it would not give him peace and only exacerbate his burgeoning anxieties. I wanted to believe his daughter's read on events was closer to the truth. We irrationally resist darker realities, not by confronting them, but ignoring them. We are not blind; we like to pretend we are.

We joined a circle that included Mom, Julie's parents, and her little sister. I shifted out of the bizarre haunts occasioned by Peachy's words and actions into the carefully measured behavior of a teenage boy relating to his girlfriend's parents.

"You did good, Richard," Mrs. Prevette said.

"I was pretty scared."

"Everybody gets scared," said Gruff. "You didn't freeze up. She's gonna be all right."

"Thank you, sir."

"She's had them before. It's a form of migraine."

"It's a headache?" I asked, wanting more information.

"Yes, but very debilitating," said Mrs. Prevette. "It lays her out. It's very infrequent. The last time was a couple of years ago."

"It's happening less and less," said Gruff, "which is a good sign, I guess. They said they expect it to stop altogether as she gets older."

"Don't count on it," Peachy mumbled.

I was anxious to convey to Julie's parents my sincerest intentions for her well-being. "I hope I didn't do anything or say anything that might have brought it on."

"Of course not!" Mrs. Prevette gave me a little hug.

Peachy said very low, "We don't have to bring it on." Those were his last words of the evening.

His face stone serious, Gruff said, "You didn't hit her in the head or anything like that, did ya?"

"No sir. No sir, I wouldn't do anything—"

"Don't torment the boy like that Bill," Mrs. Prevette rescued me, before pronouncing the ultimate accolade a mother can give her daughter's boyfriend. "You're a good boy. Bill and I are so glad to see Julie and you spending time together." Moms know what to say in front of other moms. Dads, not so much.

I was surprised and pleased to see Willie come through the doors with his mom and his little sister, Beth, who recognized her classmate, Julie's sister Lizzie. They ran squealing into each other's arms, and when Willie's sister saw that Lizzie was giggling, she took it as a good sign about Julie's condition. Their giggles turned into outright laughter, and Willie's mom chastised one of them.

"Hush, now, Elizabeth!"

Or both of them. "Which one?" Beth said, bright-eyed. "We're both Elizabeth."

"And you're both too loud. A hospital here. Sick folks."

She saw Julie's mom and immediately started backtracking, cooing over Lizzie. "Aren't you the prettiest little thing?"

"Oh no," Mrs. Prevette jumped in. "She's being too loud, and you are perfectly right to correct her. My name is Ginny."

They shook hands and Julie's mom held on to Mrs. Rowe's hand. "Thank you so much for raising a fine young man like Willie."

"Willie just did what he ought to do," the other woman demurred, though obviously tickled by Mrs. Prevette's words.

"That's exactly what I mean. And it tells me he's very blessed to be raised by parents who taught him such things. Two Elizabeths. And both so pretty."

The two Elizabeths thought that was hysterical. Still holding hands, they snickered and swung their arms back and forth like they were holding a jump rope. Who knows what eight-year-old girls are thinking?

———

In the car riding home, Mom asked me if I was "really okay."

"I'm all right. I guess."

"I'm sorry they didn't let you in to see Julie."

"I'm okay with that. I'm not family. And she can go home tomorrow."

"That's right," said Mom. "You've got the right attitude. About everything it seems."

"I don't know about everything."

"You never know," she mused aloud. "You think you have every-thing figured out and then things happen that catch you off guard, off balance. Serious things. Your daddy says Vietnam was something like that all the time. Being taken for a loop got to be a normal occurrence over there. I'm starting to think maybe it's much the same, all the time, all our days. Every day brings new things. New problems. But, new solutions too. All things are possible, right?"

"To him who believes."

"What?"

"The verse is 'All things are possible to him who believes.'"

"Oh yes. And we believe."

"Yes ma'am," I agreed.

The rest of the drive home, I considered all things might be pos-sible for Peachy.

CHAPTER 23

That night, I dreamed again.

The setting, and some of the story line, was familiar. What was new dazed and amazed me.

I feel already old and yet still absurdly young. Much like the dim and bright world wherein teenagers flop around. The future is dimly lit with bright, unavoidable questions.

I recognize the setting from my conscious life, from when I was ten.

My teammate BoDean is on first base. I am at bat.

The hard ball cuts the air between Fear the Pitcher and Fear the Catcher. I swing.

My effort is more that of desperation at bad prospects than anticipation of good ones.

My swing is far behind the ball. But I hit it! The line drive shoots past the outstretched glove of the first baseman, and right in front of the face of BoDean who has the closest look at the ball's flight but seems unaware of his need to start running.

He's so like me. Maybe all of us. We see Truth up close; it nearly knocks us over. We shrink from it. But Truth is not an option. It demands a response. He demands a response.

My Little League coach hollers at BoDean, "Run, run! Get goin', BoDean!"

He gets going, spurred not by the truth of the ball's flight, but

*by the urgency of Coach's call. We envision ourselves as indepen-
dent. But we are made to answer calls.*

I was ten in 1971, and my improbable run from the batter's box
around all the bases to home plate took less than a minute. In the dream,
it felt like it took an hour or an afternoon or even a whole day. The
dream's journey from first to home was heavy with import, as if showing me great things were at stake, are always at stake, in this life and the
life beyond. Nothing is insignificant. All things, that is, all events, all
people, even all our feelings and thoughts, have far more weight, more
meaning, than we imagine. The dream seemed to shout this.

The dream also felt more real, more substantial, than the conscious event of 1971.

*Like BoDean, I'm running, but it feels like I am airborne, at
once lofted and propelled by the cheers I hear from Donnie, Zack,
Rebecca, and a little girl jumping up and down behind the chain
link, wearing a Robins ball cap like mine, only backward. I recognize her in the dream as Julie, at age eleven.*

I know in the conscious world that she was not at that game five
years ago. But I have glowed telling her of it, and glowed brighter
when Zack and Rebecca tell her of it from their recollection.

I wonder about Time. How could he who made Time be captive to it? And we who are his children may likewise be freer than
we know from the boundaries of this time and space continuum. We
will certainly be clear of it one day when we wing away. Multitudes
are already. And if Rafer and the multitudes are already there, are not
Time and Space already altered, already disbanding, already part of
the diaspora of elements?

So maybe Julie *was* there in 1971, as she was in my dream that
night in 1976. Or maybe she is there now, as are we all who belong to
the Maker of Time.

Perhaps we are unaware of the thin veil separating real events
lived from those real events retold. Perhaps story is more pregnant
with reality than we imagine. Many testify so.

I soar to first base.

Until that at-bat in the championship game, I hadn't seen first base all season, batting seldom and always getting out. In the dream, as in the real event, I clumsily pause to step on first rather than stride overtop it on my way to second.

I make a charge toward second, only my feet are slow, my stride ponderous, because the dirt under my feet shifts. My feet shift with it, so much so that I am lost, fated to die alone between first and second.

Except that someone is holding my hand. I strain hard to turn my head, to shift my eyes to see what or who is on my right. It is a dramatic and fearfully great exertion in my dream.

And there he is.

It's Lewis. It's the boy from the Special Troop who ran beside me on the long-distance leg of the Indian War Club Relay Race.

"You can make it!" he says.

"No, I can't," I declare.

Lewis retains the look of the little boy I ran a ways with in that race, the day he spoke of simple things. But his words to me in the dream are mystically eloquent and confrontational.

"Stop countenancing the shallows of Earth's constraints! You're running as if God is some theorist's abstraction! Stop surrendering to spiritless, spineless hordes. Know that the King and the Spirit are here! Even at your side!"

"I'm just trying to get to second base," I tell him.

"Look to your left!" Lewis thunders.

I realize someone now holds my left hand as well. I labor at it; my gaze shifts laboriously, as slow as my gait. And there he is. The King. Holding my hand, running with me.

He was not flopping in sandals, nor wearing a robe, but blue jeans, white sneakers, and a white tee shirt. He had a simple, strong face in the dream, but I can't picture it now. If that disappoints anyone who hears of my dream, imagine how this dreamer feels. If he looked like anyone in particular or any race in particular, I would recount it here. He was a man.

> *"You're him, aren't you?"*
> *"I am."*
> *"I want to be safe at second base."*

I know, it's so lame. But that's what I said to the Son of Man. I suppose your communications with him have always centered on the gravest, bravest missions of eternal consequence. We'll get another chance one day, to discern and isolate eternal truths.

> *"Second base is not really what you want." He is Grace, overflowing, correcting, enlightening.*
> *"It's not?"*
> *"You want to be safe at home."*
> *The three of us fairly soar over second base, my foot treading smoothly over the bag, unlike my first base stutter-step.*
> *Just as suddenly, our soaring nosedives into an achingly slow trudge through the shifting dirt under our feet. Time more than stalls. We labor in the direction of third base, our progress intricately stitched with my tawdry questions and my companions' luminous responses.*
> *And there is BoDean, my teammate who was on first, now running the wrong way, toward me and Lewis and Jesus. Just as in the real 1971 event, we were set to collide between second and third base.*
> *"What's he doing?" I ask no one in particular, which is comical when you consider I could have directed any inquiry to the One who is the Answer.*
> *"Going the wrong way," the Answer answers.*
> *"Why would he do that?"*
> *"He thinks he hears the command, 'Go back.'"*
> *"He does," I said. "People are yelling that at us."*

"No," the Light enlightens me. "They are yelling that at you. He hears the message meant for you."

"Am I supposed to go back to second base?"

My companions speak at the same time. Lewis says, "No!" and the Lord of Life says, "That is for you to decide."

I say, "My friends and my coach and even Rafer's dad, who's really Looney-Tunes, say I should go back."

Just like the rest of the Fellowship of the Rock who were at that game, even today I can see Rafer's dad, who was coaching third, frantically waving to me, yelling at me: "Go back! Go back, son!" Our head coach too, and my hero, Zack, and his friend Rebecca are jumping up and down telling me to stop and go back.

Lewis says, "Don't listen to them. They can't recognize the eternal perspectives that hinge here, in this moment. The 'go back' message is a plea to be safe. But you are not called to be safe. You are called to collide with Fear."

"What about BoDean?"

"Are you going to collide with Fear or are you going to collide with and collapse in your own self-important questions?" Lewis challenges me. "What is this human preoccupation with questions?"

The Answer smiles. "Let them ask."

"It's just me asking," I say.

"You are asking for many," he says, "just as I answer many when I answer you."

I look to my right. "What do you mean 'human preoccupation'? You're human."

Lewis finds my observation entertaining or ridiculous or both. "You are so sure of so many things!"

I gaze back to my left. "What about BoDean?"

"He has turned, back around, and found his new, true direction," says the Life. "The call he thought he heard was a false call. He is to move, as you are, toward home."

"Will he collide with Fear?"

"He has already encountered his fear. And that has saved him."

We glide over third base, BoDean enough ahead of us to stay

clear of our path. I am so glad for him, seeing him cross home plate easily.

"The ball's back in the infield," Lewis announces, not with apprehension, but soberly. "Brace yourself."

Over my shoulder I see the Hawks' second baseman scrambling to chase down a bad throw from the outfield, and seizing the ball off the ground.

"I'm not going to make it!" I announce with apprehension, even anguish.

"Listen!" Lewis encourages me. "Everyone's telling you to go, to keep running."

It was true. All the "Stop, Richard, stop!" had morphed in a magical instant to "Go, Richard, go!"

I fret, vexed. "Maybe I'm not hearing them right."

"But you are! You know you are!" Lewis admonishes. "Run!"

"But—"

"Run toward what lies before you!"

"I will be out!" I cry.

"Finish it!" Lewis out cries me, and vanishes.

To the one on my left, I plead, "Will you leave me too?"

"I am with you always, even to the end of the age." Then he disappears. Rascal!

But I hear him: "Your eyes are not the Light. I am. I am with you."

Seconds before impact, Fear the Catcher morphs into the mammoth Hawks catcher, Booger Clark, my childhood nemesis, who had falsely prophesied that my dad would die in the jungles of Vietnam. To my ten-year-old heart, he was The Dagger. I wanted to hurt him.

The ball beats me to the plate. I slide into Booger's shin guards. I see his face dissolve back toward the countenance of Fear.

I pity him. I should say, someone invades my body and pities him, overrunning my own fear. I reach toward his face, trying to push Fear aside and pull Booger back. While his closed mitt comes down like a hammer toward my face, I punch it out of the way, *straining to get my hand to his face, which, in the dream, I take to be his soul. My punch jostles the ball free from the mitt.*

"I'm still here," I hear The Answer say to me. "Finish the course."

I put my hand on home plate.

The dream's pandemonium mirrors that of the actual 1971 event, my teammates and coach tossing me around and clapping me on my batting helmeted head. And just as on that real day, that real year, in my dream the catcher walks away, appearing smaller than he had seemed when blocking the plate.

He was smaller. And for him, this was a good thing.

I woke up.
I think this dream was the real awakening.

CHAPTER 24

The custodian, Jack Thornton, disappeared.

After Peachy saw him that night, he stopped showing up for work. The hospital's attempts to locate him were fruitless; the man seemed to have vanished, leaving only sparse belongings abandoned in the Jefferson Apartments, unit 323.

In 1952 and 1953, a man named Jan Throckmorton worked with Dr. Peachy McLeod in what was then the Belgian Congo while Peachy conducted field research on the cellular biology of various animals. At the time, Peachy was in his early fifties and Throckmorton his early thirties. The orderly who'd worked at the hospital the last few weeks looked to be about fifty. Peachy was adamant that it was the same man.

Or the same demon. It was, I suppose, a matter of perspective.

Mom and Dad and I met with Peachy, Uncle Albert, Miss Barbara, and Pastor White in one of the classrooms at Silas Baptist and discussed these things. Everyone agreed that Thornton seemed an odd man whose disappearance merited concern. But only Peachy seemed to feel there was an overt spiritual dimension to the man's appearing and disappearing.

"Even if it's the man you remember from twenty years ago, Dr. McLeod," my dad said, "and I'm not saying it isn't, but even if it is, was this guy dangerous when you knew him?"

"He was . . . he was not so much dangerous as he was mysterious," said Peachy.

"Was he possessed?" said Uncle Albert. "By a demon?"

Nothing like striking at the root of all our thinking.

274

"I don't want to believe in demons," Peachy said.

"I'm not asking you what you want to believe in."

"What does he want?" my mom asked. "Do you think he's show-ing up here, following you, to get something from you?"

"Yes," Peachy sighed. "I don't know . . . maybe."

"What would he want from you?" Miss Barbara said.

"I don't know that. If I knew that . . . I don't know that."

Even the exorcist Uncle Albert and Pastor White seemed reluc-tant to believe that Thornton was actually the same man Peachy had known twenty years before.

"And even if he is," White counseled, "are you ready to say defini-tively the man was possessed by a demon when you knew him?"

Mom said, "And who knows what's happened to the man since then?" I think she was suggesting he could have changed for the bet-ter since Peachy knew him, which of course presumes his past was more self-marred than demon marred. "Barbara says he was nothing but kind at the hospital."

"Then why are we even having this little powwow?" Peachy said. "Oh, I get it. Peachy's off his rocker. Let's all see if we can help Peachy come to his seventy-three-year-old senses."

"Dad—" Miss Barbara tried to cut him off.

"Well, let me shock you. I have all my faculties." He addressed Pastor White. "You said so the first time we talked in the church." He turned to Uncle Albert. "And you said much the same thing in the conversation we shared over pizza. Conversation, I might add, that was anchored in your contention that the multitude of UFO sight-ings reported annually are largely manifestations of demons visiting this planet. Just who is off his rocker? I don't think anyone in this room is."

He made solid enough sense that the lot of us agreed to sim-ply commit the whole matter, including the man Jack Thornton, to prayer. I write "simply" because, in the end, such a resolve, though exceedingly powerful, is not complex; we agreed to pray. The circum-stances and the suggestion by Peachy that Thornton was likely pos-sessed *was* complex, mysterious. It was one more mystery attendant to that incredible year, a year that wasn't even close to being over.

———

Julie confirmed to me in the days that followed that she had suffered a migraine.

I said, "Just a headache?" That was a mistake.

"A migraine is serious pain," she said, "and I hope you never suffer them. You're lucky I didn't throw up on you."

"I'm sorry. I didn't mean it was not . . . I know it was serious . . . You could've thrown up on me . . . I'm sorry."

"Okay, okay." She smiled a little. "That's enough groveling. I'm going to send Willie a thank-you card. He was so sweet and he really helped out."

"Willie's aces. BoDean thought you had something one of his buddies had at a party once. The ambulance guy on the phone told him to keep the guy awake until they could get there. They sang to him and that worked. That's why I ended up singing to you."

"You mean you weren't serenading me because you love me?"

"Well . . ." I took the plunge. "Yes, I was singing to you because I love you," I said with utmost sincerity.

Her expression told me she believed me and I thought she was going to tell me something close to what I'd just told her. She didn't. She asked when we were going canoeing again.

I thought she was chastising me. "I'm sorry about that. I thought it would be fun."

"I loved it. When can we go again?" She was serious. "Dad says I need to get back up on the horse."

"Come again?" I asked.

"When you fall off a horse, you need to get back up on it again," she said, "or you'll stay afraid, you know, of ever riding a horse again."

"Does he want to canoe with us?"

"You don't want to canoe with my dad," she said, answering a slightly different question.

"Well, I'd like to do something with him, sometime," I said. That wasn't entirely honest. I didn't want to do anything with him. I just thought it would be wise to ingratiate myself to the man sometime, someway.

"Don't worry about it." Julie smiled. "Something will come up, and ya'll will have a great time together. Or, something won't come up, and ya'll won't have a good time together, and that's God too. We're so young, Richard!" Her voice took on that lilt that bounced off my heart. "And it's okay to be young!"

I played a sort of sympathy card. "I thought you liked me." But it was really more a wild card of attempted manipulation.

"Whether we end up together is up to God, isn't it?" she said.

"You're being awfully philosophical about it," I murmured.

———

We had another picnic with Duffey, Caroline, Donnie, Zack, and Rebecca in the same spot by Lake Cross where we had picnicked and canoed before with BoDean.

I phoned Willie and invited him, but he said his mom wanted him to go to the new mall in Dothan and "walk around with Beth and Lizzie while Mom cleans rooms."

"Cleans rooms at the mall?"

"At the motel by the mall. Mom fills in for Miss Pearl when Miss Pearl is too sore to do the work. And Mom likes it. She always likes extra work."

"So you're walking around at the mall. Watching over your baby sister."

"I'd rather be messing around with ya'll. But least I'm not mowing grass. And Beth and Liz are funny."

"Every other guy I talk to hates being with his little sister."

"That's silly. Why would I hate Beth? And Liz is a hoot. Everything she says is funny."

"That's what Julie says too," I said. "Hey, thanks again, Willie. For being there for Julie. I mean when she conked out."

"Julie's the best," he said simply. "I love her."

If another guy had told me he loved my girlfriend, I'd be concerned. But when eleven-year-old Willie said it, it made me feel nothing but good.

"You have fun, Willie," I said.

"It'll be cool. Mom'll give me some change to buy them two some ice cream. That'll be fun."

I wondered. "Does your little sister ever get mad at you?"

"We tried that once. But Mom didn't let us go there. Said we got to stick together. And, I don't know, we just *want* to stick together. That's family, ain't it?"

———

Donnie was in the canoe with Julie and me, and Rebecca and Caroline wanted to canoe together, so that left Zack and Duffey in the third canoe. We kept the canoes much closer to shore than before, and kept sliding up alongside each other. It was an unannounced ritual, all of us keeping one eye on Julie but also just enjoying each other's "canoe company." It's like going to a bowling alley with friends. It's not as much fun if you don't bowl together on the same lane.

We came back onshore and tied off the canoes. Duffey and Zack said they would come back and move the canoes into the shed later.

"How do you do that?" Caroline asked. "I mean, do you just drag them across the grass here to the shed?"

"You can," Donnie said.

"But we pick them up," Duffey said. "Zack and me."

"By yourselves?" Julie asked, impressed.

"No, these little green men come out from the woods yonder and help us," Duffey said. "Course by ourselves. It ain't nothin' but a thing."

"You leave Julie alone," Caroline said, but she was enjoying the moment too. "She's nothing but kind to you. And what's that mean anyway?" She mimicked him. "It ain't nothin' but a thing."

"Means it's easy," Duffey said.

"Why don't you just say 'It's easy,' then? Instead of this thing nothin' but"—she got lost in the saying—"whatever a thing is."

"I dunno," he shrugged. "It ain't nothin' but a thing."

I've long pondered the wisdom of that phrase, which we first heard from BoDean five years before, during the summer of 1971.

The afternoon ended in the glow of time well spent, goofing off together. Julie was absolutely fine and even wanted to go farther out on the water. I told her that was a goal for another day; we had many days ahead to go farther out. That was true in multiple senses.

We'd come in three cars—Zack's Vega, Julie's Pacer, and Donnie's ancient but intrepid Impala, which he said was "just out of the shop," by which he meant his cousin Hamlin had pounded on it and prodded it in his backyard, and flung it out onto the streets of Silas and the dirt roads of Camp Sequoyah with all good intentions.

"It got us here," Caroline said, as she and Duffey had ridden with Donnie.

It cranked up, and Donnie looked relieved. Satisfied, Zack and Rebecca drove off and Julie and I pulled in behind Donnie and onto the dirt road that led out of the campground.

"How are you feeling?" I asked Julie.

"Great!" she said. "That was so much fun!"

"Yeah, it was."

"Uh-oh," she warned.

"What's the matter? You okay?"

"Not me. It's Auntie Em." It was her name for the car.

The engine died just as I saw Donnie's Impala turn the corner some ways ahead and disappear.

I didn't think of it, until a few more seconds had passed. "Honk the horn!" I said. I reached over and honked it a few times.

"Oh yeah," she said. "Hey guys!" she called, as if they were just outside her driver's window. She honked then, after I had stopped.

"That's fine," I said. "That'll do," I said louder, and she stopped honking. "If they didn't hear that, they're not going to hear any more."

"I know," she blushed, and then laughed. "Just desperation honking, I guess."

"Is there any other kind?" I tried to joke too, but I couldn't hold a smile. "I don't know anything about cars, ya know."

"I figured that." She was always direct.

Donnie's car appeared around the corner ahead, coming back.

Julie and I both said a variation of "Thank you, God" and got out of the car. I couldn't even figure out how to raise the hood, so I just stood there like a duck in thunder waiting for Duffey and Donnie to fly into the storm.

Caroline gave the command. "Pop the hood." I wasn't sure, but she seemed a little angry.

"Sure glad ya'll heard us," I said.

"No problem," Donnie said. "I don't think Zack heard. He'd a been here by now."

Julie popped the hood and Duffey looked down on the engine with an intense focus I'd only seen before in his eyes for edibles.

"You know a lot about cars?" Julie asked him.

"No. A little," he said. "But you're in luck."

He didn't elaborate right off, and Julie and I looked at each other with questions.

"I don't see nothin' right off," he announced, we thought to no one in particular. After a few seconds, he announced again, "I don't see nothing right . . ."

"Oh, did you want me to help out?" Caroline said with sharp mischief.

Duffey answered without looking her way, "You're not still sore at me, are you?"

Caroline huffed. "What makes you think I'm sore, Mr. I-know-cars-so-just-let-me-handle-it-Girlie?"

"Did you call her Girlie?" Julie asked him. "For shame, Duffey."

"That was a mistake," he said under his breath. "I know that now."

"What was that?" Caroline pressed. "Something about a mistake?"

"Are you gonna stand there on top of my case all day," Duffey said, "or are you gonna help out? I am sorry, and I shouldn't have said anything to you. You know I got a big mouth . . . Ow!" He bumped his head on the raised hood.

"Move over!" Caroline slapped my big friend's shoulder and he moved over, winking at me. "Caroline knows engines!" he said with relish, trying to recover her good graces.

Donnie looked at the engine with Caroline. "I know just a little," he said. "I'd like to help."

"Did you hear that, mister know-it-all?" Caroline said to Duffey, who was rubbing his head where he'd bumped it. "That's what a humble man says. And he offers to help. He doesn't say move over and let me show you how it's done."

"I talk too much," Duffey agreed. "I know it. I'm sorry."

Caroline's anger melted like ice cream at the fair. "You just . . . why do I care about you?"

"I don't know." Duffey was smart enough to say it and shut up.

"Is your dad a mechanic?" asked Julie.

"He might as well be," she said. "He works at the plant. But he fixes his buddies' cars for odd jobs. And for odd money. Ow." She pulled her hand back off something hot, then put it right back down near where she'd had it. "He started showing me stuff when I was old enough to bother him."

"Me and him are tearing down a Falcon engine before summer's over," Duffey said.

"So he likes Duffey?" Julie asked slyly.

"Shoot," groaned Caroline. "Pa thinks Duffey's his long lost little brother."

I high-fived Duffey.

"That makes it good for ya'll, then," said Julie.

"I guess," Caroline groaned again, still peering down deep into the engine parts.

"You guess?" Duffey sounded genuinely concerned.

"Oh, just drop that act. You know I'm crazy about you," she said without smiling. He did drop it, because he did know it.

"Everything looks good," she said, "except for this right here, which is the problem. Give me your shirt," she said to Duffey.

"I like this jersey."

"Your tee shirt, you . . ." She tried to stay mad, but it wasn't happening. "Take off your tee shirt, and then you can put your jersey back on."

He did so. She tied the tee shirt around a hose, and said, "Crank it up."

Auntie Em came to life, and we all gave a mock cheer.

"Take it into the shop," Caroline said. "Needs a new hose."

Julie told Duffey she'd get him his tee shirt back.

"That don't matter," he said. "I got what really counts. I got back in Caroline's good graces. Everything's right with the world. This is the best summer yet, in our whole life, ya'll."

I was sure Duffey was right, and the summer days and nights lengthened. We all seemed to drink in the intoxicating virtue, the innocence of those wholesome days.

CHAPTER 25

Batman and I were committed to making Eagle Scout. We had already earned all the required merit badges, and it was simply a matter now of reaching the coveted number of twenty-four total badges. Naturally, we scoured the requirements for various badges listed at the back of the Boy Scout manual. No self-respecting teenager is going to pursue the harder badges when all you need is the magic number of twenty-four. The more honorable route is pursuing badges that honestly appeal to the Scout, or is some field or interest the exploration of which expands the Scout's world. But how many teenagers think in such categories?

"I've looked them over, all of them, real good," said Batman to me over the phone. "Some of them are ridiculously hard, yeah. But some of them are insanely easy. Like Bird Study."

"Birds," I said, my voice and interest hollow. "I don't know anything about birds."

"Neither do I," he said. "So what? We didn't know anything about Lifesaving, either, but we got that."

"Because we had to. It's required for Eagle. And I almost drowned, remember?"

"All the more reason to coast now. We paid our dues, man, with those hard badges. Bird Study is easy."

I swallowed a mouthful of peanut butter and banana. That was my recurring lunch special at home that summer. "Not without a counselor, it isn't."

"That's just it," he said. "Mr. Albert and Peachy are both experts. They've bird-watched for years."

282

"Uncle Albert?"

"Yeah, that guy you said knows all about UFOs and demons and stuff like that."

"How do you know he's a bird-watcher?"

"I called Julie up," said Batman, "and asked if she knew any bird-watching people."

"You called up my special friend?"

"Oh come on, Richard, I'm not making a move or nothing. I know her from drama club. Anyway, she said, 'As a matter of fact, I do know two bird-watcher people.' She said she heard them talking about how birds are different here than in Ohio."

"You're sure the requirements are easy?" I was into easy. My life was complicated enough that summer of 1976.

"Look at them yourself."

"We'll have to see if Pastor White is willing to let Uncle Albert and Peachy be our badge counselors for it."

"Already done," Batman said with triumph. "He said if they're willing, we can go for it."

———

And so Batman and I found ourselves traipsing through the forests that bordered Camp Sequoyah looking into trees, listening to birdcalls, and jotting notes in our field manuals, which were composition spiral notebooks we hadn't filled up in school. Miss Barbara came with us, she said, "to make sure my dad doesn't overdo this hiking thing." She also seemed to know a lot about all the birds and calls. She was "tutored by Dad when I was a kid with pigtails, bare feet, and overalls."

I tried to picture her in pigtails and bare feet. "How old were you?" I asked.

"Oh, ten, maybe eleven," she said. "Before the world sneaked up on me. On me and Dad both. So what makes you like birds?"

"Oh, I don't know." Honesty rushed in. "It's an easy merit badge," I said soft enough to perhaps keep Peachy and Uncle Albert from hearing. I guessed merit badge counselors were not thrilled by Scouts going after the prize because it looks easy. And of course they have the power to complicate the process.

"But we're seeing that it really is pretty interesting," Batman hastened to add. Sometimes I thought Batman might give Doug a run for his money as a savvy political operative.

"Quite all right," said Uncle Albert who, to our embarrassment, overheard. "Nothing wrong with choosing a task that's not so hard . . . so long as nothing of value is sacrificed in the choice. I make the easy choice about lots of things all the time."

That intrigued me. "I can't think of anything harder than what you do with demons."

"What, you mean casting them out?" He shrugged. Shrugged, I tell you! "Yes, it is quite difficult. But of course, I didn't choose that calling. I told God I wanted to have the gift of encouragement. He made me an exorcist."

Peachy wanted to be funny. "It was a trade-off of sorts."

"Of course," Uncle Albert said. "I would be choosing a much more difficult path if I said to God, 'No thank you; I don't want the gift you give me.'"

"I don't get that," Peachy sputtered. "If there is a God, and he was trying to give me something I didn't want, I would tell him so."

"Of course," Uncle Albert said again. "Which is precisely what you have done."

"What's that mean?" Peachy asked with genuine curiosity. He liked Uncle Albert.

"God is offering to give you something. You don't want it. And you've been telling him so, for quite a long time."

We identified birds. And saw some. I wasn't good at actually finding them in trees, even when Uncle Albert lent me his binoculars. I did see them in flight, but not well enough to identify them.

I had more fun than I had anticipated and congratulated Batman on discovering a viable and interesting merit badge in the sea of those available to us.

"Now we just write it up," he said. "And go again with these guys sometime soon. And we're one badge closer. It's a piece of cake."

While I was digesting this merry news, Uncle Albert sobered us. "As I understand the requirements, the two of you need to write up a field notebook for me, your trusty merit badge counselor."

"Well, sir," Batman made an effort, "I think we can kinda just tell you what birds we saw, and kinda what kinda birds were in what kinda groups."

"Oh yes." Uncle Albert nodded. "Kinda that too. But requirement five does say, 'Prepare a field notebook.' I should think 'prepare' means create one; that is, write one and not just conjure one in your head. Don't you boys kinda agree?"

"Yes sir," we both answered. Nothing's ever easy. Except self-deception.

We rendezvoused with our cars at the camp's dirt parking lot. Peachy and Uncle Albert were in a heated discussion, the heat's source being the categories of doubt and certainty concerning the existence of God. They wanted to continue their duel and I wanted to listen to them joust longer, but Batman had to get home to undertake the formidable task of washing his dog. It was formidable because his dog was the biggest German shepherd in Silas County and hated being washed. So we split up, Miss Barbara driving Batman home and me listening to the combatants contest each other's view of how we human creatures perceive things, including our perceptions of views distinct from our own. Fun all around.

When Miss Barbara's Buick pulled out of the lot, Peachy, Uncle Albert, and I were still parked, the Boy Scout in the backseat and the philosophers in the front.

"You're so sure of what you know," Peachy said.

"I'm more sure," said Uncle Albert, "that things are knowable, than I am sure that I know them."

"How is that possible?"

"I don't know how any alternative is possible," Uncle Albert said, "because I am surrounded by revelation. The fact that we're debating the question of the very possibility of knowing what *is*, and what is *true*, tells me there is some perceivable truth in the computer of the universe. Otherwise we wouldn't bother with trying to work the computer."

"Some people don't," Peachy said. "Work the computer."

"And why is that?" Uncle Albert countered. "Why don't they? Because they can't? No. Because they do not care to."

"Maybe those are the smartest people," Peachy offered. "Like Nietzsche, brilliant before he went bonkers. And Beckett. They see there's either nothing to be found, or if there is, we can't find it, and so they don't waste their time looking."

"I can't speak for them," said Uncle Albert. "But I find it interesting that Peachy McLeod still seems to be on the hunt. You are. Otherwise you wouldn't be challenging me like this, would you?"

"What should I say to that?" Peachy, sighing, asked me.

I said, "I'm still trying to figure out how to tell a mockingbird from the birds it mocks."

I thought I'd said something funny. But Uncle Albert didn't take it that way.

"Maybe Peachy is too," he said. "Maybe the brilliant Nietzsche is a mockingbird. We think he sounded forth new truth, as if there is any such thing. But his mocking doesn't make the real birds any less real. In fact, his mocking singles them out as the originals. And by the way, Beckett's characters were waiting for God."

"But he didn't show up," Peachy said.

Uncle Albert looked to be thinking out loud. "True, he didn't show up in Beckett's play, in Beckett's creation. But that doesn't make him any less real in the real creation. Again, why was Beckett waiting for someone? Why does the question of God's existence merit Beckett's creative energy?"

Peachy said, "Maybe Beckett's characters are waiting to see if someone else shows up. Or something else."

Outside the car, a man's voice interjected. "You mean like me?"

CHAPTER 26

In the half-light of the day's receding, I wasn't sure until he stepped closer to the car. But it was Jack Thornton, the hospital custodian whom Peachy said was the same man he'd worked with more than twenty years before. He and another man had come up from behind the car, I reckoned. The other man stayed back; Thornton leaned directly down to the passenger side open window.

"Will you gentlemen step out of the car?" Thornton said. When we didn't respond, Thornton's companion, a tall thin man with a brown wide-brim hat pulled low on his forehead, pulled a pistol from his overall trousers pocket and pointed it in the general direction of the car.

Thornton's eyes followed our startled looks back to his companion and said, "That won't be necessary."

Of course it wouldn't be necessary; we'd seen the weapon.

The man put the pistol back and remained at an awkward distance, nervously rubbing his hands.

"The car won't miss you," Thornton jested. "Everyone exit on this side, please."

We got out, Uncle Albert sliding across the front seat and out the passenger side door.

"Look what the serpent dragged out," Peachy said.

Thornton took him somewhat literally. "I am free to move about. The human is bound, and always answers to a higher power."

"You're not free," said Peachy.

"And you *are*? This way," Thornton indicated a direction into the woods. "It's not far."

We followed him, Peachy ahead of me, and me ahead of Uncle Albert in the line. Thornton's companion, and his pistol, which I learned later was a .38 revolver, brought up the rear. Darkness was coming on. But there was enough light to make our way through the forest, between and around trees. The onset of evening was pregnant with storm, overcast. The breezes we had welcomed earlier in the afternoon now threatened a coming chill out of accord with the late summer season.

Thornton seemed anxious to talk to Peachy. "You know . . . you're odd," he said to him.

"I'm odd," said Peachy, a statement of fact.

"Yes. Different. No one else believes."

"That's not true," Peachy said. "Everybody talks about demons. Every day. You're all over the news."

"Enlighten me. Tell me what you mean, Peachy."

"Demons. Injustice . . . poverty . . . destructive pride . . ."

Thornton gave a guttural chuckle. "Your world is so academic. Those are not personal demons."

Neither Uncle Albert, nor Thornton's companion, nor I spoke. Only the two old acquaintances.

"It's all personal," said Peachy. "A man who's lynched would call it personal, whether his murder is born of ignorance, or pride, or fear, or some actual demon named Ignorance or Pride or Fear."

"I am a personal being, a power," Thornton intoned. "A personality. What your world calls, strangely, a supernatural being."

"Strangely?"

"The assumption is that I am the odd being, and the human world of shadows is the norm. It is backward."

"*You* are backward."

"You're not strong enough to anger me, Peachy."

"You don't mind if I try."

"I don't mind much of anything humans do."

"Then why are you talking to me? I must matter in some way."

"You believe," said Thornton. "We visit those who believe."

"But I don't believe. In Christ."

"No one is perfect," Thornton said.

For the first time, I heard a noise from his tall companion behind us. It was a short, hoarse sound, like he was clearing his throat.

"What I'm counting on, Peachy," Thornton said almost pleasantly, "is your helping me in this small matter. You helped me before."

"A long time ago," Peachy said low.

"What is time to those like you and me?"

"Time is your enemy. It's running out."

The gun-toting man scowled. "We have all the time. All the time in the world is with us."

"Precisely." Peachy stopped walking, turned, and fired back at the man. "All the time in the world. Only the world is collapsing in on itself. History is withering."

"I don't think so," Thornton said evenly, drawing Peachy's gaze back to the front. "It's only beginning. I don't expect you to see that. You're mortal. That's why I have to bother you so much, isn't it? When you're dead, your knowledge goes with you."

"Really?" said Peachy. "You won't come bother me in hell? I would think you two have to show up there from time to time. Or maybe you're not high enough on the food chain to get a free pass to come and go as you please?"

They made no reply. We walked in silence a few more minutes. I started to consider I might have seen Thornton's accomplice before. I didn't hazard any more looks at him right now; but there was something in his appearance and his spirit that was familiar.

Thornton was honest about one thing; our journey was not far. We came to an old cabin, not unlike the one in my concussion dream. Looking back, I wonder why the similarity did not strike me as eerie. It had an opposite effect. I felt a strange peace, as if I had been prepared for these moments.

Thornton motioned us inside, and gestured to an old couch, its cover threadbare. We three mortals sat down, Peachy and Uncle Albert on either side of me.

The beings whose mortality was still in question pulled two chairs from a desk against the wall and sat facing us, about eight or ten feet away. Close enough to intimidate us. Far enough to suggest they were not entirely comfortable being in close proximity to us.

The man in overalls took off his hat.

"Bradley," said Peachy, and I recognized him too.

"McDonald's!" I blurted before I could stop myself. It was the man whose car window we'd hit with the baseball.

"You were tailing me," Peachy said.

"You went to church." Bradley said it like it was a crime. "You traveled with church people—"

Without looking in Bradley's direction, Thornton made an indistinct sound with his mouth, and Bradley stopped talking.

Thornton's eyes fixed on me. "The young man Richard," he said.

"Leave the boy alone," said Peachy.

"I think you should turn yourself in," I said. "To the police. Or at the ranger station."

"The ranger station," Thornton said without inflection.

I was still innocent enough at fifteen to hope for a peaceful resolution. But sometimes the Fight refuses to leave.

"The very young man Richard," Thornton said again.

"Leave him be!" Peachy said.

"I'm not going to hurt him," he said, calm enough to sound like he meant it. But calm can be scary. I couldn't get out of my head what Uncle Albert had drilled in; demons are chronic liars. Except they know that we know they lie. Do they factor that into their incessant deceptions? Or are they so lost, so deviant, they deceive even themselves? They probably couldn't deceive entirely or perfectly. They couldn't do anything perfectly. Even their rebellion was and is imperfect. All of which circles back to Evil's parasitic nature. It has no intrinsic reality; it is an aberration. It feeds off the Good, a malignant tumor.

"Richard, young man!" Thornton said in a loud voice. He'd asked me something. What was it? I decided to tell him a small part of what I was thinking.

"You and your master," I said, "have a beginning and an end."

"Is that so?" said Thornton.

"You are prey. To Time."

Peachy laughed softly but loud enough.

"Shut up!" Bradley pointed the .38 at Peachy.

"Don't," Thornton advised Bradley.

"Do!" Peachy stared at the man and his .38. "Finish me!"

Bradley cocked the hammer.

Thornton leaned sharply toward Bradley and said in tones slightly different from his normal voice, "Pull the trigger and you'll live and die and live again many times to regret it." His words wheezed, blending with the sound of the night's cool stormy breezes that pushed themselves hard through the small openings in the walls around us. It sounded to me that breezes were saying, in Thornton's wheezy voice, *Many times.* For some reason, my vision blurred. I tried hard to look at Thornton. I heard it in the breezes again. *Many times.*

My vision cleared.

Bradley set the .38 in his lap again, and looked for all the world like he was getting sleepy! That didn't sit well with Thornton, who started to say something to him and then changed his mind, looking instead at me.

"Please answer my first question," he said, his voice normal again, flat.

"Your first question?" I asked politely. "I'm sorry, Mr. Thornton. I didn't hear it. What was it?"

"That's all right, Richard. It's a simple question," Thornton said. "Has Peachy ever written something down for you, or shown you anything unusual? Perhaps told you something that seemed odd?"

"You don't have to tell that demon anything," Peachy said to me.

I said, "Almost every time Peachy talks to me, it's something odd."

Peachy changed his mind. "Yes, tell him everything. Tell him everything you can possibly think of."

"I don't know what you're looking for," I told our kidnapper. And that was true. I did sense the liberty to lie to the demon or the possessed or the criminal. But I guessed, too, that the truth might be just as baffling to it, or him.

Bradley closed his eyes.

Uncle Albert, who to this point had remained silent and still, decided to announce something very startling, given our circumstances. "It is not up to you," he said to Thornton, "what happens to us. It is not your decision."

Uncle Albert's countenance was focused but still. A serene authority.

By contrast, Thornton's breathing was a little faster, slightly more labored. "I know what you are," he said to Uncle Albert. "I know what you do."

"I do nothing," said Uncle Albert. "I am not your problem. The authority of Jesus Christ is the issue—"

"If I were you, I would not trust the outcome," Thornton said quickly.

"—so he himself is your problem."

"Where would you have them go?"

"I would not have them go anywhere. It is the Most High who determines these things."

Bradley's chin dropped to his chest.

Peachy, moving much more quickly than I would have guessed he could, left his chair and lunged toward Bradley.

Thornton was quicker. He beat Peachy to the .38, grabbing it from Bradley's hand as his collaborator crumpled unconscious to the floor. Or dead. His body was so still, I couldn't tell.

"Back," Thornton commanded Peachy with the .38. "Sit." Peachy sat back down in the chair. Thornton, on his feet now, was breathing heavily.

He glared at Uncle Albert, who had not moved from his chair in the quick fracas. He pointed the .38 directly at Uncle Albert. I was sure he was going to fire. After some seconds, he lowered the gun.

"It is my decision," Thornton said. "These things are my decision."

"You don't decide anything," said Uncle Albert.

Thornton nearly shouted, "I decide . . ." He said in a lower voice, "I decide . . . a great deal."

His assertions were interrupted by the sound of something moving outside of the cabin. Thornton took a couple of quick steps toward the closed front door, pointing the .38 ahead of him, keeping us in the corner of his eye.

The door popped open and Sawdust darted in and stopped frozen in his tracks, as if taking everything in. My heart soared to see him, and then sank fast with Thornton's gun on the dog.

"Don't do it!" I shouted at Thornton. "Please," I added.

"Of course I will." He leveled the gun with more deliberate aim at Sawdust.

Sawdust snarled, and crouched, baring his teeth. At me.

"Ahhhh." Thornton took a step toward the dog. Then another. And another, coming alongside Sawdust who was staring at me with glazed eyes, still showing teeth.

Thornton talked to Sawdust. "It's different, isn't it? But it can be fun."

Uncle Albert whispered to me. "It has to find a host. Quickly."

I cried, three or four quiet tears. It didn't occur to me to wipe them away.

"Shoot him," I said. "Shoot him," I repeated.

"Of course I won't."

"Do you want the formula?" Peachy roared to life. "Or do you just want to keep playing around?"

"Yes," Thornton said.

Sawdust slouched to the unconscious Bradley on the floor and sat beside him. There was saliva, foam, on his snout. But he wasn't snarling. He appeared disinterested in all of us.

Thornton addressed Crumpler. "You don't have any more to say? I was beginning to enjoy your game."

Crumpler looked at Peachy. "He can't stop lying. A prisoner to his own lying."

"You talk to me!" said Thornton sharply. "Not him."

Crumpler did. "It is slipping away from you."

Thornton moved to Peachy, close enough to touch him. "It had better be more than a formula. It had better be a working solution."

"If I give it to you—"

"Don't do it," Uncle Albert said.

"—will you let the boy and Albert go?"

"He can't," Uncle Albert said firmly.

"I will, I will do this," Thornton almost stammered.

"It is not his decision," said Uncle Albert. "Nothing is."

"It strikes me as"—Thornton looked to be searching for a word—"bizarre. It's bizarre that you who are sitting where I've told you to sit, and listening to me *make decisions*"—he grossly emphasized the latter two words—"would claim that I don't decide things."

"I'm not claiming it," Uncle Albert spoke clearly. "I'm stating facts. I'm not hoping for outcomes. I'm stating outcomes. Before they happen. The King's children can do that."

"Says who?" Thornton hissed.

Uncle Albert didn't answer right away. I felt something weird. In my emotions. I laughed, a short sound. Then another.

They all looked at me; Peachy and Thornton like I was crazed, and Uncle Albert like I was . . . powerful.

Peachy, not Thornton, asked, "What's so funny?"

"I dunno," I said. I started to say more, but I laughed again.

"Why is he laughing, Thornton?" Uncle Albert said. "Falling to pieces?"

"He is." Thornton took a step toward me. I tried to recover, to not laugh. But I did it again.

"He is falling to pieces," he said. But he didn't look like he believed it. Not as much as I believed it.

"I dunno," I said again. "It's crazy." I started to laugh again and worked hard to cut it short. I felt a ridiculous urge to apologize, even to Thornton. I looked at him. "I'm sorry. I really am . . . but . . . something funny's going on here." I recognized my unintended twofold use of the word *funny*, and there they came again, snickers, laughs, escaping me.

It didn't feel like fear. I knew what fear felt like, and this wasn't it. This was very unlike me, the serious, cautious observer of Earth's curious phenomena.

Or was I being changed? Even in those moments, in a good way.

Thornton moved directly in front of me. "Your dog is possessed. By a great demon."

I stopped laughing. Out loud, anyway. There was still an inane amusement inside me, threatening to come back out.

I tried to answer the man. Or the demon. Even that dual possibility struck me as potentially hilarious in those moments. "I don't think it can be that great. It's in a dog."

Thornton said, "It is called Lamish. In your tongue it means 'vanisher of souls, fader of souls.' Is that funny to you?"

It was, but I was still, at great effort, successfully not laughing. "Lamish is asleep," I said.

He looked and saw the dog sleeping beside Bradley's unconscious form.

He said, "Your dog is a poor host."

A silly line came to me, a line from a silly movie. I said it. "That's not my dog."

Uncle Albert laughed. Peachy and I couldn't help it; we did too.

Something bizarre was happening to Thornton. It was like the comedy in our soul was a toxic to him. He sank to one knee. We stopped laughing.

Peachy stood suddenly, and I found myself standing as well. Thornton recovered and in a quick move was back on his feet.

"Sit down!" He pointed at Peachy with the .38. Then to me, "Sit down!"

We did.

Sawdust still slept.

Thornton's face took on a strange expression, or more accurately, lost its expression. As if his being was losing something. Emptying.

"Since then," the emptying man said, "it's not your dog. You won't mind if I destroy it."

He took two steps toward the animal, his back to me. He raised the weapon, aiming.

I didn't really stand; I moved low, as fast as I could from my seated position. I hit him, the gun fired and fell to the floor.

I heard "Ow," recognizing Peachy's laconic tone.

Thornton, uncommonly strong, easily rolled on top of me. I heard what sounded like footsteps running on the hard cabin floor. I was hopeful, thinking the others were getting away. I got both my hands up on Thornton's neck, squeezing and pushing hard under his chin, so his head was turned far to one side. With one hand he battled my grip on his neck and with the other he reached for something to the side. The gun.

As soon as he grabbed the gun, I saw a boot come down square on his hand. The gun squirted out of his grip, and was picked up by someone; I didn't see who, since my sight line was locked on Thornton again, eyes to eyes.

Thornton had not cried out, though I had heard his hand crunch under the boot. I looked up and to the side to see the boot's owner. His gaze followed mine and we both saw Miss Barbara, in something like a batter's stance, brandishing Tolkien.

Thornton said, "Peachy's daught—" just as she swung Tolkien flush into his face.

I heard a sick crack as wood and bone collided. He was still straddling me, his left hand still tightly gripping both my wrists. The twist of his head from the blow made me think his neck was broken, but he brought his head back around to look again toward Miss Barbara.

He said, "Human altruism."

She swung again, this time straight overhead, bringing the thick staff down on top of his head. His eyes closed and he collapsed on top of me, Miss Barbara breathing hard and still waving Tolkien overhead.

I wiggled out from under Thornton's considerable weight, and scrambled to my feet. Bradley and Sawdust were gone.

"Uncle Albert?" I asked, just as he and Batman rushed into the cabin. Batman had a short, thick stick in his left hand and Thornton's .38 in his right.

"They both disappeared," Uncle Albert said, "into the woods. Hand it over, Batman."

"I kinda know how to use this, sir," Batman said, reluctant to surrender the weapon. His words came out fast. "Not kinda, I just say kinda all the time. I do know how to use it. My daddy kinda taught me."

"That's kinda what I'm worried about." Uncle Albert took the gun from him.

Miss Barbara was breathing hard, standing over the man, or demon, she had struck down.

"Should I hit him again?" she asked.

Uncle Albert said, "Leave him," just as Peachy roared, "Yes!"

She did it, one more blow brought down on his head I'm sure as hard as she could bring it.

"Tarnation," Batman said low.

"He's still breathing," she said.

"That's good," Uncle Albert said. "Don't want to kill him, do you?"

Peachy said "Yes!" and Miss Barbara, not Batman, said "Kinda." To me she said, "Are you okay?"

"Yeah. Okay." I expected to find myself in some sort of shock, and kept waiting for signs of such. They weren't there.

"Help me over here, boys," Uncle Albert called from his spot beside Peachy, who was in a seated position on the floor, holding his leg.

"Yes sir." Batman moved to him. I started to, but Miss Barbara stopped me.

"Let me look at you," she said. "Nothing broken?" She gripped my arms, touched my shoulders. "Anything hurt?"

"Nothing bad."

"You're in shock."

"Could be," I said. "Feeling much better than him." I nodded toward Thornton.

"I hope I killed it," she said. "Can you kill a demon?" She looked at Uncle Albert who was examining the gunshot wound on Peachy's leg.

"Dad!" She was somehow late to recognize her dad's wound; maybe she was more in a type of shock than either Peachy or I were.

Peachy spoke in tones he must have used when she was a little girl. "I'm going to be just fine. Just grazed me."

She looked closely at his leg. "It didn't graze you. It passed through."

"Okay, it passed through," he said, grimacing as she gently fingered around the wound.

"I still don't know that," Uncle Albert said to Miss Barbara.

She shot the man a quick, confused look, and gave Batman an order. "Give me your shirt . . . and your tee shirt."

"Your question. Whether you can kill a demon," Uncle Albert clarified. "It's an inexact science, you know. The host body can become inoperable. They look to go to another. But they can't always do that, either. They are not in control."

She pressed the tee shirt squarely against the wound, tied it off with Batman's Scout shirt, and told her dad he was lucky the bullet missed the bone.

I offered my shirt to Batman, who shook his head. "Don't need a shirt. I'm burnin' up as it is."

"Put it on." Miss Barbara shot him a glance.

"Yes ma'am," he said, putting my shirt on, leaving me in my tee.

Uncle Albert told Peachy he was going to have to travel. "Pretty fast. I don't know where Bradley went or when he'll be back. We have to move, to a phone, to some authorities."

"I was born traveling fast," Peachy answered.

"What about him?" I asked about Thornton, who lay motionless on the floor.

"He's not going anywhere," said Uncle Albert. "I suspect he has a severe concussion, among other ailments. Help me put him on the couch," he said.

While I helped Uncle Albert move Thornton, Peachy shook his head and murmured about "the kindness of fools."

"He is a man," Uncle Albert said evenly to Peachy. "The demon's certainly left him now that the body is so damaged." To me he said, "You mentioned a ranger station."

"Yessir, it's close. I mean, no more than a mile. I'm not good with distances."

"Let's hope your problem is overestimating," he said.

Batman and I helped Peachy to his feet, and he put his left arm over my shoulders, his right over Batman's.

The five of us took a couple steps toward the door, and then stopped.

Sawdust had come back inside.

CHAPTER 27

He looked at us, growling very low, barely audible. He wasn't foaming at the mouth or showing teeth.

"I think we know where Thornton's demon went," Peachy said.

"Maybe," said Uncle Albert.

"Hey, boy," I said with a light voice.

"Or maybe this is Bradley's spirit," Uncle Albert mused in an academic manner. "King simply ran off, you know and we don't know—"

"Can we just focus on the demon at hand?" Miss Barbara suggested.

I proffered more solicitous tones. "C'mon, boy."

He stopped the low growl. He looked confused, as if he saw shadows we did not.

"Use his name," said Uncle Albert.

"Hey, Sawdust," I called.

Batman tried. "Sawdust . . . kinda." I gave him a quick look and he said, "Sorry," but then we both saw Sawdust react.

At either the sound of his name, or the familiar sound of Batman's favorite word, the dog's ears perked up. He looked at us, improbably, still appearing unsure of who we were. Or maybe who he was.

"Sawdust," I said again, louder, stronger.

He looked at me, cocked his head, conveying the impression he was pondering, or remembering. I hoped it was remembering.

"We must move now," Uncle Albert said. "If the dog's in the way, I'm sorry but we must—"

"We are *not* shooting that dog," Miss Barbara cut him off.

"Barbara," her father said, "the dog is gone."

It occurred to me that Sawdust might remember the sounds of some names. "Zack," I said to the dog. "Donnie. Rebecca. Zack."

One tail wag.

"That's right, boy!"

It looked good; I thought he was coming around. But in a quick move, he darted back to the doorway, turned to look at us, and then took off out the door.

I started to call his name, but stopped.

"Let's move," Uncle Albert said, and we all stepped out of the cabin. "We'll send the authorities to retrieve Mr. Thornton—"

"Oh please." Peachy frowned.

"—along with medical personnel."

"You think Sawdust'll be all right?" I asked Uncle Albert.

"I couldn't say, Richard. I wish I could. Animals' reactions to demonic presences are even more unpredictable than people's. And people are extremely problematic, as you know. I'm encouraged that he looked so confused."

"Confused?" Batman wondered, as did I, why that was encouraging.

"Confusion means deliberation, thinking what action to take. In most possessions I've seen firsthand, demons do not think. They just hate and destroy."

"Thornton seems to think a lot," I said.

"Thornton is different," Uncle Albert agreed. "Thornton is a mystery. He appears entirely sentient. Deliberative. He considers possibilities. He makes choices."

"I thought ya'll were gone," I told Batman. "How'd ya'll find us?"

"I don't know," he said. "Miss Barbara and me never saw ya'll's car behind us and we thought ya'll might have trouble—ya know, car trouble. When we kinda went back, the car was still there."

"Sawdust showed up out of the blue," said Miss Barbara, "and kept walking in and out of the woodland, back up to us. So we followed him here. We listened outside the door, and backed off to think about what to do."

"Then Sawdust ran like thunder up to the front door and jumped and hit it with his front paws and came on inside. Ya'll saw that."

"I sort of saw it," I said.

"We listened, and then we just thought we needed to get in there."

I thought of what I should say. "Thank you."

"Let's try not to talk right now," Peachy said, looking round about us. "Let's see if we hear anything. Bradley's out here somewhere, in some unfriendly state, demonized or whatever."

We were quite the sight, if anyone saw us, an odd company of five straining to discern the right direction back toward the ranger station and adjacent house. The woods and the air smelled like a storm, though it was not raining. The wind was deceptively strong, and tree branches moved, harassed by gusts. Traveling woods on a dark night is fraught with guesses. You guess that's the way to the broad path you guess is the easiest way to where you guess you need to go. You look for familiar things, but things familiar in daytime are either hidden at night or, if visible, not the same as you recall. Everything is cloaked. You have to trust some shadows.

I had just sensed a chill when Miss Barbara said it felt cold for June in Alabama.

"Don't know if you'll believe this," Uncle Albert said, "but I've noticed demonic visitations have some effect on climate. Very localized." He sounded like he was thinking out loud. "Just as the visitations are localized."

"You'd think they'd make it hotter," Miss Barbara murmured.

"Perhaps Dante was right," said Uncle Albert. "His inferno is marked by infernal coldness. Not hot fires."

"Speaking of fires . . . ," I said.

"I smell it too," Peachy concurred. "But I don't see smoke."

We had stopped, all of us looking ahead, around, and behind us.

"You doing okay?" Miss Barbara asked her dad.

"Don't fuss."

"Hard to see smoke on a night like this," Batman said.

"Ought to be able to see fire." Uncle Albert frowned. "Flame."

"Must be far away," I said.

"Too strong," he said. "The smell. Don't know if you're going to believe this either. But when demons burn something, and they burn lots of things, the smell is disproportionate to the size of the fire."

Miss Barbara was skeptical. "I find it hard to believe they can alter the laws of physics."

"That was me twenty years ago," Peachy muttered.

"I understand," Uncle Albert sighed. "I'm just relating what I've observed. My experiences. I stopped trying to persuade people years ago."

"There," Batman pointed.

"Fire?" I said.

"No, I think it's the house. The ranger's. I think the station's behind it."

I saw the light then, a tiny sliver in the distance. I felt a rush of relief. It's astonishing how such a small light, the glowing sanctuary of the ranger's home, could mean so much.

We pressed toward the light with renewed purpose.

"Everything's going to be fine, Dad," Miss Barbara said.

"Of course it is," said Peachy.

"We're going to make it, Richard," she said.

"Thanks to you," I said, feeling the weight of the night's events lift. "You showed up and laid down the law. You're my hero!" I gushed.

"I don't feel much like a hero," she said. "I feel like . . . bad."

"How so?" Uncle Albert said.

"I wanted to kill him," she said. "Maybe I did."

"I hope so," Peachy grumbled. "He's a demon."

"You can't mean that," she said quietly.

"Yes, I mean that," he said, and words erupted from him, a dam breaking. "If you don't believe your own eyes, consider that Jackalthorn's got a name, a history, and a purpose. That makes him pretty real, don't you think? Demon then. Demon now. Why is that so hard to believe? He'll chew up innocents until some bigger power takes him out, and I don't know what God is waiting for."

"But even if Jackalthorn is real," she said, "Jack Thornton is just a man. Possessed. Just before he closed them, his eyes were saying something. Mournful."

"Don't trust the host's eyes," Uncle Albert said.

"He looked so sad." Miss Barbara sounded sad herself.

"Oh, he was sad," Peachy said. "And mournful. We crashed his party."

Uncle Albert stopped walking, as did the lot of us. "I think I see our fire."

I saw it too, a small thing in the dark night, more smoke than flame, about a hundred feet to the side of the ranger's house.

The front door to the house opened. The ranger for Camp Sequoyah stepped out and waved to us.

I waved back and called out. "Mr. Franks! We need your help."

He jogged toward us, and I saw it was not Mr. Franks but Mr. Burkett.

"We must've been making a lot of noise," Batman said, "for him to hear us coming."

"It would seem so," said Uncle Albert.

Ranger Burkett reached us. "Let me do that," he said, immediately taking my spot helping Peachy walk.

I guess I was staring at him, because he asked me what I was looking at. He didn't say it mean, just kind of indifferent, flat, and terse, as Burkett always spoke.

"I just thought . . . I thought you were transferred. Somewhere else."

"I was," he said. "That was a mistake. Now I'm back."

"So Mr. Franks . . ."

"He's back in Georgia."

He addressed Uncle Albert. "What happened to y'all tonight?"

"Well . . ." Uncle Albert hesitated.

"Richard," Miss Barbara said, "run up to the house and call the operator to send an ambulance and the police."

I ran a few steps, but Burkett stopped me. "No, wait. I'll do it. My phone's a little broken and I know how to deal with it. Switch back."

I took my spot again holding up Peachy.

"Bullet wound," Uncle Albert told Burkett. "In the leg. Older guy."

The ranger ran back toward his house.

"Possible shock," Miss Barbara called out to him.

"I am not in shock. I'm doing fine."

"You are doing great," Uncle Albert said, "but you need attention."

"I'm only seventy-one."

"Seventy-three," Miss Barbara corrected.

"I know how old I am," Peachy objected.

"You're seventy-three," she said again.

"I'm . . . that's right." He laughed. "I guess I forgot a year or two in there somewhere."

It wasn't that funny, but we all laughed with him, as if someone turned a valve and the steam we'd been holding tight escaped.

Burkett ran back out and helped us bring Peachy inside the house and lay him down on a large, spacious couch.

"You want to lie on a bed, Dad?" Miss Barbara asked.

"Good grief, no." Peachy smiled. "I'm already threatening to bleed on the good man's couch."

She looked at the wound. "Your bleeding is under control. They'll be here soon."

"Shouldn't take them long," Uncle Albert agreed. "How long you think, Mr. Burkett?"

I heard a bolt lock click into place. I turned around, facing the door we'd just come through. Burkett stood there, stone-faced. He spoke.

In Jack Thornton's voice.

CHAPTER 28

I *do* decide," the demon said. "I decide a great deal."

Uncle Albert took a deliberate step toward him, but Jackalthorn in a swift move plucked a rifle off the wall beside him, cocked and pointed it. I'm not sure of Uncle Albert's intentions, but the rifle trumped them regardless.

It said, "Mr. Burkett's much younger, and more coordinated. Still, I was used to the other. I had him, many days. Long years." It raised its voice toward the back of the room, behind us. "Come out!"

Bradley stepped from the shadows that cloaked a room in the back of the cabin, staring at us while crossing the floor, and stopping alongside the demon Jackalthorn in Burkett's body. Bradley was not armed. His countenance was blank, void, as if nothing in the room threatened or interested him. Yet.

"We surely have no need of this," Jackalthorn handed the rifle to Bradley, "but it might prove useful. If our friends prove foolish."

Bradley cradled the weapon in his arms, not pointed or ready to fire. Obviously neither man, nor either demon, perceived any threat from the likes of us. That has ever been the demonic delusion. They believe their battle is against us.

Jackalthorn pulled a small wooden chair not far from the front door and sat in it, motioning to Uncle Albert. "Sit down."

Uncle Albert didn't move.

"Where you are," it said to him. "On the floor."

Uncle Albert knelt down.

"Sit," it said. "On the floor. Cross-legged. I've found that is quite comfortable."

Uncle Albert crossed his legs.

"The rest of you." He motioned. "It's a big couch. If my old friend accommodates you, you'll all fit."

Peachy sat up. Batman, Miss Barbara, and I sat on the couch with him.

I wasn't afraid. Severe crises can compel us to courage we didn't know we had, as if there is no room for paralyzing fear; the moments are too weighty with import. I don't know if it's the same for people who don't have a strong faith in a strong God.

"Are you doing okay, Dad?" Miss Barbara didn't seem afraid either.

"Just another day at the office," Peachy said, loud enough for Jackalthorn to hear.

"I like that," it said. "I always liked your humor."

Peachy scowled, apparently deciding the time was right to deride the demon in front of the rest of us. "It fakes laughter. It fakes everything. Except anguish. And that's eternal, isn't it?"

It said something then, tumbling guttural tones, but sounds like words. Like a language.

Peachy answered him in what sounded like the same tongue. My mind recorded the sound of Peachy's utterance. *Buala abua zumba.*

Jackalthorn didn't like it.

"That . . . will not do," it said grimly. "At all."

Bradley looked to be tightening his grip on the rifle.

The room's tension abruptly splintered into further apprehensions. Somebody politely knocked on the front door.

Bradley stepped toward the door. Jackalthorn grabbed the possessed man's arm, stopping him.

We waited. I thought it was probably a good idea to call out to whoever was knocking, but the adult hostages were not saying anything and I trusted their reticence.

The knocker spoke in the sing-song tones of the very young.

"Hey, Mr. Ranger Burkett, sir? I brought some of them home-grown tomatoes," Willie Rowe said through the cabin door. "I knew you was up 'cause I saw your little fire out here, so Mom said I could run these on over. . . . Mr. Burkett?"

The door creaked open a tiny crack. "I'll just set 'em down right here, just inside." Willie's arm appeared just inside the barely open door, setting a brown bag down on the floor.

Jackalthorn made a decision, grimacing, and nodding to Bradley, who seized the arm and swung the boy, slightly airborne, inside the cabin.

"Whooooaaaaa," Willie sort of sang, but not loud. He actually landed on his feet as Bradley let go of him. He stood there for three or four seconds, assessing the situation from his unique eleven-year-old perspective.

Batman said, "Hey Willie," and I said, "Willie," and the boy saw the rifle in Bradley's hand and stepped lively past Uncle Albert and over to us on the couch. Miss Barbara and I made a spot for him and when she patted the couch, he sat down.

"What's going on?" he said in a voice so even-keeled, he could have been saying "Good morning."

"It's kinda not good," Batman said.

Willie looked at Burkett and Bradley and said, "Ya'll know you got a fire happening out there, don't ya?" That was Willie's focus; there was an unattended fire outside. "Don't want no calamities happenin'."

"Thank you," Jackalthorn said evenly. I suspected the demon was unsure how to deal with the presence of this young intruder. It was obvious it did not want anything like carnage, or my friends and I would have been disposed of long before now. Jackalthorn wanted something, and it wasn't mayhem.

"Need some more light in here, too. A guy's gotta be able to see, ya'll."

Jackalthorn said, "I think the boy's right about the fire. It's time to put it out."

Bradley hesitated.

"Do it," Jackalthorn said.

"It gives us power," said Bradley.

"We've plenty of power," Jackalthorn said. "It's time. Put it out."

"But . . ."

"Hand me the rifle and put out the fire. Now!"

Bradley obeyed, surrendering the weapon and stepping out the door.

Uncle Albert spoke his first words of this encounter, engaging Jackalthorn, messing with his mind, or whatever faculty the being was using. "I think you'd be better off without him helping you."

"I might be," Jackalthorn said. "I let him start the fire. He needs it. He hasn't the power inside him that I have. No one does."

Willie spoke. "Are you sure you're a ranger?"

"I know precisely what I am."

Seeing him take Willie's question in such a serious manner confirmed to me the particular struggle demons have fathoming nuances in childlike conversation.

"You are Jackalthorn?" Uncle Albert looked almost impressed.

It fixed its look on Uncle Albert, turning its eyes first and then its head slightly, stiffly. As if it had yet to learn how to turn his eyes in this particular body.

"Yes." Proud.

"But, I'm sure, you have many names. A spirit of such power." Uncle Albert spoke like he was having conversation over coffee.

It made the guttural sounds again. Short phrases, like a list.

"Hmm," Uncle Albert looked thoughtful. He exaggerated a greatly disappointed countenance. "I don't think so. No, I do not know these names."

It looked angry, but seemed to wrestle against its own irritation.

"What has he promised you?" Uncle Albert said quietly.

"You should ask what I have promised him. It is I who give service to his lordship, who feeds his lordship, who sustains his lordship. He needs me. I have made it so."

Bradley stepped back inside, closed the door, turned the lock, and leaned his back against the frame, arms folded in front of him like he was the cabin's guardian. Jackalthorn held onto the rifle.

"You are sharp," Uncle Albert conceded.

"Yes." Jackalthorn sounded pleased again. "Wise. You agree I am wise."

"Well . . ." Uncle Albert hesitated.

"You are not." Miss Barbara, solid as ever, leaned toward it. "Believers are wise."

"You are not a believer." Jackalthorn smirked.

"How would you know what I am? Or what I am not?"

"You're wasting your time, Barbara," Peachy said quietly.

She wasn't listening. "I don't know what you are. A demon. A group of demons. Insane. Maybe you're a group of insane demons. But you're not a believer."

"Not true." It shook its head. "I, Jackalthorn, believe. As do . . ." he broke again into sounds unfamiliar. Listing names again.

"Does Jackalthorn shudder?" I asked.

It didn't answer. I asked again.

"Your question rots," it said.

"I'm . . ." Uncle Albert wanted to say something. "I'm . . ." But he couldn't. He looked at me. He pointed to his throat. He couldn't talk. He was not afraid. He simply couldn't talk.

Jackalthorn saw Uncle Albert's gesture. "This is not your ground," it said simply. "Imagine . . . maybe none of Earth is your Lord's ground."

I sensed my own capacity to speak leaving me. I *felt* it happening. I managed to say, "Demons also believe . . . and shudder."

"Rots!" it hissed. Jackalthorn's eyes rolled back in Burkett's head. Uncle Albert scrambled to get up off the floor and the man's eyes came back in place. The rifle was pointed at Uncle Albert, who froze.

Uncle Albert managed to say the word "Scripture," and could say no more.

I understood and wanted to announce the Word but couldn't. I looked around our group to see if the others might be able. Everybody looked more resigned to capture than tense with fear, a kind of semi-conscious state, like they were waiting for these moments to go away.

Only with great effort was I able to verbalize a sole syllable of Uncle Albert's word. I said, "Script—" And that was all.

I knew so many verses; in those haunted moments they were trapped inside me. I recalled them, but I couldn't announce them. The panic that should have gripped me many times but hadn't, now crept over me. But not inside me. Bible verses flew in the recesses of my mind. But I felt they couldn't escape over my tongue into the cabin's chilled atmosphere.

"When ya'll say Scripture, does that mean ya'll wanna hear some Bible?" Willie asked, an odd sounding query for such a crucial moment.

"We do *not!*" Jackalthorn answered.

In my mind's eye, Lewis appeared, the formidable Lewis who ran beside me in my dream. I still couldn't announce Scripture, but suddenly I could say a few words to Willie. My voice was quiet but clear.

"The King and the Spirit are *here* . . . even at your side." I nodded then, once to Willie.

"All's I know is some Christmas Bible." His words sounded like a throwaway line.

"Go . . ." Uncle Albert barely breathed it, his voice a rough whisper.

Miss Barbara was able to shout once in Willie's direction. "Talk!" She tried to say it again, but nothing came out.

The boy talked. "'There were in the same country shepherds, abiding in the field. Keeping watch over their flocks by night.' I got this off the *Peanuts* Christmas show."

"Go . . ." Uncle Albert breathed again.

"Go!" Miss Barbara echoed.

"'And the angel of the Lord appeared unto them.'" Willie paused, straining for what came next. I wanted to help him, I knew it was there in my head, but I couldn't locate it.

Willie found it. "'And they were sore afraid,'" he said.

"Sore afraid," Bradley mumbled, and then Jackalthorn as well, "Sore afraid," but with markedly different intonations. Jackalthorn looked angry. Bradley looked not so much afraid but stunned to stillness, his eyes on Willie, who didn't mind staring back.

What I know of Willie today tells me that if he had recognized the terror, he would have pretended he did not. He would have fought the fight with guts and guile. Maybe that is exactly what he did that night.

"You want I should keep talking?" Willie asked.

Miss Barbara suddenly had more than one word. "Crush it to . . ."—her voice gathered strength—"the maximum you can crush it, young man! You should just go ahead and crush it!"

Willie was pleased to do so. "'But the angel said unto them, "Fear not."'" His delight spilled over top of his words. "'For behold I bring you good tidings of great joy, which will be to all people.'"

Bradley sank to his knees, his face dripping sweat. To Jackalthorn, he said, "I don't think I can do this."

His master smacked the butt of the rifle into Bradley's forehead. Bradley didn't retaliate or make any sound. He went from his knees to a slouched, seated position, looking for all the world like he had decided to sit the entire confrontation out.

Uncle Albert abruptly found his voice and fearlessly told the ranger to hand over the rifle.

"It's not that easy," Burkett said, in a voice starkly different from Jackalthorn's.

"Yes it is," Uncle Albert said.

Jackalthorn reemerged; Jack Thornton's tone reentered the ranger, scowling. "You . . . countermand my commands?"

"All true commands," said Uncle Albert, "come from the One that even you believe is One. And you shudder. Give me the rifle."

"I won't," Jackalthorn said like a stubborn child. Then, in a more rational tone, "I can't."

It looked like Uncle Albert believed both assertions and was stymied. The two stared at each other, each waiting for his antagonist to speak another truth or lie, to make another move.

Uncle Albert finally said, "Redemption is possible."

"For whom?" Jackalthorn said, his face expressionless.

"For all who—" Uncle Albert's words were drowned in the sound of the front door crashing off its hinges. It slammed into the back of Bradley, toppling him, and bringing Duffey and Booger sprawling into the room and onto the floor. They'd run into the door together, breaking the lock off the frame.

A lot happened so fast and so loud, I couldn't follow it with my eyes, my senses. I pieced a lot of it together later, hearing what everyone said they'd done, and what they saw. But it's like any oversized fracas; the people who are in it can be the most unreliable sources for what actually happened.

Uncle Albert lunged at Jackalthorn and grabbed the rifle, struggling for control of the weapon. It went off; I honestly thought I heard the bullet go by my ear, but Duffey said the same thing about the bullet and *his* ear, and we were nowhere near each other. Maybe there was some ricochet in the cabin's tight spaces. I scrambled across the floor, half running, half crawling toward Duffey and Booger, who were both wrestling Bradley, fighting Bradley, trying to get a handgun the man had pulled from his trousers' deep pockets. In hindsight, maybe I should have hustled to help Uncle Albert and Batman, who had joined forces against Jackalthorn, both trying to wrest control of the rifle away from the demon.

I sensed more than saw Miss Barbara fairly drag the protesting Willie out the door. Yes, he was protesting. He was eleven. Kids can act crazy. Especially if they're brave.

Bradley was struggling to get to his feet. I tried to tackle him. He threw me off, but Duffey and Booger hit him, one up high and one down low, and just that fast Duffey was entirely on top of Bradley, besting him.

I thought I saw Miss Barbara rush back inside.

"Get his gun!" Duffey hollered.

I looked around frantically, but didn't see it. I did see Batman sitting up, too still, on the cabin floor. In shock.

"Freeze, you freak!" Miss Barbara hollered. She stood over Jackalthorn, holding Bradley's handgun to Jackalthorn's head. Jackalthorn had maneuvered on top of Uncle Albert, the exorcist straining to wrest control of the rifle from the demon.

Jackalthorn froze. Everybody did. Duffey and Booger had pinned Bradley and held him down securely.

Batman rubbed his right arm. "Ow, man."

The stillness that held the rest of us in those seconds made Uncle Albert's motion more pronounced. I still see him jerking the rifle out of Jackalthorn's grasp and bringing the rifle butt back hard beside Jackalthorn's head, knocking the demon silly but not unconscious.

"You will come over here. Now," Uncle Albert said to Bradley who still groaned under the weight of Duffey and Booger.

Duffey and Booger thought he meant them. "Me?" they both asked.

"Not you guys," Uncle Albert said. I thought he was going to laugh.

Bradley crawled on the floor over to Uncle Albert, who told him to lie facedown with his hands behind his head. He stayed in that position until the police arrived.

"Duffey," said Miss Barbara.

"Yes ma'am?"

"Get over here. Hold this gun on this freak."

"Yes ma'am." Duffey hurried over and took the gun, keeping it aimed at Jackalthorn, who was holding his head in his hands.

Willie stepped back inside the cabin. Miss Barbara glared at him. "I thought I told you to stay outside, no matter what."

"Yes ma'am, you did." But he wasn't leaving, and she dropped it.

Peachy hadn't left the couch the whole time, but his closed eyes suggested he might have left this world. But Miss Barbara checked his pulse and pronounced him unconscious just seconds before he started to come to, griping. "I'm fine . . . don't fuss." I was glad to hear his voice, but his daughter still looked gravely concerned.

"Albert," she said, "call the police and—" She saw he was already on the phone.

"That's right," he said into the receiver. "And an ambulance straightaway . . . the ranger's house at Camp Sequoyah."

"At the end of Pimlico Road," Willie told Uncle Albert.

"At the end of Pimlico Road," Uncle Albert told the operator.

"What can I do?" I asked Miss Barbara, while she physically forced her dad to lie back down on the couch.

She gave me one of the couch cushions. "Put this under Batman's head. Make him lie down, right there on the floor."

I pushed his shoulders, gentle-like, to get him to lean back. He contested my effort, referring to himself in the third person like he did when we were little kids. "Batman don't need to lay down."

His resistance folded fast, and he let me put his head down on the pillow on the hardwood floor. He said, "Batman's gonna let things go for a spell."

Peachy mumbled and moaned and came to entirely. "Must've drifted off . . . is the war over?"

"You're going to be fine," Miss Barbara said.

"I know. Is the war over?"

"Ambulance and police are on their way. It's over."

"No it's not," he said.

"Should we put Batman on the couch?" I asked.

"No," said Miss Barbara. "We're not moving him."

"Will he be all right?" It was Bradley, asking about Batman.

Peachy spat words in the man's direction. "How about you shut up."

"We don't know yet, do we?" Miss Barbara answered Bradley while she moved quickly to Batman, loosening his shirt and checking his pulse. Batman was conscious, but silent.

"It's a graze," she said, looking at his bleeding arm. "Just grazed him." She looked Batman in the eye. "You're going to be okay, Batman."

"Yes ma'am," he said softly.

"I know it hurts, but . . ." Her voice broke. She recovered. "You're going to be okay."

To me, she said, "Give me the other cushions. Off the couch."

Willie beat me to it, handing them to her. She put one under Batman's midsection. The other supplemented the one I had put under his head.

"I'm sorry about the kid," Bradley mumbled.

"Tell it to the judge," Duffey said. He glanced at me. "I always wanted to say that."

I asked him, "How did ya'll know where we were, to come here? That we were in trouble?"

Duffey said that was strange. In his own way. "Now that was funky monkey business off the wall," he blurted out. "We was fishing, Booger and me, close to here. Guess who showed up?"

"An angel?" At this point I figured anything's plausible.

"No," he said. "Well, maybe yes."

It came to me then, before he said it. "Sawdust."

"That's right!" said Duffey. "He wouldn't leave us alone."

Booger said, "He looked like . . . he looked really bad."

"It was a Lassie thing." Duffey smiled. "He wanted us to follow him; there ain't no other way to say it. We did, and once we was at the cabin, we could make out ya'll talking and so . . ."

"We just decided to crash the party." Booger grinned. He was obviously enjoying these muscular demonstrations of his newfound faith.

"What happened to Sawdust?" I said. "Where'd he go?"

Duffey shrugged. "Beats me."

The police and ambulance arrived in force, with several state troopers as well. Miss Barbara told the rescue squad quickly and clearly what she'd observed about the boy's condition, and her dad's. They strapped Batman and Peachy onto stretchers. I feared for Batman more than Peachy, probably because the talkative Batman was still silent. Shock.

Peachy motioned to his daughter, who came up close to him.

"The boy and I are going to be fine," he said to her. "I'm so proud of you."

"Thanks, Dad."

"Not just for tonight. I mean for everything. Everything you are. I'm so proud."

CHAPTER 29

Sawdust beat us to the hospital. We found him pacing outside the emergency room door. He'd been in the same spot five years before when Rafer Forrester collapsed on our Little League field and was rushed to the hospital by ambulance. And Booger was right; Sawdust looked pretty bad. Filthy and lean to the extreme, like he'd been in a war. Maybe he had. But his temperament was the Sawdust we all knew. He was sweet, gentle, and tail-wagging glad to see all of us. The only thing a shade scary about him was his obvious intelligence for a canine. Anxious about the ambulance, he asked with his eyes if everything was going to be all right. I petted him and told him it was, but he gave me his peculiar wise look that said he knew I didn't know that was the case, but he thanked me for trying to reassure him. It was like he was apologizing for asking something I could not know.

I knew Batman was roaring back to good health when I heard the medic outside the emergency room say, "That boy is *kinda* doing great."

"He's talking and everything, then?" Nurse Barbara asked.

"He kinda talked my ears off on the ride over," the medic said. "I never heard so many 'kindas' in all my life. He's gonna be fine."

Apparently the shock had worn off on the ride in the ambulance and Batman was talking up a storm with anyone who'd listen. He told me he was going to write up the whole episode as a short story or a play. I asked him later how that had turned out and he said it didn't seem to work as a story.

"What do you mean?" I asked him.

316

"It's too, I don't know . . . it's too weird. It's ridiculous. Who's going to believe it?"

"But it really happened!" I said.

"You and me know that. And the others who were there. That makes it a good newspaper article, I guess. But it doesn't make a good story. Or drama. It's too . . . bizarre."

He had that right. In two days, Batman was out of the hospital, and in three days, the newspapers had stopped commenting on the story.

When I told Peachy I thought the story might have longer legs, he said, "Nobody died. And the papers think the bad guys were caught and that it's over."

"Yeah, the bad guys were caught."

"No, the papers *think* the bad guys were caught. So they *think* it's over."

"It's not over?"

He didn't say. He didn't know. He didn't want to think otherwise.

Peachy's bullet wound developed an infection and required a longer stay in the hospital than first anticipated. But that was kind of a good thing, because he got so many visitors. He pretended to be annoyed by the attention, but he was not hard to see through anymore. A lot of us felt close to him, bound together now by many things.

The first day I visited him, I went with Uncle Albert. We waited in the hall outside Peachy's room, his door partway open, while he chatted with a man inside.

"Imagine the peace of mind from knowing it's all been taken care of," the man said.

"You sound like a pastor," Peachy replied.

"Oh, thank you."

"I hate pastors."

"Oh—"

"Except for one. And you're not him."

"Yes, well . . . if you are prepared in advance, you're not at the mercy of strangers during a difficult time in your life."

"Dying is a difficult time, isn't it?"

"But it doesn't have to be."

"Really?"

"And you can prevent emotional overspending."

"Yeah. I hate that. Emotional overspending."

"And wouldn't you like to offer peace of mind and security to all the members of your family?"

"I just have the one daughter."

"Yes, and I'm sure you'd like to offer her—"

"And I can't give her what I don't have." Peachy sounded almost wistful.

"Sir?"

"You mentioned security. Peace of mind."

"Yes. And the grounds are beautifully maintained, with perpetual care."

"Really? Beautiful care . . . all the way into perpetuity."

"You need to think it over, I'm sure. I'll just leave these materials and brochures here on the table. And if you'd like to stop by, we're at the corner of Van Buren and Eighth Street."

"Do you give discounts for walk-ins?"

I guessed the man tried to laugh, but it sounded more like he had a stubborn cough.

"You don't sound too good. But don't let it get you down. Maybe you could buy some of that peace of mind you mentioned."

"You're a card, Dr. McLeod."

The door swung open and a man dressed to the teeth in a dark suit and royal blue tie on a pressed white shirt stepped smartly, efficiently, past Uncle Albert and me and down the hallway. We walked into Peachy's room.

"Had many visitors?" said Uncle Albert.

"It's like Grand Central Station in here."

I feigned an exit. "We can come back another time."

"No, no," he spoke fast. "You two and Barbara are the only ones I really want to see."

"Who was that guy?" asked Uncle Albert.

"He sells cemetery plots."

"You can't be serious," I said, feeling bad for him. But he seemed amused by the visit.

"I'm serious as a heart attack." He laughed at his own remark. "Convenient prepurchase, the guy says."

I glanced at the brochure on his bedside table. "The facts you need to know," I said, reading, "about Before-the-Need Arrangements."

"Read the tiny print at the bottom." He was clearly amused.

I read aloud. "We sincerely apologize if this brochure was given during a time of mourning."

"Priceless, isn't it? It's like apologizing to the family for not raising the horrific specter of death to the departed one before they departed!"

Uncle Albert asked, "How's your leg feeling?"

"Like somebody shot it." He grinned. "But I've been shot before."

"Why doesn't that surprise me?" Uncle Albert smiled. "Listen, the police questioned all of us, including Barbara, for a good while. All of us except for you."

"They sent a couple guys earlier today," Peachy said. "Just a few questions. But they said they'll come back a few more times. They said all of our stories match up."

"Yes, they seemed satisfied," said Uncle Albert. "But I'm sure they'll want to get your story in its entirety."

"I'd like to have my story in its entirety, too." Peachy frowned. "But . . . I have a strange sense that the nightmare part is over. For me, anyway."

Uncle Albert nodded. "I have that sense too. That's why I'm leaving. Early tomorrow. Going to Mississippi. A friend of mine there has run into some odd things."

Peachy honestly looked sentimental at getting that news. "You've been terrific," he said. "Couldn't have made it through this without you."

"Thanks. I don't know, I think you all would have made it through whether I was in your way here or not. I won't belabor the point, but you've got to come to faith, Peachy."

Saying it straight out like that, I thought Peachy would protest. He didn't. "You're probably right," he said.

"Well, I'll leave you and Richard to talk that over. He seems to represent your best hope of coming to God."

"Probably so."

They shook hands. Uncle Albert shook mine too. "Godspeed," he said. "We must keep in touch."

"Yes sir," I said. Then the exorcist walked out of the room.

"Was he right, you think?" Peachy asked me. "Are you my best hope of coming to God?"

I didn't know how to answer. I hadn't come to see him with my missionary cap on. I had just come to see my friend. Yes, the miracle of redemption had come to me and so many of my close friends, and I hoped it would come to Peachy any day now. But I wasn't anxious for him; I don't know why. It wasn't because I didn't love him. I suppose I sensed that questions and answers were not always the touchstone of coming to Christ. This is a hopeful contemplation for me; to consider that Truth's revelation is not contingent on our dissecting it accurately.

Peachy remained not at all indifferent to his personal salvation, but simply unable to believe he could be forgiven. He was the antithesis of the postmodernist perspective that succeeded my generation. The notion of "sin" is so timid and vacuous in the twenty-first century; the notion of salvation strikes people as at least odd and likely irrelevant. Getting right with God has become more about discovering one's goodness than confessing one's sin. But Peachy could say with King David, "I know my transgressions, and my sin is ever before me." His sins were not a virus to be treated; they were a death sentence. They were Peachy's albatross; long sewn into his skin and psyche, they had taken root.

Now, this moment, when I didn't answer him, he said, "You don't know what I've done." To others, I had heard him shout such statements. Now, to me, he said the same words in a soft, matter-of-fact tone.

"It doesn't matter," I said, aiming to keep things simple, straightforward. Strategic wordplays and philosophical propositions perhaps have a place in evangelism and the life of the historical church. But they sank like stones whenever Peachy and I talked in the hospital.

"I appreciate what you're trying to do, Richard." He looked out the window and said, "If God had given me a son . . ." He looked back at me.

I didn't press it. We talked of other things. I read him pieces of original stories I was working on, and he sympathized with my fledgling attempts at honest sentiment.

"We don't manufacture pathos," he said. "We discover it."

"Is that hard?"

"For you, it's hard. For many others, it is impossible. But don't ever think it has to do with IQ or academic degrees or status. The King's gardener will discover pathos while he's clipping the hedges and tell the mightiest pathos-laden tale to the hedges he clips, long before the King discovers that his toenails need clipping."

He was surprised at how hard I laughed. "I don't think I've ever seen you laugh like this. You're out of control."

That made me laugh harder. "Peachy says . . . I'm out of control."

"Why is that . . . so funny?" he wondered, smiling with me.

"I'm not sure." I righted myself. "It's just you've never struck me as *in* control, I guess. And maybe, I'm so tired of all this demon stuff."

"You and me both. And maybe God too."

That got me going again, chuckling over a mental image of God complaining that he's tired of all this demon stuff.

It was a great first visit and I marveled at the ease I felt in the company of this remarkable seventy-three-year-old. I felt hope too, for Peachy's soul. Truth was not dependent on Peachy discovering him.

———

The second day I visited, he got serious with me almost as soon as I stepped into the room. First, I thought his serious comments were all about me. That was a mistake.

"You're gifted, Richard. The world's waiting for you to jump in and splash around . . . to send your ripples out in multiple directions."

"That's what everyone tells me to believe," I said. "But I don't know."

"I understand. You're smart enough to see they're telling you what any good teacher or preacher or parent is supposed to tell a youth."

"That's what it sounds like . . . so much sugar water."

"Hey, don't get me wrong," Peachy said. "I approve of them saying what they do to you and to every other person who's deciding if life's worth the effort."

"Is it?"

"Life, you mean?"

"Is it worth the effort?" I asked. I knew what I believed. Better, I knew Whom.

But I wanted to hear him talk. He let some seconds go by. As did I.

"Does the date July 2 mean anything to you?" said Peachy.

"No. I don't think so."

"How about if I add 1961?"

"I was born that year."

Peachy smiled. "Ah, thank you, I needed that new reference point for the year. For me, 1961 means Ernest Hemingway shoots himself. Suicide. Why do you suppose he does that?"

"Maybe, I guess, he thought life was no fun anymore. Or, life wasn't interesting anymore."

"That's right. So he ended it."

"Well," I said, "he ended *this* life."

Peachy looked out the window again. "And there is where I'm caught. He ended this life, and . . . then what? He presumed annihilation. As would I. Only I haven't his courage."

"Maybe it's not a matter of courage. Maybe it's a matter of wisdom. You suspect he might have been wrong about heaven and hell."

"Now I'm smarter than Hemingway?" He shook his head.

"I think that's a real possibility."

"Your kind opinion of me doesn't help me."

"Well, to be honest," I said, "Hemingway doesn't strike me so much as brilliant, as he does talented and hardworking."

That tickled him. "Put it this way. I will not embrace a God who would forgive what I've done." He did not raise his voice; he didn't have to. His resolution was indomitable.

Somebody knocked on Peachy's door, which, like the door to his core convictions, was cracked half open or half shut, however one chooses to view it.

"Yeah," Peachy called.

"Mr. Peachy, sir," came a young man's voice I thought I recognized as Booger.

"Come in, whoever you are," Peachy said.

The door opened all the way. Booger and BoDean walked in, looking like a seventies' teen version of Laurel and Hardy. The massive Booger had gotten a dramatic haircut, and had put spray or something in the hair that was left to keep it back, off his forehead. This made his face appear bigger, which made his smile look to be huge. Or maybe he was just a very happy young man.

BoDean was as tall as his companion, but thin and bowlegged. He was smiling too. He looked me in the eye and said, "Richard, my main man."

"How's it going, BoDean? Booger?"

"Never better," BoDean said.

"I'm saved," said Booger. And he was.

"Kind of you boys to drop by," Peachy said. I could tell he wasn't just saying that. He liked them. And something else. He found them intriguing. I had told him of their conversions.

"We just wanted to see you were all right, Mr. Peachy," said BoDean.

"And was you hurtin'," Booger added.

"I'm doing fine," Peachy said. "Feeling a little better every day. Have a seat." He gestured to the room's other chair, the one I was not in.

I stood up. "I can be moving on," I said. I figured they could both have a seat then.

"No," Booger said to me, his face more asking me than telling me not to leave. "If you can stay, that'd be great. I might need you translatin'," said Booger.

"Translating?"

"My brain's not so good at saying what I mean." Booger smiled while BoDean sat down in the chair. "Maybe you can tell Mr. Peachy what I said, when I can't tell him."

"Well," I said, "sure, I can stay if that's what you want." I sat back down in my chair.

"It's just Peachy, son," Peachy told Booger. "There's no mister to it."

"Okay, Peachy sir." Booger sat down at the bottom of Peachy's bed and one of the springs underneath sprang. Booger hauled himself back up on his feet.

"Sorry about that, Peachy sir."

He and BoDean traded places, Booger in the chair and BoDean now at the foot of Peachy's bed. Except BoDean sat on the other side, facing away from the door's entrance. He was looking out the window, apparently at nothing in particular.

"You don't mind if I sit here, do you?" BoDean asked Peachy.

"It's a big bed," Peachy said with a slight smile, enjoying the odd pair.

BoDean looked out the window and Booger shuffled in his chair, nervous. Peachy and I exchanged amused glances. And we waited.

"Peachy sir . . . you ain't saved, right?" Booger began.

"That's right."

"Okay. But you can be, if you want it. I'm gonna talk you into it, but wait . . ." It was like he stopped himself. "I'm supposed to say here that I'm gettin' ahead of myself." Booger looked at me. "Anytime you wanna translate, you can."

"I think you're doing fine," I said.

"Good. I can't never tell sometimes, but that don't matter. Long as you get what I say." He waited for Peachy to answer.

"I . . . so far . . ." Peachy wrestled for the right words. "Go on."

"There's nothing but trees out here, ya'll," BoDean announced, still looking out the window. "And grass. I mean real grass."

Booger went on. "I get it that this Jackal demon, this Thorn guy, or whatever, has been chasin' you for a long time. And I know that's gotta be a real pain in the . . . a real problem."

"So to speak," Peachy said softly.

"But he ain't your real problem," Booger continued.

"He ain't?" Peachy stammered. "He isn't?"

"No sir, Peachy sir, he ain't. No, the problem that's got you is *in* you."

Peachy seemed to be giving him his full attention. Remarkable how that happens, entirely independent of our inclination to hear it or not, when some strange one speaks truth.

"I know the problem's in me," Peachy started. "I know what I've done."

"You ain't got me yet," Booger said slowly. "It ain't what you've done. It's who you are."

"Who I am?" Peachy asked. "Who *am* I?"

"You're me."

Booger let some seconds hang before he said any more. He looked back and forth from Peachy to his own big feet.

"I done some bad things, Peachy sir. Richard can tell you that. But doin' that stuff ain't what kept me unsaved. It was me that did that." He leaned toward the bed. "I held on tight to being not saved. Just like you're doing."

"That's not it," Peachy countered. "I would like to be forgiven."

"I don't believe you," Booger said. "I'm sorry. But I don't."

"Why not?"

Booger ducked that question and answered one not asked. "The reason you don't get saved, is you think your bad stuff is bigger than God's good stuff."

Peachy didn't respond. He didn't seem angry. He looked to be weighing some things.

BoDean said, without taking his eyes from the window, "Yeah. I think that's it."

"Which is," said Booger, "pretty much where I was. If'n God's stuff is big enough to cover my sin, then my sin don't amount to as much as I thought it did."

"Maybe it does," Peachy reasoned. "Maybe our great sin shows the immensity of God's love."

"Are you telling me how to get saved, or am I telling you?" Booger was absolutely serious, and I think that was one of the most serious and funniest lines spoken by my buddies in 1976. Booger's question appeared to sink some holy talons into Peachy's resistance to grace.

"Go on," Peachy said.

"I used to think, back then, if my sins were big enough, then maybe I was my own god. I was god over myself. I didn't always see it like that, but that's the way it was. So me gettin' saved was mostly about me sayin' to God that he's God and I'm not."

Booger looked at me. "Ya'll can translate any of this."

"You're good," I said.

He looked to Peachy again. "It ain't about how big and bad I was. It's about how big and good God is. I mean to say, Peachy sir . . . you need to stop lookin' at *you* so much."

"I'd like that," Peachy said. "I'm so tired . . . of me."

"I been there," said Booger.

BoDean turned away from the window and faced Peachy. "Yeah. It's in your head."

"Excuse me?" Peachy said, not unkindly. It struck me how he gave these two fellows so much leeway, so much room to speak their mind to him. Maybe he sensed they were on a mission not of their own making. Maybe he was starting to see a way out.

"The problem. It's in your head," BoDean said again. "I don't even think that old boy wanted any stuff from your jungle work."

"Old boy?" said Peachy.

"You know, your jungle bogeyman."

"Oh yeah," Peachy nodded. "Him."

"He wants *you*. Just like he wanted me. And Booger and all us stupid souls."

"He almost got me," Peachy said, tapping his chest where his heart was. "Could've hit my heart, instead of my leg."

Booger shook his head. "Ain't no never mind neither."

Peachy was wowed. "I don't believe I've ever heard that one before."

For an instant, I thought the old man was on the verge of conversion, at epiphany's edge. Then Peachy said, "Ain't . . . no . . . never . . . mind . . . neither." He sighed. "I've never heard four negatives encased in a five-word sentence."

"All's we're saying," Booger trudged on, "is the war's in your head. The war ain't about your heart stopping, your body stopping. It's about your head. That's the real war. And you've got a hold of your own head and you ain't lettin' go."

"How am I . . ." Peachy said. "What am I holding in my own head?"

"Whatever bad things you did in that Africa place," Booger said.

BoDean said, "That's your excuse. I'm a pothead, Peachy. That was my excuse. You think what you did makes you a pothead to God?" Peachy didn't deny it. "It don't. It makes you just like us. One more run-of-the mill guy that's living like being lost is the way it's gotta be. Booger was *mad* at God and I ignored God, all our junior high and high school time so far. That don't sound like long to you, but that's nearly 'bout half our life."

"My daddy," said Booger, "come close to killing me one night with his hands, and I kinda wished at the time he did. It's hard to want to find God in that kind of mess. That was my excuse for running. I mean away from God. But see . . . he's bigger than my excuse."

"I want him to be bigger than mine," Peachy said.

"If that's true," Booger said, "then you got him. 'Cause he is. Bigger than your excuse. And he's got you. It's just a matter of time, Peachy sir. Short time."

BoDean stood up. "That's about it, ain't it?" he asked Booger.

"Believe so." Booger stood up.

"You're leaving?" Peachy looked genuinely disappointed.

"That's all we got," Booger said. "It took us the better part of all night last night to get straight what we been thinking God wants us to say to you. We just run through it. That's all."

"I'm going to go over it . . . in my head," said Peachy. "What you boys have told me."

"It'll keep you up all night." BoDean grinned. "But it's worth it."

"You smoke that stuff anymore?" Peachy asked abruptly.

"Why would I do that?" BoDean said. "I'm not stupid."

"Don't you want to?"

"Right now all I wanna smoke is God. And I feel like he's smokin' me. I mean, he's high on me gettin' high on him. Crazy, huh?"

"It doesn't sound crazy to me," Peachy said. "But I'm the man who says a real demon's been chasing me for twenty, twenty-five years."

He laughed with BoDean and Booger and I smiled, short of laughing. I was close to tears, not in the sad way, but in the sense of strange joy at these two boys sharing with Peachy. I felt something hard was melting from the heat of their hearts on fire.

I was just about to step out, just behind my friends, when Peachy whispered, "Richard."

I stepped back up to his bedside.

"I'm thinking," he said. "Maybe I know less than I think I do."

I said nothing.

"In fact, I'm sure it's true," he said. "But then, where does that leave me?"

How could I answer such things?

"See you tomorrow," I said. He nodded and I left.

CHAPTER 30

On the third day, he rose from the dead. Spiritually.

The day's start was gruesome; the police calling my mom and dad with grisly news that Jack Thornton had been found dead in the prison hospital, apparently ending his own tragic life with an overdose of stimulant chemicals he stole from the prison pharmacy. The same morning, Mr. Burkett made good an escape from the prison hospital. The police had sent someone out to Miss Barbara's house to watch the place and told her to stay put. She refused, and kept her same schedule, which included caring for her dad at Memorial Hospital.

Bradley was still securely imprisoned, physically. Spiritually, he was set free entirely, having professed Christ after Pastor White visited him. People can generally be suspicious of such prison-cell conversions. But Donnie's dad was as perceptive as anyone I knew about such things.

At the hospital, I peeked through the partway open door before I saw that Peachy already had company, a small, bespectacled man sitting in a chair to the side of Peachy's bed. The man had a tape recording device in his lap.

"Whoops," I said. "Sorry." I stepped back into the hall but Peachy called for me to come back in.

"You should hear this, Richard." To his visitor he said, "Richard is a lot like me. God help him. Is it all right if he's here?"

The man said, "Perfectly fine. Perhaps our session will flow more smoothly than it has."

I walked back in, leaving the door not quite closed.

Peachy was asking the man, "We haven't flowed?"

"Let's just say it could be better."

Peachy gestured for me to sit in another chair, on the other side of his bed.

"This fellow is from the police," Peachy said to me. "Dr. Bumgardner is a psychologist. A great guy. Extremely intelligent."

The interviewer was obviously pleased.

"I think they just want to decide," said Peachy.

"Decide?" Bumgardner asked, so I didn't have to.

"Whether I'm loony, or whether Thornton's loony, or whether we're both loony, or . . . maybe that's all. Did I leave out any options?"

Bumgardner shifted in his chair. "Well, you and Thornton could both be sane and the rest of the world could be loony."

Peachy and I loved that. "Don't let me interrupt," I said. "I'd kind of like to know what's what with all our brains."

"A tall order," Bumgardner mused. "All right then, where were we?"

"I was talking of how I felt Thornton betrayed me, years ago . . ."

"Yes, betrayal. And how that led to your feeling haunted."

"Not *feeling* haunted," Peachy clarified, "just haunted."

Bumgardner looked at the recorder, satisfied himself it was working, and then scoured some notes he'd taken. "Yes, well, you said you felt like you lived in a haunted house, surrounded by a . . . moat of regrets, as you put it."

"Yeah." Peachy looked serious, but maybe pleased by the metaphor. "A moat of regrets. So you're interested in the question of evil."

Bumgardner shook his head. "I didn't say that."

"I didn't say you said that. I just noted that you're interested in the question of evil. You are, aren't you?"

"All psychologists are."

"Sure. But we're talking about *you*."

"No, Dr. McLeod, we're talking about *you*. But as a matter of fact, I am writing a book on the subject of aberrant behavior masquerading as evil."

"Okay, okay," Peachy nodded, like someone just switched on

multiple lightbulbs. "So your work focuses on *explaining* human criminal behavior, rather than discerning the nature and sources of evil."

"Evil is an aberration," Bumgardner stated.

"Ah! To you. To me it has always appeared to be the norm."

"That's a very grim opinion."

"I can't help that." Peachy almost laughed. "If it's true, all the more reason to say it, right? We wouldn't want to be ignorant of bad news just because it's bad news."

Bumgardner wasn't sure what to say. Or maybe he was assessing Peachy's mental state. I'm sure that took a great deal of energy.

The seconds drifted into a discomforting silence. Peachy spoke again. "My hope is that God is the norm as well."

"How can God and evil both be the norm? Unless you're suggesting they are equal belligerents . . . codeterminants of history . . . a yin and a yang."

"They're not codeterminants," Peachy said, "or we'd be hacking each other to pieces right now with instruments sharper than words. God's driving the world. That's the only reason the world hasn't collapsed into chaos up to now."

"It was my impression that you are not a Christian believer."

"That's right."

"You sound like one," Bumgardner said.

"I can't help what I sound like. I'm just trying to let my reason and observations have free roam."

"Fascinating . . . I'm wondering what your childhood was like. What were you like as a young boy?"

"Young."

Bumgardner made a few notes. "You were somewhat of a recluse? You would say you spent an inordinate amount of time alone?"

I guess they were questions, but they smelled like assumptions.

"Why would I say that?" Peachy asked.

"Let's not focus on the *why*. Let's focus on the *what*, shall we? What were you like as a child?"

"I was somewhat of a recluse. I would say that I spent an inordinate amount of time alone."

"Dr. McLeod, you have a propensity to . . . toy with people. Why do you think you do that?"

"I thought we weren't talking about the *why*."

"I changed my mind."

"Oh good. That's a very healthy thing to do, Dr. Bumgardner."

"Why do you say that?"

"Because change is not loss. Change is gain."

"Doesn't it rather depend on what changes?"

"Ultimately, yes." Peachy smiled. "However it's been my observation that the vast majority of people do not really change, at their core, unless they are changing from bad to good."

"But what of people who change from good to bad?"

"That never happens."

"Never happens?" The psychologist wrinkled his brow, which struck me as an inauthentic expression. It looked like he was consciously trying to appear confounded. He seemed self-wise. And the self-wise are never confounded. That is their doom.

"You mean to say that no one changes from good to bad?" said Bumgardner. "Dr. McLeod, I've spent the better part of my career studying this precise issue, this concise question: Why do good people suddenly do bad things? Why do they commit criminal acts? Surely you do not believe that authentic change is limited to bad people changing to good people?"

"But I do!" Peachy roared. Then, in an almost inaudible whisper, "I do."

The seconds of silence lengthened; I can never gauge how many, my mind circles over time like a hawk over forest trees. We were startled by a knock on the door. It was a polite knock, one Peachy and I had heard before.

"Mr. Peachy?" Willie Rowe said from behind the almost closed door. "My mama sent you some homegrown tomatoes. I got 'em right here."

"Come in, come in." Peachy was thrilled.

I stepped to the door and opened it wide to Willie, Beth, Lizzie, and Mr. Rodriguez, who was holding his guitar.

"Hey, Richard!" Lizzie gave me a wave.

"Hey, ya'll." I grinned at them. They stepped inside, to Peachy's delight and Bumgardner's annoyance.

"Last time I tried to give away tomatoes," Willie said, "there was a demon or two in the room."

"Yes there was!" Peachy concurred, tickled.

"I think we're through here," Bumgardner muttered, standing.

"All right," Peachy said. "I hope you got what you wanted."

"Yes, well"—the psychologist was clearly frustrated—"I am led to the bizarre conclusion that you believe the only real change is what the theologians call conversion. Is that so?"

"I'm . . ." Peachy was without words. "I'm not . . ."

"Think it over," Bumgardner advised. "It's certainly what you've suggested and doggedly insisted on, whether you realize it or not."

He gave me a quick nod and stepped briskly by the three kids and the guitar man, and out the door.

Lizzie asked, "Was that guy a demon?"

"No, no," Peachy and I assured her and Beth and Willie, who had personal history to buttress such a query in his mind.

"He's just a brainy guy," I said. "He's really smart, but . . . it's like his brain is so big, it's hard for him to see around it."

"You mean he's like Mr. Peachy," Willie said harmlessly.

"No, no, he isn't . . ." I said, intending to say more.

"Yes, he is," Peachy said quietly.

Oblivious to Peachy's sentiments, or perhaps simply moving at the direction of a power beyond Peachy's sentiments or reasonings, Beth gave Willie and Lizzie a look and the three kids crowded close to the head of Peachy's bed.

Mr. Rodriguez strummed a chord. The kids started singing. Mr. Rodriguez didn't sing, he just strummed softly. I didn't sing either, just the kids.

They sang all three verses. When they started, Peachy smiled big. That was, I suspect, for their sakes more than it was telling his real feelings or thoughts in the moment. By the time they finished, it was obvious he wasn't thinking so much about them anymore.

Beth put her hand on Peachy's arm and said, "We're going to pray for you. Okay?"

"Okay."

"You don't have to say nothing," she said, "'cause Willie and me know what to say. Okay?"

"Okay."

We all closed our eyes.

"Dear God," Beth prayed, "Mr. Peachy needs to be saved. That's what you do, God. You save people."

I peeked. Peachy's eyes were still closed. I closed mine again.

"All the guys like him, God," she said. "And Richard loves him. So does Willie. So he must be okay, God. I mean, I think you must love him too. That's all."

Willie took the handoff. "God, we're asking you to pull Peachy into your family. He needs you, God. And you love him. So here we go, God. He's just like me and Richard and all of us. He's done some stuff he shouldn't have done."

"I'm a sinner." Peachy said it, spring rain soft.

Lizzie prayed then. "But your Son died for all that bad stuff."

"Jesus . . ." Peachy said.

I peeked again, seeing everyone's eyes closed except mine. I closed mine.

Then Beth again. "So, thanks Jesus, for what you did on the cross and then coming out of the grave, too."

"Jesus . . ." Peachy said.

"That's about it, God," Beth said. "Anyway, thanks."

We all opened our eyes. Willie put the brown bag on the table beside Peachy's bed.

"These here are homegrown," he said. "Ain't nothing better than homegrown tomatoes. I mean, to eat."

Peachy looked at me and said, "It's happened."

Lizzie poked Beth. "Tell him what your mom said."

"Oh yeah, I forgot." Beth addressed Peachy. "My mom said to tell you that she and her group are praying for ya'll."

"Her group?" Peachy said.

"Just some women she prays with a lot. And I mean *a lot*."

"I must thank them," Peachy said. "What's your mom's name?"

"Prudence."

"Did you get that, Richard?"

I recited his own words: "Without prudence, the world would spin down to cinders."

———

Having held Dr. Peachy McLeod's hands and taken the man the final steps to a new creation, Willie and Lizzie left, saying they had some "fun stuff they had to do." I think it involved a playground trip.

"I guess you know Thornton escaped," I said.

"It doesn't matter."

"How do you mean that?"

"It doesn't matter on two profound levels," he said. "First, it doesn't matter because God . . ." He seemed to catch his breath. "God has forgiven me. What else could matter?"

At root, he had that right. But there was still the matter of life on a fallen planet.

"Second," he said, "it doesn't matter because nobody will see him for many years."

"Come again?"

"He will disappear. I know him, that's his pattern. He has more time than we do—I mean history time, time in Earth history, to go after what he wants. He'll take that time, because his attempt this time has run its course and failed. Thank God."

"He doesn't have a lot more time if Jesus comes back soon."

"That's right!" Peachy looked like he hadn't considered that. "In one very real sense, I never want to see him again, but I wouldn't mind being next to him when that happens."

I spent the better part of the afternoon going over Scriptures about salvation with Peachy. When Booger and BoDean dropped in, neither of them seemed at all surprised by Peachy's new birth.

"What would be far-out, and like no way, man," BoDean said, "was if you could keep saying to God, 'No God . . . you are not God!' That'd be far-out."

"That's kind of what demons do," Booger said. "They just keep telling God he's not God."

"No way, man." BoDean shook his head. "Oh man . . . that's way out there."

Miss Barbara was overjoyed at Peachy's conversion. She showed him her new treasure, a quickly thickening notebook of outlines and verses that dealt with what she called "redemption according to Jesus."

"You can get a lot of good stuff from Pastor White," I said.

"Oh, I'll ask him and the others at church about lots of this," Miss Barbara said. "But I really like hearing what you think."

"Well, if there's any discrepancy," I said, "I'm wrong and they're right."

"That," she said, "your humility, is why I want to hear it from you first."

When she left us to attend to some others in the hospital, Peachy told me he had something important to tell me. I sat down beside the hospital bed.

"That's a little redundant," I said. "Everything you've ever told me is important."

"Even how to throw a winged knuckleball?" he said.

"That was important to me!" I smiled. "I needed an 'out pitch' and you gave it to me."

He was anguished over something. Or anguished at himself, maybe.

"No I didn't," he said. "What I gave you was . . . a formula. I was wrong. But it's done."

I waited for his explanation. He tensed up, looking like he wanted to cry, but had forgotten how that cathartic wonder is accomplished. He also looked as if he'd forgotten his own eternal rescue that he had only this very day seen with his own eyes and known in his new mind and new heart.

"But it was a real pitch, right?" I wanted to know.

"Satchel said it was. He showed it to me. I couldn't throw it. But you did. You remember what I said to you that day? After the game."

Of course I did. "You told me I'd made an epic endeavor. Unbelievably epic."

"And you thanked me for showing you the pitch and I said . . . what?"

"You said 'That was nothing.' You said that I had done the hard part. That I had triumphed in the moment."

"Now you know just how seriously I meant that."

"But you threw the pitch . . . at McDonald's. And Duffey couldn't catch it."

"That is the only time that pitch has worked for me, and I suspect Duffey could catch it, he just didn't. He expected it to be troublesome for him, and so it was. There are vastly more episodes of the power of suggestion than we imagine."

I didn't know what to say. He took my silence to mean I was worried about all he had ever told me.

"You're wondering," said Peachy, "how much more I've told you that is not true."

"No. I'm not. I'm wondering what I can say to you that will give you peace."

"You're too good for me," he croaked. "You should've stayed clear of me because . . . my whole life is haunted."

I thought out loud. "We're all haunted, our whole life. We just don't normally see it. But some of the haunts are benign. Angelic."

"You're starting to sound like me. Crazy."

"You're not crazy, Peachy. Unless being honest is crazy."

"But I lied to you."

"Past tense. You just told me the truth. One of many truths you've told me."

He breathed deeply. "He'll be back," he said. "He always comes back."

"But he has no teeth anymore. He can't hurt you, Peachy."

"He's not coming after me, anymore, I know that. I wish he were. But it's . . . you now."

I heard him, but that didn't seem to matter either. Nothing really matters except Christ dead and risen.

I said, "It doesn't matter, Peachy. God's got you and me both now. And so . . . nothing else matters."

"I was scared, Richard. And I was just trying to get away from him. I gave you the formula, Richard. I'm sorry. And if I could shoot myself now and have it undone, so you didn't know it, I'd pull the trigger this instant."

His demeanor and his words sobered me. But I still didn't know what he meant. "I don't get it."

"I know, but you have to. Because he thinks you have it. So when he comes . . ." He stopped and brightened. "Maybe he won't come, Richard, because he may feel his efforts were exhausted this go-round and there's no point in going after you."

"I'm not worried," I said, entirely honest in that moment. "Christ has crushed the head of the serpent."

"Yes." He nodded. "The Word is the final word."

"Yes," I said.

He pulled open the drawer at the top of the little table by his bed and handed me a single sheet of paper.

"I'm giving this to you now," he said, "since I could leave this world anytime now."

"I don't think so," I protested.

"No, no, it's true, I could go anytime. Or not. It doesn't matter. You need to know the formula, because if he comes after you, he will assume you have it, and you're holding out. Which of course, you are. You won't give it to him. But . . . I've thought about this a long time, Richard, and you will be safer if he knows you have it than if he comes to know you don't have it. You follow me? If he learns that you have it, he will not try to . . . he won't try to . . ."

"Kill me."

"I'm so sorry. I love you, Richard. You know that, I can tell, and so there's no point in not saying it. And I wish I hadn't, but I did give it to you."

I looked at the paper, a single sheet of words, numbers, and symbols aligned and written to fill roughly three quarters of the page. It was all nonsensical, except for the words *Paige* and *Cleveland* and the acronym near the bottom: K-N-U-C-K-L-E.

I had no concept of what the notations meant. Including the acronym.

"Knuckle," I read aloud.

"That's the core of the formula," he said. "The letters all mean something. You can see that when you look at the notes closer. Look it over, tonight, and I'll clarify it for you tomorrow. It's important you look at it first, by yourself. Then you'll remember it. Forever. You have to remember it, always, Richard. For your safety."

"Okay." I sensed his thinking was entirely sound on this.

It was time to ask. "What is the formula's purpose? What were you doing?"

"Cloning."

I had guessed that from what he'd shared around the campfire that night.

"I don't think it's as bad as you think," I offered. "And I know God forgives you."

"Human cloning."

I couldn't respond.

"I was sure it was impossible," he said. "Until I arrived at the formula. I'm still not convinced it works. But Jackalthorn is."

I noticed an odd symbol on the paper he'd given me. An upside-down fragmented cross, broken in three places. "What's this?"

"That's his personal sign. You need to know it. So you'll see it when . . . *if* he . . . I'm sorry, Richard."

I knew it, so I said it. "The only thing that matters, for you and for me, is that we know Jesus. Everything is going to be all right. Nothing can separate us from the love of God, which is in Christ Jesus. Nothing."

I wanted to clarify one more thing. "So . . . that pitch worked because I believed it would work."

"No," he said with uncommon verve. "That pitch works because that pitch works. I just couldn't throw it. But you can! You and Satch. Feller couldn't throw it either. It's important . . . crucial, that you know the pitch itself is real. Things are either real or they are not. They're true, or they're false." He smiled then, like he was excited to see something for the first time. "It's not a matter of our belief bringing something to pass. It's like redemption. Christ either wrought it or he did not. Our believing he wrought it is after the fact."

"Yes." I smiled with him. "It's real or it's not real. Still, we are called to believe this real redemption really applies *to us*. Personally."

"And so I do. I believe."

———

When I stopped by the next day, Peachy—true to his word—explained the formula to me, in a mix of layman's and genetic research terms. What I did not understand, I nonetheless committed to memory. I know enough of it to never forget it.

———

Peachy lived another seven joyful, peaceful years with his daughter and all his new brothers and sisters of all ages. He helped me choose Vanderbilt for my undergraduate study. He told me it was a good idea to stay close to what Flannery O'Connor called the "Christ-haunted South."

EPILOGUE

I did as Dr. Woodruff suggested. I wrote everything down. Everything that is, except the correct formula. One never knows.

I saw Dr. Woodruff in Breyer Hall and asked if he wanted to see any of it.

"No," he said. "I want to see *all* of it."

"Suit yourself," I said. "If your reading list is anywhere near the length of mine, the last thing you need is a tome documenting a colleague's teen angst."

"Quite right; I don't want to read my colleague's tome. I want to read my friend's recollections. Attach it to me. Campus mail."

"I can't."

"Why not? Don't tell me your Mac's on the fritz too. Stoddard camps out at the Geek Squad these days and—"

"I didn't type it. I wrote it longhand."

"Richard, I'm beginning to believe you are in fact haunted, not by what happened to you in 1976 but by your own eccentricities!" He laughed.

"Tell me something I don't know."

"I'd love to read it, if you don't mind handing over the massive volume at your convenience. Surely you made copies."

"One," I said. "One original, one copy."

"Why?"

"I'm not sure." That was true. "It's just very personal. I don't know . . . I'll get you a copy."

"At your convenience, Richard."

That afternoon I stopped back by his office and set the massive notebook on his desk.

"I wouldn't have believed it," he said. "I honestly thought you were pulling my leg. You're sick, Richard. You know that."

"I know that."

That was Tuesday.

Thursday morning he called to tell me he couldn't find the notebook.

"I can't for the life of me understand where it is," he said. "I carried it home, read a great deal Tuesday evening and last night, and oh, Richard, it's fascinating, my boy, it is—"

"Where did you leave it?"

"On the floor, by the head of my bed. It wouldn't fit on my crowded nightstand. This morning, it's gone. Strangest thing."

"David . . . you must have put it somewhere else."

"That's what I said to myself, but I don't believe me," he said. "I know that sounds funny but . . . there it is. I'll keep looking, of course."

"It'll show up."

"Yes, of course."

Friday afternoon, he called and said he was baffled, but it had simply disappeared.

"Maybe I could come over there and help you look."

"You're welcome to, of course," he said. "But listen, I got some grim news earlier today."

"I'm sorry to hear that."

"Oh, it's nothing to do with me." He paused. "You know the gentleman whom you met at my place? The psychology chap. Maybe you've forgotten."

"Dr. Throneberry."

"Yes. Him. Well, I'm sorry to say that the poor fellow passed away last night. They found him sitting slumped in a chair in his office at Marist. A Canadian, you'll recall. He was nearly seventy-five or so. Simply gave out, they're saying. A colleague of his called me. Another psych prof. I thought you'd like to know."

"Yes. Thanks, David."

Early that evening, Julie and I walked on the trail in McGill Park, near our home. It was more cathartic than aerobic.

"You know this getaway thing we were doing this weekend?" I said.

"*Were* doing?"

"I don't know. This is a cabin, right? I'm not sure I see the cabin thing working for us. As a getaway. I'm not real keen on old cabins."

"If a student of yours used 'real keen' in a sentence, you'd fry them."

"I'm not an ogre."

She kissed me. "We still go canoeing."

"Demons didn't haul me off to old canoes. I was thinking it might be fun to go see the Fellowship. Hear Zack preach."

"Sure. Let's do it."

I couldn't tell if she really liked the idea. I knew she liked "getting away" to cabins or beaches or anywhere. I was the curmudgeon regarding getaways.

"We don't have to go see them this weekend," I said.

"Yes we do. You need closure."

"It's not that. I got that. A long time ago. I just want to see my friends. Our friends."

"Great," she said. "Let's do it."

Julie is one of those remarkable people who finds joy in other people's plans.

"It's not like I need closure—"

"Yes you do," she said.

"—but I need to, you know, catch up. It's been too long since we've seen them."

"That's called closure. Short-term closure."

We drove to Silas Baptist Church and sat with three of the original Fellowship of Rafer's Rock: Rebecca Carson Ross; Donnie White and his wife, Charlotte; and Duffey and Caroline and their youngest, thirteen-year-old Chelsea. Rebecca and Zack's boy, Matt, was home for the weekend from Jacksonville State University.

Zack preached, in his open, transparent, humble, and strong way.

He's an excellent preacher, only he doesn't know it. Maybe that's why he's excellent.

It was his last sermon in a long series preaching through the book of Romans.

"Oh, I get it," Duffey said to me and Julie. "Ya'll come here to get the last sermon on Romans. While we've sat here for I don't know how many weeks slugging through Romans like it was the Camp mud pit—"

"Duffey!" Caroline scolded, trying to push her husband from the side, but she knocked herself off balance while he didn't budge.

He said, "Honey, be careful, now," and caught her.

Her genuine laugh set Julie and me free to laugh with her.

"You're a big old fool," she said.

"That ain't altogether true," Duffey said. "I'm not old."

"Tell 'em what you learned about Romans, you big fool," Caroline said.

"You can get the whole series online," Rebecca told me.

"Oh, Zack posts them?"

"That'll be the day. If Zack tells me he posted something on the computer, he means he put a Post-It note on the screen."

"Rebecca, he's a quality preacher. I'm so glad somebody posts them."

"Rafer does it."

"Tigger's boy?"

"He's not a boy anymore. He's got his own sound studio in Dothan."

"Tigger's boy," I said, enjoying the nostalgic sound of the name from my childhood. "We've turned some kind of corner, Rebecca."

"I feel it," she said. "It's okay."

After the service, I asked Zack if he posted his sermons on the web. I wanted to hear him say who did it.

"Rafer does that for me," he said.

"Rafer," I said too.

"Yeah," he said. It was like he knew I wanted to hear the name too. "The name sounds . . . really strange and kind of beautiful at the same time, doesn't it? Listen, we're taking the youth group on a mission trip. Up to Appalachia. Part of southwest Virginia, where the tornados hit. You should come."

"I've never been on a mission trip."

"Joining up with old Willie Rowe. He's taking some of his inner-city Jackson kids."

"Old Willie Rowe," I said. "Sounds odd, doesn't it?"

———

We sat at a huge table for lunch. Sweet tea, chicken sandwiches, too many fries, and burgers the size of Duffey's fists—which is to say, I couldn't finish mine. It was a local establishment run by a man Donnie said "needs to come to the light."

"Did you put it like that to him?" Julie was moved and amused.

"Duffey did!" Donnie said.

"So I did," Duffey said as if it were a matter of course. "But I told Shawn all the straight talk gospel stuff too."

"Shawn?" Julie asked.

"The manager of this fine establishment," said Charlotte. "He puts up with Duffey 'cause Duffey brings him customers."

"That ain't it," Duffey objected. "He likes me and I like him. It's just he ain't saved, is all. I can't make it any clearer to him. Course, God can."

"Donnie says you're a Scoutmaster," I said.

"He's an assistant Scoutmaster," Caroline clarified.

"Same thing," Julie said.

"Oh no it ain't," said Duffey. "We assistants just show up when we can and we don't have to do all that paperwork and stuff."

"He's kinda like a big Scout," Caroline said. "He plays around a lot."

"Is that true?" I asked him.

"Pretty much," he nodded. "But the boys keep me in line."

"You mean the Scouts?" Julie wanted him to say more.

"Yeah, they get me out of trouble all the time."

Matt Ross said over our laughs, "Isn't it supposed to work the other way around, Uncle Duffey?"

"Everything in my life works the other way around, Matt."

We didn't know what that meant, and I suspect Duffey didn't either, but it sounded like a pattern for many things in Duffey's life. Mine too, in a different way.

I had eaten nearly half of the jumbo burger; that is, nearly done with my lunch effort and resolved to ask for a take-home box, when my cell sounded in my pocket.

"Don't answer it, sweetheart." Julie gave me a puppy dog look.

I didn't recognize the number; in such cases, I normally turn the phone off. But I felt a sudden urgency, more like panic, that I needed to answer. I punched the button, my nerves threatening to overtake me.

"Hello." I expected to hear a voice familiar and threatening.

"Richard." The voice was familiar and sweet. But I wasn't sure.

"Who is this?"

"This is Willie. Willie Rowe. How's it going, Richard?"

"I can't tell you how good it is to hear your voice." I told everyone who it was.

Duffey said, "Let me talk to the rascal when you're done."

To Willie I said, "This is great. I'm with everybody right now. Yeah, the whole Fellowship, pretty much. We talked about you in church. Duffey says he wants to talk to the rascal."

"Tell him he's white trash," Willie said to me.

"He says you're white trash."

Duffey snorted, tickled. "Tell him he's a boil on my backside."

"Sorry I haven't been in touch the last couple years," Willie said.

"Same here," I said. "What are you up to?"

"Same ole, same ole. Fightin' back demons," Willie said.

"Really?"

"Oh yeah. Demon Poverty. Demon Bigotry. All the old ones, still rooting around like hogs. Demon Crime. Demon Murder. All the old enemies."

"Julie and I pray for you. When God brings you to mind."

"Then I can't lose, can I?"

My nerves coasted back to normal.

"So glad you called, Willie. What made you? I mean, call me now. Today."

"Well . . . I'm fixing to take some kids with Zack to Appalachia."

"He said that. I think that's awesome, Willie."

"Wanna come? Bring Julie. Ever been on a mission trip?"

"My whole life feels like a mission trip."

"Maybe it is." He paused. He had something else to tell me. "Richard, you know a fellow named Jarvis Hornback?"

I didn't answer. So then . . . it is happening.

"Richard . . . he says he knows you. Says ya'll go way back."

"What about him?"

"Well, I don't know him, but he came in to see me yesterday at the Youth Center and said he knew you. Real nice fellow. Turns out he's gonna be up there in the same area in southwest Virginia when we're there doing the mission thing. Said he'd like to get together over there. I told him we'd be busy with the mission agenda, and he said he might could help us out. Says he knows some folks there, and he can get us connected. That's always helpful on a mission trip. Hey man, I gotta go, but you talk to Zack and see if you can make it. It'll change your life, a mission trip."

"I'm sure it will."

"Keep me posted," Willie said. "Tell those other scoundrels like Duffey and Donnie that I'll be tugging on them to go too."

"I'll tell them."

I flipped the phone shut and put the simple T-Mobile back in my pocket.

"It's past time to upgrade on your phone, Uncle Richie," said Matt. "I can hook you up."

"Matt sells those new ones, on the side," said Rebecca. "He knows his stuff."

"If and when I have to do it, you get my business," I said.

Duffey noticed I'd hung up and barked, "I told ya I wanted to talk to that rascal!"

"Oh yeah," I muttered. "A lot on my mind."

"Don't nothin' ever change?" he said, shaking his head.

"What's Willie up to?" Julie asked.

I said, "He wants to go canoeing." I didn't think it was that funny, but I was glad I said it when everybody laughed. I wanted to feel like laughing with them.

"He wants us to go on the mission trip with him and Zack."

"Cool," said Julie. "Can we do it?"

"Well . . ." I wasn't sure where to begin.

"You gotta go," Zack said. "You too, Duffey. All ya'll."

Duffey said he wasn't sure if he could go, or wanted to go.

Zack said he understood. "People don't see it until they get there, but mission trips . . . it's like going into battle."

Duffey's eyes danced and Caroline sighed. "We'll be there."

Matt rebooted his sales pitch. "Professor Powell needs some new tech, man."

"I don't want new tech. I wish I could get rid of what I have. One day I will."

"I don't know." Matt shook his head, flashing his mom's winsome smile. "You can never go back."

"Ah," I brightened. "Thomas Wolfe."

"I thought it was Yogi Berra." Matt shrugged. "Either way. I don't think you can circle back around once you've been out there where it's happening."

I thought that was an odd way to state what I thought he meant, and was going to say so when our server, Megan, showed up at my elbow putting some sort of pastry dessert in front of me.

"What's this?"

"It's from Jarvis," Megan chirped.

"Who's Jarvis?"

"In the kitchen. A cook. He says he knows you."

She plucked a whipped cream can from her apron pocket and made a collapsing, fragmented cross on the pastry. Broken in three places.

I jumped up, hitting the table, overturning a cup of coffee. Running to the door through which Megan and her cohorts entered the dining area, I heard Julie calling after me, and Duffey belting out "Whoa!" and Chelsea let go a short shriek that turned to laughter.

I invaded the kitchen, a very busy space with lots of Megan look-alikes shuffling plates and barking orders. An old guy over a stove asked me who I was.

"Where's Jarvis?" I said.

"Are you the inspector?"

"Jarvis, the cook," I said fast. "Where is he?"

"Jarvis is on break." The old guy pointed. "He just stepped out there in the alley to smoke."

.I ran to the back door, aware that a couple of guys were right behind me.

I stepped through the door and stood alone in the alley. Nobody. Zack and Duffey came out right after me.

"Who we looking for?" Duffey looked around, ready to storm the castle.

"What is it, Richard?" Zack said.

The fear I should have felt at my first recognition came now in a wave. My stomach gave way; I doubled over and retched but nothing came out.

"Hey." Zack put his arm softly on my shoulders. "Sit down." He took me down, gentle, and I leaned against the diner's brick wall.

"Talk to us, buddy," Duffey said, sitting on the other side of me.

"I should have known," I said. "I should have seen it. I should have seen it coming."

"Seen what?" Zack said.

"I'm okay," I said, and I felt I was, standing up suddenly. We needed to go. "C'mon guys," I said, opening the door back to the kitchen. We walked in and there were Donnie, Charlotte, Caroline, Matt, Julie, and Chelsea dodging the servers, cooks, dishwashers, and one harried manager, Shawn.

"What do you mean, he quit?" Shawn asked a server.

"I thought he was on break," the old cook said.

"He was on break all right," I said. "For thirty-five years."

"Who are you?" Shawn asked me. "Duffey, your friends gotta get out of the kitchen area, please." He was already ushering us out, while Duffey was preoccupied.

"How long do you smoke that meat?" Duffey asked the old cook.

"Long as they let us," the old guy smiled.

Caroline lassoed her husband. "Let's go, honey."

"Man that smells good." Duffey left, but not before bonding with the cook.

In the restaurant dining room, Shawn started to say something to the other customers, to assure them, but they weren't even looking our way. A demon from hell could have cooked their chicken biscuit and they wouldn't care, as long as they had fries with it.

"How long had this Jarvis guy been working here?" I asked Shawn.

"Three days!" he said, upset. "We needed a cook fast and he showed up with no references and I gave him a break. What kind of world is this?"

"Fallen," Duffey said, loudly, emphatically. "Totally cracked, about six ways from Sunday, and coming apart more every day. You ready to come to Jesus?"

"Are you ever gonna eat here without asking me that?" Shawn tried to frown, but Duffey's grin thwarted him, and he smiled too.

Duffey clapped him on the back. "Getting pretty bad down here, Shawn. My buddy Richard here's about to clue me in on some more of the real war, and one day all this'll be over and won't nothing matter but whether you know the Man."

"Whatever. I appreciate your business, Duffey man." Shawn hustled back toward the kitchen door.

"Shawn," I said.

"Yeah."

"What was Jarvis's last name?"

"Thornback."

"You're sure?"

"Sure I'm sure. I thought it was something made up, and now I know it was. Everything happens to me." He disappeared in the kitchen.

"That's my line," I said under my breath.

Donnie walked back over from the cashier. "We're all set. We can go."

"So are we doing this mission trip thing?" Charlotte asked.

"I don't think—" Donnie started.

"Yes," I said. "Definitely."

Peachy was right: without prudence, the world flies apart.

It's about looking ahead and factoring wisdom into what you see approaching. My horizon perspective remains the same as I discovered in 1976. There is an ebb and flow to the clash of evil and innocence. We see them both, darkness and light, many times in our life, roaring in like the surf, foaming and crashing on the sands. But they are not the same waters as humanist mystics would have us believe.

Jackalthorn mentioned in one of our encounters that brilliant people are the easiest to deceive. It was never his goal to convey "truth," but apparently truth is too powerful a force to be entirely hidden by fallen angels.

Good and Evil are not two sides of the same Intelligence. Good is not Evil on its good days. Nor is Evil the dark side of Good.

They are discrete; the clear Creator and the distinct Rebel, with their attendant warriors.

———

Early Christians used to say in the Lord's Prayer, "Deliver us from the Evil One." Today we pray, "Deliver us from evil." We have stripped evil of its distinct personality and personhood. The devil and his minions are ideas, excesses, and deprivations. They are not beings.

The writer Flannery O'Connor, a believer, was asked why she often used graphic, violent, horrific images and themes in her fiction. She said she wanted to convey truth to a world that preferred artificial sentiment. "And for the hard of hearing, you have to shout."

Truth shouted. At Bethlehem, Golgotha, and Joseph of Arimathea's loaned tomb.

So the demons rage in death throes.

I have heard them.

I have also heard the joyful sound.

The Lamb wins.

ABOUT THE AUTHOR

Rusty Whitener's first novel *A Season of Miracles* earned two Christy Award nominations and *ForeWord Reviews'* 2010 Book of the Year Gold award in the religious fiction category. His screenplays have also garnered multiple awards, including the Kairos Prize as first runner up at the 2009 Movieguide Awards in Beverly Hills for *Touched*, the story on which his first novel was based. *A Season of Miracles* was filmed in 2012 by Elevating Entertainment Motion Pictures and is set for release in the summer of 2013 (www.aseasonofmiraclesmovie.com).

Whitener (www.rustywhitener.com) has appeared in many screen and television roles, usually playing the villain. He appreciated the chance to play a heroic figure in the movie *Decision* (2011) opposite Natalie Grant.

A 2004 graduate of Gordon-Conwell Theological Seminary (DMin), Rusty served as a pastor for twelve years in Pulaski, Virginia, where he lives with his wife, Rebecca.

ALSO BY RUSTY WHITENER

Praise for *A Season of Miracles:*

"A very special book. Baseball, inspiration, and childhood memories—a great combination. I couldn't put it down!"

—**Richard Sterban,** bass singer for The Oak Ridge Boys

"*A Season of Miracles* is a must-read . . . I was reacquainted with my childhood. A touching, challenging, and beautiful story about how God can use the unlikeliest among us to draw us to him."

—**Matt Diaz,** outfielder, New York Yankees

"Rusty Whitener has knocked one out of the ballpark his first time at bat! With every word, readers will be transported to a simpler time when coming of age was about learning the finer lessons of life, of miracles, and the hope God breathes into each of his children."

—**Eva Marie Everson,** author of *Unconditional* and *Chasing Sunsets*

Now, also a major motion picture from *Elevating Entertainment*, and starring:
John Schneider
Grayson Russell
&
Andrew Wilson
Williams

For more on Rusty Whitener, *A Season of Miracles*, or the movie, visit:
rustywhitener.com • aseasonofmiraclesbook.com • aseasonofmiraclesmovie.com